Finish 1:

IN THE
COUNTRY OF DESIRE

ALSO BY LESLIE GARRETT

The Beasts

IN THE
COUNTRY OF DESIRE

LESLIE GARRETT

HarperCollins*Publishers*

HarperCollins books may be purchased for educational, business, or sales promotional use. For information, please call or write: Special Markets Department, HarperCollins Publishers, Inc., 10 East 53rd Street, New York, NY 10022. Telephone: (212) 207-7528; Fax: (212) 207-7222.

FIRST EDITION

Designed by Alma Hochhauser Orenstein

Library of Congress Cataloging-in-Publication Data

Garrett, Leslie, 1932–
   In the country of desire / by Leslie Garrett.—1st ed.
      p.   cm.
   ISBN 0-06-016880-3
   I. Title.
PS3557.A723515   1992
813'.54—dc20   91-58541

92 93 94 95 96 ❖/HC 10 9 8 7 6 5 4 3 2 1

In loving memory of my grandmother, Florence Bradley,
August 26, 1886–July 21, 1959

And for my brother Bob, who was there during most of
my long, difficult journey back, and who, when he saved
my life, made it possible for that journey to take place.

CONTENTS

This is a work of fiction, and all characters
and incidents are imaginary.

WILLA GOES TO THE CITY OF TERRIBLE NIGHT

When one pale October morning in 1980 a young girl named Willa Rhineman, who never knew her mother, came down to discover her grandmother dead in her rocking chair on the porch, she knew the time had come to set out for the city to find her.

Willa looked at the gray-haired woman whose mouth remained open as if she were still trying to tell her what to do. Willa sighed. "I guess I can't just leave you there" she said.

Since all her grandmother had told her when Willa's grandfather died was that dead people were put in holes in the ground, she carried her off the porch and through the woods to a clearing. Then she returned to the house for a pick and shovel.

By the time she had finished digging the hole, the sky was clear and a warm sun had risen to nearly the top of the trees; dew was on the old woman's lips, beyond which Willa could see clumps of dirt already in her mouth. Ants walked up her long hair when Willa lifted her.

She did not know she was supposed to speak some words over the finished grave or quote verses from the Bible. Instead she ran back to the house, where she replaced the pick and shovel beside the barren flower garden that had been her grandfather's failed dream when he died. She had to hurry now, she realized, if she were to reach the city in daylight, for she knew it was not a place to arrive in after dark.

It was Willa's grandmother who had told her what little she knew about the city: that it contained many evil and frightening people, much mayhem and terrible devisings against strangers. She had said that should Willa ever be foolish enough to go there she would flee it as one would a wild beast or a murderer in the night.

She packed her clothes and the money she had taken from her

grandmother's purse in small amounts over the years—along with forty-three one-dollar bills she had hidden away in her grandfather's hollowed-out Bible—in one small suitcase, and still there was room to spare. Her personal possessions were few even for a young girl, as if the usual accumulations for comfort, adornment and amusement had been eliminated in preparation for this day that she had often imagined.

The black dress she wore, which was the only dress she owned that was suitable for the trip, was almost shapeless on her; made of a strong, rough material and woven at a time when cloth was intended to last, it had been sewn by her grandmother from her grandfather's overcoat after his death two years before. She had measured it to allow for Willa's full growth, but now, at sixteen, Willa was no taller than the five feet she had been then, and was as thin and narrow-shouldered, so that it was still much too large for her. It was only the second time she had worn it, and she was anxious to be out of it again soon.

Even though she had been born there and had never had any other home, she walked away from the old house certain she could not only put it behind her but put it out of her mind forever.

A large hen appeared from around the side of the house and ran flapping its wings and screeching behind her, as if demanding to go with her. She turned and made a stern face at it and waved her arms until it went scurrying back, shrieking louder than before. She had let loose her grandmother's small stock of farm animals, hoping they could take care of themselves, but now she wasn't confident they could. She imagined them later as they lay stiff and with feet skyward like stone garden ornaments toppled. But there wasn't anything else she could do to help them. She had to hurry now that it had begun.

Willa stood on the empty highway watching the pickup truck turn onto a dirt road. It tossed a high spume of dust, then began rocking impudently in the ruts as if to further humiliate her before it disappeared in the surrounding countryside; for already she was lost.

It had taken her an hour to get the first ride. She had seemed perhaps too disturbing a sight—a small girl in an oversized black dress with a suitcase, alone on a country road, and with an expression of such intense seriousness as is seldom seen on the face of a child—for those few cars that had looked as if they were about to stop had in fact, once they got close, speeded up and passed her. When the old pickup came to a stop twenty yards past her, idling there as if shivering in the damp and chilly air, she ran to it, the suitcase beating her leg with each step. The cabin was so high she had to reach up to open the door, and by the time she climbed in, dragging the suitcase after her, she was breathing heavily. The occupants of the truck had done nothing to help her—they just sat watching with expressions of vague interest.

The truck started up with gears squealing, jerking forward and stopping, and then forward again, as if in cartoon parody of this beginning of her journey; and when she found herself squeezed into the cabin next to the young farmer, wife and child, she felt her nerves had already been called upon to endure too much.

Since the occupants of the truck did not ask her any questions and did not seem interested in her at all, they had gone several miles in silence before she sneaked a look at their seamed, ageless faces, the wife's under a tiny hat with flowers on it for going to town. Country people with little curiosity. She had seen a few before and was glad to be leaving them. Only the child—a sickly-looking boy of about three with a face as drawn and expressionless as those of his parents—seemed to find her of interest, for he sat with his head straining awkwardly up at her, a glazed apple on a stick he was holding ignored for the moment as he stared at her with his mouth open, breathing loudly.

She waited for him to speak, but he just sat there in silence except for his harsh breathing. Made uncomfortable by his silent, patient scrutiny, she turned away, pretending interest in the uneventful countryside. A moment later her body stiffened when she felt his hand on her arm as he drew himself up to stand next to her. Then she felt his face close to hers, his mouth open wider still as he stared at her. She endured it for as long as she could, then turned back to him, intending to express her disapproval with a look. But when their eyes met—his steady, unblinking—she jerked her head back and looked again out the window. Even so, she could not help but be aware of his persistent interest in her, nor could she shut out the sound of his labored breathing. This time when she turned back to him it was with an expression of pleading, but that didn't make any impression on him either. It was like looking into the depthless eyes of a dead person. When she felt she could not stand it any longer, she broke the silence by speaking to the couple for the first time.

"It was sure nice of you to give me a ride. I'm on my way to live in the city. I've never been there before."

She waited, and when no response came, tried again. "I'm going there to find my momma. Her name's Madeleine. Mine's Willa."

But there was still no reply as they bounced up and down on their seats with the rigid formality of mimes in dance.

At that moment a road sign appeared, and Willa leaned forward to see how far she still had to go, but she could not find the name of the city on it as it swept past. She put her cheek to the passenger window, her palms against it, as she strained to look back at the fleeing sign. But by then it was gone, as if whisked by too quickly in order to frustrate her. She fixed her eyes ahead on the road, so as not to miss the next sign, and when finally after ten minutes it came, the only names on it were those of towns she had never heard of.

Willa had never even been out of the county before and was so uninformed about such things that she could not decide if it was too early in the journey for the name of the city to appear on the signs. She was about to ask the driver about it when she felt the child's sticky hand press against her cheek, putting his wet imprint on her. She jerked away from it. Then he lifted his other hand and pushed the glistening candy at her, and she drew her head back farther still until it was against the door and she had no space left into which to retreat.

They stayed like that for minutes, Willa's neck muscles straining and beginning to ache, the child standing so effortlessly despite the truck's rocking that she thought he could be endowed with some unnatural power that would allow him to remain like that forever.

It was then that Willa had the disturbing feeling that the child knew something about her she did not know, that there was some message he was trying to communicate to her in a language she did not yet understand. She was so preoccupied by this thought that she did not act in time to stop him when he lowered the candy onto the shoulder of her dress, as if he were anointing her. She stared at him, unable to protest in words such an outrageous affront. Then she twisted away, throwing him off balance and into his mother's lap.

Willa stared at the stain, which had ruined the only dress she had brought with her. She rubbed it, but the more she tried to get it out the worse it became, and now her fingers were stained with it too.

She was so busy trying to repair the damage that she almost missed the next road sign when it slid into view. But what she saw—the name of a town she recognized—was enough for her to realize that they were headed not for the city, but in the opposite direction.

It was late afternoon and still she did not have another ride. Vehicles appeared on a rise in the road, then whipped past her. Her feet were sore and her weary bones spoke to her, urging relief.

As the sun began fading behind the trees, even fewer cars appeared, as if someone had put out the word to avoid her; and now no one seemed even to consider stopping. As each car passed, dust rose around her like hands risen to erase her; a silence followed which after a while became frightening to her. All she could hear was the wind whispering from tree to tree. The birds standing in the trees seemed to be watching her. Dragging the suitcase, she began to limp up the highway toward what she feared then might be the unattainable city.

■ ■ ■

There is a street in the city dedicated to lonely men. It serves not the ordinary loneliness of ordinary men, which is wistful and longing, but that loneliness which deadens the spirit and makes the mind and body scream. And yet these are the quietest of men.

Vernon Monday had discovered the street shortly after coming to the city three years before; now he was there most nights and on those afternoons when he had time between jobs as a messenger for the Mercury Delivery Service.

He was nearly twenty-one, but it had never occurred to him that there was any other job he could do: he had no skills or training, and there was nothing he wanted to be. He had his furnished room, which he had made comfortable and attractive with purchases carefully selected over the years (a rocking chair, lace curtains, a bright patchwork coverlet for the bed, a framed photograph of a child sitting by a waterfall), and since he neither smoked nor drank and ate his meals in cheap restaurants, the small salary and tips he earned were more than sufficient for his needs. He had never had a girlfriend, nor made love to a woman, and long ago had reconciled himself to the fact they would remain permanently outside his life.

For Vernon was a strikingly ugly man who had experienced painful rejection; from earliest adolescence he had seen in the expressions of too many women and girls the reflection of revulsion at a loathsomeness that was without real definition. Except for his abnormally protuberant eyes, thick lips and red hair wildly resistant to the discipline of comb or brush, it was more a sense of ugliness than the summation of those parts that proclaimed him so unwholesome. It was in his slouching posture and slow movements and gestures, as if each had to be commanded out of him by an intense concentration of will; in his hesitant and groping speech, each word as though squeezed from him with extreme effort; and in a voice that sounded like someone moaning in a well. It was as if an essential part—some cohesive element—had been left out of him at birth. As if he were unfinished.

They are of all kinds, these men that come to that street without mirth—of all ages, all professions. Some are expensively dressed, carrying briefcases at noon, others, who are poor, garnish bills with coins as evidence of sacrifice for their pleasure. Some appear casual, while others have the furtive look of hiders where there is nowhere to hide. Some are handsome in disturbingly unnatural ways, and others, like Vernon, disfigured of mind or body, whose lives seem destined to be permanently joined to shadows.

What is your desire? the street seems to say. Whatever it is, it can be satisfied here. For the moment. For a price.

It was to one of the buildings on this street that Vernon came this late October afternoon: the Climax Cinema. There was little interest for him in the street's other enticements: the adult book and magazine stores, the shops with their curious and sometimes arcane accessories of desire, the record stores which sold, among other items, disembodied simulations of passion, and the lingerie and costume establishments, where desire could be transformed into other personalities, other times. For only in those darkened houses with the moving figures on the screen could he without fear hold those images that were to him liquescent: they would drain off the screen into him, and he would carry them back with him to his bed for his solitary celebrations.

That was his only passion now, and it was as necessary to him as are the condoned passions to other men. There was no possibility of rejection in it, no recognition of his abnormality, no fear or even the remembrance of fear: shedding his ugliness, he found there only conquest, completion and joy. They were moments given to him perfectly shaped, moments he controlled and of which he was the master, as he was master of nothing in the real world. So satisfactory had it become, so much a part of his life now, that those other, long-ago desires had disappeared into it as objects are devoured by a fog.

Purchasing a ticket from a woman in a glass-topped booth, he passed into the familiar delivering darkness, where love and desire were waiting to seize him.

2

It was nearly dusk by the time Willa arrived in the city. She had finally gotten a ride in a large black car driven by a bald, middle-aged man who informed her that he was a minister at the Pillar of Fire Holy Tabernacle in the city. When he asked her why a young girl was hitchhiking alone to the city and she told him she was going there to find her mother, he did not seem to realize that she did not know where to find her, for he was the kind of person who seldom heard what others said, and did not even listen to the answers to his own questions. He informed her that when she got to the city she should get into a taxi immediately and go straight to her mother's house, for only a precious mother could be trusted in a place that preyed on innocent girls alone, with no one to protect them. He told her that girls like her were frequently drugged and disappeared without a trace, to wake up in heathen countries where they were forced to become the love slaves of niggers and other Godless people. He said his church collected statistics on such things and he knew it to be a fact.

He asked her if she had been saved for Jesus, and when she answered "Sir, I don't mean to be rude, but my grandmother was a great one for all of that, and now that she's dead I don't have to listen to it anymore. I never needed Jesus. All I need is my mother and I'll be just fine" he seemed for once to have heard her, for his lips drew immediately tight and his eyes hardened, and they drove the rest of the way in silence.

■ ■ ■

Vernon got up slowly from where he had been lying on his side in bed. For a moment he looked as if he were in pain. Then the expression drained away and he sat without emotion, unable as always to make an enduring connection with feeling or thought. He was staring at the framed dime-store photograph on the wall of a child sitting beside a waterfall. He appeared to be trying to establish contact with the smiling figure, but the boy's eyes looked through him.

He gathered up the soiled shirt on the bed beside him. It was so hardened from use that when, with his slow walk, he carried it to the drawer to deposit it among the other old shirts, it looked like a corpse outspread in his arms. All of the shirts were due to go to the laundromat the next day; he took them there twice a year. But now they resembled bodies in a mass grave, some with arms raised as if reaching up to him.

Sometimes he would go out at night and follow people. In his closet were a rain slicker that came to his ankles and a rubber hat like a small umbrella that he used on nights of inclement weather; for Vernon's health was delicate and he was often the victim of migrant germs and viruses and had twice been to charity clinics to recover from pneumonia. He seldom thought of death, but sickness—and hospitals, especially—terrified him.

He would follow people for hours at night. He would sit beside them in hotel lobbies, at nearby tables in restaurants and cafeterias; he would linger close as they stood at bus stops and subway stations. Sometimes he would travel with them on public conveyances, sitting behind them or standing as near as he dared. He never touched them, never spoke to them. Now and then he would follow the same person all night. There were times when he accompanied them to their doors: so silent was he that they would have been startled had they turned to discover him there, so close that he could have been their shadows left behind by closed doors.

If he could, he would snatch some personal possession from them: a discarded handkerchief, a carelessly kept glove or scarf, anything he could stealthily siphon off from their lives into his. Later in his room he would take these out to touch, to dwell on with satisfaction that those possessions thought mislaid by their owners—lost in the ordinary effluences of daily living—were there with him, handled and gazed upon by someone whose appearance in their lives they never suspected. Only on occasion—for he was an expert in such matters and knew that their potency diminished with use—would he take them out of the box where he kept them in the rear of his closet and bring them to bed with him for the night.

There were over a dozen items now—including a sweater a woman had laid aside in a coffee shop while searching in her large bag—and he would draw back the covers of his bed and arrange them the length of it on the side next to his. The sweater formed the chest of his partner for the night, the sleeves arranged like arms in the position of one at rest; a scarf on the pillow folded sideways, one glove representing a hand, and other items constructed the outline of a body. He would get into bed naked, turn out the lamp beside him, and lie awake next to the dim outline for a while like he slept—on his back—arms parallel to his body and looking up at the ceiling. He would remain that way, very still, eyes open in the darkness. Then he would turn onto his side and place his arm carefully over the outline. He would smile at it, then close his eyes and talk to it until he slept.

But tonight he was restless again. He needed to follow. He got up, put on his long, heavy overcoat, wound a thick scarf around his neck, buttoned the overcoat to the top, and went out again seeking someone to join in the night.

3

After the minister dropped Willa off in the city, she walked a long way among towering buildings and bright lights to where the buildings began to get smaller and increasingly dirty; for she had thought that by following the trail of lessening wealth she would eventually come to low-rent neighborhoods, where she could find a cheap room for the night or however long it took to find her mother. What it brought her to finally was silence and stillness, a total absence of people as night began in what she saw was a section of abandoned small factories and warehouses, closed diners and bars. She slowed down after a while, then stopped. For the first time since she was a small child, she felt insignificant and powerless. She listened to the wind rattling a loose window, and in a large darkened window above her she saw broadshouldered machinery in shadows, like creatures come there to look at her.

Not sure of the way, she turned back in the general direction from which she had come, all silence around her in the cavernous streets, except for the sound of her own footsteps and blown newspapers scratching the sides of buildings. Several times she looked anxiously behind her, but there was only the empty street, chains with large padlocks hanging like bracelets from doors and gates, and unlighted neon signs—DINER   BAR   EATS—as if turned off to signal something dire, something coming from which everyone else had fled.

She came to a street of old hotels and closed nightclubs and movie theaters, where she saw Condemned signs and official announcements fixed to doors as admonition against entry. She had counted on finding a furnished room, for she had been told by her grandmother of the opulence of city hotels and had come to think of them as places far beyond her means. But here on this expiring street, with its fading signs and exhausted doorways, she reasoned no sane person would pay more than a few dollars to spend the night. She was tired and the suitcase was becoming heavier with each step, but she was also becoming more confident that this day of bad beginnings would come to a better end. She was lifted up by the sight of the old hotels and the thought that equity, if not grace or great fortune, had at last come her way. Turning into the doorway of a hotel, she decided she would celebrate by the extravagance of spending as much as five dollars for both a room and bath. She would sleep and set out refreshed in the morning.

But the moment she entered the lobby she knew something was wrong. Women with faces like masks sat on wooden folding chairs, as if awaiting visitors toward whose arrival they were finally indifferent. A few turned to look at her, but most continued to stare off. They were young women and some not so young, some fat and some thin. A few had made attempts at adornment with towering hairdos; but little could be done with the way they were dressed, Willa realized, when she saw that they waited without exception in what was not much more than underwear: halters and short pants. She hesitated until a fat woman with small eyes and a large forehead who was standing behind the desk leaned forward, a parapet of huge breasts slowly unfolding on the desk, and signaled Willa to approach her.

She advanced with her suitcase to the desk. She put it down and, despite her tiredness, presented to the woman a genuine smile. For she was grateful for the first sign of attention she had received since arriving in the city. She waited, but her smile was not returned as the woman leaned over the desk, staring down at the suitcase. She looked at it a long time; then she looked back up at Willa. "Did you come for the weekend, honey?" she asked.

"No, ma'am. Just for the night, if you please."

"Uh-huh" was the woman's only response. She smiled over Willa's head at the other women, most of whom were inspecting various parts of their bodies or staring into the distance. She looked back at Willa, indicating the suitcase. "You bring your nightie and things in that bag?" she asked.

"Ma'am?"

The woman's breasts were enclosed in a man's undershirt. Willa could see the large nipples, like eyes staring at her. The breasts slid slowly across the desk toward her, and despite her desire not to, she looked at them. After a minute, Willa realized the woman's gaze had followed hers, looking down with raised eyebrows at her own breasts. "Uh-uh" she said in a manner that seemed to Willa to be some kind of warning. Then the breasts withdrew back across the desk as slowly as they had come.

Willa's legs ached. Near to exhaustion, her patience drained too, she said "Ma'am, I came in here to rent a room. If you have one, please let me know. If not, say so and I'll be on my way."

The woman straightened up. She said "Girlie, if you'd come to sell, we might have done business, but we don't rent rooms around here."

She had been walking the streets around the city's center for hours, always keeping the tall lighted buildings in sight so that she would not become lost.

She had discovered that there were no rooms for rent in the slum areas. Dark-skinned people on doorsteps watched her, becoming silent and still when she approached, as if she brought with her something like a wind over grass which with its passing would restore them to movement. She hurried away from them finally to wander with sinking hope the deserted streets in which she saw only empty houses and shops with broken windows, old closed nightclubs with posters bleeding on their walls, doors sealed with boards of X's, and abandoned bars and restaurant windows, behind which she could see in shadows mounds of refuse and indications that something had wrenched objects out of them. When she stopped to rest under a streetlight, her shadow lay down where she would not dare to sleep.

Sitting now in an all-night diner in the city's center, she was for the first time doubting her dream, which is to say, for the first time doubting herself. The paper plate in front of her had contained a thick sandwich on a long loaf of bread, of which now not a crumb remained, for so reluctant was she to spend any of her small cache of money that she had put off eating all day. An unfinished cup of weak coffee had been pushed aside on the table, unsatisfying to one who had since childhood, both morning and night, drunk her coffee black and strong.

It was hot in the diner. Thick steam rose from urns and food cooking noisily on a grill, and several times her eyelids lowered and she nodded downward toward sleep.

She had discovered old hotels all around there with long stairways on which drunks slept and old women huddled with their possessions around them. Her hopes had been lifted momentarily at the sight of one hotel that looked not so disreputable, but when she inquired at the desk they were dashed again when she learned that a room there cost thirty dollars a night. That information had astonished and outraged her.

She had gone at last in desperation to one of the hotels with drunks and cripples sleeping on the stairs, but even there they had wanted twelve dollars for a room, and one look at the people inside had convinced her that she would probably be murdered in her bed if she were unwise enough to stay there.

She had sufficient money to last her for a while. She hoped the money she carried hidden in her grandfather's hollowed-out Bible would last her for a while. She had taken the Bible after her grandfather died, and inside it had found the only photograph she had ever seen of her mother and small packages sealed in tinfoil she knew by then were condoms. She had wondered at the time: Had he been doing it with another lady on the sly? She would not have blamed him if he had been, for she could not imagine him doing it with the old woman for years. She had never loved her grandfather, who she hardly knew; but the quiet, strange man had always been of distant interest to her. He was as handsome as the old woman was ugly, and looked much younger than her. He was also kind and gentle, while her grandmother was stern and unforgiving. He gave the impression that he might have had dreams at one time, whereas Willa could not imagine her grandmother ever having had a dream. Willa even felt grateful to her grandfather later, as it was the condoms she discovered in his Bible that had given her the idea of how she could earn the money she needed when the time arrived for her to leave.

So when the first boy came in the spring night she was ready, her grandmother asleep and the house dark as the boy called up to Willa's room, where she lay waiting. She heard him again as he waded back through the long, bowing grass at the edge of the woods. Then she got up and opened the Bible and followed him to where he stood waiting beside a tree at the edge of the woods. He turned when he saw her, and she followed him again.

That was the albino boy she had seen watching her when she went with her grandmother to the roadside store. He worked there, and each time they turned onto the road he was standing in clean overalls outside the door, or in the dust beside the porch. He never spoke to them, nor did her grandmother ever seem to notice him; but as they passed, he turned with them: white hair, skin as if glowing in the light, eyes like pink flowers following them. When one afternoon she had a moment alone with him to offer her invitation, he just nodded.

He led her that night along a path through the woods, across a field where the only sound was grass hissing at their feet. When he entered a thick copse of trees, it seemed to swallow him.

She had followed him into a place that was silent and dark, for the trees were so close and profuse overhead that moonlight hung here and there like long ladders lowered through the leaves, and only an occasional star could be seen peeking in on them.

He stood silent and like a white ghost against a tree waiting for her. He held out the dollar, which she took coming up to him, and they lay down together like two sides of a shadow tearing apart.

He came twice more, then never again. But after him there were other boys; and although she had not thought of it at the time, each one had something that set him apart, some imperfection that drew him along the crooked course to below her window and to the copse, where he melted with her beneath the tree. Each with his dollar, and both of them knowing he might never come again. There was a mentally retarded boy who made the long journey from beyond the mills; there were cripples on crutches and a boy who dragged his clubfoot through the leaves. A mute came three times to throw pennies at her window, and there was a blind boy she had to lead by the hand all the way to the copse, and who traced her face with his hand as if he were reading a message carved on the wall of a cave. There were some who were disfigured or had blemishes that made others shun them, and those who were among the ugliest for miles around. She once searched between them in the darkness on the ground with her hand for the hand of one boy, which was not there.

She never felt anything. She seldom thought of them afterward.

There was only a small supply of condoms in the Bible, and she did not know how to get more; so after the first few boys came and left, she insisted that the ones who came later bring with them not only a dollar but a condom as well. She had even watched, curious, as they turned modestly away from her to put on the condoms, then recovered their boldness once it was done. When they were finished, she left quickly so they could unburden themselves alone.

One night when she entered the copse, she saw a used condom tied to a branch of the tree; the next night, a second one had joined it. Every night after that a new condom appeared, so that by summer's end condoms were hanging not only from every low branch of the tree but they had leaped, as if alive and proliferating, to neighboring trees; and by the time the cool nights of autumn arrived they were everywhere overhead. It was as if the trees were bleeding, or issuing a more solemn fruit than any tree had ever borne before. She watched them over the boys' shoulders dripping like stains down the night.

Finally, the boys stopped coming. The nights had turned cold, leaves falling among those small hanging corpses, which were by then the sole occupants of the copse.

It was a strange, lonely winter for her. Now and then she thought she heard voices calling to her from the copse in the late night or in the morning when she had not come fully out of sleep.

One early morning she went to the copse. Mist crawled on its floor. She stood under the trees, where the condoms hung in the cold dawn as still as stalactites in an immemorial cavern. She sat under them, and after a while the sun came up as bright and iridescent as the sun on a cold country morning can be. The mist cleared, and the warm sunlight that fell on the stiff, hanging condoms began to soften them; after a while she discerned slight stirrings among them. Then, gradually, more and more of them began moving, until they were all twisting and swaying in the wind. They seemed to her to be dancing.

She thought of all the babies hanging there in the trees waiting to be born.

Someone shook her and she awoke with her head on the table, confused and not knowing where she was. Then she smelled the grease and the onions and hamburgers frying on the grill. She could not have slept for more than a few minutes.

A large man in a dirty apron and undershirt was standing over her. He had tattoos over every inch of his arms and hands. He shook her again. "Sister, you planning to spend the night here?"

She reached to locate the suitcase beside her against the wall, was relieved when she found it. She got up and staggered out onto the street.

It was colder, and the shock of the air helped to revive her. But she was even more tired now than she had been before, and pulling up the heavy collar of her dress for warmth, she set out again, not knowing in which direction to go or even whether it mattered anymore.

She had been walking for nearly an hour, circling the same well-lighted block at the city's center. She had seen the same things many times: the same buildings, the same stores, the same offices closed and waiting, the same restaurants where, in the chill air, steam clung to windows as food was cooking inside. All that changed were the people, bent by the cold, hurrying around her.

She walked with intentional slowness, stopping to put down the suitcase and rest on each corner. When people turned to look at her, she would pick it up and resume walking. She would do this, she had decided, until morning, when daylight would release her.

She could have gone back to the highway, returned to the house to live out her days feeding on insects in the weeds that had grown up around the house since her grandfather's death. Grown old there. But she knew her mother was somewhere in the city to welcome her and share her life with her. To go back would be to relinquish the dream that had for so long sustained her. Reentering that house would be like closing the door of a dungeon behind her. She would die there, her only neighbor her grandmother's bones.

She stopped again on a corner to put down the suitcase. A traffic light turned colors twice, and vehicles arrived, paused, and then, as if come there only to look at her, drove on. She thought of crossing the street, but she already knew what was there.

She was about to move off again when a bus slid up hissing steam around her. Its doors folded open in front of her; warmth flowed out of it. It stood waiting.

She had hoped to sleep, or at least rest, on the bus. She would ride to the end, then back, through the night. There were not many people, and she had chosen a seat away from the others, slid into it slumped and huddled to gather her body's warmth. Leaning her head on the window, she was shocked by its coldness, and she rolled it away.

After a while the city began to change. The buildings got smaller and assumed more familiar shapes. The sky came up to surprise her. She closed her eyes, and when she opened them again the moon was following her.

The bus was moving more slowly. It revealed streets where trees stood in naked isolation. Blocks of buildings slid up, pulling other blocks behind them. She saw one building with a sign on it: Apartment for Rent. She began to rise in her seat.

Another sign appeared, then another. She put her hand to the window, her face against it. For a while there were no more signs; then she saw scatterings of them drifting off as if on a wind, and others bobbing toward her, with the bus's rocking, out of the night. She was erect in her seat as the thought came to her that where there were apartments for rent, there might be rooms too.

She jumped up and, as she had seen others do, pulled the overhead cord. She picked up her suitcase, but the bus did not stop, as it had for the others. The signs were gone now, the night unblemished for as far as she could see, and afraid that the bus would continue on with her still on it, she reached up and yanked again and again on the cord. But the bus gave no indication that it was about to slow down. She turned to the aisle and, staggering as the bus swayed, stepped into it. She shouted to the driver "Sir! Let me off here!"

All she saw was his face as he looked back at her in a long mirror above his head. He did not answer.

"Oh, sir! Let me off. *I'm talking to you.*"

She lifted her foot, about to step forward, when the bus reached the end of a long block and jerked to a sudden halt. She pitched forward down the aisle, momentum and the suitcase carrying her nearly all the way to the driver. She grabbed a pole, which swung her around, so that she was facing the steps.

Dazed, she went down the steps to the door and pulled at the long pole to open it. She pulled again. She swiveled her head back at the driver, terrified now that the bus would speed off again with her on it. *"It won't open."*

"Push."

The door opened easily, smoothly, before her as she stumbled out onto the pavement. She watched the bus moving off, nodding in potholes, and when it was gone, she turned to face the street.

After the noise of the city, the stillness was disquieting to her. It made her think of fears she thought she had left behind in childhood. High up, two birds drifted, balancing their wings on currents of air.

She looked around. She had felt as if something was watching her, but there was no sign of anyone nearby.

She went back to where the Apartment for Rent signs were and began following them. They led her like signposts without directions on them. But her tiredness had vanished and the feeling of helplessness was gone, for she felt she was now near the end of her long journey and night.

She turned again, still suspecting that someone was following her. But once more there was no one there. After a while, her feeling of well-being overcame caution; an attitude of jauntiness came into her steps. She began swinging the suitcase.

Even the cold did not bother her now, and when a couple approached near a corner, she called to the man "Sir, do you know where there's any rooms to rent around here?"

He pointed. "If they was snakes, they'd have bit you."

She craned her neck around the corner to where she saw three signs on a well-lighted block:

ROOMS FOR RENT

■ ■ ■

When Vernon turned onto the street, she was standing still in front of his building, staring at it—a forlorn figure forsaken in an inundation of night.

He had never followed anyone to his own door before. When he saw that she had put down the suitcase beside her on the pavement, he knew she was not going any farther. He decided to pass her, enter his building, and end that night of following. He left the shadows and approached the entrance and was startled when she spoke to him in the unguarded manner of someone who has never been in a city before. "Excuse me, sir, but do you live here?"

For a moment he was frightened that she had seen him following her. His deep voice struggled out of him, quavering. "Yes."

"Well, I've been trying to find someone to rent me a room, but no one answers their door. You would think that if they had rooms to rent, they'd stay home and rent them."

Vernon stepped into his doorway. He did not move. His voice emerged from the shadows. "It's late. They don't open their doors to strangers this time of night."

"You mean I've got to wait here till morning before I can even see someone?" She sank slowly onto the suitcase at her feet. He watched her.

After a few minutes, she looked back up at him. Her voice was without inflection, as if unwilling to convey anything of hope. "Do you think your landlady would come to her door just this once to rent me a room?" But she knew the answer before he spoke it.

"She's asleep. After she's gone to bed, she doesn't answer her door to anyone."

She looked back at the street. "It's cold" she said.

He did not comment.

She spoke facing the street. "There's no place in all of this city for me to stay tonight. I came a long way just to get this far."

Then Vernon watched her body straighten, her face turn to him, revealing an expression that told him she saw him as more significant than the stranger encountered in a chance meeting he had been to her moments before. He drew his head back against the door frame as far as it would go; only his chin could be seen in the light from the street. He heard her say "Do you live here by yourself?"

"Yes."

She got up and went to him and stood close to him, looking up into his face without shadows between them. He might have pulled away when she did so, except that she took his hand in a way that had in it the familiarity of friendship. He tensed, but he allowed her to hold it. It was as if she now owned it.

She said "If you let me sleep in your room tonight, I'd let you do the thing to me." When she pulled his hand, he came out of the shadows.

They went through the doorway and along the hall and up the

stairs, both so silent they might have been experts in silence. They went up as strangers, but they went hand in hand.

They entered an attic room which, although it had a low ceiling and was austerely furnished, had something soft and feminine about it. There were doilies on the table and bureau, lace curtains, and seraphic figures dancing around a cloth lampshade. There was a small oval mirror with a rococo gilt frame on the wall, but it was hung so high that one could not see oneself in it.

Willa went to a rocking chair, sat in it and began rocking.

Vernon stepped into a large closet and slowly and carefully hung up his overcoat, then his long scarf on a separate hanger. He closed the door slowly, as though inside stood someone he was being careful not to harm.

Willa stopped rocking to watch him. When he turned to face her, she saw him for the first time in full light. He was ugly, but she had seen uglier. She smiled at him, but he just stood there against the closet, bent forward at the waist, looking at her with large, unblinking eyes. She got up from the rocking chair and took the suitcase and sat with it beside her on the bed. She bounced up and down experimentally a few times, then stopped. She looked at him. "Well" she said. "Well, here we are, just the two of us."

He sat down in the rocking chair, but he did not rock.

Willa waited for him to speak. She had the impression that had she chosen, he would have remained in the chair looking at her, silent, for the rest of the night. She had always preferred silence when alone—and nearly always when she was with others—but this silence was different.

After a few minutes, she felt her eyes closing, even as she sat upright. She started dozing, then shook herself awake. She bounced on the mattress again just to make noise.

He still sat in the rocking chair watching her, now bent forward from the waist. She smiled at him, but he did not smile back.

Finally she said "Do you have a balloon? I have to get some sleep pretty soon."

She waited, but his only response was a look of puzzlement. Then she understood and smiled indulgently, like a mother amused at the ignorance of her child. "If you're not the strangest boy" she said. "I bet you don't even know what balloons are for. They're so people don't get babies. I learned that a long time ago." She turned to the suitcase and pushed back the lid. She took out the Bible and opened it.

When she looked up to give him the condom, she saw that his eyes had grown even larger; he was staring at it. When he didn't put out his hand to take it, she tossed the condom into his lap, where his hand went quickly to hide it.

She rearranged herself on the bed. Then she smiled at him again. She was waiting for something to happen, but still he did not move. Finally she reached over and turned out the bedside lamp, which left him nearly in darkness; the light from the window came in onto the bed and part of her where she sat. She got up and went to the other side of the bed, in shadows. She knelt down out of sight behind the bed to take off her clothes. "Hurry up" she called. "We don't have all night." She clambered up naked into the deep, soft mattress, then sighed. "Oh God" she moaned. "Oh Jesus, thank you."

She turned onto her back into the light from the window, arms wide, legs spread, small breasts and hips: a frail figure of curious inconcupiscence.

But so exhausted was she, so long had been this most consummate of all her days, that after a few minutes her eyelids fluttered, closed slowly, and her breathing eased into the breath of peace. She drifted off in the position in which she had arranged herself for him, crucified by sleep.

She began to snore.

It might have been for five or ten minutes that Vernon remained in the chair without moving; not even a breath could be heard coming from him. With his pale face and hands, he might have been a marble statue brought there and put in the chair as a monument to him.

The rocking chair began to move slowly and steadily in the soft carpet. Then it began to rock quickly, and a moment later more quickly still, until finally the chair was rocking frantically and there was the sound of wood squeaking. Abruptly, it stopped.

For a while there was no further movement, only silence again in the room. Then he stirred. There was the sound of tinfoil ripping.

He went to her so silently he might have been her shadow come there tardily to join her.

4

Willa spent part of the next morning preparing herself for meeting her mother. In a discount store she bought a pleated red dress that looked more like a girl's party dress than one suitable for an adventure, a white purse with a strap to keep the photograph and money in, and a gray straw hat with a blue ribbon and plastic apples, oranges and peaches garnishing the brim. The saleslady who helped her told her she looked darling in them. Looking in the store mirror, she saw a pretty, smiling girl she had never seen before.

Hurrying away with the packages, she stopped at a bin that held a large mound of gloves in summer styles and colors. They looked like hands applauding her. She lingered over the bin for a few minutes, then tried on a pair. She had never worn gloves, and although she thought they made her look very ladylike, her hands felt uncomfortable and clumsy in them, so she put them back reluctantly.

Moving quickly toward the exit, she saw a sign near the door announcing a three-dollar sale of moccasins and loafers, which were lined up slanting on wire racks beneath the sign. The shoes she was wearing were the kind her grandmother had always bought for her since she was ten: black, almost square-shaped, with laces and short, sturdy heels. She found a pair of loafers that fit her, paid for them and left the store in such a hurry that she nearly forgot her change. She needed an overcoat too, but they were too expensive and she had decided to wait.

She went quickly and smiling back to her room. All of her purchases combined had cost less than twenty dollars.

▌ ▌ ▌

She had left Vernon's room that morning while he was still asleep, covered by a blanket in the rocking chair. His mouth was open and his arms were outside the blanket, hands folded in his lap. He sat so still he could have been mistaken for dead, except that his eyelids fluttered now and then and several times an expression came over his face that showed fear come to him in his dreams. She stood watching him for a few minutes, then smiling and shaking her head, she left.

Everything seemed much easier in daylight. She had found a room in another of the houses on the street for only fifteen dollars a week. It was a clean, cheerful room, with a window overlooking a garden. Now she sat on the edge of the bed wearing the new dress, loafers and hat. The purse lay beside her as she studied the photograph she had found in her grandfather's Bible for perhaps the hundredth time. What she was looking for was her own face in the features of the pretty girl who looked no older than she was now.

One night when she was three, a woman she was certain was her mother appeared to her in a dream. The woman leaned over her, looked into her eyes. Then she went away.

Willa had never seen the woman in the dream clearly. What she saw was her dim figure dressed all in white and her own child's face looking up at her and her arms reaching up to her. Now she tried to imagine the face of the girl in the photograph on the woman in the dream.

It was a snapshot of a girl standing against a railing on a raised wooden walkway. Behind her was an ocean with white curls of foam riding in on the surf. Two clouds hung over her in an otherwise cloudless sky, and in the distance was a sign—Million Dollar Pier— above a structure that looked old and joyless and could have been the remains of an ancient city. Waves hugged the pier's wooden pilings, frozen there to attest to other times. But the girl in the photograph seemed separated from all of it. She was glaring into the lens of the camera as if to inform those who would one day see her there that she was not there by choice. She was not a child, but she held a child's doll in her arms.

Willa lowered the photograph, thoughtful as always after looking at it so long, so intensely. She remembered then, as she had so often in the past, that moment in the dream when she heard the woman call her name.

She put the photograph into her purse with the money and sat looking around at the room. The house was quiet, perhaps empty, on a Saturday morning.

There are not many things one can look at for long in a furnished room, and after a while she got up to begin that search which fear of failure, she knew, had been causing her to delay.

■ ■ ■

Before Vernon opened his eyes that morning, he knew the girl would be gone. He sat up straight in the rocking chair, blinking slowly. The room was more silent than ever before; he sensed an emptiness in it where the girl had once been. It became stronger and then was alive. It moved. It stood across from him finally, watching him.

Nothing in his experience had prepared him for her staying. He was even grateful she was gone, for that way she remained unchanged in his mind. He wet his lips as he recalled kneeling on the bed bent over her as she slept. He remembered the softness of her skin as he brushed along it with his lips. He put out his tongue, tasting it. He kissed her hair, her eyes and her mouth. Then he drew back. She was smiling. He smiled back. He sought to test the texture of her breast with a finger, but when he touched it, her head rolled to the side; the smile became a frown. He waited, then kissed her mouth again to see if the smile would return. It did. He placed his face next to hers on the pillow, eyes open.

He lay like that for a while; then, slowly lifting one leg at a time, he placed himself between the tangents of her legs. He stayed there, a motionless rider in moonlight, then lowered his body onto hers, barely touching her.

He had not even penetrated her when he reared up. He became an equestrian turned to stone. Stifling his moans, tremor after tremor going through him, he twisted above her.

Breathing hoarsely, he lowered himself nearly onto her. He put his face next to hers. He was making a low sound, like weeping, when she moved and murmured something he could not understand, and he became instantly silent and still. When after a few minutes she did not speak again, he turned his face to her so close that his lips touched her ear. He kissed her cheek. Sighing, he lay face down in her hair. He had lost all sense of time, was drifting, when he heard her say clearly "Momma?"

His eyes opened.

"Momma?" she called again. "Is that you?"

He stiffened. Her arms wound slowly around his neck, then dropped away as she returned to sleep.

He saw himself slip from the bed, step back into shadows.

Now the girl was gone, and he sat in the rocking chair staring at the spot in the bed that bore her imperfect imprint. Finally he got up.

He dressed, folded the blanket and put it back on the closet shelf.

He took down his overcoat and scarf and put them on, then left the room.

He walked up the street slowly, toward the two houses with Rooms to Rent signs on them. He stopped in front of the first house, looked carefully at it, and moved on. He came to the second house, where under the sign a smaller sign had been newly added: No Vacancies. Turning, he went back to his house and stepped into the doorway, where he could watch the street unnoticed.

He saw her return to the house carrying packages. When later she came out again and went off down the street swinging a purse, he followed her.

II

THE PAST
AS A
HUNTER

5

It was for some of them a time of hard times. A great war had come over the land, passed, and left in its wake a new generation of wandering men. It was 1947 when Willa's grandmother, Lydia Wier, who was then seven months a widow at thirty-eight, sat on her porch watching a tall stranger appear out of the trees. He carried a wooden toolbox and a dented tin suitcase and wore a suit so covered with dust that she knew he had walked all the way from town. She noticed this, as she noticed most things—and retained them—because it told her she could hire him for even less money than she had planned to offer.

He walked up the long path to the house with a limp. She already knew he had had half of one foot blown off in the war; what she had not known, and saw now, was that the first two fingers on his right hand were gone too.

The felt hat he wore tilted back on his head was also covered with dust; a cigarette slanted from his lips; and even with his limp, and carrying the suitcase and toolbox, he walked with a swaggering gait. He began smiling at her even before he got to the porch steps. It was a genuine, full-faced smile, but she did not return it. She thought he had probably gotten too many unearned things out of life already with nothing more than that smile. He had thin, delicate lips, which she judged immediately to be a sign of weakness, dark eyes with long, curving eyelashes any woman would have envied, and a small, square chin so perfect it seemed unnatural, as if chiseled out of stone. A lock of black hair curled on his forehead. He was, she decided, too handsome. Handsome men never did any work they did not have to do. She knew. Her own father had been one.

He came to a stop, holding the suitcase and toolbox at his side. She nodded.

"Good afternoon, Mrs. Wier" he said. "My name's Emil Rhineman. Pastor Cooley sent me about the job."

She nodded again but did not answer him. She had already decided to reject him—turn him back through the dust from which he had come—when he did something unexpected: instead of standing respectfully where he was or coming onto the porch to face her—either of which would have established his proper place as a supplicant come seeking her favor—he swung the suitcase and toolbox onto the top step and sat down on the one beneath it. He took off his hat and began fanning himself with it.

He said "You wouldn't have a drink of something cool and sweet, would you, ma'am? That's a son of a gun of a long walk from town on a hot day like this."

She stiffened, hesitated. But she got up finally, went into the house and came back through the squeaking screen door a minute later with a small glass of tap water. She did not bend to give it to him, but he did not rise either to take it; he reached up for it with his maimed hand, as if the hand were no different from anyone else's.

She noticed he had thrown the stub of his cigarette into the dust of the yard. But she did not say anything about that either. A few scraggly shrubs grew there, languishing in the hard soil and gnat-swarming air.

He noticed her watching his hand. He was used to people being curious about it. "If you're worried about this" he said, and he held up the hand palm forward, the three remaining fingers upright, "I can work as good as any man with it. I was born on a farm, and I know machinery too."

"It isn't a farm. There's a few livestock. Some acres of corn and tomatoes and beans. It's all my husband left me except for the insurance, a pension from his church and a little money."

She stopped. It was more than she had offered to tell anyone about herself in years. She began rocking faster.

He smiled again. It was such an eager, trusting smile—as if it had never occurred to him that such generous good humor would get him anything but goodwill in return—that she decided he was not very bright. That was not, she decided too, an undesirable quality in this case.

He said "Well, if that isn't a coincidence, Mrs. Wier. We have something in common, you and me. I got a small pension too from the army for when I was wounded in the war. It happened on an island in the Pacific called Okinawa."

The new pastor of her dead husband's former church had recommended him. He had been working for small wages for the church and around the town since he arrived there three months ago. He was said to be reliable and do good work, although he was known to go off periodically, no one knew where. The women of the town liked him, but he had never been known to show more interest in them than to joke and gossip, although they probably would not have objected if he had. She decided that a man with a steady income of his own—who would not require much in wages—was not one, after all, to be rejected out of hand.

She said "I can't pay much. Just a place to live in the shed out back, meals and maybe a few dollars a week. It's all I can afford."

He dismissed that as unimportant with a wave of his hand. "What it is, Mrs. Wier, is that as soon as Pastor Cooley told me about you—and about your unfortunate circumstances—I knew right away that I wanted that job working around your lovely hearth and home here." He said it like that. *Hearth and home. Lovely.* She noted it but said nothing.

He went on. "You see—and I'm going to be honest with you—in the past there were times—and I'll admit that even now the temptation comes on me now and then—when I've indulged myself in wicked ways. It happened after I came out of the war, which, as you can imagine, left many men maimed like me, both in their spirits as well as their bodies. I come from a good, God-fearing family, and I won't be so indelicate as to tell you all the evil and wayward things I did over there. Let's just say it led me into habits and behavior that were foreign to my upbringing and my conscience too. And when I come out, I'm ashamed to say, I didn't leave them habits behind me, as more fortunate men were able to do. I hesitate to tell you such things, but I'm talking about drinking and gambling and dancing away the night, and yes—and forgive me if this offends a good lady like you—even loose living with women. But I've put all that behind me. I haven't had a drink or done any of them other things for over a year—or do I want to."

She recalled Pastor Cooley telling her of his mysterious disappearances. They weren't a mystery anymore—not to her. But she kept her silence about that too. She could handle that problem when she came to it.

"What I'm trying to say" he continued, "is that when Pastor Cooley told me about you and your situation, I knew we could come to an agreement of—should I say?—mutual benefit."

He paused to impress her with the phrase. She was not impressed. Her stiff posture and stolid expression told him so, as they were meant to. But he was not deterred. He went on. "What I'm trying to say is that wages are secondary to me. What's important is that I live a good, healthy life and at the same time get away from towns and all their temptations—get back, you could say, to the decent ways I was raised in. And if at the same time I can help a good woman like Pastor Cooley told me you are, a Christian woman to boot, who knows the way back to virtue, then all the better, is what I say. I'm twenty-eight now, and I lost those years in the war as well, so I think I better put a handle on my life right now, before it's too late and I'm like those other poor souls roaming around the country from place to place with no direction to their lives. I can say for a fact, Mrs. Wier, that you won't be sorry if you hire me."

There was not much of what he had told her that she believed. She wanted to say so, but stopped herself in time. She said instead "All I want is an honest day's work. It was my late husband who did all the soul-saving around here."

He had never been to Okinawa, nor anywhere else outside the country, unless an army training camp in Kansas would be considered outside the country. It was there that he had been crippled in one of those bizarre misalliances incurred by him with such uncanny regularity that they had maimed his personality as well as his body along the way. He knew that a cruel and ironic fate had stalked him nearly all the days of his adult life. What he did not know was that its name was Emil Rhineman.

It happened during training. His squad had completed an exercise and was resting behind a line of foxholes overlooking a field. On the field were cardboard cutout figures of Hirohito, Hitler and Mussolini. A new squad of recruits crouched behind sandbag parapets in the waist-deep excavations. On the sergeant's commands, they stood up, drew their hand grenades from their belts and, arms far back, awaited the order to release the firing pins. Then the command came, and their arms sliced upward and forward, releasing a rain of metal objects that rose in slow parabolas, turning and twisting, and then dropped in explosions that blew the breath from the earth and sent the sundered caricatures tottering and billowing across the field.

Dust rose; fell in unusual silence. The men had ducked back into the foxholes. Seconds later they arose slowly. They stood still for a moment, then became animated, calling to one another, cursing the torn and fallen dictators with imprecations they imagined delivering to the real enemy when the true time of valor came. They climbed out of the foxholes laughing, embracing, slapping one another on the backs, sending mock punches into shoulders. They had been farm boys, clerks—young men taken from uneventful jobs and lives; now they experienced for the first time the exhilaration of those given the power of righteous destruction and death's bestowal.

Another squad came forward and climbed into the foxholes. The veterans went off, still shouting and gesticulating, to join the others newly baptized in war, who stood in clusters talking or squatted smoking as they looked out at the scene where more caricatures were being raised and another round of mock death would soon descend.

Emil stood to the side of them, smoking against a tree. He was easygoing and friendly and popular among them; but they noticed that now and then he went off in his mind to somewhere else. He was at best a mediocre trainee, unconverted to their common dream of glory, of lives given for the love of God and country. The fact was, he was terrified. Given his luck in the past, he was certain he would die in the first battle. He could not care less for the appeals to patriotism, the religious ganglia delivered by the chaplain, the shibboleths, pep talks and movies they showed him of the enemy's inhuman deeds, the warning that unless defeated, the enemy would occupy their cities, rape their women and enslave them. He did not believe for one second that there was any cause worth dying for. He could think only of how he could avoid the horror. He wanted a woman desperately, for women had always protected him; given him comfort and forgetfulness when life's injustices descended on him. He thought of them lovingly, aching for them, for there he was deprived of them.

It was the grenades that had sent him dreaming this time. In his mind he had retreated from them: from the explosions, the sight of earth bellying up in upheaval, metal pelting the earth like large raindrops. He was thinking other, pleasant thoughts as he stood leaning against the tree. Looking off but unseeing. The tree had a low limb, and he lifted himself onto it. Sat there. Began dreaming again.

Someone shouted it several times: "Live grenade!" It was a scream with the intensity of fear in it.

Emil turned listlessly toward the sound. He began smiling as he watched the men running away, scattering. He thought, *Why are they running?* Then he heard another voice, the sergeant's, yelling "Grenade, damn it, Rhineman! Get the fuck out of there!"

The grenade bounced down the incline as if hurrying to meet him. It came to a stop only yards from the tree.

There was no time to climb down, and if there had been, he could not have moved. He just sat there, staring horrified at it. He put out his hand palm forward—but this too he did listlessly, dreamily, for it was a moment in which he felt that the grenade's force could be miraculously stayed by the hand. He believed that as the world burst apart around him.

The force blew him out of the tree. He rose, as ponderous as a child's parody of a bird, an object hurled high that plummeted with arms wheeling, tumbling end over end. He looked to be embracing the earth when he fell on it.

He lay still for so long, so crumpled and only reminiscently human, that when they got to him they thought he was dead.

He was not a good patient, but he was a good convalescent. He had escaped death and believed that for once a benevolent providence—if even now demanding a price—had visited him. And when at last he was able to, he was sitting up in bed laughing and joking—and at times manically chattering—with the nurses and the other, more gloomily disposed men in the ward.

He was up and about in good time, swinging down the hall on crutches, calling cheerfully into rooms where men without limbs, or wrapped and as still as mummies, lay with tubes crawling into their bodies. He once sat by a quadruple amputee, trying to cheer him up. And the fact that the stump of a man never spoke to him, even turned his face away from him, did not diminish Emil's good humor.

One night in the laundry room he managed clumsily, getting down off his crutches, to make love to one of the nurses, who met him there most evenings during the rest of his convalescence. There were other nurses he could have had too, but he was faithful to that one, who was cheerful and provided him with the extra attention and privileges he would not have had otherwise. He assured her each night of his fidelity, for he prided himself on certain refinements in manners and morals, and he had a strong need that each woman, as her turn came, be made aware of his virtues, believe in them as much as he needed to believe in them.

He was visited by a doctor who told him he could be discharged in a few days. Emil nodded, anxious to put the army, with all its deprivations and its demeaning attitude toward enlisted men, behind him as quickly as possible. But he hid his real feelings at first, knowing the army's perverse habit of denying the soldier whatever would most please him.

The doctor told him they wanted to give him a metal device—an artificial foot fitted to his stump—but it would mean he would have to stay on at the hospital for therapy and instruction in its use. He refused to listen to the doctor's assurances and placations. The interview ended when Emil began screaming that all he wanted from the army was what he was entitled to: his freedom.

He compromised. He submitted finally to the indignity of a thick, ugly shoe, which told all who might see him in it that he was a cripple. He wore it out of the hospital, then bought a pair of two-tone wing-tip shoes, packed the right one with toilet paper and left the offending pair in the men's room of the bus station. He left for Kansas City certain he had left behind on the floor of the cubicle not only his last connection with the army and the war but the major privations and miseries of his life as well.

He was wrong, as he always was when he was most confident of coming good fortune. He had only his severance pay and a pension too small to live on, and now he saw the world moving around him, indifferent to him. Even the women passed him over in favor of those on leave from the war or about to go off to it. He knew he would never go home; he had sworn when he was drafted that he would not return. So with no aims, no goals, he boarded a bus to San Diego, where he had heard there was good money to be made in the factories now booming due to the war.

But even there he found disappointment; providence had only winked at him, after all, and gone on. Fooled him once more. For the well-paying jobs were not available, he discovered, to cripples. He could have claimed preference as a veteran had he been willing to reveal the reason for his quick discharge without once having seen combat; but his pride would not allow him to endure that humiliation at a time when every man in uniform was thought a hero.

He drove trucks for a while; he swept out factories. He lived in a cheap downtown hotel and spent his nights drinking in bars that were busy with jukebox music, conversation and laughter. He moved restlessly among them, unwilling, unable, to make friends. He discovered he now had to pay whores for what he needed above all else: the solace of women. One night, drunk on whiskey, he beat a whore nearly senseless (he claimed later not to remember doing it); and although it was minor excitement in that city at that time, he might have gone to jail anyway if he had not—swaying in the hotel-room doorway—pleaded with two policemen that he was a veteran returned from the Pacific. He held up his maimed hand as evidence of it; and although he could see that the policemen were wavering, the thought that he might be sent to jail or even to prison so terrified him that he found himself begging to be released. He began crying.

The young whore had been taken from the room. He knew she was not permanently injured, although her face and dress were covered with blood from where he had broken her nose. He could only hope she was waiting with the other policeman when he asked the two officers to shut the door of the room. Then he went to the bed, sat on it and took off his sock and his shoe. He showed his half foot to them.

As they started out of the room, one of them turned back, saying

"We'll see that the girl keeps quiet, but you get out of town by morning." He closed the door quietly behind him.

He would remember that room till his dying day, and the shame he felt. He would remember the light from the hotel sign outside his window flashing on and off on the rug. The girl had gone away limping, but now alone in the room, staring down, he realized that it was not from her injuries she had limped: one of her high-heeled shoes lay capsized on the rug. He sat as the police had left him: cross-legged and motionless, mouth twisted as he stared down at the small, pale obloquy that was the truncated half of a foot he had offered up to them for his freedom. He noted for the first time the unhealed thin scar at the point of surgical severance, like a wild animal's claw imprinted on his flesh. He fondled the foot. Then he leaned over it and began talking to it.

He went through the rest of the war like that: alone, bitterly wandering. He brought uneasy ghosts into bed with him each night; they lay next to him, forbidding him to sleep.

There were other occasions when he might have gone to jail, other acts of violence and drunkenness; but each time that ritual revelation, the silent unveiling of the foot—sitting on a bed or drunk on the street, begging retreat to alleys and doorways—saved him.

It had occurred to him that he could try to pass himself off as a wounded veteran returned from overseas. Few women would question it. But his milieu was cheap bars, hotel lobbies, penny arcades and movie theaters; and each time he determined to do it, he backed away. For everywhere were servicemen, some in civilian clothes on leave, who might overhear him; and the possibility of being asked questions, pinned to details, places, names, dates—his fear that some stranger would expose him as bogus—was too great a price to pay, no matter what momentary relief it brought him.

He was living in a hotel in the Loop in Chicago when V-J Day arrived. He went out onto a street jammed with people, where high above him office workers threw ticker tape and confetti out of windows; it was as if the windows had grown arms in his absence. He watched a hat drifting down on erratic currents of air; a brassiere descended, fluttering and billowing. He saw flocks of balloons fly away off the tops of buildings.

He was soon in the thick of it, drunk with the rest of them, a fifth of Old Granddad raised to strangers, as their bottles were to him. Cars stalled in the packed streets, horns blaring and drunken celebrants rocking them as if to shake their occupants into the spirit of it all. Some of the drivers gave up and joined the partiers, while others remained inside, doors locked and windows down, as they watched bottle-wielding partiers swarming over their cars, lying and sitting and standing on them, taking both car and occupants into captivity. People danced on the roofs of cars, did swan dives into the cushioning crowds. A few leaped with abandonment into a sea of heads and shoulders, and here and there couples danced in the street with the ease and unawareness of dancers in their own parlors. He saw a naked woman holding an open champagne bottle, standing with arms and legs outspread on a car roof, as annunciatory as a goddess above the cheering crowd.

It was his liberation too, his release from loneliness and angry nights. The war was over, and soon no one would care anymore who had been where or done what. He grabbed women out of the wayward crowd, snatched them from doorsteps and kissed them, bending them far backward in a movie lover's exaggerated embrace before wandering off to other brief, nameless encounters. He was wildly drunk, but everyone else was drunk too. Women were swept into passionate entanglements, drawn along by the crowd, locked in embraces with strangers. A sailor's hand caressed a girl's white-pantied rear while he kissed her. A drunken girl with torn panties around one ankle sat weeping against a lamppost. She called to Emil, but he just stared at her, then went on.

He ended his celebration that night in his hotel room with a bottle and two women and awoke the next morning alone, sick and trembling. He went into the bathroom and vomited into the toilet, then staggered to his trousers to find that his wallet and nearly all of his money was gone.

He emerged from the hotel in the early morning onto a street changed to silence. Debris was everywhere. A store window was broken and boarded up. Hundreds of beer and whiskey bottles littered the street and sidewalk, stood upright on window ledges, doorsteps, the hoods of cars. Only a few people were about, looking as dazed and silent as wanderers in a dream.

During the years that followed, he roamed that part of the country to find that those jobs he had depended on during the war were no longer there. He followed signs to the inevitable Not Hiring. All around him stood closed factories, stilled and silent, dreaming of destruction. For a while he did not notice the other men who had joined him, come as if from a secret place of those like him who were crippled and disfigured and sent wandering. They had the look of desperate, violent men disenfranchised by lies and for whom there was no appeal, recourse or retribution. He avoided them.

He avoided too after a while the large cities whose anonymity had always depressed him, the nightly rounds of bars, bitter women to whose disappointment and anger he briefly joined his own, jobs so menial and demanding he felt they were squeezing the last remnant of spirit out of him. At twenty-seven, he felt he was growing old before the appointed years.

He journeyed south for the first time. He hitchhiked to Oklahoma and through Texas, where he turned back out of the dust and the mantislike oil drills preying on the land to the dense marshlands and cypresses weeping over Louisiana, then up through white-mansioned and cabin-weary Mississippi into Alabama and Georgia. The hostile cities of the North were behind him; the sun, red clay and calm of rural Georgia began to revive him. He slept in a field one night under a sky so jammed with bright stars that it was as if he were seeing the night for the first time. Cows slept half hidden imbedded in tall grass all around him, and slim white clouds drifted like the bones of night above him. He discovered peace of a sort in that field.

When he found a job the next day in a nearby town as a janitor in the county courthouse, he thought the time had come when he could stop wandering. On payday a month later, he bought a suit for the first time since leaving his civilian clothes at the training camp to be mailed back to his family—all that remained of him now in their possession. He bought a felt hat such as gangsters in the movies of his youth had worn; he turned the brim down on one side the way George Raft did. He thought of his new image as signifying a new life in which he would leave the old life of the outsider behind.

That night he left his room in the courthouse basement dressed in his new clothes and went to the juke joints outside of town, where in the bars joined hip-to-hip on a dirt road there was music and pretty girls with wild hair and bright laughter dancing barefoot in that frenetic, vertical style of the time in the South which was like upright rabbits hopping on the plank floors.

It was not long before he became a favorite in the bars, both with their owners, who were usually uncommunicative and suspicious of strangers and town people unwise enough to wander in; and with the rough, fun-loving men who found in him a pleasant companion who shared with them the joy of drinking and laughter and dancing and lusts unencumbered by thoughts of retribution. And at the end of the night, he danced off with the prettiest girls.

He was happy, and he might have stayed there if one night he had not taken into his basement room and the small cot he slept on the fourteen-year-old daughter of the town's mayor, who had pursued him from the first moment she saw him working around the courthouse.

One night. And when after it was over and she told him she had done nothing to protect herself, he understood too that she had been a virgin. Done nothing, she explained, because she loved him and trusted him. She said it with confidence in him, as if she knew him. Lying next to her, he stared at her. She said it would be all right so long as they loved each other—and he kept staring. She smiled at him, eyes shining with love.

The next day he bought a box of Trojans. He had never used condoms voluntarily before.

He had decided to remain there, nested, thoughtless of any need beyond those that arose nightly and were satisfied by her and in the roadside bars he still frequented. He put on weight. His face took on a healthy color for the first time in years. He grew solid on uneventfulness.

Until the night two months later when she came to him frightened, believing in him but needing to be told she could believe in him. Something hardened in him at the arrival at last of that which he had known that first night would come, must come, given the temper and auguries of his life. She came to him and told him he had on that first night seated a permanent passion in her womb. She smiled weakly, a small girl with shoulders hunched in humility before him.

He made love to her, held her, comforted her. She raised a tear-stained but valiant face, a child's face, to his. She was happy later when she told him her plans for them, talked on through the night, while he lay beside her in the dimness, removed from her. She kissed his maimed hand; then she crawled to the foot of the cot and, bending over the foot, kissed it too. As he watched her, all he felt at first was curiosity. Then he felt loathing for her. He thought of those country girls dancing brightly beyond the town, hanging laughter all over the night, going out with their lovers into the woods beyond the bars. They were free. She smiled at him from where she was kneeling at the foot of the cot when he told her he would marry her. He even felt a moment of pity for her.

But he knew what statutory rape meant too, the consequences should he not marry her, and before dawn he was on the highway with his suitcase, walking quickly, then hitchhiking north.

He changed his name for a while. Once more he took any job he could find, living quietly, always heading north. He had left with only the few dollars he had in his pocket.

He was certain the law had been alerted about him, that his name and description had been published in every town he was forced to stop in along the way. He had dreams in which they came for him. He feared many things, but he feared the law and prison most. Washing dishes, sweeping and mopping the floors of restaurants and bars for a few dollars, his meals and a place to sleep, he made slow progress. What better-paying jobs he might have had required the answers to questions, a history, a social security number, a real name; the few dollars left from the jobs took him only to the next town, the next stop in his slow escape to the North.

He arrived hungry and cold one early morning at a small town in North Carolina. He had slept by the road the night before, not eaten most of the previous day. The town was asleep, not a person abroad in it; silent even in early light in a way that made clear to him more forcefully than anything had previously the fact of his aloneness.

He roamed the town envious—hating the people he knew were sleeping unblemished by fear in the houses he passed. He sat on a bench—too hungry, too defeated to go on—to wait for the town's awakening. When well after dawn he saw a diner opening, he was its first customer.

The owner of the diner had no job for him, but he sent him to the home of a minister who offered him work repairing the roof of his church.

The tall, stout minister came to the back door to interview him; and to Emil's surprise he dismissed as of no importance the crippled hand when he held it up to show it to him. They went to the church a few blocks away, where Emil inspected the roof and declared he could repair it so that it would be as good as new.

He began to come alive again that morning; for if there was one thing he had always enjoyed, felt a sense of pride and accomplishment in, it was working with his hands: he could fix or build anything a skilled artisan could. It was pleasant work in the open and under the sun that, until the kindly minister had assured him otherwise, he had thought had been forever precluded from his life.

He stayed in the town for a month, happier by far than at any time since he was a boy, since the world had begun to close in on him. And it was there too, for the first time other than to avoid jail, that he claimed a week later that his mutilation had occurred in the war.

He had not meant to; he had hoped that day in Chicago to leave all of it behind. But the war had been over for two years, there was little chance of his being found out in the lie, and the soft-spoken minister had told him so often that he was a worthy and even excellent young man that he had come to believe it himself. Released from the past, seizing the most exotic name he could recall from the war, he informed his employer one morning that he had been wounded on the island of Okinawa in the Pacific.

Given his nature—what had been suppressed in him so long—once the lie was out of his mouth, others followed: he recounted vividly those battles he had read about in the newspapers, come during his period of exile to be obsessed by; those he had sat watching on lonely afternoons and evenings in *The Movietone News of the World*. He told it so convincingly that he came to believe it himself.

For the first time in Emil's life he was in awe of himself, of his power to sway others to see his imaginings with him, to make them believe in him as much as he wanted to believe in himself. It made him feel virtuous, even vindicated.

That morning, sitting on the ladder leaning against the church roof and for the first time taking off the shoe and sock in something other than shame, he revealed the foot to the benign and gravely watching man.

The minister provided his room and board until the job was completed, so that when he was paid he had enough money left to take a bus the rest of the way north.

But the day he left, he once again experienced that fear that had haunted him all the way up from Georgia through the Carolinas: that even there in that quiet town where he had known only kindness, at that moment while he waited for his bus in the restaurant, ladling sugar into his coffee from a fly-specked bowl at the Formica table, the dreaded sheriff would appear. He would shove the handcuffed and terrified Emil through the door and into a cell, where he would await the coming of judgment out of Georgia.

He hurried onto the bus and to the back, where he stretched out below window level until it had rolled, languid and rocking, not only out of the town but past that point where his imagination seemed almost like reality. He had bought a ticket to Philadelphia, but he did not stay there. Broke again when he arrived, he walked out of the bus terminal down Arch Street, past the winos waiting on curbs and in doorways, onto Race Street in Chinatown, where a wall of impassive eyes followed him, then onto the bridge where the busy Delaware River passed like film below him.

He got a ride on the tailgate of a truck going south again, but now within the safety of northern sovereignty, looking across land that was fertile but less rich and vibrant than that of Georgia. It occurred to him then for the first time that with all the traveling he had done, he had not progressed an inch in betterment, nor had the journey really taken him anywhere.

That was what he was thinking when he felt the truck dip, then rise, bringing into sight a town not unlike that town in North Carolina, and at its center, on a hill, stood a church with a large cross held up like a hand against the sky. But this was a much bigger church than the other: whiter, richer.

He jumped from the truck before it regained speed off the incline and, stopping only to wave to the driver, crossed the highway onto a dusty road, which in minutes carried him down into the town.

He headed straight for the church.

He presented himself to the minister as not only a veteran who had served his country—given to it part of his youth and his body (as he exaggerated his limp and held up the hand for the man to see)—but also as a skilled craftsman expert at any job a man could perform with his hands. He smiled a smile that was a combination of frankness and good-will no longer contrived: it contained a firm belief in the goodwill of others toward him.

The town was named Pineville, New Jersey. Its neat houses had porches and lawns bellying down to the sidewalks, with here and there garden ornaments of cranes, swans, pretty girls holding parasols and grinning Negro footmen in livery. The downtown was a row of one- and two-story buildings along eight blocks of a main street ending abruptly in a wall of woods. Beyond the woods, barely acknowledged by the town, were factories, which for years had been slowly eating up the countryside, soiling its rivers and streams, blackening its fields. It was a town too fastidious to be closely associated with that disreputable source from which its former affluence had been derived. Now the fac-tories were nearly all empty, the mills grinding out a bare existence. But it was a town that had survived before the factories came, and would do so again.

It did not take him long to win over Pastor Cooley—a man, he understood now, who like his North Carolina brother had come to his calling through a need to believe in goodness within every man, and who was therefore susceptible to accepting any facsimile of goodness presented him. Emil had learned in North Carolina the first important lesson of his life: that he could become what he succeeded in making others perceive him to be. So that quite soon, under the pastor's spon-sorship, he was busily and happily—if not prosperously—engaged in whatever work was needed to be done around Pineville. Circulating, smiling, he was soon calling people by their first names, stopping some-times (but only with those he knew were too old or too young to have been there) to tell again of the war in the Pacific and his own modest contribution to it. For Emil was by nature disposed to find happiness in small and uneventful ways; and in that he was like them.

He moved into a boarding house and within a month was able to buy some of his own tools—those of the trade he had at last found; and he even designed and built a wooden toolbox with drawers and compartments; and upon the side of which he painted what was for him not only a signature but a declaration of peace long after the other armistice was signed:

EMIL RHINEMAN
REPAIRS & ODD JOBS DAY OR NIGHT

Once more he would have stayed happily fixed to a place that accepted him: it was all he wanted from life now—all he thought he wanted, that is, until having achieved it, the other needs summoned him again.

It was during his second month there that it began—a time during which he lived soberly, even celibately, for he was not about to repeat the mistake he had made in Georgia by impregnating yet another town girl (for she was not the first he had fled in the night, only the first minor) with what he now thought of as his anxious seed. Nor did he want to diminish that image of healthy young manhood he now enjoyed in the town, for he had regained as well a measure of self-respect.

One night, only weeks after he had finished and first proudly displayed the emblem toolbox—as if by putting his name on it he could make it a fact—having heard of the settlement, he set out from his boarding house onto a road abutting the woods at one end and the wandering Whitewater River on the other. Minutes later he stood on the lip of Milltown.

It was called that, but it had never officially been given a name, for to do so for the residents of Pineville would have signified if not approbation, at least a conditional acceptance. They preferred to pretend it was not there.

At one end of that backwoods community created for the pleasure and entertainment of the workers in the factories around it, there was a row of wooden shacks and cribs, the homes and places of employment of black women and girls available for from three to ten dollars. Cutthroat poker, craps and roulette could be played in the kitchens. White lightning and marijuana could be purchased at any door. At the other end were the bars where only the white locals and workers were welcome; the same services were provided more expensively, but without anxiety and danger.

It was there, that night, that Emil saw again the familiar dirt road, the haphazard wooden bars, heard the music coming up off the street. A place assembled hastily, which could be as quickly dismantled. There too he saw dancers, men and women drinking at crude wooden bars, the lights from open doorways and windows casting dancing shadows onto the road—all he thought he had left behind forever the night he fled that town in Georgia.

But it was not quite the same here: gone was the exuberance, the wild laughter of young girls and rollicking men—as if northerners could not accept pleasure without paying a price in gloom.

On a high hill at the end of the road was a Negro church, which seemed oblivious to or defiant of the sin that was occurring below it. The Mount Calvary Baptist Church of Jesus Joyful, proclaimed the crude hand-lettered sign; and having announced it, the church set about the serious business of religious joy. Music lifted up from it, voices ecstatic in hymn rising above the sounds of revelry below. He saw the Negroes through the tall windows, tambourines raised and clattering, a piano pounding and arms shaking at heaven as if to invite down that God they hoped would be coming for them soon. He could see women in tall hairdos high-stepping in the windows, several wailing and with their arms raised emerging onto a wooden porch, which began shaking over the very precipice of perdition, then swayed as others joined them in such religious frenzy that the frail porch seemed in danger of collapsing and plunging them down the hill to join the sinners below.

He drank little and quietly that night, then returned to his room sober. The second time he went, he joined the dancers. Around midnight he bought a bottle and rented one of the cabins half hidden in the woods, where he spent most of the night drinking and making love to one of the girls. He left her sleeping and, while it was still dark, made his way unsteadily on the highway back to his room.

What kept him away for a week after that was fear: he awoke the next morning still drunk and remembered the dancing, the release later in the floating and pale whiskey-shimmering night in which he saw the face of another girl as he undressed slowly in front of her, watching her, then forced her to her knees and made her fellate him. She resisted at first, then submitted. Afterward she wept. When she left, he found someone else to take her place. He was terrified that one night he might do something in unguarded drunkenness that would bring the law upon him and reveal his fugitive past. He had never considered the likelihood of the southern girl's parents choosing abortion over bastardy, which would have guaranteed their silence. Such a probability would have occurred to another but not to Emil, whose every immoral act and crime erected in him a need for atonement, which he then feared would in fact be realized.

Then he went again. He spent the weekend, renting a cabin for the two nights. He danced both nights in that odd, halting step that made him rock to the music more from side to side than forward and back, and he flirted and held the prettiest girls in his arms and gave them kisses that were without promises but which kept them for him as candidates for the night's end. During the day he left the cabin only to eat and bring a new girl back with him to replace the one who had left that morning. He did not drink heavily: he drank beer, nursing a half-dozen bottles through the night. He returned to his room Sunday night sober and proud.

That weekend convinced him he had gained some control over his life at last, demonstrated that discipline was not totally lacking in him. He was a man with a trade, a home of sorts now. He began to think of renting a small shop, with his name over the door, winning the respect of neighbors. That rectification, even rectitude, was something well within his powers to achieve.

He believed it so firmly that, after a month of weekends like the first one, he rewarded himself the next weekend when he relaxed his rule about liquor; he drank moderately and without mishap, although he was weaving when he left Monday morning toward dawn to make his way back to the room.

By the following weekend he was well known there—so sought after as company by the male regulars as well as the women that drink after drink was bought him, and was bought by him in return, for anything else was unthinkable in good company.

He remembered dancing; he remembered the pretty girl so unlike the rough mill girls and whores and workers' daughters who came there every weekend; he remembered pursuing her, excluding the others, who saw him for the first time in serious courtship. He remembered the beginning and the middle of the night, but that was all he remembered until he awoke in his cabin and recognized her in his bed.

"Oh, Jesus!" he whispered.

He remembered it all then as he moved carefully off the bed, went naked to the foot of it, where he stared down at her.

She was a girl he had spoken to briefly once in Pineville, dressed that day in the crisp blue uniform of the town's Catholic high school. The daughter of a man he had worked for.

He was sick. He needed to throw up and almost did, but forced it back for fear it would wake her. Then he remembered the demand she had made of him and brought his hand to the condom, which had slid nearly off his penis and was hanging with his discharge still in it. It swayed as he moved on tiptoe toward his clothes.

He did not even try to dress in the cabin. He gathered up his clothes and went into the now quiet, nearly deserted morning and, within the dense shadows of the woods, covered his nakedness in stages which kept appearing and disappearing until only a pale face and hands came into view, still and waiting within the sanctuary of the woods.

He emerged among trees under a bright cusp of moon and moved so quickly and quietly and bent close to the ground that he might have been thought a madman prowling those corridors of night. He stopped when he got to the road, to be certain no one was there, then quickly and in silence hurried along it toward the far woods and the highway.

He had put the incriminating condom in his pocket. When he got on the highway, he took it out and, running and raising it like a frail flag, flung it away.

For two days he left his room only to hurry to the hall bathroom and back. He told his landlady he was ill and did not want to see anyone; he asked her to leave his meals outside his door.

He lay on his bed fully clothed and waited again for the footsteps, the raised voices talking about him, the pounding on the door that surely then would send him into the arms of the law and perhaps even back to Georgia.

When he was calm enough to go out, he went directly to Pastor Cooley's house to collect money still owed him for work he had done. After explaining that he had to leave Pineville for his health's sake and return to an environment more like the one in which he had been raised ("return to the soil" as he said), he was told of the widow Lydia Wier and how since her husband—Pastor Cooley's predecessor—had died suddenly of a heart attack seven months earlier at the age of sixty-nine, she had need of a man like Emil around her place.

He dreaded a return to a life of wandering; if there was some way he could do it, he wanted to remain in that town where he had found welcome. He decided that since the girl would not want it known that she went to Milltown, she would probably keep quiet and nothing more would come of it. He would get a second chance. He would hide out for a month and, if all went well, return to that town that was the nearest thing he had found to a home.

■ ■ ■

Emil came out through the screen door in front of Lydia Wier and went down the porch steps, where she stopped and stood watching him as still as a caryatid erected in that unlikely place.

He was about to go around the house to the shed when she called "One more thing, Mr. Rhineman." He stopped. "There won't be any smoking or drinking on this property. There never has been, never will be."

"No, ma'am. I told you I was through with all that."

When he was gone, she sat down and resumed the rocking he had interrupted.

She discovered he was as good as his word. For a week she kept watch on him at the windows. When he was out of sight, she went looking for him. Nor did she hesitate, but went straight up to him: she did not want him to think that feminine reticence was part of her character. It was not, nor had he thought so for a moment. But she never found him dawdling, as she had others who had come under her strict scrutiny. He was skilled and dependable and attentive to a degree that was unusual for most hired men, to say nothing of one who had appeared out of nowhere. He did his work quickly and happily, which was inexplicable to her, for she hated what was required of her outside the house and would have sold the place after her husband's death if there had been anyone willing to buy it for what it was worth or if she had had anywhere else she wanted to go. But she had never considered a more adventurous or romantic existence, as another woman might have who had married a childless widower thirty-one years her senior; she had little imagination and no desire for a life out of the ordinary.

She did not want to marry again. She would not have married her first husband except for her father urging her to when at twenty-five no one else had asked her. She had closed her eyes each time he mounted her, turned her head to the wall until he came sweating to its end. She did not want any more of that, either.

What annoyed her about Emil was his good-natured acceptance of her close watch over him. Even in the face of her rigid and unfriendly approach, he always stopped work to smile at her and greet her pleasantly, as if he were genuinely happy to see her. Several times he began telling her about the war and his travels after it was over, and although she made her disinterest obvious, he continued his prattling as if unaware of her displeasure. It confirmed to her what she had suspected about him the first day: that he was not only unintelligent but was easily aroused to frivolousness and embarrassing candor. It never occurred to her that his effusiveness was the expression of one as anxious to please others as her disinclination to please anyone was part of her.

Two weeks after his arrival, she observed him from her bedroom window as he stood nearly hidden behind a tree just inside the woods flanking her property to the east. She might not have noticed him had she not seen the wheelbarrow and shovel first, then smoke drifting out from behind a tree. A minute later he stepped from behind the tree, stripped his cigarette, pinched off the end, and ground it beneath the heel of his shoe as country boys and soldiers are taught to do. He looked around both ways, then glanced up quickly at the house and the window behind which she stood watching. Satisfied that he had escaped discovery, he took up the wheelbarrow and hurried off around the side of the barn with it.

She stood at the window after he had gone, still holding the lace curtain behind which she had hidden; then she closed the curtains, just as she had closed her mind to the possibility of firing or even reprimanding him for his defiance. When dealing with those who served her, Lydia Wier was not known for her charity or forbearance, nor was she even marginally tolerant of an affront to her intelligence. Years before in Pineville, a merchant had tried to deceive her in a matter so trivial another would have chosen not to mention it; but from that day on she took her business to a competitor, even though she had dealt with the first storekeeper for years. This time, however, she not only did not confront Emil with his deception but, seeing him sneak cigarettes on other occasions, kept silent then too. She told herself that a hired man so hardworking and dependable would be next to impossible to replace, especially at the wages she was willing to pay; that so long as he did not smoke on the grounds, she would pretend not to notice and overlook it. (Thinking it over, she noted his bizarre sense of honor in that he had in fact followed her instructions by stepping off her property into the woods to smoke.) Satisfied with her motives, she put it out of her mind.

Emil stayed not only for the month but through the summer and into the fall.

He had performed some wonders during that time. The two vehicles that until then had gone uncared for since her husband's death now stood in what had once been a stable, not only serviced by Emil at small expense to her but (as much as a ten-year-old Ford pickup and an only slightly newer Nash Rambler could) were now gleaming from the attention he gave them in his spare time.

By then her suspicions about him had—if not disappeared—lessened to the point where she exchanged an occasional pleasantry with him; she surprised herself several times by smiling at his crude but inoffensive attempts at humor; and once, on an unseasonably mild day, while seated in her rocker on the porch in the last light of afternoon, she even invited him to join her. He sat on the top step and began telling her one of his stories of the army—but this time with less enthusiasm, she noted, than on previous occasions. After a while he stopped talking, and they sat with only the sound of rocking as they watched the light bleeding slowly out of the sky. The sun had inched down between the tall pines, and the shadows had begun moving out of the woods toward them when they heard the howlings of two dogs far off beyond the highway in such high, plaintive discourse that it carried distinctly to them over the clear autumn air. It was then that she became aware that for the first time since she had known Emil he was voluntarily silent; became aware too that he was looking up at her with an expression that was part curiosity, part admiration. When she looked down at him, catching him at it, he turned quickly away. For a moment she was confused, even disturbed in a way she could not have anticipated, did not understand. She forced herself to look away from him, then got up and, pulling her sweater tightly around her, went into the house, leaving him there alone.

That night, for one of the few times she could recall, she was unable to sleep. She lay until morning thinking about him. Several days later she wondered if he might be more than the characterless, superficial young man she had thought him to be from the first moment she met him. She began to wonder if there might be something in him worth cultivating.

After that, on those days still mild enough for him to work outdoors, she once again, but more frequently than before, stood behind the curtains in her bedroom watching him. She observed him while standing for several days, then brought a chair to the window and began watching from there.

On the first cold night of the winter, she was reading her Bible before the fire when she put down the book and looked off into space. She was listening to the wind and to the house's contractions as it came alive in the winter with a sound like breathing. She heard the chair on the porch begin rocking slowly in the wind, as if she were out there awaiting someone's arrival. Then she became aware of another sound: footsteps going away from the window toward the shed.

She could not guess how long he had been there, nor what could have compelled him to stand unannounced beneath the window in the cold; if he had come to talk to her for some reason, he had decided against it and gone back to the shed. She heard the door shut with what she sensed was reluctance.

He had all the necessities: besides a cot to sleep on, she had provided a chair, a table and a kerosene lamp. There was a sink, a chamber pot and a kerosene heater. But he had left the warmth of the shed to stand in obvious indecision outside her window. Reluctance, indecision, lack of confidence—they were qualities she had never thought of him possessing; her recognition of them now surprised and shocked her, as if he had begun revealing to her unseen in the night parts of himself she had not noticed or wanted to notice before in daylight.

She got up and put on her coat and went out through the kitchen to where she saw his light on in the shed. She went down the back porch steps to where her footsteps crunching on the newly hardened ground announced her approach. She watched as his shadow through the window rose up on the wall from where he had been sitting on the cot. Then she saw it go down. She knocked, and the shadow rose again and traveled across the wall to the door. The door opened, and he stood facing her.

She spoke to him out of the shadows. She spoke quickly, even harshly. "There's no reason for you to sit out here by yourself. If you want, you can come share the parlor with me."

Having said it, she did not wait for an answer; she turned and walked quickly away, her footsteps retracing their sounds. By the time she had reached the porch steps, his door had closed and his footsteps were hurrying after hers.

He came to the house each night after that. She always heard him even before she heard his footsteps on the front porch steps. But even though he sat across from her for a few hours each night, there was little conversation: he seemed uneasy in this new and unaccustomed intimacy between them—perhaps reluctant, she thought, to go beyond the limitations she had defined for him the first night. She would have welcomed the conversation, the opportunity to establish a more cordial and relaxed relationship between them; but once that condition of silence she had herself imposed on their evenings had been established, she had no idea how to countermand it.

Except for her Bible, the only things she kept in the house to read were some old *Saturday Evening Post*s on the table beside his chair. She had shown them to him the first night, and he had seemed pleased at first, opening one and holding it high in front of his face like someone who had little experience at handling reading matter. He turned the pages loudly, as if to demonstrate to her his enthusiasm; then after a while he began turning them quickly and often, so that she realized his only interest was in the pictures. A little later she heard his enthusiasm for the pictures ending too as the pages began turning slowly, and now and then ceased altogether when she knew he was not looking at the magazine at all. He let the fourth one fall into his lap.

She looked up. "I don't have anything else for you to read. The only reading material my husband and I kept were those magazines and our Bibles. I keep my husband's Bible upstairs if you—"

"No newspapers?"

"I'm afraid not."

"What did you and him do at night, then?"

She sensed the implication, even impertinence, in the question and decided it was best to ignore it. She returned to her own reading. She heard him speak—a little louder, bolder, and with something of the petulance of a child in his tone.

"Don't trouble yourself getting any Bibles for me. I had enough of all that when I was a boy to last me the rest of my life."

She was surprised that the remark did not anger her; surprised too that it suggested a shift in his attitude—no longer submitting to the total control over him he had allowed her before. It was as if he were signaling new conditions if he were to continue to come there each night; conditions, she felt—and the thought frightened her—predicated on a male prerogative of dominance. But she did not say anything.

He stood up. "I'm going out for a while" he announced. He had not asked her permission to leave, nor did he explain when he went out the door without another word to her.

She lowered the Bible the moment she heard the door close; she sat staring into the fire. When after a few minutes she turned in her chair to the window, she did not see him outside on the porch, but she saw the smoke from his cigarette as it was blown by the wind past the window.

■ ■ ■

The next few nights were like the first, except that now when he picked up the magazines he no longer pretended interest in them; he riffled through them noisily, announcing his annoyed impatience not just with the periodical but with the character of those evenings. He got up and was halfway to the door when she spoke in a voice she almost did not recognize as her own.

"You can smoke here. For tonight, at least."

She lowered her head over the Bible, heard him hesitate, pause longer than he need have, then return to his chair.

He did not pick up the magazines, he made no more pretenses. He just sat looking at her and smoking and flicking his ashes into the fireplace. She bent her head lower over the book when she felt her face flushing from more than the fire, into which he had thrown another log. She did not dare look; she was barely breathing when she heard him get out of the chair and not come to her but circle around her chair and stand with his hands on the back of it, on either side of her head. Even then she could not look up; nor did she move as she felt his fingers begin deftly, as though he were expert at it—and the thought ran through her: *this is what he knows; this is the thing he does best*—removing the pins from her long hair, unwinding it, letting it down slowly around her. The room was so still, and her senses now so acute, that she heard one of the hairpins fall on the bare wooden floor beyond the rug.

When her hair was all down, he began arranging it: lifting it and shaping it in some manner he patiently and as if with no thought of her was now designing to please himself. When he was finished, having given a few last touches to it, he put his hands on her shoulders. He left them there so long that she knew he could not help but feel her trembling beneath them. Without her knowing how it had happened, the control had passed from her to him. But that no longer mattered. He lifted his hands as if inviting her to go if she chose to. He waited. She did not move.

"Go upstairs" he said finally.

She did not hesitate, did not even think about it as she rose, put aside the Bible, and went up the steps without a word.

When he heard her moving around in her room, he moved from his chair to hers, which was larger and had wide, cushioned armrests. It was his face the fire warmed now, for the chair was closer to it. He pulled the table beside him to in front of him, then put his feet on it and looked between them into the fire. He lit a cigarette, flicking the match into the fire, and sat silently smoking, lured by the flames into thought.

He thought of the long journey that had brought him all the way from that tree on the Kansas plain to there. The lonely nights. The fear. And finally, to that place where loneliness and fear had not followed, and where he need no longer be uncertain. He had found a true place of refuge at last.

When he could no longer hear her moving around in her room, when all he heard was the wind and the fire, he still did not get up to go to her. There was no need to, no hurry. He knew where she was now, what she was feeling and thinking. He knew she was not going to go elsewhere.

He finished a second cigarette, then got up and threw it into the fireplace. He watched the flames devour it, then turned and went up the stairs.

The lights were out in the room, but the curtains were drawn. She was lying beneath the covers in the large bed with her back to him, looking at the night.

He started into the room, then stopped; for when she turned her face slowly to him what he saw there was not desire but an expression of defiance, even hatred.

He began to undress in the doorway, thinking, I'll change that too in a minute.

* * *

But that night did not change her. He was the one who was changed by it. He had not made her love him, even need him. She never again had the kind of desire for him that had given him power over her that night. She wanted him infrequently after that, and only in ways that humiliated him. It was a new experience for him. And it set him questioning not himself but her.

As the weeks passed, he had less and less interest in that work that had brought him such happiness before. The weather forced him indoors now—usually in the stable, repairing and painting—but that did not account for his lack of enthusiasm, nor for the fact that he would stop for long periods and stare into space. For the first time in his life he was struggling to find an answer to something for which he felt his powers of reasoning and insight were inadequate. He tried, but he always returned to the same unsatisfactory explanation. *She's just a cold woman, that's all it is. They get like that at her age. They don't use it for a long time, they don't know what to do with it when they get a chance to.* But even he did not believe it when he remembered that night and the passion she had shown him.

Never again was he able to seduce her; now it was she who chose the time when they made love. He remembered the next night, when he had gotten up as she sat reading her Bible and had stood behind her, as he had the previous night. But this time when he had put out his hand to touch her hair, she reached up and pushed it firmly aside. He had attempted to arouse her: he reached down with the intention of eventually fondling her breasts and placed his hands over her dress on them. She had just turned her face up to him and stared at him until his hands slid off her and down the chair to his sides.

It was not the first time a woman had removed Emil's impertinent hands from her breasts. He understood the rules: that they had to make a pretense of reluctance. In the past others had done that and then surrendered. But this time he did not doubt the rejection; his knowledge of her—and that look she had given him of total and irrevocable indifference—defeated him. She defeated him, who had never before doubted his ability to make a woman who needed love desire him.

He had stood for a minute, first embarrassed, then furious, as she continued reading as if he were not even in the room. He did not know whether to return to his chair as if nothing had happened or remain where he was, melting away with shame and useless anger. He turned finally and hurried out the door, slamming it behind him, and went back to the shed. He slammed that door too, then fell onto the cot, reliving the insult. She had reduced him in a minute back into what he had been before: the hired man.

He wanted to hurt her, to humiliate her as she had humiliated him. To use her, as she had used him. He imagined scenes in which she came to him begging him to love her, in which she was on her knees before him, pleading with him to allow her to have him. He made her kiss his hands, crying out for him afterward—He stopped. He sat up on the side of the cot, eyes filled with unexplained fear. He turned out the lamp and in darkness released himself, crying out.

The following night he stayed away from the house. He lay on his cot smoking, listening to the sounds the trees made in the wind. Hours after it was dark, he got up and went to the window. He was hoping to find her looking over for him from the side parlor window, or see her shadow as it moved anxiously back and forth on the wall. But there was no sign of her, although the lights were on in the parlor and he knew she was there.

Two nights later he appeared again.

She did not greet him, did not even look up from her reading as he went to his chair and sat down in it.

It was an experience unlike any he had ever had before. It was worse than the indifference the women during the war had shown him, for then it had not been him the women had rejected but his status in a world gone awry which had made of him an outcast. Now not even that remnant foot served him when two weeks later, after he had made love to her, he pushed aside the covers on his side of the bed to reveal the foot to her for the first time.

"I lost that in the war" he said. "I left it on the beach at Okinawa with my two fingers." He held the remaining fingers up in the light from the window—as if she had not seen them before—then lowered them.

He knew that something was wrong but was not certain what. He had not expected from her the reaction he got from others after he had invented and perfected the story; what he had expected was at least some acknowledgment of (for some part of him still believed it each time he told it) a sacrifice made for those like her who had remained safely behind. What he received was not that but a look of impatience before she turned away from him. He did not understand it, but she was giving him something: an opportunity to save what dignity he still possessed, although she had expected no more of him than what she heard him say next.

"They were going to give me a medal for it. They would have, but they said they needed more than the one witness—a corporal who was my buddy and who was all that was left of our platoon besides me. They said I saved him, but what I said was, him and those other men—the dead ones—were the ones saved me. I said I was proud just to have served with such a brave—"

She turned and stared at him, and he stopped. His mouth remained open on the unspoken words. Her eyes finally made him look away. Then he spoke—for he had to—with what dignity and manhood she had left him. "You don't believe me?"

"No."

He sat up abruptly, tossed back the covers, and started to scramble out of the bed. Then he stopped, sitting on the side of the bed, his back to her. "What do you believe about me?"

"Not much that I haven't seen. Now come to bed. It's late." She turned away.

He lay down again, but as far away from her as he could get, his back to hers.

"It's true" he said later as she slept.

He wondered now why he put up with what he could only perceive as an attempt to destroy his manhood. He could not have known that it was not that at all. It was simply that the rules she lived by and the personality they had shaped were the opposite of his. She saw only what she saw, knew only what she knew, had no interest in reconstructing reality in order to soften its harshness. She had chosen truth over the self-serving lie long ago, and she had never had reason or inclination to compromise with it since then.

Nor did he understand why he did not leave and return to Pineville: enough time had passed, there was surely no danger now. He told himself finally that it was his need to break the pride and arrogance of the woman that kept him there; that he wanted to open her life to humiliation and submission to him just as she was attempting to degrade him and make his life meaningless. For after the night when he had tried again to take down her hair—reconstruct the scene of her seduction—and she had relegated him to his former status as hired man with no privileges other than those she chose to grant him, the only way he knew when she wanted him was by going to the parlor at night and finding she was not in her chair.

He would hear her moving around in her bedroom. He would sit down in his chair. He would wait. He would hate himself for it, but after a period of time which he imagined each time to be longer than the last, he would hear her leave her room, come down the stairs. He would look up to find her standing in front of him with her hair already down, no longer allowing him even that much participation in the decision nor any preparation for the act other than his ascent to the room, following her. Nor could he detect any reticence in her, any hesitancy: she would not even sit down across from him for a minute to grant him the illusion of his acquiescence when he got up to follow her; she would just stand there, expressionless except for a suggestion of impatience if he hesitated too long. She would look down at him not commanding his compliance but neither doubting for a moment it would come when she turned, still wordless, and mounted the stairs.

It was not her presence but her absence from the room, then, that told him each time she would allow him to come again to her bed. She would have him wordlessly still, but not without passion, not quietly, as she responded to his passion with expressions of her own stored up for him.

It always surprised him when, afterward, he saw the hardness had gone from her and been replaced by what was, if not acceptance of him—certainly not tenderness—an almost affectionate tolerance. And perhaps that was her real power over him, although he had not discovered that yet either: that at that moment when he wanted to hate her, he could only feel gratitude. It was not until later that his memory aroused him again to hatred. And shame at the gratitude he had felt for the small favor that was her partial acceptance of him.

Now there were nights, as he sat alone in the parlor listening to her getting ready above, when he waited for her in excited anticipation of that moment of silent command and his unprotesting submission to it. He thought during those times of all the women he had had, mostly faceless now: those he had humbled with his own indifference and occasional cruelty in the long journey that had brought him at last to this house. He wondered for the first time how many of them he had made hate him, even at the moment they loved him.

One night as she stood over him he saw his hands trembling in his lap. For only the second time in his life, he had difficulty sleeping. When he did sleep, his dreams were filled with her. He decided finally that he did not have to endure it, would not any longer.

He felt good as he walked to the house that night and saw that the light was on in her room, where, he knew now—knowing her habits if little else about her—she was taking the pins out of her hair, letting it down with her rough fingers, smiling (he imagined) into the mirror, not at herself but at the thought of him waiting for her, his predictability. He was smiling himself in the light that fell on him from the window as he passed through it onto the darkness of the porch. He went in and sat where he had waited for her many times before.

But this time when she came to him and stood over him he pretended not to notice her as he stared into the flames in the fireplace—free of her already, he was certain. He let her stand there, silent, waiting for him, before he looked up and spoke. "Not tonight, lady. I've had all I can take. If you want me again, you know where I'll be." He had rehearsed the speech, memorized it.

He expected a response, waited for it. But all he saw were her eyebrows raised quizzically, what could have been a shrug of indifference.

He got up then, attempting to go past her, but he moved more cautiously than he had imagined he would during that act that was to have been his final demonstration of independence. He had anticipated the moment as one in which he displayed dignity and strength, rejecting her physically as he put his hands on her not out of the desire she had come to expect of him, but in denial that he had any desire for her now. But instead of moving her out of his way, cut off from the door between her and the fireplace and the chair, he was forced to squeeze past her, bend his body to accommodate hers—for hers did not move an inch to allow him to pass. Nor did her amused eyes leave his for a moment as he went by her.

He managed to slide past her and leave her standing motionless in front of the fire. He turned his back to her and, quickly and with some dignity, went to the door; not bothering to close it, he went through it, leaving her—his only witness—behind.

He went to the shed, fell onto the cot, lit a cigarette and lay smiling. He sent smoke rings hurtling into the light from the lamp; grinning, feeling confident, he felt his pride restored for the first time in so long that he could not remember for a moment when it had all begun. After a while he put out the cigarette, turned off the lamp and, with his back to the window, went easily into sleep.

He waited the next night for her to come to him everything changed: she now the supplicant, hair down and surrendering both her pride and her body without conditions. But she did not come that night or the next. He watched both nights as the light went on in the parlor, but there was no sign of her, no sound from the house.

It took him several days to begin telling himself that all she wanted from him was that he allow her to have back some part of her pride. He had proven his independence from her, shown her the strength she had thought lacking in him, and now all that was needed was that she be given the opportunity to take him back with her dignity restored.

But when the next night he returned to the parlor it was as if nothing had happened between them. She did not take her hair down in front of him as he had imagined by then she would; she did not get up to lead him off to her room, holding on to his hand this time. What she did was nod to him, look up from her Bible only long enough to inquire about a job he had begun that morning. He wanted to leave then, would have, had he known how. But all he could do was sit across from her in the chair waiting for the hours to pass, rooted there, unable to go before the appointed time.

And when it came, when she put down the Bible, got up and left the room to go close up the house—only then, alone in the parlor, did he know he could leave.

That night he hated her.

The following night he stayed away from the house, sat again on the cot full of rage and hatred for her. When it was time, he turned off the lamp and sat at the table looking up through his window at her bedroom, which was still dark, still without invitation. Later he saw the bedroom light go on, her shadow move briefly across the wall; then it went off, its darkness lifting the darkness below the window up to meet it.

He sat looking up at the united darkness of the house, then got up from the table. He felt for the duplicate keys in his pocket: one for each of the vehicles. He left the shed and went to the stable. Pulling back the large doors, he did not even have to think about it when he chose her Rambler and noisily—not bothering to stop and close the doors behind him—drove off.

He stopped the car at the edge of the woods, at the last point from which he could still see the house, and turning in the seat, he looked back at it waiting to see the light go on in her window. But the dark window remained steadfast.

He gunned the motor and sent the car speeding along the dirt road toward the highway, where he turned onto it sharply, wheels squealing, and headed back in the direction of Pineville, toward Milltown.

It was after four when Lydia awoke to the sound of the phone ringing at an hour when no call had come since the night her late husband had died. She hurried down to the phone on the kitchen wall, confused even before she heard the man's voice speaking her name. It was not the kind of voice she was accustomed to hearing, either on the phone or anywhere else.

"Mrs. Wier? This Lydia Wier?"

"Yes."

"Listen closely, Mrs. Wier, and if you're not interested, hang up. We have a man here says he knows you, is a friend of yours. We haven't called the police yet, because he says we won't have to. He says he works for you, that you'd help him if we called you. I don't know why you'd bother to even give him the time of day, but—"

She heard Emil in the background shouting at the man, hysterical. Then the shouting stopped at what sounded like a blow against flesh and a chair falling. She waited out the silence that followed with her eyes closed, leaning her head against the wall. When the man returned to the phone, she asked him "What did he do?"

"Mrs. Wier, for what this prize specimen done, as far as I'm concerned they should lock him up and throw away the key."

She heard Emil's voice protesting, high-pitched from fear. She asked impatiently "Just what is it he did?"

"He beat up a girl. Did a good job on her too. Like he's done it before."

Emil's voice reached her screeching denial.

"Where are you?" she asked.

"The Good Times Bar in Milltown. Do you know where that is?"

"Yes. Don't do anything until I get there. We'll talk. I'm sure we can settle this without the police."

"We're not waiting all night, ma'am."

"I'm leaving in five minutes."

She did, driving more quickly and recklessly than she had ever been compelled to drive before. She came upon Milltown in its full silence. All the bars and houses had closed, lights off, as if drawn into the frost-breathing woods surrounding them. She paused at the foot of the dirt road where directly before her on its hieratic perch was the Negro church, silent too, two high, darkened windows like eyes raised questioningly at her arrival. She drove up the road, the pickup rocking on stones half embedded in the hard-packed earth. The truck moved slowly, like a vehicle in unfamiliar terrain sent to explore a place where others had disappeared without a trace or explanation. Now and then she leaned forward to peer through the window. Then she saw him.

A tall man stepped out from the shadows of a bar doorway onto the side of the road. He did not signal to her; he did not have to. She pulled onto the opposite side of the road and crossed to him without any sign of recognition from either of them, for that was unnecessary too.

"Where is he?" she asked.

"In one of the cabins out back. He's beat up a little."

He turned and she turned with him, her shadow pivoting with his on the gray, barren ground. They went past a row of bars into the woods where she saw cabins clustered behind the trees. They proceeded in silent single file until they emerged from the woods through the porticoes of two trees onto the wooden steps of one of the numbered cabins. He turned there, waiting for her to catch up to him, noting that she did so without hurrying. He had heard of her.

She went into the small one-room cabin where the only light was a bare bulb hanging at the end of a cord from the ceiling. She saw Emil immediately, slumped in a chair, blood at the side of his mouth and clutching his stomach as if holding something inside of him that might otherwise fall out. He looked up, squinting at her through an eyelid so swollen that at first he did not recognize her standing beyond the bright light. A man stood to the side of him with one hand resting lightly on his shoulder; it was enough to keep Emil from rising and going to her when he saw who it was.

She heard the woman before she bothered to look at her: whining more than crying, like an animal cowering and frightened even after the time of danger has passed. The man beside Lydia went to the woman and lifted her chin to show Lydia a face distorted by bruises and tears and dark streaks of mascara. She was about thirty, although it was not easy to tell behind the swollen lips and closed eye. Lydia noticed that all her wounds were on the right side of her face.

She turned back to Emil, who straightened up in the chair and began looking wildly at her. He lunged forward unexpectedly, shaking off the hand on his shoulder and going onto his knees. He began crawling toward her as he pleaded in a high voice "Mrs. Wier, please help me. They'll put me in prison. You don't know what I—"

"*Shut up.*"

Her voice startled the two men. The woman stopped crying.

"Get up" she said to him. "For once in your life, Emil, be a man."

He crawled back to the chair and, like a child, climbed up into it, where he sat subdued again beneath the restraining hand.

She turned back to the man. "Get that woman out of here" she told him.

He looked at the other man, who left Emil and helped the woman up from where she sat on the bed and led her hobbling and twisting like a dwarf out the door.

Lydia waited until she heard their footsteps receding on the hard ground outside, until they were lost even as sounds in the night. She turned to the remaining man. "I'm sure you don't want the police involved in this any more than we do."

He sat on the bed. He did not answer for seconds. "No" he said finally.

"Good." She seemed to relax then, was even convivial as she said "I know you people have a private arrangement with the mill owners and those politicians in Pineville. Don't bother to deny it."

He did not, but he remained silent. She did not wait for his answer, though, did not need it as she continued. "It can go on like that. Nothing need change—"

She paused and after a moment he nodded, as if they did not need further explanations between them. She went on. "Good. Now what would it take to make this never to have happened?"

Emil leaned forward to see better through his swollen eyelid as the two were talking. For a while his expression was one of bewilderment, then of astonishment, then the beginning of hope as he listened.

"How much?" she repeated. The man had not answered her—still did not.

Finally he spoke. "It's a felony. That girl's been beaten to within an inch—"

She interrupted him. "That's not the first beating she's had. Or the last. And we both know it's not that whore you want to help here. Otherwise, you would never have called me. Now, how much do you want?"

He shrugged; he even laughed. "OK. Five hundred."

"I'll give you two or wash my hands of the whole matter."

Emil stiffened. He started to speak, then stopped. Lydia and the man stared at each other, both silent for a long time, until finally it was the man who spoke again.

"OK. Two hundred. But you're not getting any bargain in him, lady. You ask me, you should have him locked up yourself."

She ignored the remark; just glanced at Emil, who sat looking down now, hands clasped between his legs. She looked back at the man. "You'll have the money in the morning. I don't keep that kind of cash—"

He waved her explanation aside. "We've got the girl. Just don't make it too early in the morning. We're late risers around here." He was leaning on his elbow on the bed smiling up at her. But Lydia turned away from him, dismissing him as she crossed to Emil, who was staring at her as if seeing her for the first time.

"Get up" she told him. "We're leaving."

He hesitated, looking at the man who was still watching Lydia; he only glanced at Emil and nodded. The man continued watching until they were through the door.

Emil followed her through the path between the trees and onto the lot made smooth and colorless as glass in the fading morning moonlight. He looked like her own shadow come erect and following her as they walked, neither speaking, to the road, where she turned to him. He stopped too.

"Where did you park the car?" she asked.

He nodded to between two bars where its grayness merged with the gray soil like an aberration beneath the earth grown out of it.

She stepped onto the road. "Can you drive?" she asked him.

He nodded again and they went off in different directions to their vehicles. She waited in hers, the lights on, until she saw the Rambler nose slowly from between the bars, pause, then dip onto the road.

They drove slowly all the way back in the mellowing night. When they reached the highway, she stopped at it, and he halted also behind her; he turned slowly with her onto the highway and proceeded so close and in such concerted agreement with the pickup's every movement that the two vehicles might have been one.

There was no other traffic at that time of the morning, so that their slow and concordant progress had something solemn and processional about it. Emil rolled down his window, was chilled by the cold morning air. He saw the dawn hanging beyond the trees, some pale stars pulsing faintly so that it seemed they might fade away and die at any moment. Minutes later both headlights went out—first hers, then his—hurrying back out of the night.

It was full dawn by the time they pulled off the highway onto the road leading to the house. The lights were still on in her bedroom, the kitchen and the parlor. She drove past the house to in front of the shed, where she waited inside the pickup until he drew up alongside her. Then they both got out and she leading, went into the shed.

She was standing inside the doorway as he went past her and sat down slowly, carefully, on the side of the cot. He touched his eye cautiously, winced, then looked up at her through it, even though the lid had nearly closed it entirely now. He touched his stomach too, exploring it. He was in pain, but he was smiling when he spoke. "I don't know how you—"

She was leaning against the table watching him. "For once in your life, Emil" she told him, "be smart and don't say anything. I did it because I was able to. And because it had to be done. Just as you, more's the pity, seem always unable to do what you are able to. But we'll change all of that."

"I just wanted to thank—"

"I told you to shut up."

He did; but he need not have spoken, because his face said the words for him as he looked in astonishment at her for the second time that night as he saw her reach back with both hands and begin taking the pins out of her hair dropping them one by one on the floor; saw the long hair coming down and noticed for the first time how fine, even beautiful, it was as it hung curving over her shoulders to her waist. He looked on in amazement but in a way unamazed now by this woman who had until then hidden from him all that she was revealing to him now. So that when she turned and went out of the shed, leaving the door open behind her, there was no amazement left in him when he got up to follow her.

They became man and wife a week later, but with no bridesmaids for her, no best man for him. They had only two witnesses—a gardener and Pastor Cooley's wife—with Pastor Cooley officiating in the parlor of his home.

It was a short, simple ceremony, at Lydia's request. And minutes after it was over they were on their way back to the house.

Seven months later—almost nine months to the day of the first time Emil made love to Lydia—their daughter, Madeleine, was born.

6

The only thing Willa knew about her mother in the city was that she came there with a man named Orlo Haines. It was not until Willa was ten that she overheard her grandmother and grandfather talking about him in hushed tones. When she went to her grandmother later to ask about him, her grandmother said it was none of Willa's business and of no consequence anyway. But Willa had heard enough to suspect that Orlo Haines was her father—and given her nature and need, once she suspected it she came quickly to believe it.

She had to use all the discipline she had taught herself in order to hide from the old woman her happiness that a father had risen so fortuitously from the past. It had been on her mother until then that she had concentrated her hopes and fantasies. Not only had a father been so much less real to her (for she had seen her mother in the dream) but her grandmother had told Willa at five that her mother had refused to reveal the name of her father. And Willa had believed it then, because even though she did not trust her grandmother, she had thought her one virtue was that so moral a person would not lie.

The old couple did not have a car, and there was no telephone or television in the house. They owned an old radio, but the programs they turned on had only preachers and religious music on them. Willa was forbidden to listen to the radio on her own, and since she was almost never alone in the house for long, she did not have any opportunity to plug it in and tune in other programs. Therefore, for years Willa knew little of the world except what she learned on those trips to the roadside store and what the old woman told her. Even the mail was delivered to a tin mailbox standing at the foot of the path that led onto the property off a dirt road skirting the woods; and Willa was never allowed to go near there when the little mail car came rocking along the road in the morning.

Willa had been to the neighboring town of Pineville with her grandmother once in a taxi, for all the good that did her; for her grandmother had kept Willa at her side nearly all the time, holding on to her with hands that Willa had learned early were amazingly strong for an old woman. The trips to the store did not start until Willa was twelve—until her grandfather's illness made it necessary for her grandmother to take her instead of him to help carry packages on the long walk back to the house. It had occurred to Willa that her grandfather was also withdrawn from the world. But unlike Willa, he had always seemed content with his isolation.

When Willa was a child, her grandmother had told her stories of kidnappers and murderers who cruised the highway looking for children. She told her that any child who wandered too far from its guardian or went onto the highway alone would never be heard from again. For years after that Willa had feared the highway and stayed away from it; she even had nightmares in which the kidnappers and murderers ventured beyond the highway to come lurking beneath her window in the darkest moods of night.

But that had been during Willa's childhood. At twelve—after their first trip to the roadside store—Willa began to cultivate a conservative adventurousness that brought her finally to the edge of the highway, and even to walks in the woods beside it. She came to the conclusion that her grandmother's stories had been exaggerated to keep her from other dangers should she wander too far from the house alone. She gained confidence and decided to investigate the world further.

Willa was four when her grandmother took her in the taxi to Pineville; she was twelve when she made her first trip there alone, avoiding the highway by taking the dirt road which was mostly unused since the highway had been built and ran past the house along the edge of the woods. She went at night after her grandmother had sunk into that deep sleep from which few things could wake her.

It was three miles on the highway to Pineville; four by the meandering dirt road. When she emerged from it in the center of the town in her handmade dress and with her hair pinned back in the severe style in which her grandmother wore hers, she looked like an apparition from the distant past; and for a while, she acted like one.

It was on that first night while investigating the town and its people that she discovered the Little America Café. She had been drawn into it when while passing she saw to her astonishment through the window a box on a ledge behind the counter with moving pictures of tiny people on it; as she went through the door, she heard their voices as well. She walked to the counter and slid onto a stool without taking her eyes from the box for an instant, it so fascinated her. Only when the counterman asked for her order did she look around at the other people in the restaurant and ask for a cup of black coffee; when he told her they did not serve coffee to children, she ordered a glass of milk instead.

She stayed for an hour that night watching the box, and after that the café became her favorite place in the town. It was there that she learned by watching and listening to the people and the box much of what her grandmother had kept her ignorant of until then—and about the world beyond the town, which she had seen before only through her grandmother's eyes.

So when she finally learned about Orlo Haines it was to the Little America Café that she went to look for his name in the thick book that sat on a stand beside the telephone booth inside the door.

Willa had learned about telephones on that first visit with her grandmother to Pineville. What she had not known until then was that there was a book that contained the names, addresses and phone numbers of people who lived in the city.

She had looked up her mother's name the first time she realized the book's purpose, but no Madeleine Rhineman appeared among the countless people listed. Willa was not surprised at the omission of her mother's name: having disappeared into the large city, even Willa knew she was unlikely to publish her whereabouts. But this night when she looked, turning the pages laboriously through the alphabet her grandmother had taught her, Orlo Haines's name was there.

She wrote the address and telephone number on a piece of paper with a pencil she had brought from the house. She wrote it all out slowly, the printed letters and numbers slanting and leaning against one another—some small, some large—in that erratic style of writing her grandmother had allowed her from the rudiments of an education she had given her.

It took her five minutes, and when she was done she put the piece of paper carefully into the pocket of her dress. She did not remove her hand from where it pressed against the piece of paper until she got it safely back to the house. She did not investigate the town that night: she had come for only that one purpose.

She could, of course, have phoned Orlo Haines from the café; she had come prepared with money stolen from her grandmother should she decide to do so. But not only had Willa never used a telephone before but she felt that in her excitement and fear she might fail to convince Orlo Haines that she was his daughter, and thereby lose her one chance to persuade him. She had decided that only a letter could achieve her goal, which now was not only to ask Orlo Haines the whereabouts of her mother but to let him know as well that she was his daughter.

It took her two nights to compose the letter, hiding it away each time so that it would not be discovered by the old woman the next day. It began, "Deer Daddy I gues your suprize to heer from me—" But when it was finally done and she read it over, she knew that something was missing. She had told him how much she missed both him and her mother, of her desire to join them as soon as he sent word to do so; but she had also written, thinking it over, allowing for the possibility that after all those years he and her mother might no longer be together, that if that was the case, although she wanted to know him and visit him and be the daughter to him circumstances had not allowed her to be all those years, she wanted to know anyway where her mother was and how she might contact her. She wrote at the bottom of the letter, "HURY HURY HURY."

But knowing that something was missing, something left unsaid or undone, she did not seal the letter, nor even affix to it the postage stamp she had stolen out of her grandmother's desk.

She was staring off, trying to solve this most important problem of her life, when she saw on her bureau the only photograph she had of herself: a snapshot her grandmother had taken of her when she was three. In it she was seated in her grandmother's rocking chair on the porch wearing a pinafore dress and black shoes with buckles that came to above her ankles. Framing her face was a sunbonnet whose ribbon was tied in a bow below her chin, and perhaps because of the glare of the sun she was leaning forward, eyes narrowed and glowering fiercely from within the sunbonnet. She enclosed the photograph with the letter and at the bottom of the letter beneath her name wrote, "Woodnt yu like to hav a prety dauter like this?"

She was out not at the mailbox, where she knew her grandmother would come to meet the mailman as his small car came nodding up the rock-filled and hollowing road, but a quarter of a mile past that, waiting out of sight at the edge of the woods behind a tree.

Before the sun was up a quarter of the way toward its zenith she saw the brightly colored car coming, raising a fin of dust behind it; saw it pause where her grandmother stood tall and erect and not advancing a step to meet it, not even giving a sign of recognition as far as Willa could see to the middle-aged, plump man who was leaning out of his window saying something to her in his slow passing. Then she saw her grandmother turn and go back up the path to the house as the car continued on.

Willa stepped out into the middle of the road. There was no way for the car to pass her on the narrow road, even if the driver had wanted to. And if the vehicle evidenced anything of its occupant's feelings at the sight of Willa standing clutching a letter in her fist and facing him in the middle of the road, it was that of curiosity as the car slowed down gradually until it came to a stop in front of her. She stepped around it to the passenger window to which the man was beginning to lean over from the driver's side and stuck the letter through it. He took it, looked at it, then waited. For it seemed apparent there was something after all that she had to say. She did finally.

"I live in that white house back there on the other side of the woods. My name's Willa Rhineman. That letter—it's the most important letter of my life and it's no one's business but mine, so I don't want you to deliver the answer when it comes to where you usually deliver our letters. I'm going to wait here for you starting tomorrow morning, and I want you to deliver it only to me."

It was a very long speech for Willa at that time; she had rehearsed it. Now, having delivered it, she had nothing more to say for the moment. She stood looking at him.

The man was half reclining across the car, his face partly out the window; but he did not move or speak either, for he was waiting for her to say more. Then it occurred to him that she was waiting for his assurance that it would be done. He said "All right. There's no regulation against that as long as that letter's addressed to you."

"It won't be addressed to anyone else" she said. "I'll be here every morning before this time to meet you. You don't come earlier sometimes, do you?" The possibility had just occurred to her.

"Nope. Always about this time. Rain or shine. Neither snow nor rain nor heat nor gloom of night—" He was quoting the postal service's motto, but he did not finish. It nearly always brought a smile from others when they heard it, but there was no smile from this child. It had never happened to him before, for he had been with the post office for nearly twenty years and prided himself on his friendly service and his customers' usual friendliness in return. But now one of them—a little girl, at that—had ignored his cordiality. Not taking his eyes off her, he began to withdraw from the window back to his seat. But she stopped him before he managed to get there.

"How long will it take to get my answer back here to me? I'll be here starting tomorrow, but I'd just like to know."

He looked at the front of the envelope. And when he answered, it was not from outside the window: he stayed where he was and said in a loud voice so as to be heard from inside "A day there and a day back at the earliest. But don't count on it."

"I'll be here the morning after tomorrow, then. And after that until it comes. Just don't deliver it to anyone else. That's all you have to remember."

This time he did not linger. And he drove away more quickly than he had come.

Willa stood watching the car until it disappeared beyond the bend in the road. She watched until the dust settled, as if to satisfy herself that it was not going to return. Then she turned and went back into the woods.

She was there every morning standing behind the tree. And only when the car passed their mailbox did she step forward not onto the road now but to the side of it. She did not speak, just presented herself. Nor did the postman say anything to her. He slowed down and shook his head at her to indicate that the letter had not come.

The first morning that she waited she left as soon as he had passed. The following morning she was still standing there minutes later. By the fourth morning she remained there long after the car had gone.

The letter came on the sixth morning. She knew it had arrived when she saw the car moving toward her more quickly than on previous mornings, then slow down more than usual as it drew close to her. By then, although she tried not to show it, she could feel her heart beating rapidly. The car stopped across from her.

The impassive imposture that had hidden her anxiety until then deserted her. She broke into a big smile as she ran to the window where the man was waving a white envelope at her; he wore an expression that was part pleasure for her, part relief for himself.

She snatched the envelope from him and turning, running, was nearly back in the woods before she thought to stop. She turned back to him. "Thanks" she shouted. "Thanks, mister."

He smiled, waved, and was on his way quickly, the little car moving faster than on previous mornings, tilting and rocking down the road in what resembled either a happy departure or an escape.

Willa sat on the ground in the woods to read the letter. But she did not open it right away. She had until now done her best to control her emotions, hold back her feelings; she did not want disappointment to plunge her into one of the depressions to which she was occasionally subject, and during which she sometimes even thought she would kill herself if the time ever came when she knew she would never find her mother and that her life would never change. Now she was trying to regain that control and bring calm to this moment in which she not only held in her hand the only letter ever written to her but held also the knowledge that inside the envelope was a message that might reveal the whereabouts of her mother.

She laid the envelope in her lap, looking at it. She reached for it several times but each time drew back. She made a fist of her hands and slid them under her where she sat. Her eyes never left the envelope. When at last she picked up the envelope, her hands were trembling. She was licking her dry lips with her tongue as she ripped the flap open, tore the envelope down the side in her haste. She felt joy—and then fear—as she read the one sentence the letter contained:

Little girl, I'm not your daddy and I don't know where your mother is and don't bother me anymore.

■ ■ ■

Now Willa stepped off a bus in a suburban section of the city. She paused on the sidewalk to straighten the hat, which had started to slide off her head. When she reached up for it, the purse at her wrist slipped down to her elbow. The hat was again crooked when she moved up the quiet, tree-burgeoning street.

She saw lawns in front of each house. Each house had a porch. Each had a garage with a gravel driveway. The houses were separated by narrow strips of grass, but they were all alike. Turtle Lane was the name of the street, and she went up it following the highly visible numbers beside each door, counting them off aloud as she moved nearer to the home of Orlo Haines and her first meeting with someone who had known her mother in the city.

She crossed a street to a new row of houses, then stopped, confused for a moment. For the last house on the previous block had been numbered 138, but the numbers on this block began at 200. She went on, shaking her head at the perplexities of life in the city.

The only thing different about Orlo Haines's house was that it had a swing on the porch. As Willa went onto the porch, she saw that the swing was made of plastic. It had two red bucket seats molded into the shape of behinds. The swing was supported by two ropes that hung from the roof of the porch. Head turned to the swing, examining it, she knocked on the door, even though a doorbell was within reach. A minute later a middle-aged black man holding a can of beer came to the door. When Willa's head turned slowly away from the swing, her mouth opened and she stared wide-eyed at him.

"Well? You want somethin', girl?"

She continued to stare.

"You deaf, child?"

"You're not him" she said finally.

"Who's him?"

"I'm looking for a Mr. Orlo Haines."

"That's me."

"You can't be him."

"Well if I ain't, my momma's sure in for a big surprise. Who are you, girl? What do you want?"

"I'm Willa."

"Willa who?"

"Madeleine's daughter. Rhineman."

The beer can he was about to drink from lowered suddenly from the man's mouth. Orlo Haines looked quickly over his shoulder into the house; then he closed the door firmly behind him and stepped onto the porch. He began whispering "My God, girl, you gonna be hounding me all my life?"

"Can I come in?"

"You crazy? I got my family in there. They don't know nothin' about all that. Go away now. I don't need you to come around here stirrin' things up that's better forgotten. I told you I'm not your father. I told you in my letter."

"I know that" Willa said. "If I didn't before, I've got no doubts about it now."

"Then go away. Leave me in peace. You got no right—I work for the city now—"

"I don't care about that. I just want to find my mother."

"I told you that too. I don't know where she is. My God, I haven't seen your mother, girl, in sixteen years."

Willa stood firm, holding her ground. And Orlo knew that what he confronted in this determined child was more than he was prepared to handle at the moment.

"You were her boyfriend" she said. "She came here with you. If anybody would know about her, you would."

"We were only together a little while, child. We weren't together long enough to matter."

She did not move. She might have been planted there. Nor did her implacable expression alter by so much as an eyelash. Orlo shifted from one foot to the other. He stared back at her. Finally it was he who looked away.

"Look" he said. "If you'll go away, don't call me or write me again or nothin', maybe I could think of somethin' later could help you. OK?"

She still did not move, did not change the character or intensity of her expression. He thought it not inconceivable that should he go back into the house, close the door behind him, turn on the TV and forget her, the next morning when he opened his door she would still be standing there, not having moved an inch or relaxed a muscle. He thought that; then he knew it to be a fact.

"Look" he said. "Maybe I can help you some way. Maybe I can."

She relaxed. "That's all I want" she said. "I'm not asking for the moon." She looked over at the swing. "Can I sit on it? I was traveling all yesterday and I'm still a little stiff from it."

"Sure" he said, still in a hushed voice. "But not for long. You can't stay here for long."

She smiled at him then. "Thanks, Orlo" she said. "I didn't come here to cause you any trouble."

She went to the swing and fit herself into one of the plastic behinds. She held on to the rope and began to swing. After a few minutes she asked "What's my mother like, Orlo? Is she beautiful?"

"She was a nice-lookin' chick."

"Is she smart?"

"Smart's some, not smart's some others. The same as the rest of us. Look, girl, you can't stay here. My wife's maybe comin' out that door any minute."

"I wouldn't mind meeting her."

"*You crazy?*"

Willa winced. She appeared to be in pain. She leaned over and began taking off one of her loafers. She said "It's this foot of mine. It never bothered me before, but maybe all that walking I did yesterday and today's done something to it." She slowly and carefully unpeeled a white ankle-length sock from the foot, lifting it off until Orlo stared down at her foot. In all other respects it was a normal foot, but where there should have been toes there were only five dead digits of flesh and bone entwining like worms crawling over each other.

Willa noted his expression. "Don't worry about them" she said. "These toes are just fine." She lifted the foot up to in front of her face. She smiled over it at Orlo as she said "They're unusual. That's what I always liked about them. What do you think, Orlo?"

Orlo went to her and put his hand firmly around her arm. He

leaned down to her so she would be sure to hear him. "You get out of here" he said, face close to hers. "You go away right now. I'm not foolin' with you anymore."

She did not challenge him. She seemed to yield to his superior strength. Her manner even changed to submissiveness, resignation. "All right" she said. "I'm going. You don't have to hurt me."

He was convinced; but the moment his hand left Willa's arm, that arm and the other one went around the rope, fingers locking. She spoke just as deliberately and with just as much force as he had a minute before. "I'm not going" she said. "I'm not going anywhere until you tell me what I want to know."

He moved to pull her up out of the seat, yank her away from the support to which she was clinging so tenaciously. He could easily have done it, he knew. But she stopped him with her next words.

"You do that" she said "and I'll start screaming. This whole neighborhood will hear it. And when your wife comes out of that door, we'll see what I have to say to her too."

Orlo knew when he was beaten. He had always known when he was beaten, all his life, he thought. It was why he had been here, in a salt-and-pepper neighborhood, working for the city for ten years, endlessly emptying money each day from out of the identical iron faces of parking meters. It had not always been like that, he thought; but it was because he always knew when he was defeated that it was like that now.

"All right" he said. "But not here."

"Where?"

"I'll buy you some ice cream."

■ ■ ■

Orlo's Pinto rose on a steep concrete ramp, then leveled, and Willa saw stretching in front of her an enormous parking lot filled with cars, and beyond that a semicircle of stores like long arms reaching out to embrace her. People looking very small at that distance moved like objects in a mechanical game going in and coming out of doors. As they drew nearer, Willa saw that they were nearly all carrying packages. Some staggered out of the larger stores under loads of bags; others, wheeling wire carts, when they reached their cars were lifting trunks, opening doors, and pouring the bags and packages into them.

They got out of the car, and Orlo led her across the lot to the walkway where all the stores now presented themselves to her in unusual formations of glass, chrome and fake woodwork. As Orlo hurried her on, she turned her head to look back at a sign fashioned out of imitation wood: The Lasso Bar and Lounge. The *L* was a cowboy boot around which had descended a whirling lariat. No one was in the boot, and no hand could be seen throwing the rope. Orlo had hesitated there, as if considering its suitability, then deciding against it, went on. Willa hurried behind him past doors opening and closing for shoppers with no one there to make it happen. He turned in under another sign:

CIRCUS TIME ICE CREAM PARLOR

She followed, running to catch up, for Orlo seemed to want to keep as much distance between them as possible until they were inside.

They went toward an empty table, past small stuffed lions and tigers and elephants and monkeys fixed to the floor. A child tottered toward them wearing a large bib with the words *Circus Time* on it. It pushed Willa aside to get at a stuffed tiger which it then stooped to throw its arms around and hug. Willa watched, then joined Orlo at the table.

She took off her hat, which for the tenth time that day had slipped onto the side of her head, and put it on the seat next to hers.

Willa had seen a circus on the television at the Little America Café; she had seen clowns in it. Now one came to their table in billowing costume, white collar circling high on its neck, red shoes and tall pointed hat. It had a clown's smiling face painted over its own face, which was not smiling as it looked down at her over a pad and poised pen. She could not tell whether it was a man or woman until it spoke to her in a deep voice.

"You decided what you want yet?"

Willa looked up into black eyes that were not smiling either, then picked up a large menu which had a long list of items on it. Rather than slowly groping for meaning in its printed words, she looked at Orlo over the menu. She did not lower it to see him; she raised herself up in her chair to speak over it. "Would you order for me, Orlo? Something big. I'm starving." She saw a small mountain of confection that one child had partially demolished, but she saw by the listless manner in which he picked at it with his spoon that he had admitted defeat in the face of Circus Time's munificence. She said "One of those, Orlo. Whatever they call them."

Orlo ordered and the clown lowered his pad and pen and walked off slowly, as if his feet ached.

Willa put her elbows on the table, locked her fingers, rested her chin on her hands, and leaned forward toward Orlo. "Where's my mother, Orlo?" she asked.

"I don't know."

"Why don't you know?"

"She left me, man."

"Why did she leave you?"

She waited for the answer, which Orlo seemed disinclined, or reluctant, to give. She said "Orlo, do you want me to go back to your house? Maybe talk to your wife about all this instead of you?"

"Look. Things happened back then."

"What things happened?"

"Oh, shit. OK. You want to know about your mother? She left me for this cat Chatto Hoffman. We were only together a few weeks when she moved in with him. Look, girl" he began, then stopped. He looked frightened. He resumed after a moment of silence. "He's evil, man. He's scary. It was like he didn't have any feelings, any conscience. All he dug was sex and drugs and doin' his number on people. Scaring people. He did head games on people. It was like he could look into your head, read your mind—and what he saw there he despised. He did some things back then I don't even like to think about now. Anyway, I thought your mother was a lady—I looked up to her. But the minute Chatto showed up she couldn't keep her eyes off him. She shamed me. She turned out to be no better than the rest of them."

He leaned back. He said "You wanted to know about your mother? Now you know about your goddamn mother. Satisfied?"

"Is that why you didn't want to talk about it? Because you were ashamed of what happened?"

"No. No. Don't you understand nothing, girl? Because he's still around. *Because he'd come after me, even after all this time, if he knew I was talking to you about what happened back then.*"

Willa took out of her purse a small spiral notebook and a pen and laid them beside her on the table. She had bought them that morning. She handed the notebook and pen to Orlo and said "That Chatto Hoffman. Write down his address."

He said "He didn't have no address. He never had any permanent address to speak of. Cats like him lived at other people's addresses."

The clown returned with their ice-cream sundaes on a tray. He served them, but neither Orlo nor Willa looked at them. Neither spoke until the clown went off like a whisper on his cloth feet. When he was gone, Willa said "All right. Then who else was there you can give me an address of now? Think, Orlo."

Orlo hesitated. Then he said "Look—" but did not go on. A few seconds later he opened his mouth, then closed it again. Finally he shook his head emphatically. "No way. No way. Look, I don't want to get involved in it. You want to do that, be my guest. Just leave me out of it. I have a good job with the city now. I have kids. A mortgage. My wife's studying for her real estate license. No way, girl, am I gonna rock the boat with risings from the past." He stared at her, defying her.

To Orlo's surprise, Willa did not say anything. She took her spoon and lifted the cherry from its large bed of whipped cream atop the sundae. She put it into her mouth and chewed it slowly and carefully, only once looking up at Orlo and smiling. When she finished the cherry, she took up the napkin beside her, which had a red clown's hat printed on it, and wiped her mouth. She looked over at the counter behind which the concoctions were being made: at another man there in a clown costume who was preparing something; then at the cash register and a man who was wearing a lion tamer's uniform. He had a whip in his broad belt and wore a large false pointed mustache. She called to him. "Sir!" He looked up from a newspaper he was reading. "Could you come here, please?"

The man put down his newspaper and started toward them. Willa smiled at Orlo again.

Willa looked up at the man when he was at her side. She said "Sir, excuse me, but the clown didn't bring me a cherry with my sundae. I thought I was going to get a cherry with it."

The man looked down. Then he looked around at the counterman, who was watching them. He turned back to Willa. "I'm sorry" he said. "Nothing like this has ever—George has been making our Daring Young Man on the Flying Trapeze for three months now. I'll see that you—" He turned to go off toward the counter, but Willa stopped him.

"Just a minute" she said. He turned back. Willa looked at Orlo. "Would you like another cherry on yours, Orlo? They look good."

"No" Orlo answered when the man looked at him.

"All right." She looked back at the man. "Just one."

He went to the counter and began talking and shaking his head at the confused counterman, who was talking back to him. Finally the counterman bent down and came up with a small dish and handed it to the manager, who returned to Willa with it. He leaned over Willa and, with a spoon lying across the plate, scooped up the cherry that sat there and placed it with a flourish atop her sundae. "We aim to satisfy" he said. He smiled at Willa, who smiled back.

She said "Thank you, sir. I didn't mean to be a nuisance."

"No trouble at all, young lady" he said, then went happily off.

Only then did Willa turn back to Orlo, who had been watching it all with an expression of complete bewilderment. She said, leaning across the table at Orlo, "Orlo, I want the name of someone who could put me in touch with this Chatto Hoffman. I'd like an address too, please." Orlo started to get up but eased slowly back down when he heard her say "Or I go to the police—or maybe your wife first—and tell them you tried to force me to do the thing with you. I saw on the television once how a girl did that."

Orlo said "Who's gonna believe that shit? Even my wife wouldn't believe I'd go messing around with—"

"Orlo" she said. "Orlo. Listen to me, Orlo. I'll tell you who would believe it. Who would believe it is anyone who heard that man who just left—or that clown who waited on us—tell them you were in here this afternoon buying ice cream for a young girl who's all alone in the city and doesn't have any friends or relatives to protect her." She leaned back. She was not smiling now.

She pushed the notebook and pen across the table to him. "Write them down. All the names and addresses you can think of. If you do that you won't hear from me again."

Orlo pointed to a sign down the curving walkway. Willa had shown him the address of her rooming house written on the first page of her notebook. "The bus stops there" Orlo said. "It'll take you back to the city."

"Are you sure it goes to that address?" Willa asked. She was still unsure of herself traveling in the city and had to return to the place she had been in order to start out for where she wanted to go next.

"Yeah, Willa" Orlo said. "It'll take you right there." He sounded tired. "I'm going now" he said.

"All right, Orlo. No hard feelings."

He did not answer. He stepped onto the parking lot and shoulders hunched, began walking away. Willa watched him for a moment, then called "Oh, Orlo!"

He turned to face her. "What?"

"You almost broke a little girl's heart with that letter of yours. You know that, Orlo?"

He did not say a word as shoulders still hunched, he walked quickly away.

Smiling, Willa turned. She began to run to the bus sign because she knew by now that things could happen quickly in the city, and she did not want to take a chance on missing her bus. She saw people gathered there, and she wanted to be certain of getting a seat for the long ride back. Running, purse banging against her side, she put her hand to her head so that the hat would not fall off. But it was not there.

"Oh, Jesus!" she cried and began running back to the ice-cream parlor.

* * *

She went to their table where the two sundaes—one uneaten—had not yet been cleared away. She yanked out the chair next to the one that had been hers, but there was no hat on it now. She got down on her knees and searched under the table, then looked on the three other chairs, and finally at the floor around the table. Her hat was gone.

She went to the manager, who had been watching her. "Have you seen the hat I was wearing when I came in here? It was a straw hat with a ribbon and lots of apples and oranges and things all around it. I put it on that chair there."

He shook his head. "I was at the cash register counting the receipts for my change of shift. You can ask Mirabel, though."

"Who?"

"Mirabel the clown. The one that waited on you." He pointed to where the clown was waiting on a family of four.

Willa went to him and said "Mister—" She waited, but he continued talking to his customers and writing in his pad. "Mister" she repeated, looking up at the tall man and tugging at his clown's sleeve. She tugged twice more before he looked down.

"Yeah?"

She told the clown the same thing she had told the manager.

"I haven't got to your table yet" he said. "You look for it?"

"*Of course I looked for it.* I wouldn't be asking you if I hadn't looked for it first."

"Can't help you, then" he said, and turned away.

Willa stood there, expression drawn, diminished in spirit despite her success with Orlo. Then she shrugged and moved off toward the door, saying to herself as she went through it "Isn't that something? If you're not careful, they'd steal the eyes right out of your head in this city."

The bus was not there, but she began to run anyway as she spoke to herself again. "On my first day too. Oh, well. Easy come, easy go."

7

Early that evening Vernon drove a ten-year-old dark Chevrolet onto a street of small shops and factories. Most of the shops were closed, their display windows shadowy in the failing light as mannequins with pupilless eyes stood pointing in mute inquiry at the empty street.

A few shops had lights on in rear rooms, where women could be seen draping material on the forms of more mannequins. Vernon stopped in front of one of them. On both sides of the street the shadowy figures seemed to be watching him.

He had followed the girl earlier back to her rooming house in the car, and then, knowing she had finished her search for that day, driven on to where he waited now on the silent street. His long overcoat was buttoned to the neck, and he held his right hand to his side as if he were wounded there.

A year ago Vernon's employer had selected him from among a dozen messengers for a position that gave him not only a degree of prestige but an increase in salary as well. He had chosen Vernon because he was the one he most trusted to deliver packages in the company van to customers in less accessible areas of the city or on the outskirts. He had taught Vernon to drive and accompanied him to the Department of Motor Vehicles, where Vernon took the driver's test and passed it. Vernon had done it all as he did everything: slowly and with intense thoroughness. After that he came to know the city even better than he had before; with his shadowing of others, he came to know it as well as anyone.

The car he was in now belonged to his landlady. It had been left to her in the will of an older sister who was widowed and childless. But Vernon's landlady could not drive and was not in good health, and since she knew Vernon—her longest established tenant—to be careful and dependable, they agreed that in exchange for his use of the car—the keys to which she turned over to him—he would drive her on occasional visits to old friends in distant parts of the city, on her monthly visits to her doctor, and once a week to the supermarket, where he waited for her in the car and then carried her packages to it and back to the house. Since the old woman had no other use for the car, it seemed to her she had gotten the best of the bargain; for she knew Vernon would seldom use it for himself, would almost never even take it from the garage where she kept it except for repairs and to have it serviced.

That day Vernon had used it. He had followed the girl on foot that morning to a bus stop near their street, where he stayed close enough to overhear her ask directions of a man waiting for a bus. She had looked down at a notebook in her hand before asking "Could you tell me how to get to a place called Turtle Lane? Someone told me I should take a bus to a place called Village Park and when I got off there I'd find it. He said the bus comes by here."

Vernon had not waited to hear the rest. He had hurried—as much as he was capable of hurrying—the two blocks to the garage and driven the car back to where he waited on the other side of the street a half-block away from where she was sitting on a bench.

The buses to Village Park, Vernon knew, came only once an hour. But even so, he could have lost her by going for the car. He had decided to do so because following someone within the anonymity and distractions of the city was less difficult than following long distances into less populated areas.

When her bus came and she boarded it, he knew he had made the right decision as he pulled out from the curb and moved close to the rear of the bus. Before long he had adjusted to the new technique of following, which served him as the other technique did: it joined him to her.

By the end of the day he had come to know some of her story: he had learned that, like him, she was alone in the world; but unlike him, she had a mother she loved and for whom she was looking. He had seen her maneuvering of the black man, had been in awe of her for accomplishing what he would have been too frightened to even try. She was strong, determined and resourceful; she confronted situations, whereas Vernon could only reflect them. For the first time he felt something more than lust for faceless women, something more than the imagined coupling of a nameless body with his. It disturbed him, he was not comfortable with it yet, but it excited him in a different way than his other following had.

Now Vernon got out of the car and stepped onto the street of mannequins. He locked the car and, still holding his hand to his side, approached the door of the shop. He leaned forward and looked into it through the window, where in a lighted rear room he watched for a moment the women working among the still figures of mannequins. Mannequins waited: they were silent and submissive.

He knocked several times before one of the women heard him; she detached herself from the form on which she had been working and looked through the intervening darkness of the shop to see who was knocking. She stepped into the darkness, then appeared out of it looking over the gilt lettering on the window. She smiled and opened the door.

But although she held the door wide in invitation, Vernon did not go in. He remained where he was as he spoke. "Do you remember me, Miss Godman?"

She was a small, sturdy woman in her mid-thirties; she seemed especially sturdy before the cadaverous Vernon. But she had a friendly manner, accepting and generous. She said "Of course I remember you, Vernon. You deliver our patterns."

"I've come for it" he said.

She seemed puzzled, but she motioned him inside. Locking the door, she led him into the rear room.

Three women were there, one kneeling before a dressmaker's dummy with an unfinished dress on it, the others arranging finished dresses on mannequins. The women were too busy to look at him, but one of the mannequins seemed to stare at him over the kneeling woman's head. Vernon stared back at it.

"What is it you came for, Vernon?" Miss Godman asked, looking up at him. "Did you forget something on one of your deliveries? Do we owe the service some money?"

He continued to stare at the mannequin. Then he looked down at Miss Godman. "I came for that mannequin" he said, pointing at it. "The one you don't use anymore. I want to buy it."

She turned to the corner at which Vernon was pointing and at the mannequin he had been watching, which was older and shabbier than the others and had a crack in its side. It was the crack that had first inspired him to own it, but he hadn't had the courage to ask for it before.

"I should have thrown that old thing out long ago" she said. "Do you want it for your mother, Vernon? Is she a dressmaker?"

He had not thought until then what reason he could give for wanting to own a mannequin. "Yes" he said. "It's for my mother. She needs it to replace her broken one."

He began staring at the mannequin again.

"Take it" she said.

He turned back to her. "What?"

"Take the old thing. You can have it."

"No" he said. "I can't just take it."

"Nonsense. It's not worth anything to me."

"I can't just take it" he repeated. "I have to buy it. I have to own it."

The kneeling woman looked up at those words. She stared at him, a jetty of pins suddenly still at her lips.

"I have to buy it" Vernon said again.

She shrugged. "All right. Five dollars would be fair. Although I'd be happy just to get rid of it."

But he was already taking out an old wallet with his left hand from the left pocket of his overcoat. She had not noticed until then that he kept his right hand pressed to his side. "Is something wrong with your side, Vernon?"

"It's only a cramp." He laid the wallet on a board filled with sketches of dresses and fumbled with it until he had extracted a five dollar bill. He held it out to her.

She took the bill, folded it and stuck it into the neckline of her dress. She said "You should have your side looked at, Vernon. One never knows when something—"

But he was no longer listening to her, perhaps was no longer aware of her existence—or her existence was now of no further interest to him—as he stepped past her and went to the mannequin. He put his arms under its arms, which yielded rigidly. His face pressed close to its face; a hairless head without features looked back at him. It was not heavy, but as he lifted it in his awkward hold it tilted backward like a woman declining an embrace. He swung it around, clinging to it, and with it preceding him he moved past the watching women, through the doorway, and to the outer door.

He stopped there, not wanting to put the mannequin down as his left hand searched for the lock to the door, his right elbow now pressed to his side. He could not find the lock, but still he did not put the mannequin down; he just waited in the near darkness, the four women gathered at the other doorway watching.

Miss Godman came out finally and reached around Vernon and the mannequin. She opened the door and stepped back and watched as he carried the mannequin onto the street. He did not notice that she locked the door quickly behind him.

He laid the mannequin face up on the rear floor of the car so that it could not be easily seen from the street. When he attempted to close the door, the mannequin's pedestal, flush with it, lifted the mannequin on the bump in the middle of the floor. It rose partway, as if sitting up to look at him; then it settled again. He locked the door and drove back to his rooming house.

He waited outside in the car. He was waiting not only for full darkness but for the hour when he knew his landlady would be asleep. When it came, he lifted the mannequin from the back and struggling with it went into the house and up the stairs to his room. He knew he did not have to return the car to the garage; parking was allowed on the street and he had left it there overnight before undisturbed. His was one of the few remaining safe neighborhoods in the city.

He stood the mannequin at the foot of the bed. Then he backed off from it and went to different parts of the room to observe it. He adjusted its angle several times. Finally satisfied, he went to the rocking chair where he had left his overcoat, took the girl's hat from inside it and laid it on the dresser. He opened the closet door and, as carefully as he could, hung the overcoat and scarf on separate hangers. He closed the door and turned back to the room, where he stood looking at the mannequin a moment.

He removed his clothes in the near darkness, putting them over the arm of the rocking chair. When he was naked, he turned to the bureau, took the hat, and went to the mannequin with it.

He studied the mannequin in the darkness from different angles, then put the hat on it. In the light from the window, he adjusted the hat until he was satisfied that was how the girl wore it. Then he raised the mannequin's arms.

He moved to the window and drew the lace curtains so that in the diminished light the mannequin could have been mistaken for the girl. Then he went to the bed, drew back the covers, and got into it on his back, where he lay looking up at the dim hatted figure.

He placed his hands palms down on his thin, hairless chest, then lowered them slowly the length of his body. He sighed. He was looking into the hidden face of the mannequin, which was lifting its arms in recognition of him.

8

Now in the winter a year later both of them sat in the chairs reading Bibles before the fireplace, within the aura of the flames, the one with her propensity for silence, the other uneasily learning it. Each in the unbeleaguered evenings committed to an hour of reckoning with God. It was a price Lydia had exacted from Emil on the first day of their marriage, even before their wedding night began, not for her body (which she offered to him without conditions finally, still taking down her hair, but with an eagerness at last equal to his own); nor was it out of obligation to her (for she did not press him to feel any); nor to assure the installation of peace into their evenings (for he felt from the first moment of that first evening its promissory presence). Not any of these, which both he and Lydia would have recognized to be an unequal bargain, offering him too convenient a reason for its cancellation, but— without a word spoken by them—a contract for his reconstruction, his eventual safe harboring.

The magazines had been banished from the house. There was no question of his returning to drinking; no compromise could be made with that, he knew, not even for an occasional beer when he went to town. She still allowed him his cigarettes, although never again in the house. In the new ritual, he would get up, take down his overcoat from the clothes tree beside the door, go onto the porch and smoke there looking out at the night. He was not aware of it at first, but he even—as he had done the first time—stepped out of sight of her to the side of the window where the smoke drifted past the window signaling not only his station there, but his acceptance of it as well.

He told himself that for the first time in his life he was at peace

with himself and the world. For the first time in his life he felt contentment. He felt safe.

No one believed their alliance would last: not the people of the
town, not even Emil at first during his newly acquired honest discourses
with himself, those first confrontations with his history of frail resolve.
Only Lydia had known; she had known from the first, and in time she
made him know it too. She had told him the morning they returned
from Milltown that she would change his life, and he was surprised not
so much at her keeping that promise as at the ease with which he had
lent himself to it. She had made him believe that he had virtues, even
strengths, which before, in his pursuit of unconditional sensations and
his fear of responsibility, he would have denied. He had never before
known a moment of genuine self-respect, and that was the most important thing she had given him. It was gratitude too that bound him
finally to her.

There was an old console radio in the house that she had him bring
down from the attic and put in a corner of the parlor—a domed skull
with a cloth face filtering its voice and a lighted mouth exposing its
teeth of numbers. Her first husband had listened to the evening news
on it, the weather and farm reports. Now it was resurrected, with religious programs coming out of it like exuberant crusaders descended on
a place full of revelers: comedies, crooners, soap operas, game shows,
and commercial jingles for toothpaste and hair tonic. Exhortations to
faith mingled with studio laughter and commented upon dramas
unfolding, unseen. Castigating preachers denounced phantom illicit
lovers, who were then also banished by the turn of the knob. Emil's
favorite radio program from the past was "Amos 'n' Andy," but that too
was swept away by her in favor of church choirs assembling God's messages. They listened together.

There were nights, however (those on which she took down her
hair), when they would turn off the lights in the room, only the fire in
the fireplace and the radio's face watching them, and tune into dance
music coming to them from twenty-five miles away in a ballroom atop
one of Atlantic City's luxury hotels. They would come together in the
middle of the room like shadow dancers highlighted from behind by the
fire, dance silently and with a formal, stately elegance transported from
another time.

Emil's new wife surprised him the first time they danced together
there; she had a natural grace when dancing that all his years on dance
floors had never given him. She possessed serenity while dancing, which
is the assurance of grace in movement. She led him easily into new

rhythms, where he discovered in her arms those rhythms in himself. It would have seemed to a passerby looking in at the window a quiet, strange dance, the dance of somnambulists come together with identical dreams.

One evening toward the end of the winter, their daughter asleep above them in her crib, Lydia put away her Bible and Emil laid his aside too and sat, face turned full to her, in anticipation of an announcement. He sensed her moods now; sensed that this night something had changed for him.

She said "They'll be hiring at the knitting mill in the spring. You'll start there then. It's been arranged."

He had known all along that that time would come; she would turn him out now into the world of other people. She would release him, apprenticed in discipline, out of sanctuary; and only he knew the fear that was in him at the thought that the moment was near.

"I have work to do here in the spring" he said. "I've still got—"

She interrupted him. "You've done all that needs to be done. I've hired a good, reliable colored boy who will be coming to do what needs to be done around here. I'll oversee the migrants when it's time to harvest."

"You've hired a boy to replace me?"

"He's nineteen. Pastor Cooley recommended him from the colored church in Milltown. He teaches Sunday school there."

"A mill, Lydia? I'll be working in Milltown?"

"Not there. It's a mile east of Pineville, just off the highway."

"What will I be doing?"

"Is that important?"

"No."

"It's settled then."

Their daughter cried and Lydia went up to her, leaving him to thoughts that were for the first time since their marriage hidden from her, stored with guilt and misgivings away from her because she would have had no tolerance for them. It had become more important to him that he appear strong in her eyes than that he be strong in fact. He got up and went to her where she sat on the side of their bed rocking the child.

Since Madeleine's birth, Emil had held back any strong feelings he might have had for her; for although he had been moved by the sight of the child he had made, he had been frightened by her too. She was as beautiful as he was handsome; and even at three months, she seemed with her good nature and exuberance so much like him in his youth that it was as if Lydia had had no part in her making. He felt a bond between himself and his daughter that was potentially too strong for him to accept; he sensed its power to bind him to his new life in a fuller and more final way than any bond that held him now to Lydia. The child represented to him the potential for luring him into ultimate surrender, the final relinquishment of himself to another, for which he was not yet prepared.

He sat on the bed next to them, watching mother and daughter. The bed had become chastened.

After a while the child went back to sleep, and Lydia turned to Emil and held her out to him. It was an offering she had made before, and one from which he had always drawn back. But this time he took Madeleine in his arms, looked down at her. She awoke at the awkward transfer from her mother's arms to his, began to cry, then stopped as she looked up at Emil with trusting eyes. He felt at that moment that his lost innocence had been passed on to her, and was alive and growing in her. He saw it there as she placed her hand on his.

This time Emil not only did not refuse the child but arose with her in his arms and, with his wife beside him, went to the crib and lay Madeleine back in it. He drew the covers up over her and, holding his wife's hand, stood looking down at his daughter. He knew well the feel of Lydia's large, rough hand, but now it felt harder, like a rock in his hand.

The first morning in spring, Emil got up to go to his new job at the knitting mill. Lydia had bought him a lunch box, which was on the kitchen table waiting for him with his lunch and his Bible inside.

It was not a job designed to give anyone contentment. Women stood at a long table where knit dresses, sweaters and skirts were laid out in tall piles in front of them. He watched as they folded them and put them into boxes, like parts of women to be sealed up and sent off. At the far end of the hangarlike room there were machines with large spools feeding trembling skeins of yarn. All day he could hear the machines unceasingly whining. The sound followed him out of the mill; it traveled back for a while with him on the road home.

Rows of women sat bent over sewing machines, as if listening to what the machines were whispering to them. They lifted pieces not yet assembled out of canvas bins, held them together beneath the needles, slid them through and out into other bins beside them. Other pieces rose to follow.

Emil was given a cart. He wheeled it along the aisles, supplying the women with new bins of unassembled pieces and picking up the ones piled high with finished garments. He pushed bins of dresses with arms dangling at the side, like the bodies of women he was hurrying away.

At noon he lunched on a high, sloping lawn that overlooked the highway at the front of the building. He ate quickly, then spent the rest of the time reading his Bible. He did not speak to the women; he sat away from them under a stunted sapling. He breathed deeply before he went back into the mill.

On the Friday before the Memorial Day weekend, he sat on the lawn watching a caravan of cars going to the shore as the summer tourist season began. By mid-June there were lines of them coming and going: to Atlantic City, Cape May, Ocean City, Wildwood—concatenations of resort towns spread out along the seaboard on both sides of Atlantic City. Car horns began honking in the late morning, and shouts of vacationers drifted up through the mill's large, open windows. He could hear them from inside the house at night—more distant, unreal. There were nights when he imagined the vacationers were gathered in front of their property, feet shuffling in the dust of the road as the curious sightseers discussed them. He drove to work on the dirt road parallel to the highway, where he watched the cars moving like strange gardens blooming with beach chairs, picnic baskets, painted buckets and shovels, parasols, striped beach balls and inflated rubber animals that would be the vacationers' companions in the ocean. Children sprouted between them on the packed seats. When Emil's Rambler dipped on the road's inclines, he could see boats on car roofs sailing over the tops of trees. The tourists came and went endlessly through the heart of the summer.

Weekend partiers came too: young people from the cities singing and laughing, calling and waving to the locals who stood watching them beside the highway. There were nights when Emil sat alone on the porch listening to them and remembered that Georgia town, the wooden bars in moonlight shaking with excitement, juke music of heartbreak, pretty girls with smooth, shining faces dancing like tall rabbits on the plank floors. He heard the big, barefoot country boys whooping and stomping, saw the wooden floors buckling, sending the glasses on the beer-kegs-and-plank bars dancing too.

He awoke one morning in a silence that was suddenly defined, made sentient, by the absence of the vacationers' sounds: they were not abroad yet, and all he could hear was the occasional lone car on the highway.

He got out of bed naked and went to the open window. He could hear Lydia in the kitchen: pans rattling, drawers opening and closing. Looking down, he saw Lester Kane, the young black man who had come to work for them three months before. He was sitting on a chair in front of the shed reading a Bible as he waited for Lydia to bring his breakfast on a tray to the top of the back-porch steps. He had been invited to eat in the kitchen before they ate, but he preferred to take his meals alone in the shed were he lived. He always ate quickly and then left the tray next to the kitchen door for Lydia to find. He came and went so soundlessly that Emil often did not know when he was near. He seldom spoke to either of them except when they spoke to him, and Emil had not exchanged more than a dozen words with him.

Now Lester sat as he did every morning—not shy, but aloof from them, so that Emil felt again the uneasiness he had always felt at the sight of him. It was as if he were expressing by his detachment from them an indifference that was also a judgment. He was not as talented as Emil was at the work, took none of the pleasure Emil had always felt in it; but he worked without malingering, and if his aloofness bothered Emil, it was a virtue in Lydia's eyes. Emil knew that what Lydia found most satisfying about him—what made him an ideal employee to her—was that she never felt any need to acknowledge him as a person, was not compelled to form even a cursory relationship with him based on his identity as a man.

Emil stood at the window longer than he had intended to. He had pulled the lace curtain over the lower part of his body, so that if the young man looked up he would not see him standing naked. Lester did not look up, though; he never did on those mornings when Emil stood there naked looking down at him. After a while, Emil left the window, dressed, and went down to breakfast.

Breakfast was always a silent time for them. Lydia shuttled from stove to table and finally joined him, with little more than nods and gestures between them. They did not speak at all when he took up the lunch box and, exchanging nods with her, went out of the kitchen into the early morning sunlight.

It was the first Friday of the month—a payday—and Emil received his envelope from the payroll clerk while passing him with a bin. He took it in silence, as did all the others, for the mill management frowned on idle conversation. The women's heads went up, then down again to their sewing machines as they took their pay. Emil opened the envelope at lunchtime, sitting on the hill.

He did not read his Bible that noon, and his lunch remained uneaten as he sat leaning over his raised knees looking down at the passing cars. Some of the vacationers waved and shouted at the workers sprawled on the grass, and they waved back and called greetings in return. Only Emil was silent and expressionless, watching each car as it passed. Ten minutes before the lunch break was over, he stood up, and in response to a convertible full of young weekenders, raised his right hand high, not in greeting, but palm forward, its three fingers wide and stiffly erect. He did not lower his arm as the car passed, but followed it with the raised hand in what might have been a sign of benediction. He repeated the gesture with another car a few minutes later, and then with a third—always silent, always pivoting, and with the hand raised high until they were gone.

When the buzzer sounded for them to return to work, he went into the mill, but not back to his bins; he went instead to his foreman, who was huddled with another foreman in front of one of the large machines. He communicated more with gestures than with words, for the whining of the machines drowned out nearly all speech. The foreman understood finally that he was ill; he nodded his consent to Emil, who turned away and went out a side exit to the Rambler and drove off down the inclining road.

But this time he did not turn onto the dirt road toward home. He drove instead to where the road intersected the highway, and pausing only for an opening in the traffic, fitted the car in and became a constituent of it.

He pulled onto a gravel lot five miles down the highway. A wooden building stood on it, even in daylight its electric signs announcing on and off in the window, Pabst Blue Ribbon—Budweiser. Another sign was blinking over a small building joined to the larger one at its hip: Liquor to Go.

He went into the dark, nearly empty bar and ordered a beer. The barman took a chilled bottle from the freezer, uncapped it with a levering motion on the bottle opener beneath the bar, poured, and took the dollar Emil had put down next to his glass. He rang up the sale on a clattering, bell-ringing cash register and placed two quarters in front of Emil without another word between them.

Emil drank the beer with his head lowered over the glass. Now and then he looked down the length of the bar at the barman, who was standing at the end of it watching him. He finished the beer quickly, then raised his arm for another. The barman served him, maintaining the silence between them.

Emil got off his stool unsteadily after the fourth beer. Feet back, he leaned forward, supporting himself on the bar, fingers curling over its raised edge. He looked down at his hands and smiled at them. He did not raise his head, but twisted it to the side toward the barman, smiled at him, then looked back at his hands. He did it again as the barman began wiping glasses, pretending not to notice him. He looked away each time Emil smiled at him.

Finally, Emil straightened up and went across the bar and down a wide ramp into the package store, where he bought a pint of Old Granddad, returned to the car and drank half of it. He was still smiling as he drove off.

An hour later he saw the ocean rising to meet him; the beach and the boardwalk followed as he entered Atlantic City and turned onto Atlantic Avenue, where blocks of square buildings seemed to go drifting backward beside him. He rolled down his window so that he could smell and taste the salt air. The ocean breeze brought the distant piping of a calliope to him. A minute later he saw Steel Pier lifting up on the boardwalk, heard clearly the shouts and screams of riders on the roller coaster, laughter as it went clattering and with chains clinking in slow ascent, screaming as it plunged into a steep fall.

He turned off Atlantic onto Pennsylvania Avenue, where he craned his neck down each street at the boardwalk, and the ocean moved closer and became bigger. He watched as large, rearing waves came shuffling like bears to the shore, broke with the sound of something being crushed gently under them. Smaller waves hurried in as if anxious to display their white hats.

He turned into a parking lot, where he handed his car keys to a boy dressed only in a shirt and swimming trunks. He took off his own shirt and tied it around his neck, then walked off the lot bare-chested among people in bathing suits, wearing sunglasses and wide-brimmed straw hats. More of them came down the ramps off the boardwalk, under which bathers emerged out of the darkness and the damp sand dancing barefoot on the scorching street and sidewalk. They struggled on tiptoes toward the awnings of refreshment stands, then came away dancing again with armloads of hot dogs, hamburgers, boxes of popcorn and soft drinks. Some licked melting ice-cream cones as they went. Emil laughed watching them. He stopped several times to tilt the bottle of bourbon in its brown paper bag, then shoved it back into his hip pocket.

He passed small hotels and rooming houses—one with a sign declaring Mrs. Brown's Fine Home Cooking—where old vacationers, disinclined to share in all that had brought them there, sat in rocking chairs on balconies, stubbornly rocking. They were all fully dressed and looked down on the others as if they had grudges against them. Their stares told them they would like them to go away.

He turned into the open doorway of a bar. He sat down in cool dimness, smiling at the busy barman at the far end of the bar as if he had something he was waiting to tell him. But when the barman got to him, Emil just ordered a shot and a beer and sat silently watching him. He looked up at a sign behind the bar:

LIVE BAND
DANCING NIGHTLY

Nearly everyone in the bar was barefoot and in bathing suits; some had left behind them dark, skeletal imprints of wet feet on the concrete floor. Sand was everywhere—even under Emil's hand on the bar. When he left, sand went crunching with him beneath his feet.

He went up the ramp onto the crowded boardwalk, where people passed him with sprightly steps. He stopped to watch large, hooded wicker chairs on wheels being pushed by elderly black men shouting "Comin' through! Comin' through!" as if they owned the boardwalk by possession of the important-looking chairs. The ponderous chairs had high backs fanning up like giant oysters in which could be seen small, huddled old faces looking out.

He crossed the boardwalk, conscious of voices and shadows moving in its interstices beneath him, then walked down a flight of worn wooden steps onto the beach. He headed straight for the ocean, his feet sinking in sand with each step as he weaved between clusters of people until he reached the water's edge.

He stood for a while staring out at the ocean and the sky, breathing deeply, then sat down on the wet sand and took off his shoes and socks. He tied the laces together, slung the shoes over his shoulder, then got up and began walking.

He walked slowly, planting his feet ankle-deep in the surf, letting it pull at his feet as it rushed back to the ocean; behind him in the wet sand his footprints were drawn back with the tide. He began to walk faster in the surf; then he was running. The people grew smaller behind him.

He was alone on the beach now, running with no one near him or even within hearing distance behind him. He ran tilting and hobbling, like a large crab scurrying upright along the surface, head back and mouth open, taking in the palpable air. When he reached the jagged, hunched rocks crawling onto the beach several miles away, he climbed onto one and sat there staring off, so motionless he might have been thought a statue from antiquity washed up out of the deep. After a while, he got up and ran back.

He was tired, and he sat down again on the sand at the edge of the ocean, leaned back on his elbows and raised his face to the sun. He closed his eyes. He let the warmth of the sun envelop him and felt the ocean pulling at his feet, drawing the sickness down out of his body. He could feel the crippled foot being cleansed by it.

When he opened his eyes, the voices behind him on the beach had diminished; the sun was low as thinning groups of bathers gathered up their possessions and called in their children, who ran dripping out of the water, sand exploding around them with each step. Adults stood in groups shaking out their blankets, performing precise dances toward and away from one another until the blankets were reduced to small, manageable squares. They trudged off loaded down with beach gear, tilting like tenpins in the sand.

Emil put on his socks and shoes and got up. He entered the darkness beneath the boardwalk, then ducked behind a rotting wooden piling to finish the bottle. He dropped it in its bag among crumpled cigarette packages, paper cups, Popsicle sticks, Dixie cups with photographs of movie stars fading on their lids, and condoms laid out in relentless remembrance. It was cold there, and he put on his shirt and moved quickly onto the street.

He went into one of the small hotels with a sign over its narrow door: Family Rates. Some of the people gathered in the lobby were already dressed and waiting for others to come down and join them for dinner. They sat on overstuffed chairs and a leather couch in a room with a large rubber plant in the doorway; most sat leaning close to the tiny screen of a Motorola television, whose picture wavered, blurred and faded in and out, as if the performers on the screen were reluctant to remain with them for long. Children, still sleepy from naps, tilted against their parents' shoulders, one sucking his thumb as he gazed with a melancholy expression at the screen.

Emil registered, took his key from a sport-shirted desk clerk and went back out the door, onto the street and into a liquor store. He bought a fifth of Old Granddad, and on the street pulled his shirt out of his trousers, opened the three bottom buttons and hid the bottle as best as he could in his side pocket. Returning to the hotel, he hurried past the desk clerk up to his room.

He had been given a room like a monk's cell, furnished with only a single bed, a bureau, a wooden chair. The window was propped up by a stick and looked onto an alley and a windowless brick wall.

He opened the bottle and drank from it sitting on the side of the bed. He sat facing the window, seldom moving except to raise the bottle to his mouth. He heard families talking, moving around him in the hallway, beyond the walls. Someone had written in large, scrawling letters on the wall next to the window:

IF GOD IS DELIVERANCE,
WHY DOESN'T HE
DELIVER ME FROM PAIN?

He watched the last light of day fading away, the shadows of evening spilling like ink slowly down the brick wall. He watched until the wall had turned as dark as the night.

He got up then and switched on the light. He placed the bottle on the bureau, holding it steady for a few seconds to make certain it did not fall. He staggered slightly, but steadied himself on the bureau. He tucked his shirt back into his trousers, straightened his collar and combed his hair with his hands. There was no mirror in the room, but he stood for minutes as if staring at his reflection on the wall behind the bureau.

When he emerged back onto the street, signs everywhere were blinking slowly, invitationally, but he knew where he was going as he walked up the street and into the bar he had been in that afternoon.

The bar was still dim, but it was no longer so quiet; its clientele of bathers and daytime drinkers had been replaced by young people in summer clothes. A spotlight was on in the rear, revealing a dance floor surrounded by tables. A band was unpacking its instruments on a plat-form at the dance floor's far end.

He went to the bar and ordered from a new bartender—a dark-haired man in a wide-necked sport shirt, eyes hidden behind dark glasses.

At another time, in another place, Emil would within minutes have had the barman laughing, listening to his stories, serving him drinks on the house; now he felt no ease in these surroundings that had once been so natural to him, no real happiness at the expectation of abandonment they offered. As the barman came bending low over the bar to serve him again, he saw a small reflection of himself in the dark lenses. He began to feel frightened, and for the first time in over a year he felt alone.

The band began playing, and he turned to it. Young couples came hand in hand onto the dance floor, but when they started dancing it was in a way he had never seen before: not joined at the cheeks, nor belly pressed against belly, not with joy in the release of music, not wildly shouting in the night like the southern country dancers, but as people removed from one another, only touching in passing. It was a dance characterized by style more than endurance, and by a disinclination to engage in any passion other than the abstract one to which they responded in the music. He turned away from it.

Because he felt panic building, heard a voice begin to scream somewhere inside of him, he forced himself to smile at the barman as he poured Emil's third drink. Emil said in a voice he realized was not his "Just keep 'em comin', ole buddy." The voice had a southern accent.

Below the glasses the barman's mouth crinkled into a slight smile. But Emil knew that the eyes behind the glasses were not smiling—nor did the man reply as he moved silently away down the bar.

Emil finished the drink in one swallow, then lifted his arm as a signal for another. Like something on casters, the barman worked his way back with Emil's brand, poured, and picking up his two dollars, began to turn to the cash register when Emil waved him away with a sign that the change was for him.

A young girl approached the bar, ponytail bobbing behind her. She signaled to the barman, who waved to her smiling and came leaning across the bar, ear turned to hear her above the music. She shouted her order into the ear, and he nodded and began mixing her drink below the bar.

The girl turned away to watch the dancing, her ponytail swinging in a way that announced sexual arrogance and self-assurance—qualities that in the past had always been a challenge to Emil. She was drumming her fingers on the bar to the music, nodding her head to it. He leaned forward and stilled her hand by placing his own hand over it. She turned to him, annoyed at first; but when she saw his pleasant, unaggressive smile she smiled back, even as she removed her hand from under his. Then she turned her back to him, again watching the dancers. Seconds later she was nodding her head and moving her body to the music.

Emil leaned close to her. He had to shout to be heard. "I only have one foot, but I bet I could dance to that there music all night." She turned a startled face to him. He nodded solemnly. "No joke" he said, raising his foot. "I lost half this here foot in the war."

"No kidding?" the girl said. "That's a shame. It must be tough." She turned back to the dance floor, head nodding.

"It ain't so bad as all that" he shouted into her ear. "I can dance with it. I can pick banjo with it, too. Of course, I never did learn to pick banjo real good."

He lifted his glass to her in a salute at the moment the barman came up with her drink. She smiled at Emil before she went off.

He had wanted to detain her, buy her a drink, make her laugh, dance with her until he had the lights shining in her eyes—do all those things he had once done so effortlessly without ever thinking he needed to do them. But he had hesitated, uncertain, unable to go beyond the first stages of flirtation. Afraid of what was unknown waiting for him there. He made himself smile as he turned back to the barman. "Does she, or don't she, ole buddy?" he asked as the barman served him.

"Don't they all, pal?" he answered as he took Emil's money and moved off.

Emil looked for the girl. He saw her at a table with a young man and another girl. A tall boy approached her, and she sprang up and went bobbing onto the dance floor with him.

He turned back in time to stop the barman as he was passing. He caught his sleeve and brought him down aslant to him. "Hey, good buddy" he began.

The man's eyebrows above the sunglasses lifted in either exclamation or annoyance, which Emil saw but preferred not to notice. Then he saw him look down at Emil's fingers holding his sleeve, and Emil let go of it. He said "I bet I know a story you never heard before. Listen here a minute, and I'll—"

"Look, pal, I'd like to, but maybe you noticed, I'm busy here."

"This won't take but a minute. Listen. Just listen." He heard the note of pleading in his voice, but he hurried into the old story—one he had told dozens of times and which had never failed to evoke laughter, good fellowship, love for him. That it might not do so this time caused his sense of panic to grow. He felt his throat tightening as he began the story.

"This fellow was taking his pet duck for a walk when he comes to this movie house, where he sees they're showing a movie he wanted to see for a long time. But the movie's about to start, it's the last time they'll be showing it, and there's no time to take the duck home, so he buys a ticket and goes up to the ticket man with it. 'You can't bring that duck in here' the man tells him. He doesn't know what to do until he gets an idea and goes around the corner and stuffs that ole duck in his pants and buttons his coat over it. Then he goes into the movie house and sits down next to a woman and her boyfriend to enjoy the show. After a while, the duck starts to move, and he knows it needs air, so he unzips his fly and lets it stick its head up. The woman looks over. She turns to her boyfriend and nudges him. 'Do you see what I see?' she asks. He looks over and shrugs. 'So what?' he says. 'If you've seen one cock, you've seen them all.' 'Maybe so' she says 'but this one's eating my popcorn.'"

He waited somewhere distant in his mind for the laughter. But there was only silence from the barman and a weak smile, which was more humiliating to him than no laugther at all. The barman looked down to where Emil was again holding his wrist—had been throughout the story—to keep him there. He released it, and the barman drifted away.

He turned toward the dance floor, pretending an interest in the dancers that he did not feel. He thought, I don't have any joy in me anymore. I'm afraid to feel it now.

He got up and went weaving among packed tables to where the girl sat. He pulled up a chair from an adjacent table and sat down, an uninvited guest at the table where the girl and her two friends were talking and laughing. The girl's back was to him. He tapped her on the shoulder. She turned, but the smile she had prepared for another was replaced by slight annoyance when she saw who it was.

"Let's have us that dance now" he said.

"What?"

"A dance. I can show you what real dancing is."

"Hey, look" she said, "I'm sorry. I don't feel like dancing now. Another time, huh?"

A young man came to the table, leaned into the girl's now uptilted, eager face; and without a thought, Emil knew, for him, she went off with the young man, already dancing. He turned back to see her friends—heads together and whispering—looking at him.

He got up. "What the fuck's wrong with you?" he shouted.

They looked startled, stopped talking.

He staggered backward. "What's the matter, you never seen a man ask a girl to dance before?" He knocked over the chair as he turned and went off, not away from the tables and the dancing, but to the edge of the dance floor.

He forced himself to go up to the first girl he saw sitting alone. She was not attractive, and he knew that was why he had approached her. In the past, he would have gone from the rejection of one pretty girl to one even prettier. And he would not have given the first one another thought.

He sat down behind the girl. When he put out his hand to touch her on the shoulder, it was like someone else's hand reaching for her. He had the sensation that he had slipped out of himself and was standing unseen behind himself listening. He heard himself say "I've been looking for you, Deliverance."

She looked back at him through unfathomable, vague eyes. He thought of cows he had seen with such eyes. "Huh?" she said.

"Isn't your name Deliverance?"

"No, it isn't." She turned her dead eyes slowly back to the dancers.

"Dance with me, Deliverance" he said.

She answered him over her shoulder. "I'm waiting for someone."

"So am I" he said. "I'm waiting for Deliverance. Do you know what happens when I dance? I fly away."

She still did not turn to him as she said in a shrill voice "Oh, sure! Boy! Some people!"

He got up. He put his hand on her arm and started to pull her up—not roughly, but firmly. "Come on" he said.

"Hey!" she said. She tried to pull away, but he held on to her.

"All I want is to dance with you" he said. "Just dance." Again he heard the tone of pleading in his voice. He smiled at her, but he could feel the smile wavering. He put his hands to his face and felt it beginning to crumble and fall away. He lowered his hands and fought back the panic, and the smile returned, like something burning his face. "Please?" he asked in a voice that was no more than a whisper.

She stared at him, examining him with eyes he knew had never seen anything at all. Finally she shrugged and got up, and they went onto the dance floor.

He did not hear the music, not a note of it. He heard instead under the fierce light the whining guitars, the music of other nights. Beyond the glare of the spotlight he saw young country dancers moving up and down with curious beauty. He threw back his head, then raising his good foot, arm firmly around the girl's waist, he brought the foot crashing onto the floor. "*Ah-haaaaaaaaaaaaaaaaaaaaaaaaaaaaaaaaaa- aaaaaaaaaaaaaaaaaaa!*" he yelled, and charged into the midst of the dancers, who were already moving back to avoid him.

He felt the girl pull away from him, stand back; both were still then, as the others stood still also, away from them. The music had stopped. Every eye was on him.

He ran from the bar into the hotel lobby and back to the room. He pushed the door firmly shut and turned the lock as if sealing something away. He grabbed the bottle from the bureau, sat down on the bed and began rocking back and forth. After a while, he got up and turned out the light.

When the bottle was empty, he got up; staggering out the door and along the hallway, he plunged, nearly falling, down the stairs into the lobby. He passed the desk clerk, who was dozing; huddled shapes with silver masks gathered around the television in the dark room. As he swerved to avoid walking into the rubber plant, the desk clerk awoke and raised his arm to him. But Emil was out the door before he could speak.

He went to an all-night drugstore and bought a pack of razor blades and a bottle of fifty aspirins. Then he went to the liquor store and purchased another bottle, not bothering to hide it this time as he went back through the door of the hotel, where the clerk was talking to a stout middle-aged couple. The woman wore a black velvet gown, and the man, evening clothes, and now in out of the ocean breeze, they were both perspiring heavily. A little boy in a sailor suit sat half-asleep on the floor holding the man's trouser leg.

The clerk looked up as Emil was passing him. He called to him "Sir! Sir! Just a minute, please. I want to—"

But Emil was gone up the stairs before he could finish.

He locked the door again. He put the packages on the bureau and took off all his clothes. He brought the chair to the bed and sat on the bed in front of it, where he opened the bottle of bourbon and the aspirin bottle. He peeled the waxed paper from one of the razor blades and laid it next to the aspirins. Then he leaned back on the bed drinking and looking at them.

He was surprised at how calm he felt. The decision made, everything assembled, he now felt peace, even happiness. For the first time in his life he did not fear pain; imminent death did not frighten him. But when he reached for the aspirin bottle, his hand would not touch it.

He drank a third of the bourbon trying to get the bottle of aspirin to his lips; but even when he was able to touch it, he lowered it before it reached his mouth. He had wanted death, but now that the moment was near, he was afraid again.

He got up, turned off the light and fell onto the bed face down. He drew his legs up and his arms in and bent his head into his chest. He began trembling. Then he slept.

The silence woke him. That and the cooler air coming through the window from the ocean. He listened to the ocean, the street's silence in the deserted morning. Loneliness invaded him.

He sat up in the fear-filled silence and began drinking again.

When he raised the aspirin bottle, his hand shook, but he managed to bring the bottle to his mouth. Washing the aspirins down with the bourbon, he chewed the first mouthful. The taste was so bad, he swallowed the next mouthful whole. After that it was easy.

He finished them quickly, before courage could leave him. Once done, there was nothing to fear anymore.

He picked up the razor blade, brought the foot onto the bed and made an incision full-circle above the ankle. He turned his head away when he saw the blood rising, stopped, then forced himself to look again until it was done. He lowered the foot to the floor so that he would not see it bleeding.

He made the same kind of incision on his hand at the wrist, looking away again when he saw the blood.

He finished the bourbon with his left hand, holding the right one to the side, where he could not see it, then lay back on the bed waiting for death to come. There was no pain: only a pleasant tingling at his wrist and ankle. He drifted into sleep, drunk and smiling.

He awoke to first daylight knowing he did not want to die. Fear had woken him this time. And nausea: he barely had time to lean over the side of the bed before he vomited on the floor. He vomited repeatedly and convulsively until the bile and residue of aspirins lay below him in a puddle he stared down at in disbelief.

When he attempted to get off the bed, he found there was not enough strength left in him to do it. He tried to raise himself up and felt the sheet rising with him where it stuck to his flesh in dried blood. He turned over and pulled the sheet free of the bed, then rolled back again to the edge. He reached out for the chair.

He was crawling off the bed, using the chair for support, when it fell away from under him and he crashed to the floor, the sheet sliding down slowly behind him. He got onto his knees and began crawling toward the door, the sheet following him. It stopped when he stopped.

He dragged himself upright until he sat leaning against the door, then stretched his arm up it toward the lock. He could not reach it. His fingers traveled up the door again and again, smearing it with blood where his wrist touched it. He fell back exhausted, face pressed to the door.

He sat for a while with his eyes closed, the only sign of life his slow breathing; then his eyes opened and he put his mouth to the door. He tried to call for help through the door, but although his mouth opened and closed, the only sound that emerged was a nearly inaudible squeaking. He rested his face against the door and closed his eyes again. He felt himself slipping away.

What woke him this time was the sound of his hand faintly knocking on the door; it beat slowly, almost casually, as if it had a will of its own now and had determined it would save him. He pulled himself upright and continued knocking in that slow, steady rhythm that might have seemed unremarkable to anyone passing had it not persisted. When he heard a door open down the hallway, he knocked more loudly, then stopped to listen.

He heard footsteps coming toward him, then a man and a woman talking outside the door. He began the slow knocking again, stopped again. When the man spoke to him through the door, the only answer he could make was the faint squeaking sound. He began knocking again as he heard them go running toward the stairs.

He continued knocking, but now even more weakly; he was fading away again when he heard footsteps and more voices coming up the stairs. Someone called his name through the door.

They had to push back both the door and his legs to get to him. He watched as the lower half of his naked body moved around him. He shifted his head out of the way to the side, against the doorjamb, so that when the door swung open the top half of his body was leaning into the hallway. It fell forward onto the floor.

He could not rise. He lay where he was, looking up at the desk clerk and the stout couple, who were now in bathing suits. The small boy was clutching the bunched flesh of his mother's thigh as he pressed a beach ball to his chest; he stared down, eyes nearly as wild as Emil's, as Emil raised his head trying to speak. But all they heard was the squeaking, and all he saw was the ball as it fell from the child's hand and came bouncing toward him.

■ ■ ■

Two weeks later he was back at the mill, but no longer picking up carts and bringing other ones back. A new job was created for him in which he cared for the lawn, landscaped the grounds around the mill and handled minor repairs around the building.

It was not a job that led anywhere, but he had no desire to go anywhere beyond it, just as Lydia, from the beginning, had never considered the possibility of his achieving anything beyond daily occupation. He understood then finally that what he was at the mill, both now as well as before Atlantic City, was what she had arranged for him. There was no need for him to feel grateful for her intervention: her deployment of his life had been from the first the agreement between them.

He had freedom of movement and privacy in the new job, and during the winter especially there were hours in the day when he was not needed and could be alone. He spent that time in the boiler room, where they had given him a desk, a chair and a hot plate on which he could make coffee and heat up the lunches Lydia prepared for him each morning. In fair weather he was seen sitting on the now meticulously cut lawn under new saplings, among his modest creations of sculpted shrubbery, always alone and always reading his Bible. He seemed to the workers not so much aloof as apart from their concerns and interests. During the cold days, he read the Bible at his desk, or stood for long stretches of time looking out the high, small window at the sky and the fields and woods beyond the highway. Except for the window, it was like his room in the basement of the courthouse in Georgia.

It was during his first week in the new job that they left the church of Lydia's birth—the church of her parents, the one her late husband had served most of his life. That church which with its civil resolutions she now thought was no longer a strong enough restraint on Emil's darkly fluctuant character. What was required was not the mannequin Presbyterians among whom she had been raised, but something darker, more primal.

It became a resolution that they leave behind for a while tranquil adherence, tradition and allegiance as she took them one night bumping in the pickup outside of the town—as well as the precincts of respectability. Emil, in a severe new black suit Lydia had bought for him, clutched his Bible, silent and contemplative in the darkening countryside, as Lydia drove, looking straight ahead. Soon they arrived at the Ball Creek Church of the Pentecost on the other side of the Whitewater River, on the other side, too, of sanity—and perhaps salvation—at least in the eyes of the Presbyterians, whose church was as different from this as the softly churning water in the river was different from the nervous depths of the polluted creek bottom.

She delivered him there with that same practicality with which she had assigned each element of rectitude to his life. She did it not in cold blood, nor with passion, but sensibly, as the severest means available for a lasting conversion. There were times when he feared her more than he had ever feared anyone or anything on earth.

That night Emil got up among the newly saved, the reborn. Among others who were speaking in tongues. He stood before a blind preacher, who told him that Jesus would heal him as, with the others shouting hallelujahs, he received God's visitation. He fell to his knees and rocked with them, and with them tore pieces of God's flesh from his body. He collapsed onto the floor and, writhing and speaking in tongues, disappeared.

He was baptized in the Whitewater River on his thirtieth birthday, along with four children and an old man.

9

At three Willa was a precocious and inquisitive child, although more reserved than most children of that age. She had been talking for twenty months. Then one morning she stopped.

She withdrew. She no longer relied on her grandmother to satisfy her curiosity but instead began conducting investigations of the world around her on her own and in silence. Her grandmother, who had not questioned her withdrawal, sometimes found her watching while standing under the kitchen table. Once she opened a closet door and Willa was inside with her eye at the keyhole. She hid behind furniture to observe them.

When Willa resumed talking a year later, it was as if she had matured by much more than that year in the interval. She was less trusting and more secretive, where before she had only seemed shy. She was more sure of herself and seldom sought out her grandmother for information anymore. It was as if she had initiated the year of silence and withdrawal to settle questions she had about her surroundings and family and had discovered they were not what she had thought them to be.

■ ■ ■

The morning after she saw Orlo Haines, Willa was in bed in her room waiting for a phone call. The new dress was draped over the back of the chair, the purse hung by its strap from the chair's arm, and the loafers were lined up in front of it. It looked like a new, faceless Willa waiting to be filled in.

As she turned on her side to look out the window, she thought again of the names Orlo had given her the previous afternoon:

Chatto Hoffman
Mary Vandel
Sylvia Rosenberg

Mary Vandel was the only one for whom Orlo knew an address. He said she had been a friend of her mother's. He had never met Sylvia Rosenberg but had heard that Willa's mother had been ill at one time and had lived with her for a while.

After Willa arrived back in the city, she had taken another bus to the neighborhood in which Mary Vandel lived. It was like a city within the city. It had parks, nightclubs, bars, and streets full of bookstores and shops displaying in their windows exotic costumes and jewelry and paintings that looked to Willa like objects exploding on canvases. Past these there were quiet residential streets with small trees and cobblestone streets and old brick houses newly restored.

Then she came to a street of crumbling old buildings, refuse and glass from smashed windows scattered on the sidewalk. She took out her notebook to check the name of the street, then went down it looking at the numbers, which here were mostly broken or missing, fallen with the same acquiescence with which the buildings had surrendered themselves to the street. She stopped in front of a house where there was no number but which, with her new knowledge of such things, she decided must be the one where Mary Vandel lived.

She went up the steep steps holding on to a concrete railing that had crumbled away, exposing veins of thick wire and pipes embedded in the foundation. There was no bell, but one side of a wide double door leaned outward on loose hinges. She pulled at the door, which opened easily, and went into a foyer and then a hallway. She heard voices beyond where the hallway turned and made her way toward them.

She stood facing an open door and a kitchen lit only by candles in the center of which was a long box laid out on two rows of chairs. She saw girls seated on chairs at the head of the box, some grouped around it, looking into it, and others standing back against the walls. They were all (except one, a woman seated at the head of the box) about Willa's age, and were shabbily dressed. Willa stayed where she was, for she sensed that this was an occasion at which a stranger wandering in would not be welcome. Then one girl, who looked a few years older than the others, noticed her. She put a finger to her lips and raised her hand to Willa as a signal to her to be silent and not come any farther. Detaching herself from the others, she came into the hall with an expression that suggested that Willa was not only welcome but expected. She put her hand on Willa's arm in a way that was friendly, even intimate.

"Welcome to Madeleine House" she whispered.

Willa wondered whether the name of the house the girl had just spoken—her mother's name—was more than a coincidence. She was about to inquire about it when the girl signaled another request for silence. Even so, Willa said "I came to see Mary Vandel."

"Come with me" the girl said, and hand around Willa's arm, she led her into the room.

No one looked at her. They were all watching the box in which there was obviously something they had come there to see. In the light from the candles, the girls' shadows hung back on the walls like a second set of congregants. The girls looked puny compared to their tall shadows.

The older girl led Willa to the head of the box, and Willa looked into it. It contained the body of a young girl.

"That can't be her" Willa said in her normal voice. "Mary Vandel's a grown woman, not a girl."

The girls stirred. Some of them drew back farther into the shadows. The woman seated at the head of the coffin, who was in her thirties, tall and erect, spoke with her face thrust forward between two candles. "What is this girl doing here, Heather?"

"She's looking for Mary, Penny. She's a runaway."

"Just a minute. I never—" Willa began. But the woman interrupted.

"Take her outside. I'll talk to her in my office."

Without a word to Willa, the girl called Heather took her arm again and led her back out of the room.

"I'm not running away from anywhere" Willa said in the hall. "I just came here to talk to Mary Vandel."

"I'm sorry about that" Heather said. "Please, just wait here. Penny will talk to you." She started to leave.

Willa called after her "Who was that dead girl in the box?"

Heather turned back. "That was Linda. She was one of us." She hurried back inside.

The woman came out a few minutes later. She hardly glanced at Willa. She said "Follow me" and headed toward a wide wooden stairway. Willa followed.

They went into a room on the second floor with a sign on the door:

PENNY MARKMAN
DIRECTOR
MADELEINE HOUSE

The only furniture in the room was a desk and a chair, an old leather couch and a metal filing cabinet. Penny sat behind the desk and nodded Willa toward the couch. Willa sat down on it slowly, looking around.

Penny picked up a pen and a pad of paper off the desk, then looked directly at Willa for the first time. "What is your name?"

"I'm Willa Rhineman."

"When did you run away, Willa?"

"Look. Ma'am. There's been some mistake. I only came here to see Mary Vandel about something."

Penny put down the pen. "Oh? Do you know Mary?"

"I never met her. But my mother knew her. That's why I came here. I'm looking for my mother."

Penny leaned back in her swivel chair. "I see. Well, unfortunately Mary doesn't come here these days."

"I was told by someone that she lived here."

"She used to live here for a while when she first bought the house—the Lord knows why. But that was before it became Madeleine House and I came here to run it. She hasn't been here at all for over a year. She turned it into a home for runaway girls. It's one of her many charities. Mary Vandel is a saint."

"I don't know anything about that" Willa said. "I'm just trying to find my mother."

"I'm afraid I can't help you."

"This place" Willa asked. "How did it get its name?"

"It was named after a runaway Mary knew in the sixties. She lived in this building at one time."

Willa asked "What happened to her?"

"I don't know. Mary seldom spoke about her. Just some girl, I suppose, who came and went. There were many of them back then."

Willa got up. She felt smaller standing in front of the large desk. "If you'll give me Mary Vandel's address, I'll go see her there."

"I'm afraid I can't do that."

"Why don't you call her, then, and tell her I'm here? She'll remember my mother. Just tell her who I am and that I'm looking for Madeleine Rhineman."

"It's a private number, and she only takes calls from close friends and business associates."

"What is she—a recluse?"

"She has retired. She's not well."

"Look, ma'am" Willa said, "this is important. I have to talk to Mary Vandel. Today." She planted herself, legs spread, hands balled into fists on the front of the desk. She leaned forward at the neck.

Penny studied her a moment, then sighed. She wrote something on a piece of paper. "Here. It's the address of the Carousel Club. Mary owns it. She used to be in there nearly every night. Maybe she still goes. I'm afraid that is the best I can do for you." She smiled, but it was not a genuine smile, and Willa did not return it.

Willa put the paper into her purse, went to the door, opened it, then stopped. She turned back. "That girl down there—how did she die?"

"Unfortunately, some of our girls wander back to old bad habits, old illusions. With Linda it was drugs. Too much at one time. The fatal illusion is that illusion can be heightened to the infinite power. No such equation exists. But I have the feeling you don't know much about such things."

"No, ma'am. I don't know much about a lot of things. But I'm learning."

She left the door open behind her.

The Carousel Club was a nightclub on a narrow street of expensive restaurants and bars. When Willa went through the door, she came upon a scene unlike any she could have imagined. It took her a moment to adjust to the dimness, but when she did she saw a long bar in front and empty tables and a bare stage in the back. On its walls was a continuous mural depicting grotesquely fat bodies and vacuous faces looking down on the patrons. One of the faces had a serpentine tongue curling out of it, licking an ice-cream cone below eyes blank as coins. A carousel carried more of the fat people on wooden animals that were dwarfed by their flabby bodies. While the small beasts strained under them, the riders displayed an insane abandonment; one of them was beating his wooden giraffe with his belt. The arm of a rider snatched a brass ring from the snoutlike nose of an onlooker, and a braceleted hand held a slab of blood-dripping meat in front of another onlooker, who was lunging at it with long fingers like claws and a wide, ravening mouth. The mural bore a title written in ornate script: "The Square Fair."

Sitting and standing at the bar were men wearing dresses and women's wigs and jewelry. Willa watched them walking with soft steps, exaggerated feminine gestures and made-up faces. Then she saw there were women there too, in men's suits, shirts and ties. The women were larger than the men, robust where the men were delicate, deep-voiced where the others were shrill. But Willa knew that even in the men's clothes and with their short hair, they were not really men, just as the men were only probationary women. There were girls there too, some not much older than Willa, who did not attempt to disguise their sex: they were clearly feminine and yielding in the arms of the tough-looking women. One girl sat leaning against the chest of a woman who was wearing a man's suit and smoking a cigarette in a long holder, her arm over the girl's shoulder, hand clasping her breast. Willa sat on a stool next to them, then looked away when they both glared at her.

A bartender came dancing up to her wearing a woman's blouse and pendant earrings, and Willa asked "Could you tell me if Mary Vandel will be coming in here today?"

"Oh, no, honey. Mary doesn't come here anymore. Not for the longest time."

"Sir, I've got an important message for Mary Vandel, but they told me at Madeleine House I'd have to come here to find her."

"No one's seen Mary in a coon's age, sweetie. You'd do better writing a letter."

Willa took out her notebook and pen. "Where does she live? Maybe I'll just go see her instead. I have to get this message to her today."

"Are you a friend of Mary's?" It was the voice of the woman in the man's suit, with the cigarette holder, and it was not friendly.

"You could say she's a friend of my family" Willa said.

Another voice came from behind Willa. "I never knew Mary to have square friends. *Oooooh,* I bet she's been keeping secrets from us!" Willa turned to look into a man's face heavily painted with rouge, lipstick and blue eye shadow. He wore a blonde wig.

Willa turned back to the bartender, who kept pushing up slipping bracelets on both wrists. He seemed to be the only pleasant person there. "Mary Vandel and my mother were friends" she explained "when my mother lived here."

"She's come looking for her butch mother!" someone declared behind Willa, and began clapping to a tune. She turned to see a bald man in his forties wearing a blue taffeta dress, with a long purse hanging by its strap from his arm. He was not wearing a wig, and he had on men's horn-rimmed glasses, so that his incomplete transition gave him a bizarre appearance even in those surroundings. He started dancing around Willa. When he began singing too, she knew he was as crazy as he looked.

How ya gonna keep 'em down on the farm
After they've seen Par-ee?

Willa turned back to the bartender. "Sir, Mary Vandel and my mother were friends, like I told you. I'm sure if you told her I was here, she'd want to see me. Why don't you just call her and ask her?"

"I can't, precious" he said. "I'd like to help you but I just can't. I'd get fired if I did."

Willa turned around and spoke to two others who had been listening. "Do you know Mary Vandel's address? Just tell me the name of the street if you don't know the number. I'll find it."

The woman in the man's suit answered for them. "It's like this, Little Bo Peep: Mary's retired now. No one sees her. And she doesn't welcome uninvited callers. The people around here love Mary. There's not one of us hasn't been done a favor or been helped by her at some time or another. We don't intrude on her privacy and we don't help others do it."

Willa got down slowly from her stool. She felt tired—even more tired than she had felt the previous evening while looking for the room. She opened her mouth to say something more, then closed it.

She went to the door and opened it, letting daylight in. She looked back down the bar where a line of faces leaned out, watching her. Behind them the crazy man started singing again. As she closed the door, the words followed her out:

How ya gonna keep 'em away from harm?
That's a mys-tery ...

She had been walking all over the neighborhood inquiring where Mary Vandel lived, but no one knew—or would tell her—and no one would suggest anyone who could. When she came to a small park, she sat down on a bench to rest, discouraged and tired.

A derelict was sleeping on the bench across from her. His shoes were under his head for a pillow, socks stuffed into them. She watched a large bug travel his face with leisurely inquisitiveness; when it reached the edge of his white beard, it started back over the terrain it had just covered. She watched it until it walked off his face.

She was about to leave when she saw a man enter the park and begin making his way around it, performing in an unusual way for the people on the benches. He wore a tall hat, sky-blue overalls and white gloves. His face was painted white. He faced the benches, then slid up to them as if on air. He rowed boats that were not there, looked out of invisible windows, felt his way along unseen walls, walked up and down illusions of stairs, climbed ropes made out of air. After each brief performance, he took off his hat and people put money into it. He brought silence with him, then just as quickly took it away.

He came to Willa's bench and stood in front of her. He was smiling broadly, challenging her to smile with him. When she did not, he made a downhearted face in imitation of hers, then fluttering his gloved fingers, he raised them slowly, the sad face disappearing below the fingers and a smile appearing, as if he were making it with a wave of his hand. When he saw that all Willa could manage was a wan smile in return, he went down on one knee in front of her. He touched her on the shoulder and tilted his head to the side, studying her; then putting a finger below her chin, he lifted her face lightly until she was looking at him. He got up.

Bending forward at the waist, his arms rising above his head, he brought them down and around again time after time, swimming placidly in unseen waters. He turned his face to hers, grinning at her, challenging her to defy logic too, until at last he succeeded in drawing a smile from her. Then he drew a laugh from her as he held his nose with two fingers, raised his other hand over his head and, bending it at the wrist, waved good-bye to her as he disappeared under the water.

He jumped to his feet, made a low bow to her, then swept off his hat and held it out to her. She took some coins from her purse and dropped them into his hat. He raised the hat in a wide arc and placed it back on his head without spilling the coins.

She signaled him with her hand to come closer. One of the boys who had lain with her under the baby tree was a mute, and she thought he was one too. "Sir" she said, "have you been doing that around here for long?"

He nodded.

She drew him closer with her hand. She said "I guess you get to know a lot of people that way."

He nodded vigorously. He drew his hands far apart to convey the idea of quantity.

"Do you know Mary Vandel?"

He shook his head, then made a sad face in imitation of her disappointed expression.

"Have you ever heard of Mary Vandel?" she asked.

He nodded.

"Do you know where she lives?"

He nodded again, then framed his smiling face with his hands, in imitation of hers.

She got off the bench. She took out her notebook and pen and held them out to him. "Could you write down her address for me, please? I'd really appreciate it."

He shook his head. But before she could be disappointed again, he held out his hand to her. She hesitated, but when he wiggled his fingers for her to take it, she reached out and put her hand in his. Skipping, he led her to the edge of the park. She had to skip too, to keep up.

He pointed down a street several blocks to where a wide avenue transected it. She pointed too. "She lives on that street?"

He nodded.

"Which way?"

He pointed to the left.

"How many blocks? Approximately?"

He held up four fingers. He hesitated. Then he held up one more, shrugged, and made a grinning face that apologized for the imprecision.

"Thanks, mister" she said as she moved off.

She turned and waved to him when she had crossed the street. He waved back with his fingers.

A policeman directed her to it. All she saw at first was a high stone wall with an iron gate built into it at the side. Wrought from the black iron in the crown of the gate were the letters *MV*. She went to it and looked in.

It was a large white house across a wide cobblestone courtyard. There was a fountain in the center of the courtyard, a statue of a naked woman standing ankle-deep in the water, which rose and fell like a sheer curtain over it. The statue's arms were reaching out of the water, its veiled face lifted to the sky.

She turned the handle on the gate, but it was locked. There was no bell. She went to the side of it, where there was a hole in the shape of a large face cut into the stone wall. A small wire-covered hole shaped like a mouth was in the center of it. She studied it for a minute, then pushed a button next to the mouth. When she pushed it again, the mouth spoke to her.

"Yes? Who is it?"

She stared at it.

"Who is it?" came a woman's voice again, harsh, impatient.

She had to rise onto her toes to place her mouth to the wire hole. She spoke into it. "Hello? Hello?"

The voice came again, as if it had not heard her, or was trying to confuse her. "Is someone there?"

"*Yes*" she yelled into it. "*I'm here. I'm talking to you.*"

The voice did not answer. There was no sound at all. She pushed the button again but this time only once. The voice returned. "Goddamn it, who's there?"

This time she was prepared, her mouth as close to the hole as she could get. "I'm here to see Mary Vandel. Hello? Hello?"

"If you kids don't—"

"*I'm not kids! Can't you hear me? Why can't you hear me?*"

"—go away I'm going to call—"

She pushed the button again, hoping that would help. It cut off the voice. She released it and the voice came back: "—cops."

Realizing how the device worked, she hurried to push the button again and hold it there as she shouted "*Don't go away. It's me. It's me!*"

"Who's me?" the voice asked. It was no longer angry. It was quietly ironic.

In her excitement not to lose the voice again, to get as close to it as she could, Willa had gone up as far as she could on one foot, her other leg raised on the wall. She looked as if she were trying to climb into the hole. Her mouth was pressed against the wire mouth. "It's Willa Rhineman" she said. "Is this Mary Vandel?"

There was a long pause. "No."

"I want to speak to Mary Vandel. It's very important."

"Does she know you?"

"Not exactly. But—"

"I'm sorry. Unless you have an appointment—"

"Please, lady" she said. "I've got to—"

"Don't bother us anymore."

There was a click, then silence. Willa stared at the mouth as she slid down and away from it. She slumped against the wall. It was minutes later before she moved again.

She stepped back and looked at the gate and the wall. There was no way she could climb over them and no other entrance to the courtyard. She was not even certain now if it would be worth trying. There was only one thing left to do.

She took out her notebook and wrote a note on the ledge of the hole and put it through a slot marked MAIL at the foot of the gate. She wrote in large letters on the overleaf: "FOR MARY VANDEL PERSONEL." It said:

IM MADELEINE RHINEMANS DAUTER END I WAS TOL YOU WERE HER FREND END I AM LOOKIGN FOR HER. PLESE HELP ME FINE MY MOTHER BY CALLIGN THIS TELEFON WILLA RHINEMAN 546-3690.

* * *

Now Willa turned back from the window. She sat up in bed and listened. She had heard the phone ringing in the hallway below.

She heard her landlady's door open, heard her go to the phone, answer it. Heard her put down the phone. Willa held her breath in the silence that followed. It seemed like a much longer silence than it was.

Finally she heard her landlady climbing the stairs, her obese body and the asthma that was probably killing her announcing her with each halted step. She stood wheezing at the top of the stairs before coming down the hall to Willa's door.

Willa was already into her dress. She was barefoot.

The landlady knocked. "There's a phone call for you, Miss Rhineman."

"I'm coming!" Willa shouted through the door. "Tell her I'm coming!" She waited, standing next to the door, until she heard the woman make her slow progress back down the stairs, heard her speak a few words into the phone, then close her door behind her. Then Willa ran down the stairs to the phone.

"Hello?"

"Willa?" It was a woman's voice, strong and deep, but with something about it—inertia, a lack of enduring interest—that made Willa anxious to please it. She tried to hold the speaker's interest with good humor.

"It sure is, Miss Vandel. This is Willa. I'm glad you called. I've been wanting to meet you."

The voice ignored Willa's effort at friendliness, withheld any feelings of its own it might have had. "Can you come to the house tonight at eight?"

"I sure can."

"I'll speak to you then." She hung up.

Willa stood for a moment grinning into the phone. Then she replaced the receiver and ran two steps at a time back to her room.

10

When the girl finally came out of her building that morning, Vernon followed her to a diner, where she had breakfast. But instead of continuing on, she went back to her rooming house. He waited an hour, and when she did not come out again or appear at any of the front windows, he went through an alley to the rear of the house, where a strip of land separated that block from the one behind it. He stood next to a tree that was large enough for him to hide behind if necessary, and there, in the middle one of the three second-story windows, he saw her.

She was sitting in a chair by the window, elbow on the window ledge, looking out. She seemed to Vernon to be in lonely isolation there in the center of nine empty windows. He imagined himself in the room with her, embracing her. He stroked the tree.

He had spent most of the night awake with the mannequin, whispering to it as it stood at the foot of his bed. He had gotten up once and knelt naked beside it with his head on its hip, his arms circling its waist. He was careful not to look at it closely.

But in the light of morning, it was not the same. The mannequin's pupilless eyes saw nothing, and its raised arm no longer seemed to be summoning him. He put it in the closet and sat down in the rocking chair. By the time he left the room, he knew what he must do.

Now the girl got up from the window. Vernon watched her disappear from sight, as if to lie down. He had overheard her conversation at Mary Vandel's gate the day before, had seen her write the note and put it into the mailbox. He knew now she was waiting for an answer to it. He hesitated before leaving, perhaps losing his connection with her for that day; but he knew she had to see Mary Vandel and so knew too where he could find her later.

Vernon studied the people he followed. He noted details about them, for that is what he took home with him. When the girl had returned the previous morning, he had recognized the shopping bag she was carrying. It had on it a colored logo, the bottom part of which was a smiling woman; forming a crown over her head were the words *Miller's Discount Department Store.*

He had bought his curtains and the rocking chair there. It was only four blocks away, and it was open on Sunday.

Miller's had prospered by advertising its prices as the lowest of any store in the city. This was true not only because it sold inferior merchandise and imperfect goods at reduced prices, but also because it wasted no money on comfort, adornment or convenience. It offered no enticements, no balm for the senses such as other stores provided; there were no carpets on the floors, no fluorescent lighting, no elevators or artful displays of merchandise. Nearly everything it sold was in bins or on counters or hung without pretext of design in long rows of racks. Accompanying each item was a hand-lettered cardboard sign that said Sale. It was more like a warehouse than a store. It was this barrenness and lack of luxury that had drawn Vernon to it. Miller's did not intimidate him as did other stores; he did not feel so much like an inferior, upon whom eyes turned in condescension and suspicion.

He went to the toy department first, where on counters stacked with plastic airplanes and tractors, dolls standing in boxes like prisoners behind cellophane windows, games and coloring books, he found what he was seeking: a watercolor set. He paid for it, then holding it in front of him so that he would not be mistaken for a shoplifter, he went down the aisle to a wide doorway over which was a sign: Women's Wear.

He hesitated there, afraid for the first time in Miller's. He saw women going casually about their shopping in that place where it had always seemed to him men were unwelcome: a place that contained intimate items not intended for male eyes and in which he would almost certainly be looked at with scorn.

He stopped in the doorway. He turned to leave, then turned back. When he moved onto the threshold, he stood staring straight ahead. He was very still. His eyes did not blink. When he finally stepped forward, his movements were stiff and uncertain. He could have been mistaken for a blind man.

He went into the first of long rows of racks laid out like spines down the center of the room. He moved slowly, looking at the dresses hanging like stored husks of women. He touched some. When he turned into the next row, a woman in a blue smock was standing there. He stopped. He did not move.

She was a tall, gray-haired woman who might have been a grandmother, and when she stepped up to him and smiled, his tense muscles relaxed slightly.

"Can I help you?" she asked. She smiled at him like the kindly mother he had longed for as a boy but never had.

He answered "I want to buy a dress and a purse for someone."

"What did you have in mind?"

"I want the same kind of dress and purse a girl bought here yesterday morning. I want them exactly like hers."

"Can you describe them?"

He did. He added a description of the girl, even to the clothes she had been wearing then. The woman's eyebrows went up, impressed by a man who could describe women's clothes in such detail. "I think we can find them" she said. "There were two of us here yesterday. Miss Kingsley must have waited on her. Come along and we'll ask her."

He followed, moving much more slowly than the saleswoman. When he caught up with her, she was waiting with a younger woman in front of a long counter with a cash register on it.

"This is Miss Kingsley" she told him. "She remembers your friend. She'll take care of you."

He did not look at the older woman as she went off, nor at the younger one when she spoke to him.

"Those items were on special, sir. But I'm sure we have some left. Follow me."

He followed her slowly, eyes down. He seemed to be stepping only in her footsteps. She waited for him beside a large bin. She lifted a purse from the bin which was like the girl's but was blue.

"Hers is white" he said. "It's a white purse."

She reached in again and withdrew a white purse. She held it up, and he looked at it and nodded. She walked off quickly, signaling him with a finger to follow her. This time he skipped steps to keep up with her.

When he reached her, she was inside a row of racks. He did not follow her as she went down it flipping dresses which seemed to him to come alive, motioning to him as she passed. She stopped.

"How tall is she?" she called to him.

He held up a hand to indicate the size, and she turned back and began flipping through the dresses in front of her. He looked as if he were in pain as he watched the dresses coming alive in the rack. He turned around and looked away.

Then he heard her returning, something suspiring traveling with her. She stepped in front of him and held up a red dress like the girl's.

"You're lucky" she said. "This is the last one in red. Isn't it adorable? That little girl looked so cute in it. Is this for her mother?"

"No" he said. "It's for someone else."

"I just know she'll love it" the woman said and headed back to the counter.

Vernon waited at the counter while she was writing the sales slip. He looked elsewhere, as if he had no part in the purchase. When he rested his hand behind him on the counter, it touched something soft. He turned to look, then snatched his hand away from a pile of panties and brassieres on display.

The woman called to him "Does she need some of those?" She had finished writing and looked up to see him staring at the items on the counter as if he could not believe they were really there. She went to him behind the unpackaged lingerie. He did not look at her, but he nodded.

She found the right sizes and laid them aside. "They're on special" she said. "Three for five dollars. Would you like two more pair?"

"No" he said. "I only want her to wear one."

She stared at him. He began blinking.

After she had rung up the sale and given him his change, she said "I just remembered your friend bought a hat too. Would you like one of those?"

"She has a hat" he said, and hurried away from the woman and out of the store hugging his packages to him.

He returned to check the girl's window, where he saw her get up to drink a glass of water at the sink and disappear again, then went on to his room with the packages.

When he opened the closet door, the mannequin was standing inside facing him. He took it out and put it at the side of the bed, then took a cloth-covered box with flowers painted on it from a bureau drawer and sat down with it on the side of the bed, facing the mannequin.

He opened one of the bags and took the brassiere out of it. He held it to the chest of the mannequin, then stood up to bring the straps behind it. It did not fit. He loosened the straps and raised the mannequin's arms and put them through the straps. When he leaned over the mannequin and reached behind it to close the clasp, they seemed to be embracing.

With the brassiere fitted to the mannequin, he sat down, opened the cloth-covered box and took out a pair of scissors and a needle and thread. He threaded the needle quickly, holding it up to the light, for he had been taught to do his own sewing as a child and had done so ever since. He stuck the threaded needle in the bed beside him, picked up the scissors and cut the panties down both sides. Holding the needle in his mouth and bending forward, he brought the panties up between the mannequin's legs to its waist. Letting them fall on one side, he reached into the box and took out a pincushion in the shape of a large strawberry, and holding a half-dozen pins in his mouth, he used them to fit the panties around the mannequin's waist. He sewed them there quickly, leaning forward as he finished each side to bite off the thread. When he was finished, he straightened up to look at them. He ran his hand over them.

He stood up and, taking the hat off the mannequin, put it on the bed. He raised the mannequin's arms above its head and brought the dress down over it. He replaced the hat and fixed the arms. He hung the purse over its right wrist.

He took his drinking glass off the night table, went with it into the hall bathroom and returned to the room and sat down on the side of the bed.

He looked up at the blank face before taking the watercolor set out of its bag. He opened it, picked up the brush and began painting the girl's features on the face of the mannequin.

11

It was his daughter, Madeleine, who brought joy back into Emil's life. For a while he thought he had found it in Jesus the night he abandoned himself to him writhing on the floor of the Ball Creek Church of the Pentecost, but it soon faded away, just as the people on the Atlantic City dance floor had proven to be a chimera devolved out of dreams and insubstantialities. What remained after Ball Creek was only a semblance of peace, a disinclination to hope or even remember happiness, until Madeleine entered his life.

Two months later he and Lydia returned to the First Presbyterian Church of Pineville. Lydia believed the purging had delivered him, that the baptism in the Whitewater River had washed away more than his sins, and that her own sacrifice during those months was a fair exchange for their return to sameness. She believed in equilibrium for the same reason she believed in God; she might not have believed in God if she had not thought that his highest purpose was order and stability. Joy to her was not a necessary—nor even a desired—component of life, for few things in her experience were less lasting than joy; few things created more disorder and eventual sorrow. Even those joyful occasions she had experienced as a girl had grown dim over the years.

After they returned from Ball Creek, there were people in the town of Pineville who said that Lydia Wier had married one man but another now slept in her bed. There were young women and girls who said that if that were so, she had been cheated. Neither thought had occurred to Lydia, who had precisely the husband and life she had intended to have from the first.

Emil no longer dreamed of those southern nights, those wooden bars where he found abandonment, the suspension of the world under the lights and in the mist of music where the clear laughter of the slender southern girls called to him. He thought of those southern girls sometimes when he made love to Lydia; he thought of them briefly and then tried to forget them. Since Madeleine's birth, the sensuous woman he had known Lydia to be after their marriage was seldom there; by the fourth year of the marriage, she was gone. One night, while making love to Lydia, he thought of her body as a mountain he was trying to climb. Her time of fertility had passed by then, her body as bare of promise as it was of excitement. When he thought of the southern country girls after that, they were florid and plump, burgeoning like ripe fruit.

He retreated into a world where Lydia could not follow him. It was like a room he closed himself into sometimes and would not come out of for hours, sometimes for days. He opened the door and stepped into it, stood safely there, half remembering, half not needing memory.

When Lydia thought about the changes in Emil, it was to note that the wildness had left him at last, that his near death in Atlantic City and return to virtue at Ball Creek had matured and sobered him, and that the demons he had lived with in concordance for so long were finally gone. She saw no need to probe into his periods of silence and withdrawal, for they were to her no more than the reflection of peace that her efforts and the coming of God to him had brought about. The deeper man she had sensed in him had emerged. He was someone now, she knew, who was not whole, with areas identified as inculpate excised from him. She did not take personal pride in his refiguration, did not credit herself with unusual moral merit or excellence; she felt she was guided more by certitude than strength. It was not, she thought, the rigorous application of a strong will upon a weak one that affected the change, but of one more cognizant and able to act in the other's name. That an effacement was the price paid for the change was not a factor she thought was of any importance.

Madeleine's early childhood was as free of disturbances as her father's young manhood had been full of turbulence and crisis. She was growing into a beautiful young girl of grace and intelligence, with a trusting good nature and love of laughter so like her father had once had that it was as if those qualities he had thought had died in him had been resurrected in her. At the age of four, she surprised him by being there.

Part of the happiness Emil experienced in the belated coming of love for his daughter was that for the first time in his life he felt virtuous. Sexual fidelity to Lydia had not made him feel so, nor had the fact that he had not had a drink since that day in Atlantic City nor had his brief surrender to religion. He knew that his monogamy and sobriety had their roots in fear, and in the weariness a man feels in the third decade of a life devoted to unremitting indulgence. His being born again at Ball Creek, he realized later, had been yet another surrender to indulgence. He had hungered not so much to love Jesus as to have Jesus love him.

With Madeleine, all that changed. For the first time in Emil's life, he found in himself the ability to love selflessly and experienced the feeling of virtue that grows out of it. All he wanted was that she accept his love. He did not realize that what he received in return was his acceptance of himself at last.

For Lydia it was the last ingredient necessary to form that amalgam toward which she had directed so much of her thought and effort. She had watched Emil in the early years, when Madeleine was an infant and then a toddler, observing her as someone who was distant from him. He never bathed or fed her, did not play with her or talk to her as other fathers did with their children. When he could not avoid being aware of her, it was as if he would not allow himself to penetrate beyond that acknowledgment to the fact of her relationship to him. He had withdrawn that part of himself he had once displayed so recklessly to Lydia and others, but his daughter had not yet become even that real to him. His realization that he was Madeleine's father, the love Lydia saw growing between them day after day, put the final seal of virtue on her life as well.

■ ■ ■

They came out of the woods hand in hand, arms swinging, laughing, the five-year-old girl's face lifted to her tall father's, she talking to him as they waded through the uneven grass. They seemed more like friends of the same age than father and daughter out on a Sunday stroll; more like happy conspirators bent on secrets between them. They held in their free hands wildflowers they had picked along the way, and now and then Madeleine lifted hers as if offering them to the sun. It was the child who did most of the talking, the father leaning down at times to hear her, listening with grave interest—not as an adult listens to a child but with full attention to what she was saying. More like, Lydia thought as she observed them from the kitchen window, she was the adult who was instructing and informing him. Now and then he would laugh loudly at something she said.

Lydia withdrew from the window as they approached the back steps. She heard the girl say loudly "Oh, Daddy, you're such a clown sometimes." She said that, Lydia thought, like the adult to the child, mock-censuring with an amused indulgence that tried to soften the real criticism behind the remark. The girl, Lydia thought not for the first time, assumed on occasion the grave manner that Emil, in his now infrequent dark moments, still lapsed into. She imitated it as if, Lydia thought—thinking more about them every day—the girl now and then set herself up before him as a mirror in which he could see himself in his less attractive moods. The girl did it, she thought, as a considerate means of instructing him. The girl. More and more Lydia found herself thinking of Madeleine as *the girl*. More and more she had difficulty thinking of her as her own daughter as well as his.

She busied herself setting the table as they came to the screen door. Madeleine went through it first, running. She held her flowers up to Lydia in a fist. "We picked them for you, Mother" she said.

Madeleine's manner lately was almost formal with Lydia. Lydia had noted that change and resented it. She could not remember the last time she and Madeleine had laughed together.

Lydia took the flowers from Madeleine and put them in a glass of water in the center of the table. Emil held his.

"Give yours to her too" Madeleine said to him. "We picked them for her, didn't we?" She said it with less than full conviction, and Lydia wondered whether that was the impression Madeleine had intended to convey. The largest flower—a dandelion—was in Madeleine's hair.

"Wash your hands" Lydia said to her. "Then sit down. I've been holding this roast in the oven for twenty minutes, waiting for you two. It's probably ruined by now."

Madeleine dragged a chair to the sink, kneeled on it and, stretching to reach the faucet, began washing her hands. Emil was at his usual place at the table, watching her. Her head was bowed to the afternoon sunlight coming through the window, and her black hair shone. She turned off the faucet and climbed down from the chair and began to drag it back to her place at the table. Lydia spoke with her back to Madeleine.

"Don't drag, Madeleine. Lift."

Madeleine put her arms around the chair and began carrying it. Halfway there she stopped and, resting the chair on the floor, did a pantomime for Emil's amusement of tiptoeing in place behind Lydia. He laughed.

"Stop dawdling" Lydia said, still without turning, and Emil laughed again as Madeleine tiptoed with the chair the rest of the way to the table. When minutes later Lydia was saying grace, Emil and Madeleine looked at each other from under their bowed heads and began laughing again at Madeleine's performance.

That evening they sat in the parlor before a television set Emil had bought after winning over Lydia's objections to its purchase. The light in the room was dim, and the figures moved fuzzily on the small screen.

A cumbersome couch with an ornately carved wooden frame which Lydia had exiled to the attic after her first husband's death had been brought down to accommodate the expanded family; but Lydia still sat in her own chair, erect and removed, as though staring into a fire that was no longer there, part of her in an unchanged place. Now the chair that Emil had once occupied across from her was vacant as in the evenings he and Madeleine sat together on the couch.

Lydia's interest in what was happening on the television screen was perfunctory: it wandered restless among other concerns. Only two changes had been made among the furnishings in the house since her first husband's death, and yet the reappearance of the large, ugly couch and the coming of their first television set had changed all of it. She had submitted to those changes uneasily and with misgivings.

It was Madeleine who had manipulated her father into the purchase of the television; Lydia had consented to its purchase only after they agreed to her conditions of what they would watch, for how long, and at what times. Lydia was too practical not to realize that even she had to make some compromises while raising a child, and Emil and Madeleine had gone off happily to buy the new television, convinced they had won a victory over her. What neither understood was that Lydia allowed compromise but never victory.

She had insisted that they keep the old radio that she and Emil had once danced to, with which they had dialed into the world as if their parlor were a stage she could turn back into reality by the twist of a knob when she decided the moment should pass. Now the large console radio with its cloth mouth stood turned at an angle, nearly facing the television, which with its low sound and flickerings was like another mouth murmuring to it in the near darkness. Only Lydia was aware of the two objects' uncomfortable coexistence; only she ever turned the radio on, listened to it alone; only she ever thought of their disparateness, that each stood unresolved and inimicable in a separate time. Only in her had the uneasy thought risen that time no longer seemed insoluble.

She turned to where Emil and Madeleine sat laughing together on the couch, then to the screen, where a man was singing and dancing in a woman's costume, wearing makeup. He had large, false breasts and wore a hat that looked like a tall basket of fruit. He sang in an uncanny falsetto that brought tittering laughter from Madeleine, and she saw Emil's face as if laved in silver, mouth opening and closing with laughter. The light from the screen isolated the faces of father and daughter, made images of them on their dark perch across from her, like a portrait hung in the air. She saw herself as another portrait in the room—shrouded, unseen, a replicate burdened with awareness.

She leaned forward in her chair toward the screen, her hand turning silver as it reached for the knob. "It's past your bedtime, Madeleine" she said.

"Oh, Mother!"

"Lydia—" Emil said, hoping to bargain for Madeleine.

Lydia's hand lingered, then like something startled in the pale light, dove out of sight. The sound ceased, and the image shrank slowly and died.

"Oh, Mother! Daddy, can't you—"

"Up! This minute!" Lydia's harsh expression appeared under the light from the floor lamp she had turned on beside her chair. Confronted with it, Madeleine hesitated, then started crawling off the couch beneath Emil's hand. When he leaned down to kiss her good night, her arms went around his neck, reluctant to release him.

"Now, Madeleine" Lydia commanded.

"Good night, Daddy."

"Good night, gorgeous."

She went to her mother, where on tiptoe she kissed the offered cheek.

"Go and get ready" Lydia said. "I'll be up in a minute."

Madeleine's fingers lingered along the furniture as she went; releasing the last piece, she began climbing the stairs.

Emil was surprised when he went up an hour later to find Lydia at her dresser with her hair down and in the negligé she had bought for their wedding night. She had not worn it a dozen times since then, nor had the hair come down as emblem half that number of times. She was brushing it in the mirror as Emil undressed. Putting on the pajamas she had bought him a year after their marriage and finally insisted he wear, he sat down on the side of the bed. Her reflection looked over at him.

"I've told you before, Emil, you're spoiling the child. I won't tolerate that kind of defiance from her much longer."

"She has spirit. That's life in her."

"All the more reason to curb it before it gets out of hand." She put down the brush in a way that made him understand the discussion was ended. She smiled at him in the mirror, and he forced himself to smile back at her before turning away.

"Do you know" she asked in a voice that anticipated no answer and did not require one, "what can happen when what you call spirit is allowed to get out of hand? Don't you remember, Emil? Was it that long ago?" She got up and went to the bed where the covers were already drawn and lay down on his side of it as he sat looking into his hands.

"Come to bed" she said.

He did not move.

She said "I saved you, Emil. I'll continue to keep you safe as long as you understand what the rules are."

It was the first time she had spoken to him directly about it, the first time she had claimed her right to him in words. He felt her hand on his shoulder turning him toward her. She forced him to look at her. She said slowly, quietly "In every relationship between a man and a woman, there is one who is strong in things where the other is weak. It's the duty of the strong one to direct the one who is weak—just as it's the need of the weak one to be directed."

"What does the strong one need?" he asked.

"Only that."

On Madeleine's first day at school, it was Emil who took time from his job and escorted her there; it was he who had bought her school clothes, with reasonable adherence to Lydia's instructions that they be sensibly priced and of durable material. He went with Madeleine to Pineville one Saturday afternoon, to the new department store recently opened there.

What he discovered that afternoon was not only something with which Lydia would not have credited him, but that he had never suspected was in him: that he, who had never shopped for any female before, had not only a shrewdness about it but taste, and even a feeling for fashion, as he selected from among the many clothes displayed there for young girls. By purchasing her clothes from among the denims and corduroys, he satisfied Lydia's requirements; his own and Madeleine's desires were met in that they were individually styled and more brightly colored and innovative than those Lydia would have chosen. He assembled her outfits with care, searching out each item rather than accept those matching combinations put together by others: created *in toto* by people never seen, to be worn by children they would never know. It was that sense that he was creating ensembles for Madeleine—and in a way creating her out of them—that he felt most intensely that afternoon. It was that prescience of the young lady she would one day become that guided his selections, the future woman hinted at that he wanted to express.

As each outfit was completed, he sent Madeleine into one of the narrow cubicles where the women went to try on their clothes behind curtains. The first time she returned through the curtains, it was with more self-possession than any of the women emerging around her had; she posed for Emil in unconscious imitation of the women she had seen on television displaying clothes for men—and with something of their flirtatiousness. She modeled powder-blue overalls with silver buckles on the straps and a small bird in flight embroidered above the breast, a white peasant blouse with slightly billowing shoulders and, set on her head at a jaunty angle, a gray beret. She looked like a vital young woman on her way to a fashionable but casual party.

After that, throughout her grammar school years, Madeleine was dressed by her father in a style that set her apart from the other children; had she been anything other than the friendly and unassuming child she was, she might have been thought to be displaying herself as superior to them. As it happened, there was only a succession of boys stricken with puppy love, and initial envy (then quick acceptance) from the girls.

Emil became a familiar parent to Madeleine's teachers; it was he, almost always alone, who attended PTA meetings in the evenings; it was he they called when Madeleine had to be taken home ill. He sought them out for advice when she had problems that were beyond his knowledge and understanding.

When from the ages of eleven to thirteen Madeleine wanted to be a poet, Lydia dismissed the ambition as a childish fancy she would soon outgrow. Emil encouraged her, praising the romantic and idealistic poems, while her mother responded to them either with condescension or in a way that implied that such frivolousness could only result in unhappiness and disillusionment. Lydia believed that the only respectable literature was religious literature, and there was no permanent place in her house for the books of those poets she believed were, for the most part, persons with disordered and often diseased minds, and whose lives, from what she knew of them, were lived immorally and always ended in tragedy. That after a while Madeleine stopped showing Lydia her poems—even hid them so that Lydia would not read them without her knowledge—gave Lydia only a feeling of relief.

Lydia told herself that at her age she had earned some peace at last and that she could afford to avoid those minor skirmishes that were no real threat to the way of life she had made for them. She withdrew more into her church and into an even more intense religious involvement than she had had before. Since she saw no serious flaw in Madeleine— no hint certainly of those darkly improvident traits that might have come to her from her father—she was glad to be relieved of so much of the responsibility for Madeleine's education and rearing. For it was to Emil—not Madeleine—that her first allegiance and concern belonged.

That Lydia had never felt lasting love for Madeleine, any tenderness that lasted beyond the first year after her birth, was to her not an unnatural state, not a condition for which she felt the slightest need to scrutinize herself morally. It never occurred to her to question whether a human factor was missing in a woman who had taken a husband without love, and bore a child with whom that same emotional bond was absent. Duty, she would have said, was the only genuine expression of what others call love. She had witnessed during her own girlhood—and carried within her the scars of it even now—love's conversion to betrayal. At eighteen, she had experienced her own mother's early death from cancer; she knew that day with a cold certainty that the man who was her father, and who had once been a husband to her mother in love, felt neither love nor loss—only relief—at the death of the woman his infidelities and drunkenness had driven to despair. He had not waited a year before marrying a woman twenty years his junior, who in her turn had married him without love. And when he died ten years later from a liver so diseased it was like a scourge had invaded his body with dire recollection, that wife did not pause long enough even to honor duty, to say nothing of love, instead selling what was left unclaimed by creditors of what had once been a prosperous farm. Neither Lydia nor her two younger brothers, whom Lydia had raised, ever saw her again.

■ ■ ■

During Madeleine's grammar school years a curious ritual began between her and her father: every school day at noon she would wait, either inside the doorway, standing on tiptoe to see out of the window, or with the other children at one of the school-yard tables, where on mild days they ate lunch. She sat away from the others, primly attentive that at the last minute she not soil or wrinkle her dress, occasionally getting up to look for her father's Rambler as it drove up the street and parked outside the gate. The moment he appeared, she would swing open the heavy metal door or rise waving before she ran from the bench to meet him. She would always hurry, abandoning decorum as her lunch box banged at her side. He would wave back smiling broadly, leaning across the seat to the passenger window.

She would always open the car door herself, climb up onto the seat and slam the door behind her. During those first years, only the top of her head could be seen from outside the car as they sat side by side, talking and eating. Later the lunch box was replaced by paper bags, and the girl who still ran to him ran more carefully, aware that her body was beginning to develop contours that were changing her from a child into a young woman. She would sit with her elbow resting on the edge of the open window now, head thrown back when she laughed at something he said. Before they parted, they would kiss and hug as they had in the beginning; but now the girl no longer had to reach up to encircle his neck, and her arms fit fully around him. She would wave to him as she ran back at the sound of the school buzzer, just as she had as a child.

When at that time the other girls began to tease her, joking and exclaiming about her handsome lunch date in the overly expressive way teenage girls do to convey approval, Madeleine laughed too. But she never entered into that spirit of well-intentioned teasing; and although by then they had come to know Emil—a few of them developing crushes on Madeleine's young father, who seemed in spirit nearer their own age than their parents'—none of them were ever invited to join them.

By the time Madeleine entered high school, the mill, which had prospered and grown, had promoted Emil and given him two assistants. His responsibilities had expanded to the maintenance of machinery as well as the general repair and upkeep of the grounds and building. His office was elevated too from the basement room to one just off the factory.

Lydia was elected an elder of her church.

Those who saw them together in the town said that the pretty girl (who unlike most girls her age always carried herself tall and erect) and the youthful-appearing man went about more like sweethearts than father and daughter. Madeleine was physically mature for her age; at a distance Emil might have been mistaken for her older brother. It was Madeleine who gave the impression of being the more self-assured of the two, less inclined to display exuberant feelings in public, more in control of those emotions the father sometimes seemed unable to discipline. Unlike him, she could temper her love for him before others, was more aware than he of her responsibility to do so. The right proportions of strength and character from Lydia and good looks and easy access to laughter from Emil had been passed on to her; the combination resulted in a modification of those excesses that had resulted in major flaws in her parents. She was plainly her father's daughter in personality and looks; it was her mother's common sense that held the seams in place.

Only Lydia saw the child who was still struggling to survive a while longer in Madeleine; Emil saw only the beautiful girl he had raised, who as she matured was more of a companion, confidant and friend to him than daughter. She gave him the love and warmth Lydia had always denied him, as well as the respect he knew Lydia would never give. Because Madeleine gave what Lydia had for so long denied, he had begun to depend on her more than she depended on him. He knew he had come to need her more than he needed Lydia. There were moments when the thought made him feel uneasy, hinting at loss, the emptiness of that day when she would leave them and he would sink back into that compromise with life that had been the substance of his existence with Lydia from the first. In the meantime, Madeleine gave him the only real happiness he had ever known.

One day after Emil returned from the mill, as usual an hour earlier than when Madeleine arrived on the school bus at the highway where he met her, he went to her room and closed the door behind him. He sat in a chair beside the table she used as a desk, his back to the window. There was a picture of a male movie star on the wall. Emil had not been to a movie since before his marriage to Lydia, and so he had no idea who the effeminate blonde young man was who was so different from the dark and ruggedly masculine Clark Gable and Errol Flynn and the too handsome but also manly Robert Taylor, who had been the romantic idols of the girls of his generation. He got up and went to the picture to study the face. He looked into the eyes, which seemed to him to contain nothing; at the perfect teeth and features, which seemed finally to result in vacuousness. The man's smile, the way his mouth turned down sharply at the corners, looked to Emil to be cynical, flaunting some truth about himself he was certain would never be discerned by the young girls who adored him. Emil had never seen the photograph before: it had been hung recently. An intruder had slipped into his house whom he had not known was present until then. And although he was prepared to be tolerant of a teenage girl's enthusiasm for unattainable movie stars, he was disappointed in Madeleine for having chosen this one. It was not until minutes later that he realized the movie star's picture had replaced a photograph of Edna St. Vincent Millay, who had been Madeleine's only idol until then.

He moved to the bureau, where he ran his fingers across Madeleine's comb and brush, a lapis lazuli set he had given her for Christmas the year before. He looked at his face of five years before smiling in a framed photograph: the perfect, square chin which she had inherited from him, the lock of hair which like hers fell curving like a comma over his forehead. He went to the closet next to the bureau and opened it. Every one of the dresses hanging there he had bought for her and helped her select; absent from Madeleine's body there was a quality of sadness about them. He ran his hand over them before closing the door.

He returned to the chair and sat down again. He became aware of an unusual quiet in the room, in the house. The stillness disturbed him; it made him afraid. He leaned his head back, so that for minutes he saw only the ceiling; then he lowered it again to take in the sparse furniture, the clean, neatly kept room. He knew then as surely as he had ever known anything that something had been lost to him that day, just as something else, which had as much sorrow as happiness in it, had been found.

He got up, went to the bed, and lay down on it. He reached up and pulled down the covers partway. Then he turned onto his side and lay with his hand and his face touching the pillow.

He did not sleep that night. He lay beside Lydia, who was sunk into that deep sleep that was in her like death. He could feel her cold foot on his, could see one wrinkled hand clutching the covers to her. Her hair had receded and rose high now, like a lion's mane, over her long forehead.

He got up around three and, even though it was cool in the April morning, went out of the house barefoot and in his pajamas.

He did not stop at the porch, but went off it onto the hard, rocky soil. He stood for a moment looking at the trees, whose branches were waving in the wind as if they had gathered there to greet him. He walked toward the woods on thick grass that bent before him and was slippery with heavy dew; as the grass became taller, his feet disappeared slowly beneath him. At the edge of the woods he could hear the wind, stopped to listen to it. Then he stepped between two trees which, close together and straight, made a portal into the woods.

Above him as he went, bright slices of moon slid between the leaves. He stopped when he heard a creature break the silence and go skittering among things fallen and dead on the ground. He listened until it dragged its sound away into silence. After a while, it occurred to him that every living thing in the woods had its own place of silence to which it could retreat. Only the sounds of the leaves and the wind were constant; only they, like presences, kept a watch over all the rest.

When he raised his maimed hand to look at it in the moonlight, he seemed to be saluting the sky. He held it there, flexing and unflexing the three fingers as if trying to scratch something out of the sky. In the silence of objects come alive with occasional sounds, with his hand framing the sky, he recalled for the first time in years the embattled Kansas plain. He heard the grenades bursting again, saw the rain of torn earth returning to earth. He felt the limb of a phantom tree beneath him, felt his bowel open and murmur to him as he watched the small metal object hurrying down the incline to join him, then come to a stop, waiting for him. He saw his hand raised then too, as if in greeting, surrendering to an inevitability that until the last moment, he knew now, he had sought desperately to disbelieve. He felt himself lifting up off the limb, rising in such a ring of glorious silence that he remembered for the first time that he had thought he was rising to heaven.

He lowered the hand quickly now, as if erasing those memories, and, turning on bare feet which for the first time that night felt the cold and the hardness of the ground, walked quickly out of the woods to where he saw the dark and silent house waiting.

He went onto the porch and through the door without hesitation. He moved in easy intimacy with objects through the darkness to the stairs. He climbed the stairs with canny silence, even though his happiness made him feel carefree.

He moved down the hall quickly and into Madeleine's room, where he stood with his back to the closed door, watching her.

She slept facing him, half out of the covers, pajama top twisted around her. She had her fingers in her hair. When he whispered her name, she moved, then was still again. He spoke her name louder, but in no more than a whisper. She opened her eyes. His hand had remained on the doorknob, but at that moment he took it away.

She sat up. It took her seconds to recognize him in the shadows, to realize he was there. "Daddy, is that you?"

He stepped into the light from the window.

"What's wrong?" she asked. "Is something wrong?"

"No. Nothing."

She lay back again, smiling at him from the pillow as he went to the bed and stood looking down at her. "I love you" he said.

"I know, Daddy. I love you too."

"No matter what happens, understand that it's because I love you."

"What do you mean?"

"Don't say anything. Just lay there."

She watched him sit down on the side of the bed and heard more than saw him take off his pajamas, drop the top, slide the bottoms to the floor. She stared at his long naked back. Then he turned to her. He leaned down and kissed her on the mouth.

"No, Daddy. Please. I don't like this."

"Be quiet. I just want to hold you."

She did not move away; nor did her arms lift from her sides as he drew down the covers and lay down next to her, holding her to him. She could feel him trembling, and with that part of her mind that was capable of understanding, she felt pity for him. When he took her hand and guided it to him, she did what she knew she had to do for him.

"Please, Daddy" she said when he came again the next night. "We shouldn't."

"We'll just talk. I just want to hold you and talk to you tonight."

* * *

Nothing changed outwardly, but everything had changed just the same. Much that had been before they both knew, would never be the same again: constancy had changed to inconstancy, changing everything else. A new awareness had grown overnight inside both of them, altering their perception of themselves in relation to others.

Nor did anything change in the attitudes of others when they saw them together. It surprised them the first morning, and arose daily after that for Madeleine when she tried to close her mind to what she thought her face must reveal, to keep out of it those thoughts that infringed from the night with specific names but uncertain conclusions, admonishments she thought would be announced with rollings of thunder where higher judgments are made. How could she condemn herself and exempt her father from condemnation? It had taken the daughter fourteen years to discover about her father what her mother had known the first day she met him. The trust she had always had in him was nearly all gone now. He did not seem to Madeleine during the day any different from the father and friend he had always been to her: she still loved him for who he was during the day, even as she saw clinging to him what he was to her at night. She thought for a while that if she waited and was patient with him, it would eventually stop, and after that even the memory of it would go away.

Emil's surprise that morning when he found that outwardly nothing had changed, that nothing had been detected as different about them, was replaced during the days that followed with the watchfulness of one not fully confident that no clue had been left unnoticed at the scene of the crime. What he had begun—even if he had been able to acknowledge it as a sin—could not be called by the other—society's—name. That, even he understood, was taboo: that act he had not committed, nor had he allowed himself to consider its eventuality. He wanted to, but he knew there was a line he must never cross, beyond which nothing could ever be retrieved or rectified. He did not feel guilt, even though he knew he was supposed to. What he felt was happiness—and gratitude for the only love ever to come into his life.

He felt other things too. He bought a camera, the first the family ever owned. He told Lydia that Madeleine was no longer a child and that the family should be recorded before that time came when family would be only a word. There was one photograph of them in a frame on the mantelpiece. They had all gone together to town, dressed in their best clothes, hair combed, and posed in a studio where they were frozen into a second of immutable time; posed on a couch with a canvas backdrop painted to look like a living room behind them and out of range of the camera, photographs of other families on the walls looking down on them like people in a gallery. Their photograph incontestable, testifying: Madeleine at three held in her mother's lap as if at any moment to be handed to another out of sight of the camera; Emil not touching them, his smile too determinedly offered up to be genuine. Now, he told Lydia, they would be fixed in their moments, detailing the days of their journey out of life.

Now they gathered outside in the late afternoon light, in front of the house. The rocking chair was brought off the porch for Lydia, then rejected and carried back up again: Emil was composing. He sat mother and daughter on the steps, leaning against the porch railing. He moved them from place to place, and they obeyed him. Even Lydia obeyed him.

Finally satisfied, Emil sent Madeleine to find Lester. After fifteen years, the black man who had come to work for Lydia and Emil as a young man was still unknown to them, but not to Madeleine: she spoke to him, made him laugh at times, even confided in him. She was fluid with him within the boundaries he allowed. Emil never forgot those mornings he had stood in the window clothed only in a lace curtain and stared down at the black boy bent over his Bible. Lester was now a deacon in his church, as Lydia was a deaconess in hers. But those churches that were united in spirituality were, in the real world, miles apart. Lester was heavier now; his hair, less lustrous, retreated a few inches over a fierce forehead. But only in a vague way were Emil and Lydia aware of the change. As he had from the beginning, Lester left every Saturday at noon, silently except for a word seeking permission from Lydia. He returned with the sun Monday morning, once more in his place in the shed's doorway, reading his Bible as he waited for Lydia to come through the recalcitrantly squeaking screen door with his breakfast on a tray.

"Hurry up, Lester" Lydia called to him now. "Where do you always get to when I need you?"

Madeleine was leading him. "He was working, Mother" she said.

"Come along, then. We're waiting."

Lester walked faster but in his own time and in his own way, demonstrating the point beyond which he would not compromise dignity. He nodded to both of them with stiff formality, addressing them as if he had just that moment met them: "Mister Rhineman, Mrs. Rhineman." He turned slightly to face Emil.

Emil placed the new camera in his hand. Lester glanced at it as it rested on his pale palm. Then he looked up again questioningly at Emil.

"We need you to take our picture" Emil said. "Can you do that?"

"I can."

"Wait. Don't take it until I tell you."

Emil herded Madeleine and Lydia back to the porch steps. He stepped into the center of the group, then out again to move Lydia back and a little to the side. He glanced up at the sun, which was dimming behind slowly passing clouds. He put his arms around Lydia and Madeleine, told them to smile.

The sun appeared between two clouds, sending a feeble, fast-moving light over them. "Now!" Emil called to Lester. "Take it now!"

Lester did, but again in his own way and time. He lowered his head over the viewfinder, the square eye looking back up at him, showing them held upside down in its integuments. He put his right hand in front to shield the camera from light, poised a finger above it, touched the button, held it down and released it in one swift and sure movement that with its casual expertise, refuted all they thought they knew about him, and still went unnoticed. He straightened up and held the camera out to Emil. Then he walked off.

Lydia's smile in the photograph appears like something carved on her face: something unwillingly given, which will in a moment be taken away. She is tilting her head back, chin high. She had let down her hair at Emil's request, but it rises unnaturally high over her receding broad forehead, giving her a fiercer appearance than she had intended. Madeleine is smiling in valiance, accommodating the occasion. This time Emil's smile is genuine, spreading outward to the edges of the others' restraint. He is hugging them, tilting Lydia, causing Madeleine to stumble momentarily. He is holding them physically together until the moment when his creation will be recorded in more than the uncertain annals of memory.

They only took two other pictures that afternoon: one snapped by Emil, the other by Lydia. Emil's shows this: Lydia and Madeleine side by side but staring ahead at the lens of the camera as if each unaware of the other being there. In the picture Lester took, Lydia's right shoulder and part of that side of her body are out of the frame to where Emil moved her seconds before the picture was snapped; in the second photograph, taken by Emil, a fourth of her body and face are not there. In the next one, taken by Lydia, there is only Emil and Madeleine. The first page of the family photo album begun that day shows the photographs in that order: Lydia disappearing. She had posed unwillingly for the photographs, outwardly impatient with it all but also shy and uncomfortable, unaccustomed to the restraints imposed and uncertain of what a photograph might reveal of her. She was relieved when Emil never asked her to pose again for that album, which eventually was filled to the last page with only pictures of Madeleine alone and Emil and Madeleine together.

*   *   *

She let him take off her pajama tops one night, draw the bottoms to her knees. He had promised he would not touch her. He just looked at her. She closed her eyes as he stared at her.

Early one morning, Emil stopped as he was passing his bedroom window and saw Madeleine and Lester talking below. She stood with her back against the wall of the shed, arms folded beneath her breasts. He had never seen—perhaps never noticed—them talking intimately before. He stepped back to where they could not see him.

He heard Madeleine laugh, saw a smile come to the face of the black man, whose expression Emil could not remember ever being other than neutral, revealing nothing. He watched as Madeleine touched Lester casually. He stiffened, then leaned forward, crouching now behind the window. He stood up a minute later, very straight, fists clenched, when he saw Lester go into the shed, Madeleine following. The door remained open, but he experienced rage and unreasoning jealousy for the first time as he waited for it to close behind them. He expected it to.

A minute later they came out, Madeleine holding a book. She smiled and waved back at Lester as she went off. He watched Lester's face resume its neutrality.

Emil left the window only after Lester had gone off in another direction. Then he went to the bedroom door, opened it to a crack, and listened through it.

He listened to Madeleine and Lydia in brief conversation, but he could not make out the words. When he heard Madeleine coming up the stairs, he closed the door slowly to only a small crack he could see through. He put his eye to it and watched Madeleine go down the hall into her room. He knew she would not leave for school for another three hours. Before this morning, he had never known her to be up so early. Only Lydia's presence below kept him from going to her.

When he left the kitchen that morning, he did not get into the car, as he had every other morning; he turned when he reached it and looked back to see that Lydia was not at the kitchen window. Then he went around the car to the door of the shed. He knocked once. He waited. Then he went in and closed the door quietly behind him.

He had not been inside the shed since he himself had spent nights there in a time removed by more than years. He had purposely avoided it; it helped keep the past dead for him. Now as he stood in it again, he saw that there was little of his past there; nor was it anything like he had expected it to be.

The cot was still there, but it was made up expertly, a brightly colored quilt stretched tightly over it. The window curtains were hung along a rod on which Lester could open and close them. There was little visible that was personal: some toilet articles, a photograph of a middle-aged black couple Emil assumed were Lester's parents, a comb and brush set and a box that resembled a small coffin on the bureau. He went to the bureau and opened the box to see a manicuring set. He closed it with an expression of disapproval at the evidence of fastidiousness in a black man. To Emil, such concerns were effeminate, the province of perverts and the rich. He noticed that each object on the bureau was arranged in precise relationship to its neighboring object. Nothing was carelessly placed.

He went to what he knew was a narrow clothes closet built crudely against the wall. Now a curtain hung over it. He pushed the curtain aside to find only a few work clothes, a dark suit, black dress shoes and a solid dark tie folded over a hanger. He turned to face the room again.

Emil was not certain he had in fact ever smelled it, but what he had expected in the small shed when he entered it was the odor of Negro: something musty, dense and redolent of urine and sweat. What he detected instead was the odor of freshly applied detergent and disinfectant. He imagined Lester industriously scrubbing away the stench of Negro that settled wherever he did.

The only other personal possession he saw was a row of books lined up in order of size on the table in front of the window. He went to them and read the names of their authors, none of which he recognized, several of which he could not pronounce: Plato, Kant, Nietzsche, Kierkegaard, Marx, Engels, Dostoyevsky, Tolstoy, Freud, Ibsen, Balzac. It was from among these, he concluded, that Lester must have taken the book Madeleine carried back to her room.

There was nothing else to see. He left as quietly and cautiously as he had come, certain he had not left behind any sign of his having been there.

He returned to Madeleine's room alone again that afternoon. He closed the door slowly behind him as he had the first time, stood with his back to it as he had then. It occurred to him that twice that day he had entered rooms to seek answers to questions about those who were not there. He realized then too that more and more he was living alone in the house, present in body but removed from the others as far as his real feelings were concerned. Even in his early years with Lydia he had not lived so much within himself, been so silent, so secretive, about himself. He saw the book on the table and went to it.

He did not pick it up, did not touch it. He sat down in the chair and looked at it, uneasy. The thought came to him that what kept him from opening it was the same suspicion that had disturbed and frightened him earlier, although he had been unwilling to confront it until now. Now that the moment had arrived, he knew that the idea was so improbable it bordered on insanity; still, he had to know whether when he opened the book he would find a letter or message, perhaps writing on the pages themselves, that would reveal Madeleine and Lester as lovers. He knew what he would do then: kill Lester, kill her.

He drew the book to him across the table. He placed a hand on each side of it and stared down at it. He read the title on the cover: *The Poems of William Blake.* So the black man, along with his other affectations, read poetry too. Lester had in common with Madeleine what Emil had only been able to share with her from the outside. His hand shook as he turned the book's cover to reveal the first page.

There was nothing. No message, no dedication, only notes in the margins where Lester had underlined passages. He had turned over every page.

Emil began reading to see if they were love poems. After reading a few pages he frowned. Finally he closed the book, satisfied that they were not love poems. They seemed to be about God; but when had anyone ever written about God like that? If it was poetry, he decided, it was the work of a madman. Then he opened it again, angry this time. He was not certain at whom he was angry—Lester, Madeleine, or the mad poet William Blake—but he knew then that Madeleine had to be taught a lesson for the future about activities and interests from which he was excluded. He pushed back the chair, unbuttoned his shirt, put the book inside and rebuttoned the shirt.

He went down, got into the car and drove a mile up the highway. He pulled off the highway and went deep into the woods and threw the book as far as he could. It disappeared through the lower branches of some trees, creating a rupture in the leaves, which then closed, and everything was still again.

■ ■ ■

He told her to lie on her back while he opened her pajama top and drew the bottoms down again to her knees. He was kneeling over her on the bed. She turned her head away and stared out the window as he touched her breasts with the tip of his finger.

"Daddy, please stop" she whispered. "It's wrong."

"It's not" he said "if two people love each other. You love me, don't you?"

"Yes."

He traced her flesh with his finger from her hip to the top of her pubis. He lingered there, finger in the hair. He leaned over her and laid his face on the soft swell of her belly.

Her hand rose from her side and began stroking his hair. She felt him begin trembling. Tears came to her eyes as he took her hand and brought it down to him.

One afternoon in June Emil arrived home to find Lydia waiting for him in the kitchen.

"I want you to talk to your daughter" she said.

He put his lunch box on the table without looking at her. "What is it?"

"It's that your precious daughter, our model student, has failed three subjects her first year of high school." She took a paper out of her apron pocket, put it on the table in front of him. "Here. Her report card. Look at it."

He only glanced at it. But he stiffened at Lydia's next words, which sounded not angry but puzzled. "What's wrong with that girl?"

He did not say anything.

Lydia persisted. "She drags around here lately as if the weight of the world is on her shoulders. She has no energy anymore. What's happening, Emil? She talks to you. I can't get a word out of her lately. She was always distant with me, but now she ignores me. It's as if she isn't there half the time. The counselor at school can't get anything out of her either."

Emil's hand on the table clenched into a fist. It was seconds before he could answer. "She's sensitive. She thinks you don't love her."

"Oh, my Lord! She's sensitive! She thinks I don't love her! When has she shown any love or respect for me? Since she was a child it's been you, you, you—the two of you. Your private jokes. Your secrets. As if I and the rest of the world didn't matter. As if only the two of you mattered." She lowered her voice. "When she was a child, that was all right; I understood that you had things in common, because you've never been much more than a child yourself. Look at yourself, Emil. You're forty-four years old and you still haven't learned to take life seriously. You raised a daughter who can't respect you as a father because you have always treated her more like a sweetheart than a daughter. You're not a man, Emil. You never were. And that's what she knows about you that you have always refused to see."

He had begun to sink slowly into the chair; he sat now staring past her at the sink. He finally looked up at her, not angrily, not supplicatory, but in quiet inquiry. "What do you want from me? What more do you want that I haven't done?"

"What I want is what I always wanted—that you accept your place in this world."

"My place?"

"In *this* world, Emil. The real world."

"Like you" he said. He looked at her for a long time—for the first time understanding. "You hate her, don't you? Because of me, of what we've always had together. You hate her for that, don't you?"

She only hesitated a moment before answering. "Yes."

"My God!"

"Don't you dare bring the Almighty into this. God didn't make you what you are—you did. And you have infected her with your weakness, your—fantasies. The two of you are alike now; none of me is in her anymore."

"And that's why you hate her."

She did not hesitate this time before answering. "I despise her. For her weakness. Her dreaming. That unhealthy poetry she used to write. Still writes, for all I know, so little do I know about her now."

"God will punish you, Lydia, for your cold heart."

"Don't speak to me of God, I said! Not in this house of pagans. When was the last time either of you got down on your knees and prayed to him? God gives love to those who love him. For that it is you—both of you—who will suffer his wrath when your day of judgment comes."

He looked at her, as always beaten down by her. "What do you want me to do?"

"For a start, I want you to tell her she's going to summer school to make up those grades."

"I can't."

"Of course not. As always, the bad news has to come from me. Perish the thought that her wonderful father would discipline her. All right. She's in her room now. Go tell that angel of yours I want to talk to her. Her hour has come."

He went up the stairs and stood for a moment outside Madeleine's door. He knocked and she answered, but he did not go in. He told her Lydia wanted to see her, then went to his bedroom, closed the door and sat on the bed.

He told himself he was not hiding, that all he wanted was to avoid seeing Madeleine's disappointment when Lydia told her her summer was ruined. She had hoped to go to Atlantic City for a day with a group

of young people, under the supervision of the church, and he knew that
Lydia would now deny her that. He told himself it was the sight of
Madeleine's unhappiness that he wanted to avoid, not the scene to
come. Not what Lydia might come to know, or guess, or inadvertently
extract from Madeleine during the conversation. He could not face the
possibility of that ever happening.

When he heard Madeleine going down to the kitchen, he began
thinking of other things.

Madeleine stopped in the kitchen doorway, stood looking down. She
only looked up when she heard Lydia's voice.

"Look at me, miss."

She did.

Lydia pointed to a chair at the table. "Sit there."

She did, but she sat looking down.

"*Look at me*" Lydia commanded.

Madeleine raised her head. She was looking at Lydia, but her eyes
appeared out of focus, as if the mind that controlled them was going
elsewhere.

"First of all" Lydia said, "you will go to summer school this year.
And there will be precious little leisure time for you—I'll see to that."

Lydia paused as she saw the eyes coming back into focus, revealing
clarity and decisiveness, intensities she had never seen in those eyes
before. She went on. "There will be no outing at the shore, either. Not
this summer, maybe not next summer either if you don't start mending
your ways."

She stopped. She was staring at a look on Madeleine's face of not
only hatred—which she had expected—but contempt, which she had
never seen directed at her by anyone before.

When Madeleine spoke, it was in a voice that Lydia recognized as
no longer a child's but not yet that of the woman Madeleine aspired to
be; it contained derision but was uncertain of its power to wound.
"You're an ignorant old woman, Mother."

Lydia's mouth tightened. She spoke slowly, deliberately. "What was
that you just said?"

Madeleine's eyes held Lydia's, unwavering. Lydia thought she saw
something moving in them, a shadow passing. She raised her hand to
strike Madeleine, but the girl did not flinch. The hand lowered as Lydia
backed up slowly to the sink. There was silence between them as each
stared at the other.

Lydia said "If you ever say anything like that to me again—"

"You'll do what?"

"You'll see. Your days as a queen around this house are finished."

"I know what you can do to me. And why you'll be glad to do it. I've always known you hated me, and why. It's because he loves me, and he never loved you."

"Don't say that."

"You've always been jealous of me."

"Go to your room. I won't talk of such things with a child."

"I'm not a child anymore. He knows that. And he told me he never loved you."

"Damn you."

"No matter what you do to me or say to him, he'll still love me. It will always be me he loves, not you."

"You fool. You don't know anything about him. You don't know—anything. Go to your room, girl. Stay there. No supper for you. No television again until I see some changes. We're going to find out right now who is the real queen in this house."

Madeleine got up and began to run from the room. She stopped in the doorway. "He doesn't love you!" she shouted. "He never has! You're old and you're ugly. No one loves you." She ran off sobbing.

For several minutes after Madeleine had gone, Lydia stood staring at the empty doorway. Then she sank slowly onto the vacated chair.

Lydia unplugged the television that afternoon. She moved it herself into a far corner of the room and turned it so that it faced the wall. It was there with them that evening: a culprit found guilty and sent into shameful exile.

That night Lydia and Emil ate alone, in graver silence than ever before. Emil watched her carefully all through the meal, fearful that he might discover in her the beginnings of suspicions so burdened with forbidden images that even she might be unwilling to recognize them yet but that she might be forced to bring herself to face soon. He saw none. He saw only her anger at Madeleine, her need to make the girl bend or break. He left the table a man reprieved and restored to an unmerited grace, an uneasy probation.

That night they sat as they had so many nights before but had not for years—in attentive silence, across from each other in their chairs, both with their Bibles again, for Lydia had taken hers out, and Emil had returned to following her lead. On the surface, as if no time had passed since those other nights: nothing intervened to bring them to other attitudes. But Emil's mind was soon languishing in his Bible as Lydia sought instruction and solace in hers. Emil looked over at the window, where there appeared finally a picture of peaceful night. Random sounds conjured reveries out of the house's silence, returning them to a time when there was no Madeleine. Until only the two people grown older there were reminders of time.

As it had been on those other nights, Lydia announced the hour to retire by closing her Bible; she took off the metal-framed glasses she now wore when reading. She put them on top of the Bible on the table beside her as Emil got up and went around shutting up the house. Then he followed her up the stairs to the bed where for that night memory was restored to what it had once been, and the bed was timeless.

The next afternoon Emil asked Madeleine what had been said, what if anything had been revealed or suspected by Lydia during their confrontation. Madeleine spoke angrily, bitterly about her mother; Emil assured her that Lydia had acted out of her sense of what was right, what was best for Madeleine. Madeleine looked at him. She had expected a firm commitment from him against Lydia, a solid alliance, but what she saw were his alliances shifting between herself and Lydia.

Lydia had left the house to oversee Lester in some work, and they were in the upstairs hallway: there was no way Lydia could come upon them unheard. But when Madeleine went to him to put her arms around his neck for comfort, he drew back from her. He stood with his arms at his sides as she lowered hers in front of him. He felt shame for his cowardice, for what he acknowledged was fear. He put his hand on her shoulder and squeezed it and told her it would be all right, that with time and patience things would be as they had been. He thought she wanted things to be as they had been.

It was then, for the first time, that Madeleine felt the fear of being alone.

Madeleine bent to her mother's will. Lydia had demanded an apology for the things Madeleine had said to her and had at last gotten it from the beaten girl; Madeleine appeared in the kitchen doorway one afternoon, and looking down spoke the words almost inaudibly. Lydia nodded, satisfied—but not one ever to forget, she offered no word of reconciliation before Madeleine turned and left.

It was Emil who convinced Madeleine there would be no peace for any of them until the apology was given. Then, after Madeleine was humbled, he began instructing her on how to deal with the woman he had lived with and slept next to for nearly sixteen years. It did not occur to him that he was instructing her in the same duplicity, self-effacement and cowardice that had enabled him to survive uneasily with Lydia all those years.

They seemed to be strangers living politely under one roof, without intimacy but with uncanny awareness of one another. It was difficult for Madeleine—even for Lydia—but it was nearly intolerable for Emil. As the weeks went by, he was in torment that he was unable to see Madeleine alone for long. He could not touch her, tell her he loved her.

He began watching her when he thought he was not being watched. The unhappiness he saw come over her when she did not know she was being observed made her even more desirable to him than her former girlish happiness had. It drew him closer and made him love her all the more.

He went into her room one afternoon, opened her bureau drawer, took one of her slips and put it beneath his shirt. He went to the attic, dragged an old mattress into a far corner, and put a blanket he found stored in a cardboard box over it. He spread the slip out to its full length on the mattress and lay next to it with his face on it.

He tried to fight his need for her. He did not allow himself to touch her, even as a father might rightfully touch a daughter, not even as an acquaintance might casually place his hand upon another. He knew that now even the most casual physical contact between them might sweep him back into longings he could no longer control. His need to hold her, touch her shoulders, her hands, her face, was filled with tenderness as well as desire. There were times when his eyes clouded with tears at the thought of her.

One night as Lydia slept, he went down the hall in the dark to Madeleine's door. He stood close to it, hands flat against it, cheek touching it. He thought he could hear her breathing through the door, and he closed his eyes and imagined her lying there. He saw himself slipping into bed next to her, saw her opening her eyes, smiling at him, her arms reaching to draw him close to her. He brought his body to the door, pressing against it. A sound came from him that might have been a moan, or a low cry of anguish.

He still went to meet her where the school bus stopped on the highway; they could not have done otherwise without Lydia questioning it. But now they walked back in silence, and no longer hand in hand, as they had before.

He had struggled against it for days, drawn back from it each time at the last moment, until once in mid-August, before they reached the house coming back from the bus, he drew close to her and said "I'll come to you tonight. It's all right now."

He saw her flinch. She did not answer until they were on the porch, where she turned to face him. "No. I don't want you to." Then she went through the screen door, letting it close between them.

When he went to her room the next night, she was sitting up in bed before he got through the door. She spoke in a voice not loud but not a whisper either. "No. Go away."

He stood in the shadows. Then closing the door quietly behind him, he slipped back into the darkness of the hallway.

In late August, he told Madeleine he was going to take her to the shore for a day. He explained his plan; they even laughed about it. He had not been with her for two months, and she felt grateful to him, not just for making the excursion she had looked forward to possible, but for joining her finally to cheat Lydia.

The next day after work, Emil went shopping in Pineville. The last day of August was Madeleine's fifteenth birthday, and he told Lydia he was going to take Madeleine the following day after summer school to buy her a present: a pair of shoes. He told Madeleine that if he had said the present was to be a new dress, Lydia would have refused, and they laughed at how clever he had been, how easily Lydia had been fooled.

He purchased the shoes, after which he went to the department store and bought a small suitcase. He went from there to a newly opened expensive women's shop. The negligé the saleslady brought him was milk-white with a modest neckline pulled tight at the throat by a thin ribbon. She laid it out for him on the counter, where Emil untied the bow and drew down the shoulder straps and the top. His movements were very slow, very thoughtful. He stood looking down at it for so long that after a while the saleslady turned away in embarrassment and went to the other end of the counter to wait for him.

There was a new car now—a blue Chevrolet Lydia had approved—and after he had made his purchases, he went back to the car and, opening the suitcase on the front seat, took the camera out of the glove compartment and put it and his packages in the suitcase. He locked the suitcase and put it into the trunk of the car, then locked that too.

Madeleine was waiting for him on the highway the next morning. They stopped in Pineville, where he called the mill and Madeleine's school to report them both ill. Then they went on.

It was a humid, cloudy day, and they rolled down both their windows. They drove on with little conversation between them for the first fifteen miles, Emil now and then glancing over at Madeleine where she sat with her arm on the window ledge, her hair lashing against her face in the wind. As they drew nearer to the ocean, the air came to them stronger and clearer. Madeleine closed her eyes and turned her face up into the wind. She breathed the air deeply, then turned and smiled at him. He understood that the smile was her hesitant way of saying she had forgiven him: things could again be as they had once been between them. He smiled back at her.

Marshes began to appear, then canebrakes and small lakes, where fishermen sat as motionless as paintings in rowboats. They passed narrow streams rushing crookedly toward the ocean. They crossed an echoing old wooden bridge, where they saw sailboats moored below bobbing in the wakes of yachts on their way out to deep water. Madeleine leaned out her window to watch them.

They kept crossing bridges—there was more water than land around them for long stretches—and the air was fresh and damp on their faces, with the taste of salt in it Emil remembered from years before. Madeleine turned to him, smiling. "I can smell the ocean" she said.

"You can taste it too."

She put her head out the window, mouth open, eyes closed. Emil watched her. She called to him over the sound of the wind. "I *can* taste it." She leaned farther out, hair lifting behind her.

Madeleine's hand was on the seat between them. When he reached over and put his hand on hers, he felt her stiffen, and he waited for her to take it away. But it stayed there. He patted it and returned his hand to the steering wheel.

When he saw the first of the clam-and-crab bars on the roadside, he spoke to her with his eyes on the road. "Are you hungry?"

"This air makes me hungry. I could eat a horse."

He turned onto a dirt lot in front of a bar with neon beer advertisements flashing in a high, darkened window. There was no other window and the door was closed, so that no sound penetrated to them from within. It resembled a place that had been fled in the face of calamity, and where only the blinking lights told of former occupants.

They went through the door into a rush of cold air from an air conditioner. Men in work clothes and fishermen stood leaning across the bar drinking beer. Several turned to them, silent and watching, as Emil guided Madeleine to a scarred wooden booth. Then the men turned back to the bar.

A waitress came hurrying out of the kitchen, her dyed blonde hair swept up in a high tottering mass, loose sandals slapping the floor with each step. The ends of two pencils protruded from her hair; another pencil and an order pad were in her hand. She held both pad and pencil close to her face as she waited for them to order from the menu.

"Two dozen clams and two ginger ales" Emil told her, looking over the menu.

"OK." She wrote the order slowly, biting the side of her lip in con-centration. "That all?"

"May I have some crabs too, Daddy?"

Emil ordered them.

"OK" the waitress said. She read the order back to him. "That right?"

He nodded and the woman turned, still reading the order, and san-dals flapping, went back into the kitchen.

Madeleine and Emil had restrained themselves in front of her, but now that the waitress had gone, they leaned close to each other over the table, laughing. They straightened up and tried to look serious when a few heads at the bar turned to them.

"Are you enjoying yourself?" Emil asked when they managed to stop laughing.

"Yes, Daddy. Thank you for bringing me. Did you buy swimming suits? Can we go into the ocean?"

"If we do, your mother might become suspicious. We'll buy some straw hats so we don't get suntans, either."

"That's all right" she said. "I don't mind if we don't go swimming. But I want to go on all the rides."

Emil nodded and began studying the menu again.

The waitress returned slowly, carrying their orders precariously on a tray. Struggling to hold back their laughter, they sat up stiff and straight, only their eyes laughing. They watched as the waitress lowered the tray slowly onto the table. She placed their order in front of them finally with an expression of relief at a job accomplished without mishap. "OK" she said, more to the table than to her customers. She looked at Emil. "Is that OK?"

"Yes."

She turned to Madeleine: "You OK, honey? I get you something else?"

"No, thank you. 's OK."

Emil turned his head away to hide his laughter.

The waitress went off mumbling to herself.

Madeleine ate ravenously. She hardly looked up except to smile at Emil; neither spoke. Emil watched her, his expression serious when she was not looking at him, smiling when she was. He left half of his clams uneaten, then pushed the plate away. He lit a cigarette, but after a few puffs crushed it out in one of the clams. The clam moved, as if still alive at its touch. He leaned back and watched Madeleine until she was fin-ished. "Are you ready to leave?" he asked.

"Uh-huh."

"Had enough?"

"Oh, yes!" She patted her stomach to indicate its fullness.

"We'd better go then" he said, trying not to look at her.

Ten minutes later they saw Atlantic City rising in the distance. Madeleine leaned forward in her seat as buildings appeared sooner and taller than Emil remembered from before. He turned onto Atlantic Avenue, where a ferris wheel rolled over the tops of buildings as if run amok and attempting to crush them. Madeleine leaned out her window to watch patches of ocean down the streets between blocks, blue waves plunging behind the boardwalk. When he turned onto Pennsylvania Avenue, they heard the ocean's steady pounding.

He drove into a parking lot, where Madeleine waited outside her door while he went to the trunk and took out the suitcase. She seemed puzzled when he appeared carrying it.

"I thought we'd get a room to change in" he explained.

"Change into what?"

"Our beach clothes. I bought some."

"You said we couldn't go on the beach."

"I said we couldn't go into the water." He took her arm, but she pulled back. He increased the pressure until she moved forward stiffly. They walked in silence off the lot onto the crowded street.

The hotel was still there, unchanged on the outside, the smaller sign—Family Rates—hanging below the larger one; but inside the hotel the faces were all younger. The community room was still there to the side no longer dim but well-lighted under fluorescent tubes. The dwarflike television had been replaced by a large-screened color set.

Still holding Madeleine's arm, Emil guided her beside him to the desk. He resurrected the conquering smile of his former life for the middle-aged woman behind the register. She smiled back. "I'd like a room for my daughter and me just for the day" he told her.

"I have a nice double in back on the third floor. If you'll just sign—" She smiled at Madeleine as Emil bent over the register. Madeleine looked away.

The woman slapped a bell on the desk, and a boy appeared and took the key from her. Emil hesitated when the boy reached for the suitcase, then gave it to him. He took Madeleine's arm again, not looking at her, as she had not looked at him since leaving the parking lot, and they followed the boy to an elevator that had not been there before in the three-story hotel. They went in, and the boy pushed the number 3. The doors came slowly together, and they began to rise.

As they waited for their floor, the boy smiled at Emil, who nodded, then at Madeleine, who looked straight ahead at the closed doors. He hummed under his breath until the doors slid open. He went out of the elevator ahead of them, so that he did not see Emil pull Madeleine along beside him. She walked with jerking movements to the room.

"It's all right. I'll do it" Emil said to the boy, who was bending to unlock the door. Emil tipped him and waited until the boy had gone before he turned back to the door.

"I don't want to go in there" Madeleine said, looking at the floor. "I want to go home."

Emil opened the door. He picked up the suitcase and held the door open in front of her. "No nonsense, Madeleine, please" he said.

She resisted the hand on her back, which was gently forcing her forward, then gave in to it. He closed the door behind them.

"Sit down" he said as he passed her. She watched him go to the bureau and put the suitcase on top of it.

"Daddy—" she began. But he ignored her, his back to her as he opened the suitcase. She went to a chair beside one of the twin beds and sat on the edge of it. She got up and moved the chair as far away from the bed as it would go, then sat down again.

He was watching her in the mirror behind the bureau as he stood holding the suitcase open. He had been watching her every movement. He reached into the suitcase.

She sat up slowly when she saw him lift something long and white out of the suitcase. He turned to her, holding the negligé in front of him in both hands. She watched as he went to the bed and laid the negligé out across it.

"I bought this for you" he said. "I hope you like it."

Madeleine got up and walked to the bed. He stood aside for her. She picked up the negligé and held it out in front of her, examining it. She held it up to the light from the window to inspect its transparency. Then she turned back and tossed it onto the bed.

He hurried to lean over it, straightening it. He turned to her. "Please, Madeleine. I want you to wear it for me."

She was back in the chair, hands gripping its arms. "No" she said.

"Madeleine, go into the bathroom now and put it on." He pointed to a door behind her.

"I won't" she said. "I don't want to." She glared at him. Then her lips began trembling. "Please don't make me."

"Do as I say and go in there" he commanded.

She began crying. "Please, Daddy. If you really loved me—"

"It's because I love you. Please try to understand that. If you really loved me, you wouldn't hurt me like this."

She got out of the chair and pushed past him to the bed and

snatched the negligé off it. She turned to him, holding it hanging in her fists. Her eyes were cold now; they held his resolutely when minutes later he struggled to look away.

She began to undress. She took off her skirt, her blouse, her slip. She turned her brassiere around, unhooked it and let it fall to the floor. She stepped out of her panties. Then she stood naked, without moving, in front of him, looking past him as he stared down at her. His mouth opened to speak, then shut. His lips trembled. Then he jerked his head away, turned awkwardly and returned to the bureau, where he stood with his back to her, looking down.

Madeleine stared at his bent head; she did not take her eyes from it, even as she slipped the negligé over her head. She was still looking at him when she stood barefoot in the negligé.

It was too long for her. She held up the hem as she went to the bed, drew back the covers, and climbed into it.

She arranged herself on the bed with her arms at her sides, legs together. She stared up at the ceiling.

He turned and came to her and stood for a while by the side of the bed, looking at her. Then he lay down next to her. "Please don't fight me" he said. "If you love me, you won't make me suffer anymore."

She tried to make her mind die as he lowered the top of the negligé and drew each of her breasts to his mouth; she lay without protest when he lifted the gown over her hips, moved her legs apart and knelt over her. When he leaned down and kissed her, her mouth did not move beneath his. She stared past his head at the ceiling. She tried to imagine it was a stranger who lowered himself onto her.

She cried out when he entered her. He stopped, whispered to her to be quiet. The pain started again. She welcomed it finally. She heard his breathing next to her ear; it grew harsh and rapid as he began to move more quickly inside her. She imagined herself floating away.

She came back when she heard him cry out, felt his body twisting on her, stiffen, jerk up, then sink slowly back onto her, as if it came down in separate parts to claim her. He lay holding her as, in a hoarse voice, he began murmuring her name and telling her he loved her.

When later they went out onto the boardwalk, Emil won a doll for her from a man wearing a straw hat and a candy-striped shirt and pointing a cane who failed to guess his age and weight. He posed Madeleine with the doll against the boardwalk railing, a cloud-stained sky above, Million Dollar Pier like a ruined city behind her. She posed, but she refused to smile when he took the picture.

12

At dusk one evening when Willa was eight she watched a car come up the dirt road and stop by the woods beyond the house. A man got out carrying a blanket. A girl in a print dress hesitated at the door and looked in both directions down the road before hurrying with the man through the woods to the edge of the clearing.

Willa climbed into a tree close to them and watched the man spread the blanket and lie down with the girl on it. They kissed, then moved close together. Their stomachs rushed together and the girl's leg wound around the man's waist. Then they stopped and the girl pushed the man away. Willa leaned closer to hear what they said.

"Did you bring it?" the girl asked.

"Sure."

"Then put it on or you'll give me a baby."

He sat up and turned away from the girl, and Willa watched as he undid his trousers and took out the stiff man part of himself. He was holding a small packet from which he now tore away a shiny wrapper, then pulled a balloon over his man part. He turned back to the girl, who was now lying with her panties beside her and her skirt up and legs wide and waiting. The man got on top of her, pants at his knees. His bare bottom began moving. They were quiet for minutes. Then Willa was startled to hear the girl call out.

"Oh, Jimmy!" she cried. "Jimmy Jimmy Jimmy. Jimmy? Jimmy? Jim-EEEEEEEEEEEEEEEEEE!"

The man's bottom leapt and the girl's legs went around it and began to shake at the sky. Their bodies jerked and kept jerking and then were still. They lay there like the dead.

They left quickly minutes later, and Willa climbed out of the tree.

She sat under it to think about what she had seen. It was not until later that she understood the part the balloon had played in it.

■ ■ ■

A buzzer sounded and Willa opened the gate and entered Mary Vandel's courtyard. The gate closed behind her, then locked. She felt the cobblestones beneath her feet as she walked to the house past the fountain in which the statue of the naked woman stood lit with water and moonlight.

The two-story white house spread over the length of the courtyard. Willa could hear voices and music coming from inside, see people moving in rooms beyond the windows.

When she reached the house, she stood facing a thick wooden door. She looked for a bell, but there was none. There was a brass boar's head attached to the door and she reached up and pulled it and let it fall back heavily against the door, where it made a loud sound. She did it again. Then she waited, smoothing down her new dress. She regretted that she had not bought the gloves, for she had seen ladies at a ball on the television wearing them.

The woman who opened the door was in her late thirties, tall and big-boned. Her black hair was swept back and pinned behind her head. She wore dark slacks and a white blouse open wide at the neck to reveal rough, leathery skin in the hollow of her breasts. She had to look down to speak to Willa. "You're Miss Rhineman?"

Willa nodded.

"I'm Josephine Unway, Mary Vandel's secretary. Come this way. Mary said to bring you directly to her. She's resting now." It was the voice that had spoken to Willa at the gate yesterday and in the wire mouth a few minutes ago.

She led Willa into a large foyer with a marble floor. A free-hanging staircase at the far end doubled back on itself until it disappeared beyond the room's ceiling. Willa stood staring up at it until Josephine tapped her shoulder and Willa lowered her gaze. A small duplicate of the courtyard fountain and statue, water falling over it endlessly here too, stood in a niche in the wall to her left. Willa had time to look at it only for a moment as she followed Josephine to a door at the far end of the foyer. They went through it into a long hallway.

Willa's feet sank in thick carpeting as they passed an open door where people had gathered at what was obviously a party. They went by two more rooms of partiers before coming to a closed door. Josephine knocked quietly on it. She knocked again. A muffled voice came finally from beyond the door, and Willa followed Josephine into a room lit with only a blue bulb and so dark she could not see very far into it at first. What she saw finally was movement—a slight shifting from one side to the other—of a large woman lying on a divan. The woman's head turned to her. The voice that spoke was deep and without emotion, but it was not unfriendly.

"Come here. Let me see if you look like your mother." Her head lifted from the pillow on which it had been resting as Willa moved closer. She looked down at a face she could imagine was once pretty. Black bangs clung to a damp forehead. The eyes showed the weariness and resignation of one who has lived too long with pain. "Come closer" Mary said.

Willa went to the edge of the divan, where Mary studied her face. "Yes. The chin. The mouth. That noble forehead. You're Madeleine's child."

"Yes, ma'am."

Mary Vandel began to sit up. She said to Josephine, who was standing behind Willa "The child has been taught manners. How refreshing. That makes her an anachronism: one of us. The fate of everything worthwhile that endures." She was sitting up now. It had taken her a minute to do so.

Willa said "My grandmother taught me about manners. She was very strict about things like that. Miss Vandel, do you know where my mother is?"

Mary looked at Josephine. "My medicine, Jo." She turned back to Willa. "I haven't seen or heard of your mother since sixty-six, when she was living with a girl named Sylvia Rosenberg. I heard Madeleine was in the hospital before that."

"What was wrong with her?"

"She transgressed."

Willa was about to ask what that meant when Josephine appeared with what looked to Willa like a thin cigarette, which she held out to Mary. Mary took it and Josephine lit it for her with a small gold lighter. Mary drew in the smoke, held it deep inside her, then exhaled. She coughed.

"Would this Sylvia Rosenberg know where my mother is?" Willa asked.

Mary shrugged. She drew on the cigarette again—deep, quick puffs that caused the tip to flare again and again in the dim light. It was several minutes before she answered. "Sylvia? She was—nothing. A lap dog. Always hanging around the High Note begging love from the jazz musicians. A pathetic thing. One of the invisible ones. Invisible people—disappear. It was so long ago, Willa."

Willa asked "Did my mother ever talk about me?"

"No."

"Never?"

"I never knew you existed until yesterday. Your mother had secrets. I don't even know where she came from."

"She came from near a town called Pineville in New Jersey."

"It might just as well have been the moon. She was my moon goddess, Willa."

"What?"

Mary turned again to the cigarette before answering. "I loved your mother, girl. Unfortunately, she never loved me. What she loved was death."

Willa stiffened. That her mother was dead was the only possibility she had never considered. "My mother's not dead" she said. "I may not know much else about her, but I know that."

What Mary said then confused Willa not only by the words but by the strange, dreamlike way in which she said them. "We all died back then. A few of us are still here haunting the neighborhood, walking the streets, sitting in bars waiting for ghosts. We dream. The past devours us. Memory is the real tyrant."

Willa watched Mary come back from wherever she had been. The large woman struggled to get up—ponderously, slowly, until Josephine came forward and helped her to her feet. She was inches taller than the tall Josephine. Willa saw her then clearly for the first time.

The woman who stood finally before Willa was not so much fat as swollen. Her head looked grotesquely small on her large body. She was wearing an ankle-length caftan.

Mary finished the cigarette standing, and Josephine took what was left of it from her. Mary smiled down at Willa. "I'm giving a party for some close friends and business associates. You'll join us, Willa. Then we'll see what we can do about finding your mother." She put out her hand to Willa.

Willa took the hand and they left the room together.

Willa had never tasted alcohol before; she had never experienced the calm that good wine can bring. Nor had she ever known people such as those she had just met. She sat on a smaller chair next to the tall, thronelike chair on which Mary sat. A finished plate of canapés was beside her, the thin wine glass sparkling in her hand when she held it up to the light from a chandelier. The wine seen through the glass looked like pale blood.

The guests seemed to come to Mary only when she summoned

them or when by some subtle gesture or signal she let them know their approach would be welcome. Willa felt that she and Mary were more spectators than hostess and guest at the party.

Mary was on her third glass of straight gin, while Willa had not yet finished her first glass of wine. Josephine had come forward, at Mary's signal, with another of the long, thin cigarettes, and as she neared the end of it Mary began to talk of Madeleine almost as if she were there, another guest at the party. Willa was quiet, just listening. It was the first time anyone with personal knowledge of her mother had spoken to her in a way that had begun to make her appear as a living person.

"She seldom smiled. I never once heard her laugh—not even during her first weeks with Chatto, when she was so much in love with him—a time when girls are usually happy. You see, Willa, Madeleine stood out from the rest of them from the first because she did not spend her days and nights pursuing laughter. Laughter insulated the rest of them. It protected them in their fear of their collective parent, a disapproving society. What we mock we make seem less real. No one laughed at spiritual love, but romantic love was thought to be a selfish illusion. It implied ownership and the power to control: spiritual greed. Then your mother appeared, and I fell hopelessly and for the first time in love myself."

She was silent, drifting off again. Then she came back. "She was like a madonna, or perhaps a fragile princess, come among us and sitting there with us night after night at my table at the High Note. She had the quality of innocence that is unaware it is doomed. She didn't know then that it was death she was in love with. We were all aware—even Chatto, who was her lover by then—that she didn't belong there among us. Those nights: laughter and intense conversations about God, about art, about the revolution they all felt they were engaged in that would change America. It changed nothing finally, although like all revolutions it left behind many casualties. But at that time they felt only the excitement. It was contagious, that feeling of freedom in the air after the stifling air of the fifties in which we had grown up. It was there at the High Note every night—that air thick with the smell of dope, the passing of joints under the table as we listened to the great jazzmen who were like gods to us. Their music was the perfect expression of that freedom."

She was silent again. Willa waited. Then Willa said "Orlo Haines told me Chatto was an evil man."

Mary laughed. It was a loud laugh, which carried above the music and voices across the large room, causing some of the people to stop talking and turn to them. Mary said "Orlo Haines? Is that chicken still around?"

"Orlo said he was afraid of Chatto."

Mary's expression became serious. Willa watched her drifting away again. Her head went back onto the chair. She was looking up at the ceiling when she said "Ghosts. They're everywhere. They're even here in this room."

Her head tilted, and after a few minutes Willa knew she was asleep.

Willa sat watching Mary as she slept. Others in the room took quick looks at her, but no one came to wake her, no one intruded. Willa did not know whether to get up and leave—tell Josephine, who was in another part of the room, that she would come back the next day to see if Mary would help her find her mother—or sit waiting for Mary to wake up. She decided she had better ask Josephine what to do.

She finished what was left of her wine and put her glass on the table next to Mary's chair. Mary held her glass firmly in her hand as she slept. The few ounces of gin left in it tilted with the leaning glass. Willa debated whether to rescue the glass from Mary's hand but decided it did not need rescuing. She started to get up.

Mary's eyes opened. Her free hand reached over and took Willa's hand by the wrist. Willa sat down again. Mary finished her drink and held it up toward Josephine before she spoke. "Don't go" she said. "We haven't talked about finding your mother for you yet."

Willa leaned toward Mary. She felt now that if anyone could find her mother, it was Mary Vandel. "Would you do it?" she asked. "Could you help me?"

"I have contacts" Mary said. "If she can be found, we will find her."

Josephine appeared with a new glass of gin. She laid another cigarette and the gold lighter on the table, nodded to Willa and left. Mary drank off a third of the glass while Willa waited. But when Mary spoke again, she seemed to have forgotten about Madeleine, and although Willa was impatient and wanted to bring her back to the subject, she decided not to press her for fear of losing her help.

"These people" Mary said, waving her hand at the others in the room and speaking in a voice loud enough so that she seemed not to care whether they heard her or not, "I have obligations to them, and so I give these parties twice a year. But I lied to you: they're not my friends. I don't have any friends anymore except Josephine. I do business with most of them; the others are just useful to me. I've bought some of them."

Willa was puzzled. She asked "How do you buy people? I didn't think you could do that."

Mary's voice rose even louder, so that some of the others turned to them. "Everyone can be bought, girl. If not by money, then with love." She pointed to a man sitting in a chair across the room. Willa had noticed the man, who unlike the others was alone. He did not speak to anyone. He never smiled. He hardly moved except to pass the palm of his hand over his bald head. He had a mouth that was as small and compressed as a rosebud. He looked as if he were awaiting an appropriate time to leave.

"That old man" Mary said "is one of the richest and most powerful financiers in the city. Most of the people who know him fear him. Gods and powerful people are meant to be feared. But he's in his seventies, and for the past thirty years he has been impotent. He has a beautiful young wife, but he cannot make love to her; and although he has been to every specialist, no one has been able to help him. He has given up trying. Now once a week he pays a great deal of money to have girls younger than you come to him. He sits in a chair in the living room of his apartment fully dressed, and the girl—who has been instructed that she must look at him but never speak—gets naked and sits on the floor at his feet. She must reach up then and take out his limp penis and hold it in her hand for an hour looking up at him adoringly."

Willa, who had been brought another glass of wine by Josephine, had begun to raise it to her mouth as Mary spoke. Now the glass was stopped midway between her chin and mouth. She lowered it into her lap.

Mary indicated another of the guests: a tall, elegant woman Willa had stared at several times because she was so beautiful. "And that woman, an heiress," Mary said. "By the age of twenty she was the most notorious nymphomaniac in the city. Men, women, animals—she has had them in every combination, all colors, sizes and shapes. In every way imaginable her money and beauty have provided her whatever sexual gratification she desires. And although no man or creature has ever satisfied her, she goes on searching. She has been married eight times. She has been to psychiatric hospitals, where she managed each time to corrupt the staff. A year ago she paid thousands of dollars for a handsome young priest, who lasted a week. Now she is waiting for word on another priest: the oldest, most devout and yet virile one that can be found."

Mary finished her drink and put it down on the table. Willa's remained still untouched as she stared at the woman Mary had been talking about. Mary picked up the lighter and the cigarette from the table, but she did not light it. She leaned down and, touching Willa on the shoulder, brought her attention back to her. She said "Those two are among those who buy people with money. As for the other way to own people—with love—see the woman talking to that group by the window."

Willa looked and saw a woman in a tailored suit—less elegant but as beautiful as the other woman Mary had spoken about.

"That woman" Mary said "is one of the most successful attorneys in the country. Few lawyers—man or woman—are happy to hear her name mentioned as an adversary. She has been a special legal advisor to two presidents and is a senior partner in the largest law firm in the city. Her first husband committed suicide when she left him; her second died in a sanitarium for rich alcoholics. They were both so much in love with her that when she turned from them to others they could not endure the loss. Both were strong, successful men when they married her. It was her second husband who claimed she is a witch who can cast a spell over men that gives her possession of their souls. Now she has only lovers—always strong men too, at first. Toward the end of each affair—when the man is so obsessed with her he cannot deny her anything—she will only consent to let him make love to her under one condition: he must wear a paper bag over his head during the act. They all submit to this humiliation at least once before being discarded by her."

Mary raised the cigarette and lit it. She leaned back in the chair while she smoked. Some of the smoke drifted up, stretching like a hand in the dim light of the chandelier. She looked down at Willa. "And then there is a third way to own people" she said.

"What's that?" Willa asked.

"With dreams. With illusions. These are promises we want to be kept."

Willa felt sad from the stories Mary had told her. She had never imagined there were such people in the world, much less such things happening. Her grandmother's descriptions of evil had been of acts more basic, less desperate. She turned back to Mary, whose head was now tilted, her eyes closed.

"Miss Vandel" Willa said, "will you help me find my mother? I want to be with her as soon as I can."

"Patience" Mary answered without opening her eyes.

Willa touched Mary's arm and her eyes opened. But her head remained tilted back, and only her eyes were directed at Willa down the length of her body.

Willa asked "Do you think you could find something out by tomorrow? Maybe that Sylvia Rosenberg or Chatto would know something?"

Mary did not seem to be listening to her. She was straightening up in her chair. She was staring at Willa. She leaned forward and cupped Willa's chin in her hand, raising it. She turned Willa's head first one way, then another. Finally she released it. She said "You're beautiful. I didn't see that before. You're as beautiful as your mother at your age. Are all the women in your family so beautiful?"

"No, ma'am. My grandmother was pretty ugly."

"That place you're living in" Mary asked. "Is it a rooming house?"

"Yes, ma'am."

"That must be depressing."

"It's pretty nice, really."

Mary raised her hand, then waited until Josephine appeared. Mary nodded to her, and Willa saw that two of a different kind of cigarette were left on the table this time when Josephine had gone. They were smaller and wrapped in brown paper.

"Tonight" Mary said "you will sleep here. Josephine will get you whatever you need. In the morning we'll see what we can do about finding Madeleine for you. However long it takes, you'll be welcome to stay here." She picked up both cigarettes. "In the meantime" she said, "I want you to forget your troubles for a while. There's nothing for you to do now but wait."

Willa awoke hours later on a couch in another part of the room. Everyone was gone—even Mary. She remembered Mary lighting the cigarette for her, showing her how to swallow the smoke so that it went deep inside her; how to hold it there and then let it come up so she could swallow it again. She told Willa to lean back and close her eyes and imagine she was a cloud drifting in the sky. But before Willa could do that, Mary reached over and flicked Willa's wine glass with her fingernail. The glass rang with the sound of small bells. Shapes of light came out of it, like tiny people coming alive at the sound of the bells. Willa smiled at them. She closed her eyes and leaned her head back on the chair. She listened to the party music, the voices of the people fading. Beautiful objects—flowers and birds and trees and clouds—bloomed in bright colors out of the darkness of her mind, drifted away waving like friends with promises to return. Other objects just as brilliant rose out of the darkness in turn. She let herself float away.

It took her a minute now to recall Mary's invitation to stay with her. She sat up, too weak for a few seconds to stand. Then she lowered herself slowly onto unsteady legs.

She could not have gotten back to her rooming house, she knew, if she wanted to. She needed to find a bed and sleep. When she began to walk across the large room to the door, the room stretched away in front of her. She stopped twice to rest before she reached the door and stepped into the long hallway. She listened, but there was no sound of anyone awake in the house.

As far as Willa could remember, Josephine had not told her where she could sleep. The house was too large, and she was too exhausted to go exploring. She moved down the hall instead to the door of the room Josephine had taken her into to meet Mary. She knocked softly, waited, knocked again and went in.

She saw Mary immediately in the blue light, still in her caftan, asleep on the divan. A small figure was curled up naked beside her. It lay on its side like a child turned to its mother in sleep for protection.

When she got to the divan, Willa saw that the girl beside Mary was Heather, who had led her to the edge of the coffin at Madeleine House.

13

Vernon waited in the doorway of a closed shop across the street from Mary Vandel's house until the last guest had left and all the rooms but one had gone dark. Only when he was certain the girl was not coming out did he return to his room.

He could not sleep. Not even the mannequin standing at the foot of the bed could soothe his nerves, and at seven-thirty he got up and went down to the hall phone and called his supervisor to say he would be in the hospital all that week. He had been in the hospital twice before but otherwise was so reliable he knew he would not be fired.

He returned to his room, set the alarm for ten o'clock and, settling it all in his mind, fell immediately into a deep sleep.

There were times when Vernon would sleep through an entire day, and other times when he could not sleep at all. In the past at such times he went to one of three houses he knew where he watched through the window as others slept. But since meeting the girl and following her, such solitary devices were no longer necessary.

At ten-thirty he was standing by the tree, looking up at the girl's window. He remained there for an hour, watching for her, but now not patiently, not content to absorb time as he absorbed people. For the first time he was annoyed at the girl. It seemed to him as if she had purposely removed herself from his scrutiny in order to frustrate him.

By noon he was calm again as he approached Mary Vandel's gate. He pushed the buzzer beside the wire mouthpiece. A woman answered.

"Yes?"

His voice was without emotion now as he held down the button and spoke. "Would you please move the white station wagon you have blocking the driveway across the street?" He released the button, waited.

"What white station wagon? We don't own a station wagon."

"Someone there must own it. None of your neighbors do. Maybe it belongs to someone else in the house. A guest, maybe." He watched the mouthpiece as if it were the person with whom he was having the conversation. It spoke to him.

"We only have one guest."

"Would you ask if they own a white station wagon?" he persisted in his unhurried, deep monotone.

"Oh, for God's sake! Wait a minute."

He waited, looking down at the mouthpiece. It was several minutes before the voice returned. "She says she doesn't own one either."

"Thank you."

He spent the rest of the afternoon walking back and forth across from the house. He never lost sight of the gate in the middle of the long block. By five o'clock the girl still had not come out of it.

He returned to his room, and although he lay down on the bed, by then he could not have slept had he wanted to. He did not take the mannequin out of the closet. He lay on his side looking at the window where darkness appeared in increments. He got up and went down to the tree again. Her window was dark.

He drove the car to Mary Vandel's this time, parking halfway down the block from the gate. He had passed the house once, seen the light on in the room that had stayed lit all the previous night, but he already knew he could not see anything in the room from the sidewalk. He waited.

He was standing in a doorway when a pizza delivery truck drove up and a man with a large box waited for the buzzer to sound, unlocking the gate. When the man went through the gate, Vernon was only a few steps behind him. He slipped into the courtyard and disappeared in the shadows at the other end of the gate.

He watched the delivery man leave. Then he moved across the cobblestones to the side of the window.

Three females were in the room grouped around a tall, fat woman wearing a long robe and sitting in a chair that looked like a throne. At her feet was another girl, who sat leaning her head back against the fat woman's leg, eyes closed. The girl he had been following was in a chair next to the fat woman, and a tall woman sat apart, watching them.

He had not recognized the girl at first. She wore a white blouse and white slacks. Her hair had been combed out full and loose all around her head, a lock of it curling on her forehead. A large mandala hung from a chain around her neck. She was wearing makeup—rouge, lipstick, eye shadow and face powder, which made her look unnaturally pale, almost ghostlike.

The tall woman and the two girls were eating the pizza; the fat woman had put her half-eaten slice next to a plate on which pizza crusts lay like offerings to her. The girl held a glass of wine from which she now and then drank; the tall, fat woman drank her wine from an identical long-stemmed glass.

After they finished eating, the fat woman took a thin cigarette from the pocket of her robelike dress and lit it. All four of them began smoking it.

Vernon leaned farther forward at the edge of the window. His body tensed, for he knew from watching the movies on the street what the cigarettes were, had seen there what men and women—and sometimes women with women—did when they smoked them. But nothing like that happened. The other girl and the girl he had been following got up separately and did strange, slow dances, but that was all.

Nothing happened, but Vernon saw what was happening nevertheless. He saw the girl look at the fat woman and smile. She slid off her chair and sat with the other girl at the fat woman's feet. He watched as the fat woman smiled down at her. He saw the fat woman's hand descend onto the girl's head. He saw her fingers curl into the girl's hair, saw the girl lean back, head tilted, eyes closed. The woman's hand went to the girl's neck, large fingers holding it, caressing it. He cried out, then drew away from the window, head against the stone side of the house. His fingers were at his chest when he leaned back to the window to make certain they had not heard him.

They had not. They stayed as they were even then, like people in a portrait.

He left the window finally, for it was getting late, and it was dangerous for him to remain there, exposed from the street. Besides, there was nothing more to be seen. They were not even talking. But the thought of them there—the girl apart now not only from him but from her identity as well in the white clothes, the different hairstyle and makeup—remained with him as torment and a feeling of betrayal even after he had left the courtyard and returned to his room.

He went first to his sewing box, took the scissors out of it and went down through the sleeping house to the door of the cellar. He paused, listening, to be certain there was no one down there. He had heard his landlady in the cellar that morning doing her laundry; she was fearful of the laundromat, where old people had been robbed, where all of the dark people went. Vernon listened for another minute at the door, then opened it, turned on the light, and descended the steps.

He wove through damp hanging sheets and tablecloths, wash-and-wear dresses and underwear, which trembled behind him before he got to the other side of the cellar, where a long length of clothesline hung through a metal eyelet to the floor. He cut the rope, folded it, and put it under his overcoat, where it bulged like a signature of aberration as he ascended again to his room.

He placed the mannequin at the foot of the bed, but this time he drew up a chair beside it. He climbed onto the chair. He raised the mannequin's arms as far as they would go, then bound them at the wrists with one end of the rope and threw the other end over the ceiling light fixture. He pulled on the rope, lifting the mannequin into the air, where it hung swiveling. Then he got down from the chair and sat on it.

He began talking to the mannequin—not angrily but more like an instructor to an undisciplined student—as it hung turning above him.

14

Lydia felt she had accomplished her dream when Emil's had just begun. She had accepted the imperfections in it finally, for Pastor Cooley had accomplished what no one else had been able to: he had convinced the fifty-five-year-old woman that imperfection was part of God's plan too, a test of humility for those who were stronger, more able. He had taught her to accept compromise with her dreams.

Emil had discovered a copse beyond the woods where he took Madeleine when he could. He had hollowed out the pages in his Bible and hidden condoms inside it (the one imperfection in his dream, one concession to caution). He kept the Bible wrapped in oilskin in the hollow trunk of a tree in the copse. He had replaced that Bible with another of the same edition on the bookshelf in the parlor. He had done it with confidence, having watched Lydia's relationship grow with Pastor Cooley, her new preoccupation with him and the church, the relaxation of scrutiny of those in her house who had never before experienced the freedom she now gave them. He had switched the Bibles that night with satisfaction, with a feeling of recompense, retribution, renunciation of that church and God that had led him, he felt, so cruelly with lies until now. He had made his own heaven and, in his mind, was accountable to no one for it.

Madeleine went with him to the copse each time without protest. Docile. Willing to accept the fact of her life now, which was in any case unavoidable, since she had no allies, no one she had ever been close enough to to confide in; for the one person to whom she had been almost exclusively close was the one who, had she been able to rouse herself to grievance, was the cause of that grievance.

He loved her; she knew that. Loved her as men were supposed to love women: with tenderness, with passion, then with gratitude. She saw the greater guilt as hers for being the weaker of the two at that time when she should have been the stronger. Now her shame was endorsed by the repetition of submissions to Emil's desire for her.

Lydia stood at the kitchen window watching Emil and Madeleine come out of the woods, just as she had watched them that other Sunday after-noon ten years before. Behind them was a new sign high above the highway near Pineville, the words *Jesus Is Coming to Save You* peering through the trees. But father and daughter came this time not hand in hand, not with arms swinging, only Emil holding wildflowers, Madeleine less than a head shorter than Emil now and looking down, not laughing with him. That other scene to Lydia returned, bearing the mutations of time.

Madeleine and Emil came through the still-squeaking screen door, but now Emil was first, smiling, Madeleine unsmiling and silent behind him. It was Emil now who gave Lydia the flowers, kissed her on the cheek as she stood with her back to him at the sink. He smelled of grass and other things inferent of woods and the earth.

"For my love" he said to her.

"Stop that nonsense, Emil." She shrugged his hands off her shoul-ders and lifted one of the fish out of the tub in which she was preparing to clean them. Pastor Cooley had given them to her after church ser-vices from those given him by a member of the congregation. But she was secretly pleased, for this Sunday the family had attended church together. Emil for several years had gone only sporadically and at her insistence, and Madeleine had avoided church as much as she could.

It was Madeleine this time who sat down immediately at the table; Emil put the flowers in a glass and, smiling at her, brought them to the table, where she was looking into her lap. She pulled the hem of her skirt down several times, stretching it tightly across her knees.

Madeleine's silences, her new submissiveness, pleased Lydia too; she thought them the result of the hard line she had taken with her in the weeks since their confrontation. All this Lydia considered reward for her life of dedication, that which was charged to her to accomplish for those under her sovereignty not in her own interests nor even entirely for their betterment, but rather that the principle be adhered to, the construction of one of life's most resolute concepts forced against the recalcitrance of life itself into completion and place. "Fate is attitude" is what she had often told Emil in the beginning years; more recently Madeleine had begun hearing it.

Lydia's relationship with Pastor Cooley had, through their work together, grown into one of mutual respect and spiritual union. Although she would never have thought of it that way, it was more intense than her ties to her husband, even during the first months of their marriage. She now sought Pastor Cooley's guidance and advice, opened up to him as she had never done to anyone and, now and then, knelt and prayed with him aloud in the parlor of his home as his wife listened in another room.

Now Emil sat smiling at Madeleine while she watched her mother—who had put on pink rubber gloves that went up to her elbows—take up the special knife she used for cleaning fish. Madeleine saw the knife begin grating against the fish bodies, scales flying and sparkling in the light from the window before falling onto the spread newspapers on the sideboard. The fish dropped splashing into a tub in the sink, the knife following them. Lydia split open their bellies, then drew out of them pale entrails that dripped onto the newspapers. A pyramid of fish heads was growing on the sideboard, where into the fishes' stunned eyes Madeleine's own startled eyes looked back.

Later they sat before the television in the parlor, where Madeleine now occupied Emil's former chair. Lydia remained steadfast in hers, back straight as the chair's despite time, while Emil sat on the couch in the near darkness. But this time there were no comedians in dresses with baskets of fruit on their heads; in the otherwise darkened room, war raged on the small television screen where the sound was turned low. Men toppled like flowers severed from their roots. Corpses lay half hidden, woven into the fabric of jungles. Helicopters descended in infestations, light as ballet dancers above their swollen bellies. Bodies of water erupted and the tops of palm trees exploded, flapping their long arms as they rose into the air.

Little had changed in the house, while everything was changing around them.

That night when Emil lay next to Lydia in the darkness, there was the odor of fish in the bed with them. He was hesitant still to go to Madeleine down the hall, where she lay frightened that he would. To Madeleine the odor of fish seemed to be in every room in the house.

The following afternoon Pastor Cooley knelt in the parlor of his home. He had closed the sliding doors as interdiction against entry, sign that God's work was being done, although now God was absent from his thoughts, even as he struggled to bring him into them.

He had been praying, for prayer was still solace to him, although its efficacy had become increasingly less absolute, less dependable than it had been when he was a young man—even until a few years ago, when absolutes were still unquestioned by him. He had thought then that he knew the answers to many things; now he knew he did not have the answer to anything. It was the first real secret of his life, out of which the other secret had grown; and the one thing he understood now that he had not then was the power such secrets had to make everything else surrender to them. They drew in the outer life and reshaped it as part of them. They grew larger with silence.

Pastor Cooley had also seen the war news the previous night. He had sat next to his wife watching young men dying on television. He had grieved for them and for the other young men he had seen there who might die young too. It was them—both the dead and the ones he had seen sitting next to death—he had gone to the parlor to pray for before Lydia arrived. He believed—and it was true—that he would gladly have died for them if he thought it would save them.

Now Lydia Rhineman would come to unwittingly sharpen his suffering. For she saw him as strong, possessing answers, when all his life he had never even asked questions. He had never known suffering before this. It had come to him in the faces and eyes of those young men as he watched them for the first time on the television, seen them later in photographs in magazines and newspapers (clippings hidden away in a box in the cellar), which had brought forth and then clarified for him what he had hidden from himself all those years. Lydia had with her own need invested a faith in him; that woman he had never known to surrender any part of her will to another—certainly not to any man after the death of her first husband—now had selected him as the depository of her long-dormant need to have faith in another, to give up a large portion of her will to him, who she saw as worthy of it. But he knew himself now to be the least worthy. It was only during those times when he made his own surrender, knelt in abjectness and humility, with a need at last given in to, that he felt confirmed. He could then for a moment become reconciled with himself, for it was only then that he recognized himself.

He got up, brushing off his trousers at the knees. She was at the door. In a few minutes he would have to see her, present to her that face of equanimity which was the lie of himself now. Then tonight he would have to go again and invite a humbling so that he might feel a moment of true worthiness.

Lester Kane's annual layoff was from the end of May to the end of September. There was no longer a crop to be planted then on the Rhineman property. Lydia had abandoned it six years before as only marginally profitable. The hired black man's job since then consisted mainly of upkeep and restoration. He was packing when Madeleine appeared in the open doorway.

"I'll miss you, Lester."

He did not answer. His back was to her where he bent putting books into an old suitcase. He went to the doorless closet, took down his black suit and dark tie and folded them neatly into the suitcase. He turned only then to face her. "I'll only be coming back this year and next. Then I'm quitting."

"Why?"

"I've been going to a Negro college in Alabama on a church scholarship. I'll graduate in two more years. Reverend Stokes is an old man, he'll retire, and I'll take over at Mount Calvary."

"Is that what you want to do? Be a minister?"

"It's one of the things I want to do. There are other things even more important that have to be done."

She hesitated a moment before turning in the doorway to leave. "I'll miss not having you to talk to" she said. "It will be lonely after you leave."

"There are worse things than loneliness these days. Loneliness is the least of a lot of people's problems."

She had turned and was leaving when she heard him address her by her first name; it was one of the few times he had done so.

"Take care of yourself, Madeleine."

When she was gone, he looked up from his packing. There had been something about her—in her manner—that made him think she had come to him to do more than say good-bye. She had acted as if she had something to tell him, or perhaps to seek advice from him.

But he had no time to think about it further. He returned to his packing.

One day in late October Emil went to the copse and brought the Bible back into the house. He hid it in his locked toolbox at the back of the hall closet. Then he waited.

He went to Madeleine again a week later. She was sitting up in bed. She seemed to be expecting him. He hesitated inside the door, for when he saw her face in the light from the window, the expression upon it—as if mixed with the memory of other resolves which had failed in the past—was one of uncertain power over him.

He sat down next to her on the side of the bed. "What is it?" he asked. "Why are you looking at me like that?"

But he did not wait for an answer, for he had decided that her uncertainty was, after his month's absence, no more than the reluctance he had seen in her before. He had turned away, was beginning to remove his pajama top, when his fingers stopped, frozen to the first button by her words.

"I'm pregnant."

He stood up immediately, as if an electrical shock had gone through him, leaving him like one who is afraid to move, wanting only to postpone for as long as possible that moment when he will be forced to assess that power's terrible consequences. When he finally spoke, he did not look at her. "How long has it been?"

"Two months."

She saw his back straighten, go rigid, as without another word to her he walked from the room, closing the door quietly behind him.

He went up the stairs to the attic. He did not put on the light, but he could see in the light from the attic's small window the old mattress still in the corner. He went to it and lay down on it, then slowly drew his arms and legs in to his body. He closed his eyes.

Fear had kept him from thinking until now; but it was a stronger fear that later drove him back down the stairs and into the room, where she was still waiting.

He stood over her this time, did not sit down on that bed that he understood finally had been forbidden to him by more than law. "You have to help me" he told her. "Give me time to decide what to do. Will you do that?"

"Yes."

"Do you understand why you can't tell anyone it was me? What would happen to both of us if you did?"

"Yes."

He turned, about to leave, then turned back again. "I won't be coming to you again. We have to stop now." She was silent. "We have to" he repeated.

She looked up, searching his face for what she realized then was not there, had never been there: some recognition of her, the real Madeleine, in his eyes.

He would not help her, she realized; he could not. She was alone now, she knew, and the only one who could help her was her.

Lydia sat in the pickup outside Arthur Cooley's house wondering if she had done something to offend him. She had gone to ask his advice about whether she should consult a doctor about Madeleine. Since Thanksgiving the girl had been acting more strangely than ever. She stayed in her room most of the time and had let her appearance go; she always wore one of the ugly long peasant dresses Emil told Lydia she had asked him to buy her. They were the new teenage style in imitation of those girls with long hair and boyfriends with guitars slung over their backs that now and then drifted in and out of Pineville singing folk songs and offering flowers to strangers. But Madeleine had never been one to imitate others before. She had always done what she thought would please Emil.

Lydia had on occasion in the past thought that Madeleine was not nearly as bright as she appeared to others; now she wondered if there had even been something backward about her all along.

Arthur Cooley was the only friend Lydia had made since she was a girl. Until now she had not needed friendship any more than she needed love. Both created reliance, she had believed, and emotional debts in the guise of gifts given and expected in return. But now that Madeleine was nearly grown and Emil brought to conclusion—salvaged, if possibly never to know true salvation—the emptiness she felt lately she recognized as part loneliness. She needed to align herself with the strong will of another, now that her own strength was no longer required.

She had presented herself to Arthur Cooley in a spirit of abnegation, and he had accepted his role as her mentor. But now he had withdrawn from her. She had broken for him her hard rule that what is never given cannot be rejected later.

She had thought he was strong, but now she wondered if she had deluded herself into thinking it so she could unburden herself of her own strength at last. His mind obviously elsewhere, he had not been any help in her problem with Madeleine, which to her was the same as withholding his interest in her.

She turned the ignition on the pickup, convinced that whatever his problem was, he alone of all those she had ever known was capable of solving it or rising above it.

Madeleine left the house around midnight. With the television off and the house dark, she knew that Lydia would be asleep. Emil might hear her if he was still awake, but that was no longer a consideration for her. She was only his daughter again now.

She had to lift the long peasant dress beneath her overcoat to step over rocks and twigs as she made her way along the path through the woods to the highway. She wore a cheap metal wedding band she had bought in the five-and-dime store in Pineville.

It was cold, and she had turned up the collar of her coat. A tall girl, she looked even taller in the long dark coat with its severe lines. Her understated beauty, the dark eyes, made her seem serene, even when the last thing she felt was serenity. She had pinned up her hair and wore light makeup and knew that she would not have any more trouble getting in than she had the other times. They knew her there now.

She was going to a dance hall in the back of a tavern that had opened on the highway two miles the other side of Pineville. They had a band and dancing, and although she had only drunk soft drinks, no one seemed to mind. She had been there three times, the first time two weeks ago, just after Christmas.

She had sat in a booth in the back, danced with several young men but only let one man each time join her afterward in the booth. All three of them had told her lies about themselves, but the lies had not mattered. She had refused to go to motels with them but later went with them to the back seats of their cars.

She had allowed them to kiss her repeatedly in deep passion, but when they attempted to place their hands over her coat, she stopped them. "Don't touch my breasts" she said. "They hurt." She kept the coat buttoned to her chin, and when they tried to put their hands under it and her dress, she held them away.

When eventually they became too anxious, too demanding, she offered to help them. She placed her hand on their trousers.

She looked away while doing it for them, then when it was over and before they could recover, slipped from the car and disappeared down the night of the highway.

The next morning it snowed, but that night Arthur Cooley returned to Riverton Square in the city, where winter and summer, men sat waiting on benches before a screen of high bushes in the circular park. Behind them tall luxury apartment buildings stood like walls with eyes—silent, removed. He paused at the entrance in front of a bronze statue of a goat, which stood buried to its belly in a mound of snow. Its legless shadow lay toppled on the snow beside it.

Older men circled the park, stopping occasionally before the benches where young men sat looking pointedly away. They stood in dark coats like shadows waiting to be acknowledged. When the young men turned to them, they sat down. Minutes later they got up together and their shadows accompanied them across the snow and disappeared with them into the bushes.

But Arthur Cooley was not one to do it in silence, without even a name between them. He did not want to efface himself as the others did; for what he needed each time was a declaration of himself to them. He wanted to see himself in their eyes.

He sat down next to a young man whose hand rested on the bench between them and who was looking straight ahead. Unlike Arthur, who wore a hat to hide his baldness, the young man was bareheaded. Gusts of wind lifted his long hair, revealing a high forehead. He seemed less certain of himself than the other young men, who were habitués of the park. Nor was he as young as they.

"Are you waiting for someone?" Arthur asked.

The young man turned his face slowly to him, the wind lifting his hair, then settling it on his shoulders. "Yes" he answered.

"It's cold to be waiting here alone."

"I've waited in colder places" the young man said after a minute.

"My name is Arthur."

The young man hesitated again before answering. "I'm John."

"How old are you, John?"

"Twenty—one."

Arthur knew he was lying. Either that or he had experienced too much at too early an age and it had matured him. "So many of you young men are going off to that war in Vietnam" he said. "Are you?"

For the first time the young man showed a willingness to communicate something honest about himself. "Not yet. Pretty soon, though. I've just been reclassified."

"Are you afraid of dying there?"

"I'd be a fool not to be afraid."

"I know what fear does to one, John, when there's no one to share it. I'm lonely too."

Arthur reached over and put his hand on the young man's hand. Both hands began trembling. He whispered his next words, although there was no one near enough to hear him. It was not unreasonable caution that made him whisper, however. It was to hide his excitement at what the words would finalize about him. "I could help you if you let me. I want to do that very much."

The young man looked directly at Arthur for the first time.

"If we went over there—" Arthur said. He gestured behind them.

The young man got up. "All right" he said.

Arthur rose beside him. He took his hand, and together they walked around the bench into the bushes.

He emerged from the bushes ten minutes later, now in too much of a hurry, too frightened, to remember until later seeing the terrible knee prints he had left behind in the snow.

Madeleine was returning home one afternoon out of the woods. She slowly marched through the untrodden snow, lifting her legs to the knees and planting deep holes that followed slowly behind her.

She was in her long overcoat with the collar turned up to her ears, arms circling herself, and a scaffold of long scarf wound to below her chin. Her hair was flecked with white where the trees had dropped sprinklings of snow over it. The holes followed her up the porch steps.

Lydia was waiting for her in the kitchen. "Sit down" she said.

Madeleine stood across from her at the table. She unwound the scarf. She took off her boots. Then she sat down, still wearing the coat, looking at Lydia.

"You haven't been to school in four weeks" Lydia said. "You took a note in excusing yourself supposedly written by me but which was not written by me."

"They told you that?"

"They had me down to your school to show it to me. They showed me another note dated eight weeks ago excusing you from gym. Do you have an explanation for all this?"

"I never liked gym."

"That's a lie."

"What does it matter, then? Whatever I say, you'll tell me I'm lying."

"That's because a liar is what you're becoming. And not a very good one, either."

Madeleine shrugged.

"We don't lie in this house" Lydia said.

Madeleine looked at her, eyebrows raised in exclamation as if she could not believe she had heard the words.

"Did your father know about this?"

"Ask him."

"Does he know what's been going on around here these last months?"

"If you want to know what's been going on, ask him."

"He's not here."

Madeleine was silent.

"Well, we'll get to the bottom of this one way or another" Lydia concluded.

They were waiting for him in the parlor when he returned that afternoon. He nodded to them as he proceeded toward the stairs where Lydia knew he would ascend to the attic. He had done so most days for some time now, which was for the moment inexplicable to Lydia. He would sit until dinner in the chair he had brought up there and placed in front of the small window, where he could see only a margin of sky and the tops of clouds; he would come down for dinner and then go up again afterward. Since apparently all he wanted was to be alone, doing no harm, it had seemed almost normal for him then. Now she realized that nothing had been normal in the house for some time. She called to him. "Emil!"

He stopped midway up the stairs, hand still on the railing, motionless. He turned finally with a mechanical, jerking movement and came back down the steps to the two chairs in which Madeleine and Lydia were sitting. He attempted to smile.

It was a smile Lydia remembered from the distant past: the young man who, although come as a supplicant to her porch steps, was still confident of his power to charm. But she had taken that away from him too, and now what she saw was a failed imitation of that charm. She allowed him to stand.

She asked "Did you know Madeleine hasn't been to school in four weeks? That she wrote a note in my name to get excused? And another to get out of going to gym?"

"No, Lydia."

"Do you know what's happening around here?"

"No, I don't."

"I think you're lying to me, Emil."

"No. I'm not. What reason would I have to lie?"

Her Bible was on the table next to her. She took it and held it up to him. "Swear it."

He put his hand on it. "I swear."

She turned to Madeleine, who was sitting with her legs tucked under her, the bottom half of her body hidden in the long, loose dress. Lydia studied the formation she had constructed of herself on the chair. Madeleine was staring at her father, who was looking away from her. She saw the girl's hand go to the dress and begin smoothing it out. Then the thought came to her that she wanted to disown. "Go to your room" she told Madeleine.

Emil stepped back to let Madeleine pass, the ghost of another figure in another time moving close to him, creating a frail memory in Lydia too which was soon gone.

Strength to Lydia had always meant acting in the regions of greatest fear. Virtue was defined by it. Now at a moment that she could only describe as one of self-doubt, she understood that action was also an acknowledgment of fear.

She got up more quickly than she had intended, having wanted to leave Madeleine alone longer in her room, and moving past Emil like that ghost come again out of their past, left him, after she had gone, with other presences in the room.

She went to the room where Madeleine was sitting on the side of her bed. She closed the door behind her, stood with her back to it. She said "I kept asking myself 'Why gym?' Stand up."

Madeleine got up more quickly than Lydia thought she would, as if glad that Lydia was there at last as the agent of authority.

"Take off that dress."

Madeleine lifted the dress, which rose like a large bell above her, halted a moment while she struggled out of it. She tossed it onto the bed, then stood in her slip waiting.

"The slip too."

The slip rose, the face which emerged a moment later beneath it smiling in a way that frightened Lydia. Her fear was not lessened by the fact that the girl looked smaller standing in near nakedness before the large woman. But even so, she stood defiant, even proud. As if now that this moment had come, some part of her was glad to show Lydia what was taking shape inside her.

Lydia crossed the room and sat down in the chair by the window. She put her hand out toward the table, but when she saw it was shaking, she lay it in her lap instead.

Madeleine had never seen her mother so at a loss. It was a moment of satisfaction for her. She sat back down on the bed to watch her. She respected her for a moment when she saw what effort it took her to regain control.

"How long has it been?" Lydia asked.

"Five months."

"My God! And your father knew all this time?"

"He knew. I told him."

And hid away from it, Lydia thought, in the attic. As if by hiding he could make it not have happened. She said "How did this madness get into my house? Who brought it here? Who's the father?"

Madeleine was silent.

"You won't tell me his name?"

"I won't tell you anything. You can do what you want to me, I'll do whatever you say until it's born, but you'll never know who it was."

Lydia got up and went to her and stood over her. If she had not understood the intensity of Madeleine's hatred of her before, she did now. She brought the flat of her hand around with such force that it snapped Madeleine's head back and sent her halfway across the bed. Then she turned and left the room.

Lydia took Madeleine out of school the next day, told them she was sending her out west for a while to live with one of her brothers. Then she restricted her to the house, withdrew her, in fact, from the world.

She did not take Madeleine at her word that she would submit to her will during the term of her pregnancy. She let her keep her robe, slips, underwear and nightgowns but took the rest of her clothes and locked them away in the old stable. She confined Madeleine to her room most of the day.

(Later Emil came across her unexpectedly in the hall one night, on her way to the bathroom. Not in her robe or a slip or even underwear, but naked. He turned out of his bedroom doorway and, before he realized it, was facing her. What he remembered later, what horrified him and persisted in recollection even though he tried to rid himself of it, was the bowl of swollen flesh thrust forward toward him, the thick dark womanhair below it, she standing there not in her own shame but certain of his and that it would then be conscripted into permanent memory. Another time she came out of her room and stood at the top of the stairs, one hand on the railing and wearing only panties and brassiere: a figure of dishevelment, which was intended to shock. She shifted her swollen belly so that it came to rest against the top banister, then rubbed it against it in a slow rhythmical movement intended to resemble an act of lovemaking. When Emil came into the parlor out of the kitchen and saw her, he stopped and, despite his disgust at the sight of it, his desire to flee it, stood watching for seconds before turning away. He complained to Lydia about it later but was unable and in part unwilling to express his true feelings, so that her response was "She is shameless; now let her be shamed." But it was he who was shamed, who could not rid himself of the picture of that daughter who was like a specter haunting the hallway waiting for him.)

Lydia had stopped asking questions of Madeleine, for she knew she would not get any answers; there was little communication between them as their relationship evolved into a series of silent conformities, an acquiescence on both their parts, that was like a truce observed in which there was no mention of former hostilities. But Lydia needed no answers now that she accepted what she knew was inevitable, and had set her mind on a course that would accommodate itself to inevitability.

She had gone to see Arthur Cooley first, not to seek his advice, for she could not admit even to him so blatant a failure, but to seek from him a general reparation, which might strengthen her for the ordeal ahead. But he who before had seemed to her a paladin of faith now offered her platitudes that she knew even he found unconvincing, ineffectual. He was withdrawn, like someone who was looking at shadows. Toward the end of her visit he had begun talking wildly to her: about young men dying, about how only those who exposed themselves to their greatest fear before the eyes of others could know true salvation.

So Lydia returned home in doubt. She doubted for the first time her ability to control those events that were threatening her. She had to bring Madeleine's pregnancy to conclusion herself and in secret, then give the child up for adoption in another city or state. There were books on the subject in her mother's trunk—old, thin books passed down in her family. A doctor in the neighboring town of Lebanon who had been a friend of her father's would supply what additional information was required.

She had decided not to trust anyone with the secret: not those agencies that provide services for adoption, nor her lawyer, who would advise her in the matter later.

But now she wondered if she was equal to a task that before would have been accomplished by a will so imbued with confidence that it would have considered the thing done at the moment the idea was conceived. She felt that in some way Arthur Cooley's equivocations had infected her; that the hard edge of certainty that had served her so well in the past had been blunted by him.

■ ■ ■

Lydia did not hear about it until it was over. How on Thursday night a week later Arthur had gone to a park in the city, which was empty except for a few people. How he had sat down on a bench next to a young man. He had said "My name is Arthur. Are you waiting for someone?"

She heard how the young man, who was a police vice officer, said that after a few minutes of conversation Arthur had suggested they go to a place behind the bushes, which the officer did in the performance of his assignment. He said that Arthur had gotten onto his knees in front of him. When he had attempted to perform an act of oral sodomy on him, the officer had arrested him.

She heard that at the police station he had given his name, address and occupation without hesitation but had declined to make a phone call and was released on his own recognizance pending trial.

Leaving the courtroom, he had been approached by a reporter and a newspaper photographer. They had gone down the long hallway with him, the reporter questioning him, the photographer taking pictures, but he had kept silent at the reporter's questions and had tried to hide his face from the photographer. He had hurried out of the building and into a taxi.

She heard how at noon he had registered under his own name and address at the Apollo Hotel, an old, cheap four-story hotel near the center of the city where he had not been questioned about the fact that his only luggage was a paper bag.

She heard that they had discovered later that the bag had contained a pack of razor blades and a length of nylon rope purchased in a hardware store. There had been no sign that he had brought food to the room, nor had he left the room for the nineteen hours he had been there. Found on the night table were a book of matches and what remained of a package of cigarettes, with which the police concluded he had inflicted the forty-two burn marks over all of his body, although the other occupants on the floor had not heard a sound from his room. The only blood in the room was on the windowsill, a radiator and the floor in front of the open window where he must have stood with the rope already fashioned as with one of the razor blades he sliced his penis from his body. The police found it on the floor beside the window.

The police theorized that he must then have sat on the windowsill, for his hind parts were bloodied too, the sill smeared where it traced his path off it, the rope leaping upon it as it followed him down.

He fell two stories before the rope fastened at one end to the radiator and at the other end in a noose around his neck jerked him to a halt. The force of his fall lifted one end of the radiator, pipe and all, off the floor and part of the way over the windowsill, where it lay like an accomplice leaning over the ledge, looking down. It held him there in its silver fingers.

First light revealed him to a deserted street. Not a soul was there to see him as he must have hung for a while like a marionette dancing against the dark face of the building; he was still by the time the shadows lifted and the first person came upon him, an old woman come early to scavenge and who was stilled too at the sight of such a display two stories above her.

A crowd of the poor, who seldom protest even so aberrant a work as that when presented in the public domain, soon gathered at the station of the rag lady on the sidewalk opposite the hotel. They looked but they did not speak, and not one offered to intercede in the shame of the figure now slathered in the silver light of morning, hanging with its mouth open, head tilted into its chest and eyes wide, as if looking down in astonishment at the dark menstrual flower blooming in its groin.

It was the hotel night manager who came out finally to see what had attracted that silent crowd, then turned back into the hotel at the sight of it and called the police.

They arrived minutes later, then stopped and looked up at it, silent too except for a whispered "My God!" from one of them before they rushed up to the room. There in the window they looked to the crowd like new players uncertain of their roles, until one of them leaned over and took hold of the rope and, as mute as an acolyte performing a ceremony, hoisted him like a bell.

Lydia went to church Sunday morning, but the doors were closed. Others had gathered outside, some of whom had read about it in the papers (first the story and photograph of his arrest in the Saturday evening editions, then of the suicide Sunday morning), others of whom had talked to the widow and the police who arrived at her house that morning. They had come to the church anyway to gather at the only site available at which they could display their emotions, exchange information and touch the source of mysterious misery and helplessness they felt in the presence of so inexplicable a tragedy. They needed to understand in some way that such things happen within a plan.

They lingered. They seemed reluctant to leave that pristine building whose doors had always held behind them the answers to mysteries. Those doors which, when open again, they had need to believe, would answer this one too. Only Lydia left promptly when there was nothing further to learn. She heard what there was to hear and, as if there was no mystery for her, departed without comment and no display of emotion. She left behind with them—although they were too preoccupied at the time to realize it—a mystery of her own.

She resigned her membership and position of deaconess in the church the next morning by letter, but without stating a reason. She refused to come to the phone later when called about it. She drew around her a wall of silence that even those least familiar with her realized could not be penetrated. Arthur Cooley's death had reaffirmed for her that compromise was already failure, and that the only mystery was silence.

The night before Madeleine gave birth, Emil made love to Lydia for the first time in over a year. When it was over, he lay facing her. He put his arms around her. She could feel him trembling. Then he lifted his leg over her and drew himself up her body as if seeking to merge with it or find a place where he could climb into it and disappear.

"What are you doing?" she said. "What's wrong?"

She looked past him, eyes wide.

It was Emil who heard Madeleine calling the next night. He lay awake beside Lydia as the girl's voice grew louder, more insistent. He tried not to hear it, but then she called out to him—"Daddy!"—and the word crucified him.

He did as Lydia had instructed him, served at his twin stations in the kitchen and at Madeleine's bedroom door; but when Madeleine gave birth at four in the morning, he was not there. He listened to the long silence and then the strong cry of his child announcing itself to the world, but when later he heard Lydia's heavy step on the stairs bearing the infant down to him, he fled the house and rushed into the woods, where he took up his station among other tenants of the night.

Lydia looked at the open doorway through which Emil had fled. She held the child in her arms, wrapped in a thin blanket. It had wrinkled fingers, a misshapen skull, the fierce face of a gnome. Not a sound came from it, nothing after its one annunciatory cry. It bore no resemblance to Madeleine nor to anyone she knew. It might have been a shrunken soul come back out of hell, and it clung to her as if she were its true mother.

She stood in the kitchen doorway looking at the open door, the chair fallen to the floor. There was a doll on the table.

She went to the table and stood looking down at it, a type of cheap plastic doll she had seen at carnivals and fairs. It held clumps of earth in its clenched fists, clusters of sand and bits of leaves in its matted hair. Its dress was soiled and torn. One side of its face was caved in as if it had been dealt a blow with a heavy object, and it lay on its back looking up at her out of one terrible crooked eye. Something buried and dug up again hastily much later.

She took the doll and went to the door and in the light of the kitchen held it out as if introducing it to the night.

Emil watched her from behind a tree.

"Your father has run off. Tell me why he would do that." Lydia stood over Madeleine where she had been dozing in bed. Madeleine opened her eyes.

"And left this behind" Lydia said, tossing something onto the bed beside Madeleine.

For an instant Madeleine thought Lydia had flung her dead baby at her. Then she saw that Lydia was still holding her child; the thing that lay with its plastic hand on the sheet over her breast was a doll. "What do you want now?" she asked. "What more do you want from me?"

"The truth, for a change. What is the meaning of that monstrous toy? Your father is frightened, girl. There is something he wants me to know but is afraid to tell me, so he left that behind. That's his way."

Madeleine lifted the doll to look at it. She lowered it slowly. "Go away" she said. "I'm tired of both of you."

"I will know what has been happening in this house, what I have been kept from knowing. I will know now."

"Ask him. Ask him, then."

"He knows who the father is?"

Madeleine began to laugh.

"God will damn you for your perversity" Lydia said.

"Your God's not real. You're alone, too."

She had brought Madeleine's old crib down from the attic to their room, put the sleeping child in it and gone to sit in her rocker in the still and quiet early June morning. She had left her bedroom door open so she could hear the child if it cried. She was waiting for Emil's return.

She could feel him out there. One of the shadows, waiting. Watching her.

She had suspected the truth for days. Perhaps even from the beginning it had been a dim suspicion but, until now, not one she had been willing to face; she wanted to believe there were things of which not even Emil was capable, when she of all people knew he was capable of anything. She had hoped Madeleine would provide her with some indication of his culpability at the sight of the doll; now only he could.

He returned at dawn. She heard him come in through the kitchen, go up to the attic. He came not stealthily but not announcing himself either, accepting what was and could not now be changed. He was telling her he was ready.

She went to the bedroom and picked up the child in its blanket, then climbed the stairs to the attic with it.

He was standing at the high window. Shoulders bent, head bowed, there was a strange delicacy about him there in the pale and diffusive light. She remembered nights in bed with him after lovemaking when in the darkness he had questioned her about what it was like to be a woman, and her feeling then that if he had had a choice in the matter, that is what he would have chosen to be. She had understood even then his need to reveal that about himself to her, and that with no other would he have felt that need and the confidence to confide it. Too often, she decided, she had allowed her understanding of him to cloud her judgment.

She switched on the overhead light, and in the glare of it the child opened its eyes and looked at Emil from a skull that formed a plateau on one side slightly below the other. Emil turned to them, and Lydia raised a corner of the blanket, revealing the child's foot, the toes intertwining. "Deny it" she said.

He did not.

"Damn you" she said. "Damn you to hell."

He raised his arms to her in a gesture of supplication. "Save me, Lydia" he said.

She expected to see the fear in his face, but what she saw too was complete surrender to her at last.

"Kneel" she said. "Pray with me. *Pray with me, I say.*"

When she brought the infant in to Madeleine the next morning for its feeding, she said "The child must have a name." She motioned to Madeleine, who lowered the top of her nightgown, and laid the child beside her, directing its mouth to Madeleine's breast. It held the breast with one hand and sucked voraciously.

Madeleine turned her head away. "I don't care what you call it" she said.

"She's as thin as a willow branch. I'll name her Willow."

"No. Not Willow. No more willows. No more weeping."

"Willa, then."

15

The three questions that bothered Willa the most were: Why did her mother disappear the third time? Where did she go? And why was she never heard from again?

She thought she knew why Madeleine had left the first time, gone off to the city. It was not, she knew now, because she had loved Orlo Haines and wanted to be with him; he had only been the means by which she escaped the old woman. She reasoned that if her grandmother had done half the things to Madeleine that she had done to Willa, Willa did not blame her for wanting to disappear so that she could never find her. She understood now from what Mary had told her that Madeleine was not as strong as Willa. That she was trusting, whereas Willa had been taught by the old woman that there was much evil in the world and that one must be on guard against it. Madeleine had allowed the old woman to know what she thought and felt, whereas Willa had learned early that the only way to deal with her grandmother was not to reveal anything to her: to hide from her, keep silent. Because of that, the old woman had thought she was feebleminded, but that was good.

She knew too now why Madeleine had gone off the second time, as if she had created a series of erasures of one life to reappear in another. She understood that by then the only thing Madeleine could trust was the unknown.

But why had she disappeared the third time? She knew this now from Mary: Madeleine had gone into a hospital where they had pronounced her well and released her, and for a while she had lived with Sylvia Rosenberg in another part of the city. Then she had disappeared for the third time. It was as if, in her final act of disappearing, she had miscalculated and erased herself too thoroughly, and now no one knew where she was or what had happened to her.

Willa recalled the time when she was four and her grandmother was telling her about God. Willa had asked where God lived, and her grandmother had told her he lived so far up in the sky that no one could see him. Later Willa went to the woods and climbed as far up in a tree as she could go and searched the sky for hours, but she could not see God. Now she thought that perhaps, in her own way, that was what her mother had been searching for too: the face of God that no one ever sees.

■ ■ ■

Willa was still waiting the next day, Monday, and the day after that. She never left Mary's house, saw no one but Mary, Josephine and the girl, Heather. Willa and Mary talked a great deal—about Madeleine when Willa could hold her to the subject, but mostly Mary talked about her life in the sixties and the people who had been around then and now were nearly all gone. They smoked the thin cigarettes—sometimes with Josephine and Heather, sometimes only the two of them—and Mary reentered her past. It was as if Mary's life existed for her now in that one time, only among those people.

Of the four of them, only Josephine had been there too, but she never spoke about it. Heather seldom spoke at all. She was like a pet to Mary: an object for Mary to fondle, happy just to be in Mary's presence. Willa was certain that Mary forgot Heather when Willa was with her. It was only Willa that Mary invited into her past.

Mary had Josephine buy Willa new clothes: white dresses, white slacks, white sweaters and a white and gold serape. White belts, white shoes, white scarves and a white beret. Josephine put them in the closet in Willa's room, where Willa saw them hanging with such an erect and exclusive air about them that it was as if they were awaiting someone of importance to occupy them.

"Mary expects you to wear these while you're here" Josephine told Willa, and Willa nodded. In the short time she had been there, she had come to feel a need to please Mary.

A box of exotic metal jewelry appeared on her bureau later, accompanied by a note from Mary asking her to wear it with the new outfits. Willa had observed earlier that much of the communications to the other two residents of the house came in the form of handwritten notes from Mary. The servants—a cook and a cleaning woman who arrived in the morning, worked unobtrusively and quietly and left in the evening—seemed to receive most of their instructions in the form of notes too.

Quiet, if not silence, seemed to be demanded of everyone in the house: the only time Willa had heard music was at the party Sunday night. Nor were there any other living creatures present: no pets, tropical fish, or caged birds heard singing. Mary did not allow flowers in the house. No clocks. No calendars. No newspapers or magazines. When the only phone with an outside line rang, it rang distantly in the upper room on the far side of the house that Josephine used as her office.

Willa had come down Monday night dressed for the first time in the new clothes Josephine had selected for her and laid out on her bed: white slacks, a white blouse and white loafers. She wore a replica Aztec mandala on a long chain around her neck. Josephine had put makeup on her and combed out her long hair in a style in which she had never worn it before.

Mary was waiting alone for her in the living room. She was sitting in the tall throne chair. She motioned Willa to the smaller throne chair beside her and lit one of the thin cigarettes from a silver box on the table next to her. She offered one to Willa, and they smoked in silence for a while.

"We're making progress trying to find Madeleine" Mary said finally, "although I would prefer not to tell you anything until we have definite information. I don't want to raise any false expectations."

"Yes, ma'am."

"Please, call me Mary."

"OK, Mary."

"I want us to be friends, even after this ordeal for you is over."

"Actually, it hasn't been so bad—except for the first night I came here, I mean."

"What happened that night?"

"I was scared, Mary. I mean, I never realized until then what it was really like to be alone. I was scared of the city. Of people. Of everything. I was sure someone was following me, and I couldn't find a place to stay—until I met this strange boy."

"He directed you to a room?"

"Not exactly. You see, the rooms on his street were shut down for the night, so I made this deal with him to sleep in his room for that night."

Mary had been lifting the cigarette to her lips; now she stopped short. "What sort of deal?" she asked in a voice forced low—to hide something, Willa realized, that Mary did not want her to know she was feeling. Willa was fascinated by how the cigarettes made her observe and understand things, enabled her to detect hidden meanings—thoughts behind the actions and words of others—that would have gone unnoticed at other times. She was aware that Mary, Heather and Josephine were able to do it to her, too. Like talking without words. It was most intense between her and Mary, more sporadic, less meaningful, with Josephine and Heather. Even objects had a living quality to them.

Mary asked the question again. "What kind of deal did you make with this boy?"

"Well, you know how boys are, Mary—always wanting to do the thing. I figured that if they'd pay money for it, it should be worth at least one good night's sleep."

Willa watched as the hand that was not holding the cigarette curled up on the wooden arm of her chair. It looked like a large, pale spider poised there. When she was able to bring her attention back from the spider, she continued. "But what happened was I fell asleep, I was so tired, and he slept in this rocking chair he has."

The hand relaxed; the spider disappeared.

Willa said "Mary, tell me some more about my mother."

"Madeleine—watched. Everyone else—talked. She seldom spoke. I remember my first impression of her: proud but vulnerable. A beautiful girl who could be easily hurt. She had a strong, noble chin, but her dark eyes revealed deep pools of sorrow. I wanted to protect her. I would have if she had let me."

"Where did you first meet her?"

"I was there at the High Note the night she came in with Orlo Haines. And the second time too, when Chatto Hoffman not only took her away from Orlo, but ran him out of the neighborhood."

"How did he do that? Was he bigger than Orlo?"

"It wasn't that. There were other men around who were bigger and stronger—rough men capable of great violence—who were afraid of Chatto. What Chatto had that frightened others was that he didn't fear death, and in order to beat him you would have had to kill him. He had the kind of will that inevitably dominates, a belief in himself that turned stronger men into cowards. Genghis Khan, Caesar, Alexander the Great must have been like him. Had he believed in anything else but himself, he might have become a great man. He was smarter than any of the others around, although he usually tried to hide it. Chatto, I came to understand later, had evolved from whatever early influences shaped him into someone who did not respect anything or anyone. But he could be very charming when he wanted to. Women were crazy about him; and he understood things about women that only other women are supposed to know."

"And my mother loved him?"

"Your mother was drawn to his flame."

They smoked on. Willa watched little smoke children appear in the air. She leaned forward to see them better, but was brought back by the suspirance of Mary's caftan as she shifted her body. Willa saw the outline of Mary's legs beneath the silk: twin pillars of stout flesh, thighs that could have straddled the large chair. She saw behind Mary's face the face of the pretty girl she had once been. She had recently, but inexpertly, painted her lips a bright red. They hung there like butterflies caught in dough.

"Have you thought about what you will do if you find that your mother is dead?" Mary asked.

"She's not dead. She can't be." Willa shook her head vigorously.

"Just remember, if that turns out to be the case, you always have a home here."

Heather entered with a bottle of wine and four glasses on a tray. She wore a much smaller but otherwise identical version of Mary's caftan. She poured the three of them wine and sat down on the floor at Mary's feet. She leaned her head back against Mary's leg. "It's cook's day off" she said. "Jo's ordering pizza." She spoke to Mary, ignoring Willa. Although she had been friendly to Willa at Madeleine House, she had ignored her since she had come to stay at Mary's.

Heather was a delicate, thin girl a few years older than Willa. Willa had tried to be friendly with her again, but without success. There was a quality about her that seemed to say that she had seen and done things that made her forever a stranger to girls like Willa. It was obvious she idolized Mary. Now Willa felt the beginnings of jealousy, the need to compete with Heather for Mary's favor. For the first time since the search had begun, there were long stretches of time when Willa did not think of her mother at all.

The cigarette was passed around, and Willa began drifting off again. She had spent most of the morning and part of the afternoon sitting in that same room watching television. No one else in the house ever watched it, but it was there: a color console the size of a refrigerator, sitting with its blank eye watching her now. The box at the Little America Café had been a source of excitement to her; but this morning and afternoon, as she watched program after program, a feeling of unreality had come over her. It was as if the box, having lured her with the promise of revelations, now with its sameness had ceased to reveal anything. Now, as it sat there silenced, only a gray eye at the other side of the room watching her, she found that it had the same attraction for her whether it had pictures on it or not.

Mary's voice brought her back. "Do you know what the ultimate loneliness is, Willa?"

"I don't think so, Mary."

"Then let me tell you about it, for I was once in the presence of it. When I first came to the city I lived in an old run-down hotel called the Apollo, which has since been demolished. It was a place for outcasts, miscreants, and those whose dreams had died. I was very poor, had little money for diversions or entertainment, and so I spent much of my time in my small room with only a wooden chair to sit on by the window and the bed to lie on. One early morning I awoke to a tapping on the other side of the thin partition between my room and the next. Then a woman's voice spoke to me through the wall. 'Are you listening? Are you out there listening to me?' it asked.

"I didn't answer, I just lay there awake, waiting, until the voice came again. 'Yes. You are there' it said. 'You are listening. I know it. I can feel you through the wall. Listen, then, and save me. Hear me and save me.'

"I knew there was no sense complaining to the manager, for it was the sort of hotel that tolerated madness and little derelictions, perhaps even encouraged them, and so I turned over in bed and tried not to listen.

"Then the voice came again. It said 'So you've turned away from me too, like the others. But you cannot escape me, as they have always done. I will not let you. For I'm through with all of that finally, with those who run from me because they are afraid of what I can tell them. But you—you are here with me in this night, a captive of this night too, and you will hear me.'

"'Do you know what loneliness is?' she asked. 'You think that you do, as do others in their pretty conceits, but you don't. Do you know about the scream that has no sound? The night that does not end, follows you even in the bright light of noon? Sits with you among the deep riches of day's perils? Can you even define loneliness truly? You will say that loneliness is the absence of love. But you know nothing until you understand that real loneliness is the result of unending and consuming love; that which is rather than that which is sought. So listen to me, because I can give you what God cannot.

"'This room is a coffin' she continued. 'We live here in coffins, side by side. I am lying in my coffin now, my head near to yours, our bodies so close we could touch if it were not for this wall. We are both entities in the same night, but my segment of night has engulfed me.'

"I shifted in bed, impatient, annoyed, knowing that if I answered her, acknowledged a connection between us, it would only encourage her to go on. She was speaking to me, I could tell, with her mouth close to the wall.

"'I have chosen you' she said. 'Yes, chosen. I watched you the other day as you were going out; before that I listened to you alone in your room; and so, like God, I chose you. Like God with the prophets, I have taken a chance on you.'

"'You may be my last hope of salvation' she said. 'For you see, I have been to the priests, listened to their lies, let the doctors put their white hands on me. I have wandered the halls of false felicities, listened to the agony of others all around me, heard the nurses tiptoeing, silent, afraid too. They put me into their thunder machines, sent lightning bolts screaming through my brain, probed me with minds that are like hungry hounds out of hell, looked to find me among calibrations on long tongues of paper licking out at me; sent me finally screaming away from them inside my skull—and learned nothing. They could not help me; left me with only their wet fingertips tingling on my skin, their handprints forever roaming all over me. My parents could not help me; they took me out, and then when they went off on their travels, put me away again. And when I was grown and began to scream, they could not endure it, and so they began putting me away and taking me out all over again.'

"She stopped. I waited: nothing. After a few minutes I turned over in bed and looked at the wall. Then her voice came again. 'I am tired now' she said. 'I must sleep.' After a while I went back to sleep.

"The tapping woke me again hours later. It was nearly daylight. Then her voice came, asking 'Are you listening to me? Are you still there? Does the world whirl around you too? I have watched you, studied you through the crack in my door when you were in the hall, listened to you while I crouched here by this wall like a secret wind expecting you; and I have decided that you are the one who can save me. For you see, I am the lover of Jesus.'

"She was silent for minutes, but I knew she was still there with her face pressed to the wall, her fingers exploring it. I could see our shared light at the window; the city had crawled off into silence. My hands and my feet seemed to have grown as heavy as large rocks. I spoke to her for the first time; I whispered 'I'm listening.' I even pressed my hand to the wall. And at that moment she spoke.

"'I am a big woman like you' she said to me. 'And like all big women, I have a voice inside me telling me I am ugly, even though a glance in a mirror shows me to be a woman of rare beauty. As a girl I was big too, much larger than my friends. Later, in the convent school my parents sent me to, I towered over the other girls and was even taller than most of the nuns. I always felt ungainly, more like a man in disguise than a girl among them. I used to daydream that I was so tiny I could hide under rocks. When I lived at home, my family had a speedboat. I used to race it out into the heart of the ocean just so I could feel small there. But then, then, then, they sent me away. They sent me to that place of the big flapping birds, the place of obedience, where silence is ordained. There were statues of Jesus all around us: in the hallways, in the dining room, dripping like stains off the walls behind our beds. They had us on our knees praying to him day and night. When I was twelve, he became my lover. I found passion for the first time with him.

"'I seduced him; I made him a slave of my love those first years. He was not a man then, but a boy of my own age: slender, graceful, too shy to be the aggressor in the love games I was beginning to invent for us. He came to me the first time, head bowed. He stood off from me. He knew I was evil. But still he stood there, sending waves of innocence out to me to inspire me. How could I help but desire him?

"'I had him sit down next to me on that hill. I could feel him trembling. I whispered to him words of passion; then I took his hand and drew him back down beside me. "Don't be frightened" I told him. "I am the teacher now."

"'Oh, he was so beautiful! So adoring! He trembled like a moth in my arms. "Little Lord Jesus" I said, "love me."

"'It breaks my heart to remember him as he was then in his innocence—wanting me, but afraid too. I gathered his long white robe around me; I lifted it like a curtain and put my hand where no one had ever put it before. I could feel his new manhood pulsing. It grew, crept closer to be near me.

"'He resisted me; oh, yes, he resisted. He raised his head from my shoulder and arched it toward the sky, and his mouth opened wide and a cry leapt from him that was pure agony. He began weeping as, with my hand placed on the back of his head, I lowered his face slowly onto my breast, where after a moment he began to feed on my knowledge.

"'But still he resisted me; his body lay stiff in my arms, bent like an archer's bow away from me. His precious animal shrank from me. "Little Jesus" I said as I moved him gently away from me onto his back staring up at the sky, "I love you. Little Jesus, little Jesus" I whispered as I bent over him and lifted the hem of his robe like a tent over my head. I sought him with my lips in the darkness. His buttocks felt like soft melons in my hands.

"'He resisted me still until the last second, until there was no resistance left in him, until when he cried out the second time it was with joy as he answered my love by growing like a great flower in my mouth.

"'I withdrew and spread myself out before him. I drew him over me. He was still trembling as I led him gently to me. When he entered me I exploded, and then we both became great flowers together.

"'He came to me every night after that. While the other girls slept with their safer dreams beside me, I invoked him to lie down with me. When during the day the sisters said "Jesus loves you" I smiled secretly.'

"She was silent after that for minutes. I thought I could hear her breathing. Then she said 'I can tell you all of this because there is a wall between us. But it has exhausted me. Now I will leave you alone for a while.'

"That night I heard her pacing her room. Back and forth, back and forth. She would stop, mutter to herself, then continue pacing. Her voice came again around midnight.

"'I am lying here in my hair" she said, calmer now. 'This long hair, which falls to below my waist, I have always thought was the only beautiful thing about me; and now as I lie here naked with it wrapped around me I feel like a butterfly safe in its cocoon. It is the color of honey, and it shines in the sunlight. Men have admired it, fallen in love with me because of it. I have wrapped it around them, given them exquisite pleasure with it. It is the only sex I can give them that does not feel like a betrayal of him.'

"She said later 'This hotel for the damned has been waiting for us all the time. Do you hear our screams? Did you think that any of us came here by chance? You are a fool if you do. You do not yet see them, but they are out there in the hallways; the memories that destroy us come knocking at our doors, demanding entry. They may yet call you too to return to this, your last domicile. Hear me. Believe me, for it is the one truth of life.'

"She woke me hours later, proceeding as if no time had intervened, and as if only she and I were alive and awake in the world. 'Jesus matured with me' she said. 'He became a man when I ended my days as a girl. Several times I tried to live without him. I took lovers briefly; I was even married once for less than a month. But none of them could satisfy me. I would lie with them pretending passion and then get up and go into the bathroom, where he was waiting for me.'

"She stopped. I waited. Then I heard her pacing the room again. Faster. Faster still. Then she stopped. She went back to the bed and lay down. I heard her say, as if to someone in the room, 'Come. Lie down with me. She will not mind.'

"I could hear them making love in the bed next to me on the other side of the wall. I could hear her passion building, her cries, the words of love. The bed sang in its frenzy. I heard her call out his name.

"'I've been walking the streets at night' she said later 'around this forsaken hotel. I put on dark glasses and wear a large hat that hides my face, so that people will not recognize me. And all I see is emptiness, death and deep sorrow. People whisper to me from out of the shadows. I see men and women turned to stone in the alleys. I have taken Jesus from them, so who, then, is there to save them? But despite my disguise, they recognize me. They know that I have the dirt of the ages on me.'

"She did not speak to me again that day, and that night and the next morning I heard the sounds of their lovemaking. Again and again. So many times I lost count. And as it increased in frequency, it increased too in intensity, so that I knew it had gone beyond desire, past pleasure, into some region in which she could no longer separate passion from expiation.

"The next day I stayed away from the room as much as I could. I went for a long walk, sat most of the day in the park. I hungered for sunlight. But as I walked, I saw what she had seen in that part of the city all around the hotel: men and women who had been driven beyond desperation into the living death of acceptance. I stood on the street outside the Methodist mission. They fed them there, they took them in, gave them beds for the night. Charity cheated them. It took away their rage and then turned them loose to wander. That was religion's gift to them, I understood then, as I listened to them singing hymns, heard the minister promise them Jesus' love and salvation. But love no longer interested them and they needed salvation now.

"The lovemaking stopped the next morning. I heard her pacing the room again, but now calmly. I heard her talking, but now to herself, as if discipline and discourse could bring her back into the world of normal men and women. Around eight o'clock I heard her tapping at the wall. I was standing by the window looking down at the street. But I just stood there, refusing to go to the wall. She tapped again, impatiently, as if knowing where I was and intuiting my resistance to her now. She stopped tapping, but I just stood looking down as a garbage truck came growling down the street, devouring refuse in its jaws as it went.

"The next day I found a job. I determined to leave the hotel the following week, when I had saved enough money. I worked at night in a coffeehouse, waiting tables until midnight. It was a kind of hard work I was not used to, and the first night I fell into a deep sleep as soon as I returned to the hotel and lay down. She woke me minutes later.

"'Don't sleep. Don't sleep' she spoke to me anxiously. 'I have something to tell you.'

"I was exhausted and so I broke my silence and answered her. 'Go away. I'm tired' I said.

"'You don't know what tired is' she answered. She went on. 'I went out last night' she said 'and tried to lie down with the derelicts and winos in an alley. But instead of granting me peace among them, they robbed me and then drove me away. My allowance from the estate comes tomorrow. I'll pay the rent and buy food and then go down and give the rest of the money to them. It is what he would have done had I not taken him from them.'

"She asked me then 'Do you know what happens to the winos the first time the weather turns freezing overnight? No, of course not. You have lived in sanctuaries until now, so I will tell you. It happens each year at the beginning of winter. The police anticipate it, they even look forward to it with pleasure; for I have watched them laughing as they went about it. What happens is this: in the winter the winos drain antifreeze out of cars to drink; those that can afford it buy cans of Sterno, heat it and strain it through cheesecloth into containers. These not only make them drunk but give them the illusion of warmth. The police know this, and so they send out paddy wagons to collect the winos where they have frozen overnight in doorways and alleys. They pick up the stiff carcasses and toss them like driftwood into the open back of the paddy wagons. By late morning the paddy wagons are full of them. I've seen the bodies stacked up there, waiting to be carted away. The children of the city know about it too; I have seen them in the streets playing with the frozen corpses: laughing, happy with their toys of winter. If there is ice on the sidewalk, there is a game the children play: they take a leg of the body and spin it like a top to see who can keep it turning fastest and longest.'

"It was much later that she woke me with her tapping and a single sentence—almost whispered, reverential: 'Today I will go to the maker of graven words, for I know now what I must do, and he can help me.'

"The next night, when I returned from my job, I could see as I approached it in the hall that her door had been left wide open for the first time. I heard sounds—not words, but unintelligible noises and utterances—coming from inside her room. I had intended to hurry past, but what I saw there stopped me. There were about a dozen derelicts crowded into her small room; and in the middle of them—the object of their attention—was the tall woman sitting naked in a chair in the center of the room. She had placed a floor lamp next to the chair, the shade tilted to direct the light on her. At first I could only see her face and part of her upper torso, legs and arms; for a half-dozen of the men—and several of the women too—were gathered around her. An old derelict in rags and a toothless wino stood on each side of her fondling her breasts as if they were not connected to her; another man stood excitedly working his erect penis back and forth in her cupped hand; a woman was leaning across the others, kissing her. The rest pushed and shoved for a position around her, and an old man with one arm was on his knees in front of her, inserting a finger into her. Then the women went behind her and she moved in the chair, and I saw her full-length for the first time. The long hair she had spoken of hung nearly to the floor, covering part of her naked body, while a midget sat in her lap kissing it.

"I was about to turn and rush off when she saw me. She turned toward me, and it was then that I saw the large words tattooed across her chest: *Crucify me.* She held my eyes for seconds, smiling. Then she raised her free hand and with it signaled to me to enter.

"I fled the hotel and went to an all-night movie theater. I sought comfort and soft anodynes in the darkness. But there were none. For they were there too: those—her—people. They roamed the shadows of that cheap theater, crouched, silent except for their breathing, going from one to another on their insatiable feasts. Silence was required, obviously, but now and then a muffled cry went up among them which had more in it of pain than of pleasure. But even so, I stayed, sitting hour after hour hiding in the darkness as I watched Doris Day and Rock Hudson make a comedy of desire on the screen.

"When I returned to the hotel around dawn, her door was closed; all was silent. I fell onto my bed fully clothed and plunged into the darkest, deepest sleep I have ever known.

"I awoke later that morning to see a large crow drop like a bullet onto my windowsill. It screamed at me through the glass. It beat its wings against the pane. It had gone mad and wanted to get in. I lay there terrified, praying that the glass would not break.

"Everything dies, but nothing ends. I left the hotel the next day—I had met Big Brown the pimp and moved in with him. He began to teach me his trade, but because my time at the Apollo Hotel had taught me things about the depth of human need and the unobserved darkness in all of us, I was light-years ahead of him already. There was a message about love delivered to me in that hotel, but by the time I received it, it was too late.

"It was a week later that I read about her in the papers; the people of the neighborhood spoke of little else for days, for because of the prominence of her family the newspaper and television coverage was extensive, the sensational elements of the story played up much more than they would have been had she been just another of those faceless ones among whom she had chosen to live.

"The hotel manager had found her murdered in her room. She had been strangled and her breasts had been cut off. A butcher knife had been buried to the hilt in her vagina. Most puzzling—to everyone but me—was that her hair had been cut off and left in a box on the floor.

"The night after the murder the crow appeared again—but this time on the windowsill outside Big Brown's bedroom. It stared at me with eyes glistening like stars. Then, flapping its big wings, it flew off, calling to things in the night."

There was a long silence as Mary finished her story. A cigarette went around again. Willa watched Mary's hand reaching out. It began weaving messages in Heather's hair.

Mary's story had terrified her. She looked up at Mary. Then Mary opened the lid of the silver box and took out a handful of the cigarettes. She gave them to Willa. "For later" she said, "if you want one when I'm not here."

Willa almost cried with gratitude for the thoughtful gift. She put them into the pocket of her blouse. "Thanks, Mary" she said. "You've been awful good to me."

"You're safe here" Mary said. "You're among friends now."

Heather spoke to Willa for the first time since they had met at Madeleine House. "Mary has hundreds of friends. People she's helped and who love her. She cares for people nobody else wants. I'd have been dead on the street if it hadn't been for her and Madeleine House."

Willa was grateful she only had Heather to share Mary with now.

Mary said "Heather, dance for me. Show Willa how beautifully you dance."

Heather got up and walked off a few paces. She did not move for a long time; she looked like a statue. Then her arms came out from her sides. They lifted. They began rising and falling slowly. Eyes closed, without music, Heather began dancing slowly, gracefully, in place. She did not move from the spot on which she was standing, although she now and then turned around in a full circle, and several times her knees bent and she lowered her body nearly to the floor and then up again. Her head tilted back and rotated slowly, pivoting on her slender neck; then it moved back and forth like a pendulum from shoulder to shoulder. She lifted one leg up—and down; then did the same with the other leg. She was smiling. She looked like someone dreaming a wonderful dream. It was to Willa a strange and beautiful dance—and she knew that the strangeness was part of its beauty.

The dance ended and Heather returned and sat on the floor again at Mary's feet. She leaned her head back again against Mary's leg. Willa watched as Mary's fingers crept in Heather's hair.

Mary turned her face toward Willa. Her eyes were barely visible, half-sunken in flesh. They were quiet eyes, imperturbable, confident. She said "Would you dance for me too, Willa?"

Willa arose and went to the spot Heather had vacated. For a minute she just stood there. She felt light as air, buoyant as water. Then she too raised her arms, but straight above her head. She lowered her arms slowly, fingers fluttering as if to describe leaves descending. She rose onto her toes, then down again, a dozen times. She began to sway like a frail tree in the wind. She tiptoed yards away, then back, like high-stepping birds she had once watched in the woods. She walked around in a circle, turning circles as she went. Arms out at her sides, rolling gently, bending and unbending at the waist in place, she became a large bird drifting on currents of air. Her arms lowered and she began leaping slowly around the room.

She returned to her chair, where she waited for Mary's reaction. Mary smiled at her. It was like warm waves going through her. "That was lovely, Willa" Mary said.

"Thanks, Mary."

"Will you dance for us again sometime?"

"Sure, Mary."

"We'll be looking forward to it."

"Me too. It's nice to have friends, Mary."

Mary smiled at her, and she smiled back. Then she sat watching as Mary's fingers began stroking Heather's bare arm. Seconds later Heather's eyes closed, her head fell back; it was ecstasy she was feeling. Willa shifted uneasily in her chair, then slid to the floor and took up the opposite station against Mary's other leg. Mary's hand came forward and began massaging the muscles on the back of Willa's neck, and Willa sighed.

16

Vernon was at Miller's again just before dusk, because that was when the idea came to him and it was the only store nearby open at that hour. He had come to buy the mannequin an overcoat.

He had returned late that morning from watching Mary Vandel's house, exhausted from his vigil, which had gone into its third day now. Caution had kept him from making another inquiry of anyone in the house, and he was afraid of stretching his luck too far by sneaking behind someone into the highly visible courtyard again. And although he had once caught a glimpse of the girl from the street as she passed a window, she had not emerged from the house since she entered it Sunday night. He was worried about her, and the tension was showing in his nerves.

He had slept through the afternoon, and dreading another period of watching the house from the street, he had decided that periodic checks of her rooming house would accomplish just as much, with less risk. In the meantime, he had the mannequin to keep him company.

When he went through the door, he saw only a few late shoppers; most of the salespeople stood idle near the aisles. Their eyes turned to him. Hiding his face in the collar of his overcoat, he hurried down the aisle and through the wide doorway, above which were the words Women's Wear.

He felt relieved that neither of the two salesladies there—an elderly woman facing the doorway and a younger one leaning across the counter unpacking boxes of gloves onto it—were the ones who had waited on him before.

The older woman came toward him. She was smiling, and the fact that Vernon did not return her smile did not seem to diminish her good humor. She was a small woman, whose hair was arranged in a high hornet's-nest hairdo that wobbled as she walked. Vernon stared at the hair as it came closer. The hair stopped, swaying slightly, inches from him. Then it tilted away as the woman looked up at him. He stared down at her.

"I want to buy an overcoat for someone who is this big." He held up his hand to indicate height. "It has to have a big collar. And it has to be long."

"Of course, sir. Do you know her approximate weight?"

He looked at her a moment surprised by the question, unable to answer it. He remained silent, staring down at her.

The woman waited, but when he continued to just stand there looking at her, she said "I mean, is she on the thin side or plumpish?"

"She's just right."

"What color did you have in mind?"

"It doesn't matter."

She smiled broadly as she said "Perhaps not to you, but I'm sure it does to her. What's her coloring?"

"What?"

"Is she dark?"

"She's pink."

Her smile faded. She was struggling to recapture it and speak again when he looked over her head at two rows of overcoats on racks. He pointed at them. "I know what I want" he said, and without looking at her again he brushed past her and went to the two rows. She stood watching his head and shoulders as he moved down the aisle, face turning from one row to the other as he went. Now and then he would stop, then go on.

The woman walked quickly to the younger woman at the counter. Their heads inclined. Then they moved even closer. The older woman's arms went up in the air, describing things. One arm finally pointed at Vernon, whose head they could see bobbing above the coats. The younger woman put aside the box of gloves she had been unpacking and straightened up behind the counter. She nodded at the older woman and went around the counter to where Vernon had come to a halt. He was standing still staring at a coat behind a tab that read "Extra Long." It was the only coat of its kind there and hung nearly to the floor. The woman stepped in front of him, but he continued staring, as if he could see through her.

She said "I'm Miss Perry, sir, the floor manager. Can I help you?"

He pointed around her at the coat, and she stepped aside to look at it. "I want to buy it" he said.

She took the coat from the rack and held it in front of her. It was powder blue with large white buttons to the neck and a wide collar. "It's a special sale item, sir. It can't be returned. It's last year's model."

"I don't care. I want her to wear it anyway."

"Indeed. Do you now? Well, since you're in such a hurry—"

She turned and walked off with the coat, and Vernon started after her. Then he stopped when he saw that in her hurried departure she had brushed by a section of coats, which were now twisting in front of him. They seemed to be signaling him, warning him about something.

The woman appeared again at the head of the aisle. "Sir" she called, "we're closing. Did you want this coat or not?"

Looking back over his shoulder several times, he followed her to the counter, where she put the coat in a bag and began writing up the sales slip. He paid and was about to leave when he saw the gloves on the counter. He picked up a pair of red ones and held them out to her. Despite the fact that he had chosen red gloves to go with a blue coat, she made no attempt to advise him.

He snatched up the bag and, trotting more than running, hurried from the store.

Outside, a tall man with a hooked nose and carrying a Bible approached him. "Jesus is coming" the man said. "Are you ready for him?"

"Not now" Vernon said, and hurried on.

When he got back to his room, it was evening; his landlady was asleep. He took the mannequin from the closet and put the coat on it. He buttoned the coat to the top and turned the wide collar up as far as it would go. He stepped back and tilted the hat over the mannequin's face and fitted the gloves to its hands. Then he carried it down to the car. He placed the mannequin across the front seat, where it came to rest near the passenger door. He locked the door, went around the car to the driver's side and sat down next to the mannequin.

He drove aimlessly for a while, up one busy street and down another—but slowly, and always close to the curb. Several times he drew abreast of pedestrians, as if wanting them to look at him and his passenger. A few did, then looked quickly away, at which moment he drove off and around a corner out of sight.

When he came to a wide intersection he saw a large car even older than his stopped at a red light with an elderly woman in the driver's seat. He pulled up next to it as the small woman sat staring ahead, hands on the steering wheel as if afraid to let go. She had blue hair and wore tortoiseshell glasses attached to a chain around her neck. She was watching the light and did not see Vernon when he leaned across the mannequin to the side window and looked at her. He did not move, just looked. After a moment the woman turned; she smiled at him but did not notice the mannequin in the shadows beside him. The light changed to green, and before she drove off she smiled at him again.

Although Vernon had never been on a date with a girl, he knew in a general way what men and women did and how they conducted themselves on those occasions. So when he saw a large building constructed almost entirely of glass, girls in short uniforms and on roller skates going among the cars gathered around it, and a large neon sign saying Hamburger Castle, he pulled up to it. He rolled down his window and sat waiting.

A moment later a waitress slid up to him on roller skates, wheels screeching to a precise halt. She had to lean down to take his order. Although Vernon was in full view, he knew she could only see the bottom half of the mannequin. The girl wore a hat that looked like a large hamburger with mustard and catsup dripping down its sides. Looking more at the hat bobbing above his eye level than at the girl, who spun the wheels of one of her skates while she waited for him to select from the menu, he finally ordered two hamburgers and two coffees. The girl spun the wheels again, like a race-car driver revving the motor in preparation for departure. "Right" she said, writing in her order pad. "You want everything on them burgers?"

"No onions."

She glanced down to see Vernon holding a gloved hand. "Oh. Right. Coffees regular?"

Vernon looked to his right as if in inquiry. "Yes" he said.

"Gotcha" the girl said and spun off.

While Vernon was waiting, he pulled the top of the mannequin toward him so that it was leaning across the seat, its head on his shoulder. Then he put his arm around it. He waited for the girl to return.

She slid up to the window minutes later and fitted a tray with his order to the side window. He had the money to pay her ready in his left hand, but for the moment he withheld it. "My date thinks you're pretty" he said.

She leaned down slightly, squinting. "Say, thanks a lot."

"This is our first date."

She hesitated before saying "Yeah. Well, have fun."

He placed the bills on the tray and signaled with his hand for her to keep the change. She picked it up and sailed off as if the wind was behind her.

Vernon replaced the mannequin beside the window. He ignored it as he ate both hamburgers and drank both coffees. Then he sat waiting for the waitress to return and take away the tray. She sped by several times but each time ignored him. Then he noticed other car headlights blinking to signal their waitresses, and he began blinking his. They went on and off more slowly than the others.

Minutes later she came sailing up to the window. "Everything all right? You done?"

"Yes" Vernon answered.

She had unhooked the tray and was about to go off when she hesitated. She leaned down to the window, squinting again. "Have a nice time, miss" she said.

"She will" Vernon said.

"Yeah" the girl said, stooping farther, her voice softer, more hesitant now, as Vernon backed out of the spot. As Vernon turned the car toward the exit, the girl saw a portion of face looking back at her beneath a straw hat.

He continued his cruising, but now moving away from the city. When he came to the suburbs and a block of stores, one of which had a sign—Flowers—in its window, he stopped. There were few shoppers there and most of the parking spaces were vacant, but even so he drove around the block where he saw the unlighted delivery entrances at the rear of the stores. He parked the car, locked it, and walked to the flower shop.

He emerged ten minutes later with a small box cradled in his arm. When he returned to the car, he slid across the seat to the mannequin. He opened the box and took out of it a gardenia corsage and pinned it to the lapel of the mannequin's overcoat. When he pulled away from the block, the highway was dark ahead of him except for what looked at first like a fire standing in the sky. It flickered, then faded, then leaped forward again in bright colors. He drove toward it.

He had never been to a drive-in movie before—had not been to any movies in the city except those he had gone to on the street—but he had heard about drive-ins as places where lovers went more for the intimacies the privacy of their cars allowed them than to watch films. Nearing its entrance, he pulled over to the side of the highway and laid the mannequin face down across the floor of the car. Its long coat hid it at one end, while his own coat and legs straddling it covered it at the other. Inside the drive-in, settled in his spot, he placed the mannequin upright again on the seat. He readjusted its arms, fixed the hat, which had come askew, and pulled the collar up again. Then he turned to watch the movie.

It was a feature-length animated cartoon about a deer that looked like a pretty girl and lived with other forest animals. He sat for a while waiting for the sex scenes to begin, but there were none. There were only cute animals talking in high-pitched voices. After a while he became bored and turned away from it to the mannequin.

He lifted the mannequin across the seat to him, tilted its head against his. He turned to it. He undid the top buttons of the coat and placed his hand inside it, over its breast. Then he turned it toward him and kissed it.

He sighed, then turned back to watch the movie again.

"Would you like some popcorn?" he asked it a few minutes later.

He had seen a refreshment stand just inside the entrance, where yellow popcorn bounced in a machine behind glass. Returning to the car after buying a large buttered popcorn, he slowed down as he drew up to it. Then he stopped. He stood motionless beside the rear fender.

A small black boy was beside the front passenger window. Hands grasping the door panel, he was standing on tiptoe looking inside. Only as Vernon's shadow slid forward and fell over him did the boy turn his head reluctantly away from his watching toward Vernon. He lowered himself from the window. "This your car, mister?" he asked.

"Yes."

"What that you got in there?"

"My girlfriend."

"Your *what?*"

Vernon stiffened at the words. Only the box he was holding moved, turning thinner between his fingers from the pressure, popcorn rising in it and tumbling over its sides. The boy turned away from him. He rose again on his toes to the window, looking in. He looked back one more time at Vernon, then smiling and shaking his head as he went, he walked away.

Vernon watched him until he was gone. Mouth opening and closing soundlessly, he seemed to be miming the words coming from the screen.

He drove back toward his rooming house in silence except for the sound of his fist hitting the steering wheel again and again. Now and then he talked to himself. The mannequin swayed gently beside him in shadows.

He did not sneak the mannequin to his room this time; he carried it carelessly into the house and up the stairs, its arms outstretched over his shoulders behind him, pedestal hitting the railing as he ascended. It jerked upward at every landing.

When they were inside the room, he opened the closet and pushed the mannequin into it. "You're not her" he said to it. "You couldn't even fool a little boy."

17

An unexpected consequence of Willa's birth was that it brought Lydia and Madeleine closer. It was not the result of two women sharing that experience from which all men are excluded; nor was it the compassion a mother might feel for a young daughter violated within the sacrosanct boundaries of family; nor even an alliance formed in retribution against the transgressor. Emil was exiled not only from Lydia's bed but from their room to his own makeshift quarters in the attic; but even that in Lydia's mind was not retribution or punishment. It was rather that he was now an unnecessary associate whose presence would distract her from what she knew she must do. For the child's deformity and the fact that it displayed few of the emotions of normal infants—seldom cried, was not angry or impatient, never smiled—made it clear to her that it must be kept out of sight of others or its origins would be surmised.

The night after Willa's birth Madeleine had said to Lydia from her bed "I don't want it in here with me." She had refused from the first to call Willa by name, referring to her each time as *it*.

Lydia said "She can sleep in my room. I'll take care of her."

She took Willa to the crib in her room that night, stood over her looking at her. The child's black eyes were open, looking up at her. She knew it would never be among those granted privilege from beauty; what was a signature born in its bone and flesh would mark it as one to whom easy access and easy solutions would be forbidden. Not like Emil and Madeleine, or her own father.

She pulled back its blanket to study the deformed foot, the mis-shapen skull rocking like a buoy on its pillow in its attempts to follow her. A creation imperfectly cast, alone except for her. One who would be solely dependent upon her and whom she could influence and shape. It was then she understood that Willa was her second chance; that dream she had held long ago could be made alive again.

At that moment she became aware of a sense of the room's new dimensions; it seemed larger and emptier. It was not just Emil's absence that made her feel this: something intangible had vanished from the room. It was the dead aspirations, cleared away to make way for a new one. She felt strong again, her mind unencumbered with those considerations that had for so long dissipated her will and resolve. Her focus had been restored and all was clear.

From that night on Madeleine's contacts with Willa were limited to her feedings: Lydia would bring the child to her, lay it at the girl's breast, then sit down across from them waiting for it to finish. Now and then she would reach over and fit Willa's mouth back onto the nipple, which had slipped from it. Madeleine would not have done it, had not once touched her daughter since the night she was born except to nurse her. She was unable to accept such an affront to her womanhood. Alone in that time when childhood usually dies with ceremony, she had no one to guide her to womanhood. If she ignored the child, in time it would go away.

The next morning Lydia fixed Willa's pillow and blanket in a cardboard box and carried it with her wherever she went in the house and grounds. Whenever she put the box down—on the table in the kitchen, on chairs in the other rooms, on the back porch steps or her rocking chair in the front—it was never out of sight. She noticed the child watching her, saw that it was soon following her with its clumsy head, tried even to raise its head to watch her when she moved out of its sight, and knew there was not only curiosity but some intelligence there. She seldom spoke to it, and when she did it was never in the patois in which adults usually address infants, but rather as one adult would speak to another. She felt that she was already informing it by example, that unlike her relations with others, there was no need for words here. All her adult life Lydia had resented the need for words as an instrument of communication; she felt that, unlike actions and deeds, they served more the purpose of obfuscation, deviation and confusion. Like all such people, she attributed these qualities to the speaker and not the inaccuracy with which people use language to express complex feelings and thoughts. Now there would be another in the house for whom words would assume a rightfully minor function.

As the weeks passed, she began to see parts of herself in the child. She gave it an apple to play with.

* * *

Around ten in the evening three months later Emil stood looking out the small window in the attic. It was a large attic, the other end of it windowless and in darkness, the only light from a naked blub hanging by a wire. He had scavenged all of the furnishings from among objects stored in the attic, dust-laden where he found them from a time before he had come to the house. He had fashioned out of them the spare living quarters beside which he stood now: a small cot, a bureau, a table and a single chair underneath the light bulb. He had found an old rocking chair with a broken runner; bringing up his toolbox, he had repaired it, using his tools for the first time in years. He had fixed a broken floor lamp, and running an extension cord into the overhead light socket, he put it next to the chair. He had found under some old clothes a porcelain bedpan still faintly garlanded with painted pink flowers, and next to it a copper pitcher, which now helped keep his drinking water cool. A drinking glass was the only item he had taken from the house proper.

Before placing the furniture, he had scrubbed every inch of the floor and walls of that area he intended to occupy. On hands and knees beside the bucket, he had gone over the floor time after time, uncovering successive layers of dirt until he reached the bare wood. He unwound with a broom a nest of cobwebs from the beamed ceiling. The released walls revealed their original white paint, upon which now, when he moved under the bare light, his broken shadow followed him. Where his labors had ended, walls and floor faded into the dirt and dust of an imprecise demarcation between his new quarters and the rest of the attic, where darkness ruled.

He was not unhappy. He was even relieved to be there. He admitted age and felt it for the first time, and that was a relief too. He knew that Lydia would protect him and he need only live out in peace whatever portion of life was left to him. Hope was no longer a burden.

From where he stood he could see part of the front porch and a section of the woods where the path to the highway entered it. The headlights of cars crept slowly from tree to tree.

He was about to go to his chair to wait until it was time to sleep when he heard the screen door open below, footsteps going down the porch steps. Madeleine appeared in the yard wearing her long overcoat. She had left the house without subterfuge, with no apparent interest in those inside who might hear her. She pulled up her collar and stood for a moment, hands in pockets. A girl like any other pausing to listen to the sounds of night. Moments later he experienced intense emotions again—pain and sorrow—as he watched her move off with long strides carrying no longer the girl but a woman outward.

* * *

The roadside tavern had changed since the last time Madeleine was there. It was brighter, louder, the voices inside coming out to her. There was a busy new neon sign with the words "Rainbow Tavern" crawling across it and a printed sign by the door: "This Week—LIVE JAZZ."

As she passed through the door she saw that tables had been added around the bandstand and there was no dancing. The lights had been turned low, and instead of talking among themselves, the patrons were calling out to the five musicians—four black and one white—in response to their music. The anonymous booths she had previously sat at were taken, and she had hesitated, undecided whether to leave, when she noticed a small vacant table in shadows to the side of the bandstand. She went to it and slid silently onto one of the chairs.

A young waitress wove her way to her, tray high on the column of her raised arm, and although Madeleine turned her head away toward the musicians as she ordered a beer, the waitress did not challenge her to prove her age. Minutes later she returned with the beer, and Madeleine gave her full attention to the band.

The obvious star was a tall, handsome black trumpet player with a short beard and straight hair to his shoulders. When he played solo, he placed his feet firmly apart on the floor, midsection thrust forward and head back, directing his music to the ceiling. As the audience encouraged him with applause and comments, his long fingers moved, dancing on the valves. Madeleine watched fascinated as his polished and manicured fingernails glinted against his black skin in the band's spotlight. He played with his eyes closed, building his passages higher and louder, until at the end, in a frenzy of applause, he turned away and moved off with seeming indifference to his admirers. Madeleine's beer stood untouched through each of his solos.

Three of the musicians—pianist, bassist and drummer—seemed content in their supporting roles behind the more talented trumpet player; they were there for the fun of it, laughing and talking among themselves, drinking from glasses beside them and flirting with the women weaving like cobras to the music at their tables. The fifth member of the band—the saxophonist, a stocky, light-complected black man—did not drink or flirt, looked modestly down as he played and after the lesser applause at the conclusion of each of his solos moved off to wait almost anonymously for his next appearance. His performances were workmanlike; it was clear he had none of the passion and flair that made the trumpet player such a favorite. Unlike the others, who wore casual, brightly colored clothing, he was dressed in a dark suit, white shirt and tie.

She stayed until the band stopped playing at two in the morning, then quickly left. But she was back the next night at the same table. As she had on previous visits to the tavern, she kept her overcoat on, buttoned to the top.

At the end of one of his solos, the trumpet player moved off, indifferent, as always, to the applause; but this time he looked at Madeleine and nodded. She nodded back and smiled. At the end of the set he climbed down from the bandstand and, ignoring the invitations of the other patrons to join them, went to Madeleine's table. He stood over her.

"We been bettin' about you" he said.

"Why?"

"Whether you'd be back."

"I like your music."

"It do seem to get to some people."

She looked up at the pointed irony, but he was smiling. He sat down across from her.

"Let's get us some drinks here. Playing makes my mouth dry." He moved Madeleine's beer aside with the back of his hand, then spoke to the waitress, who had appeared beside him: "Two double bourbons." He watched her move off, then turned back to Madeleine. "I'm Coley Wilson" he said.

"I'm Madeleine."

"Well, Madeleine, after we drink these fine drinks that's comin', I'm gonna play a song just for you."

He played for her fifteen minutes later, this time directing his horn at her.

When he returned to her table after the set she had not taken more than a few sips of her bourbon. She had never tasted liquor before, and the little she drank had made her dizzy.

"You too tense" he said. "You need somethin' to relax you. And I got just the thing. We got a break after this next set. We'll go have a taste then."

She had not intentionally encouraged him, but she did not refuse either. She felt like she was moving implacably in a dream: without will, but without any desire to stop either. Before the next set began she saw him go to the light-complected black saxophone player, who looked over at her as Coley spoke to him. The saxophonist shook his head, as if unwilling to do whatever Coley was asking of him. But Coley persisted, and a minute later the saxophone player took keys on a chain from his pocket and handed them to Coley.

The lights came on at the break, and the musicians climbed down into the audience, where a jukebox had begun playing. When Coley appeared at her table, he did not touch her, he just gestured, and

Madeleine got up and followed him outside. His long black hair looked more like a woman's than a man's and shone in the light of the neon sign as he passed it. With Madeleine still following, he turned the corner of the building and approached a Chevrolet sedan. He unlocked the back door and motioned her inside. Then he got in beside her. In shadows, she could barely see his face and hands.

"Madeleine" he said, "you're a very quiet chick. Most chicks, they come to hear us, they got lots to say."

She did not answer.

"Well, maybe this'll loosen you up." He took a thin cigarette from his pocket and struck a wooden match with his thumbnail; she saw his face clearly in its glare. He took several short, quick puffs, then held it out to her.

"No, thank you" she said. "I don't smoke."

He coughed up part of the smoke laughing. "Baby, this isn't *tobacco.*"

"What is it?"

"You never seen grass before?"

"What?"

"Marijuana."

He offered it to her again. She drew the smoke in, swallowed, but it came back up in a fit of coughing. Her eyes began watering.

"Just a taste at first" he said. "Slow."

She inhaled again, coughed again, but this time managed to keep most of it down. Wiping the tears from her eyes, she handed it back to him. He sat smoking for a few minutes, silent, watching her. Then he put his arm around her. She tensed, but she did not move away. She watched as his shining fingernail flicked ashes onto the floor. His fingers, more than anything else about him, spoke for him. He held the joint between two fingers and brought it to her mouth. She smoked it from his hand.

When he spoke, his voice seemed to come from far away. "We'll save this for later." He pinched out the lighted end of the joint, put the remainder into the ashtray and turned to her. He placed his forehead against hers. Then he began unbuttoning her coat.

"Don't" she said. She tried to pull his hand away, but he was too strong for her. He opened the coat and the fingers went to her blouse.

"Please don't" she said. She turned away from him, but he brought her easily back. The deft fingers had several buttons undone before she could try to push them away.

"Stop that" he said as he pulled the unbuttoned blouse away from her. He slid both hands under the blouse and undid the clasp on her brassiere. "Let me look at your jewels, girl" he said as he lifted the brassiere to her chin. When his fingers went to her breasts, they danced lightly on them. She sighed and leaned her head back against the seat.

"Be gentle" she said. "They're tender." She watched the back of his head as he bent over her, his fingers raising one breast to his mouth. Her hand lifted, hesitated, then descended to stroke his hair. She let her mind drift under the aegis of dreams.

When he attempted to lay her back along the seat, she regained her will. She struggled upright, and with the palms of her hands against his shoulders she was able to push him back. He looked stunned. His expression seemed far away. "Hey!" he said finally. "What you come with me for, if not that?"

"No. I didn't. I didn't" she said and twisted away when he reached for her again. She felt the door against her back.

"Don't you play games with me, girl." He was glaring at her, close to anger.

She began gathering her blouse around her and buttoning it. "I'm not" she said.

"Then what's all this shit you layin' on me?"

She did not answer, but to his surprise she moved back next to him. He let her hold down both his hands at the wrists. Then one of her hands rose onto his leg. Her fingers felt him where he was rigid. She opened his fly and inserted her fingers inside his shorts. "Don't touch me again" she said, "and I'll do this for you."

His mouth fell open and his eyes went wide. He seemed incapable of speech for a moment. Then he jerked away from her. "Shit!" he said, then slapped her.

She fell back against the door, hurting her shoulder. She was too stunned for a moment to cry, to realize anything about what was happening except that he had turned away from her to adjust his clothes. She could hear him mumbling to himself. Then she began crying.

"Shut up!" he said over his shoulder. "Shut your mouth up!" He turned back to her, and she cringed as his hand went past her to the door. He unlocked it and opened it. Then he pushed her out.

She fell onto the gravel lot, still crying. When she heard him get out of the other door and his footsteps on the gravel, she thought he was going to come for her again. She managed to get onto one knee. Then she heard other footsteps hurrying toward them. It was the saxophonist, who confronted Coley behind the car. He looked at Madeleine as she crouched by the fender, then back at Coley. "What did you do to her, man?"

"Get the fuck outa my way" Coley said and started past him.

"You just gonna leave her there? You crazy? You can't *do* that 'round here, man."

Coley hesitated. He looked back at her. Then he put his hand in his pocket. "Oh, shit. Yeah" he said. He tossed the keys to the other man. "Chick's a pervert, you ask me. Here, be my guest." He walked away.

Madeleine and the saxophone player stayed as they were, still and silent, for a moment—she half-risen, watching, afraid. The stocky black man had short-cropped hair, and his hands hung indecisive at his sides: the antithesis of menace. "Be quiet now" he said. "I'm not gonna hurt you. What's your name?"

She did not answer. She began backing away, eyes never leaving him. He moved cautiously toward her. "I just wanna help you" he said.

She was silent, watching him.

"Did he hurt you? Why don't you lie down in the car for a while?"

She remained silent but retreated more slowly as he advanced toward her. Behind her was the end of the gravel lot, and beyond that, the woods.

"Come on now" he said. "You lie down for a while and you'll feel better. I won't bother you."

She finally answered him. "I don't want to. I want to go home."

"Where's your car?"

"I'll get a ride on the highway."

She had stopped retreating, and he stopped too, several feet from her. He took the keys from his pocket and held them out to her at arm's length by the chain. "Look, you go back in my car there and lock the doors. Here's the keys. No one's gonna bother you. Then when we get off, I'll drive you home." He dropped the keys onto the ground and backed away.

She advanced cautiously to the keys. Still watching him, she stooped and picked them up. "He hurt me" she said.

"He won't bother you no more. Go on now. Get some sleep. I'll be back in an hour."

She nodded. He waited until she began to get back in the car, then turned and started to walk away. Her voice stopped him, stronger, no longer afraid.

"What's your name?"

"Orlo Haines." He disappeared around the side of the building.

She got into the car, locked the doors, and lay down on the back seat. She drew her arms and legs inside the coat, then pulled the collar up. She heard the music begin again inside the tavern, distant but clear. After a while it calmed her. Sweet and low, it said.

* * *

The silence woke her. Then objects began detaching themselves from the night. Cars were pulling out around her, headlights swept away. The neon sign went off.

She heard a tapping at the window and saw Orlo gesturing at her. She unlocked the door.

"Are you all right?" he asked.

She nodded and sat up.

"The other musicians're gone" he said. "I waited. I thought you wouldn't want to see Coley again."

She took the keys from her pocket and held them out to him. She saw his hand trembling when he took them from her.

"You can sit back there if it makes you feel more comfortable—or in front with me" he said.

He stepped back farther than was necessary to allow her to get out the door. She smiled at him in passing, but his eyes avoided hers.

He drove her home without any attempt at familiarity. His timidity made her feel in charge. The exaggerated courtesy he showed her was that of one unaccustomed to displaying courtesy.

When he pulled up on the dirt road outside the house, she knew he was waiting for her to leave, and at the same time wanted her to stay. He said finally that he had to get back to the city, where he had a day job in a garage, but if she wanted to they could talk for a while.

He said little at first. She sensed that he was unaccustomed to talking to women and did not know what to say. He was the kind of person who found it difficult to express his feelings and was ill at ease talking about himself. She felt he wanted to say something but had decided finally it would cause her to judge him badly. She asked him questions, and gradually he began to talk more freely.

He was twenty-six, he said, had never married, lived alone. He loved the music, loved to play it, but had nothing in common with the other musicians, no taste for the life they led. He had dropped out of college after one year but hoped to have a better life some day—a good job, a wife, a house of his own. He saved his money.

As she watched him, she saw his hand trembling again. She was turned toward him, but he did not look at her. When he left, she said good night, but he did not respond, did not even look at her before he drove away.

She could not sleep. When she heard Lydia's alarm clock go off, heard her bring Willa to her to be fed, she turned her head away. Lydia shook her shoulder, and Madeleine lowered the top of her nightgown. Lydia fitted the child's mouth to Madeleine's breast, then sat down in the shadows.

Later Madeleine lay awake thinking of Orlo. But when she tried to picture him, all she saw were his hands hanging unremembered at his sides.

She suckled Willa for the last time later that morning; when she told Lydia, she did not object. That night, before Madeleine left the house, she milked her breasts dry for the first time.

■ ■ ■

She appeared at the tavern at one o'clock. It was less crowded at that hour, and she sat in a booth. During the first break Orlo came to her. He stood. "How're you doin', Madeleine?"

"All right, Orlo."

"Maybe you shouldn't've come again. Coley don't like you bein' here."

"I didn't come to see Coley."

"Who, then?"

"You."

She knew he would not act on his own, without encouragement; she knew by the end of that night that he loved her but did not think he was worthy of her. He told her later that he had loved her from the first night.

He was like a hunk of the night; like something that tried to dissolve itself in the darkness. He sat later in the car on the dirt road, removed from her as they talked, afraid of any hopes or dreams she might inspire in him.

He deferred to her in every way. When two nights later she told him she wanted to go to the city to write poetry and songs, he believed instantly that she would be successful at it. It did not bother her that she was deceiving him, because she understood by then that those who love without hope accept lies as gifts.

It was she who finally, the next night, reached out across the seat and took his hand; it lay unresponsive under hers, inert, lifeless. When she moved next to him and lifted her face for him to kiss her, it was a chaste kiss. It was not until the next night during their second kiss that he put his hand to her breast; but when he attempted to open her blouse, she stopped him, and from then on the chaste kisses and his hand on her clothed breasts were the only intimacies he attempted. At the end of that night she intentionally, but as if by accident, brushed the back of her hand across his trousers. He was large and rigid. It occurred to her that she had done something that whores do, and the thought was not an unpleasant one to her. That he thought her beautiful and superior to him in every way, thought that he was the unworthy one, was an even more pleasant thought.

The night before the band's engagement was to end, he asked her to go to the city and live with him. He said he would be good to her and make her happy. She could write her poems and songs; he would take care of her. When she said yes, he kissed her, as face tilted upward, eyes remaining open, she stared past him through the side window.

She held the kiss, arms around him. Then as Orlo watched, she opened her blouse and removed her brassiere. He fell on her breasts like one who is famished, while her face lifted, smiling. But when he began to push her back across the seat, she stopped him. She asked if he had something to protect them, and he reached behind for his wallet. In his haste to extract it, the condom dropped on the floor. His fingers searched the darkness, where he found it minutes later. Then he turned away.

It was over in seconds. He lay like a mountain trembling on her while she smiled past him at something in the night.

Afterward she suggested they get out of the car. Standing side by side, she was several inches taller than he. She took his hand and they strolled in an unusual promenade past the house to the edge of the woods and back. He had to rise onto his toes to kiss her good night. The car drove off slowly, as if it too were weary.

She turned and looked up at the house, but the face watching them from the dark attic window had withdrawn.

When Orlo came for her after two the next morning, he parked and waited for her in the car, as she had instructed him. She watched from her bedroom window, then went down to the porch with Emil's old tin suitcase. She signaled to him to wait. It was a bright night. The moon was full.

She went back into the house and up the stairs to Lydia's door. She entered without knocking and stood for a moment beside the sleeping woman. She heard Willa shift in sleep, turning toward her. She reached down and shook Lydia by the shoulder, and Lydia opened her eyes. She did not seem surprised to see Madeleine there.

"I'm leaving" Madeleine said. "I'm going away. Someone's waiting for me outside."

Lydia got up and sat on the side of the bed, her shoulders and arms bare in her nightgown. Madeleine was surprised, as she had been before, at how large and strong her mother was. As she put her feet in her slippers and drew her robe to her from the foot of the bed, Lydia asked "Did you come to say good-bye?"

Madeleine ignored the sarcasm. "I came to tell you you can put the baby up for adoption—or do anything else you want with it. I won't ever come back."

Lydia stood. She put the robe on, then went to the crib and looked down at Willa. She spoke to Madeleine with her back to her as she pulled the blanket up around Willa. "So be it. I expected as much."

Madeleine's voice became higher and she spoke quickly, as children do trying to explain themselves. "After all, it's as much the two of yours as it is mine. More. He's the one who's responsible."

"So you went out and picked up the first man who would have you to run off with."

"It's not like that. His name's Orlo Haines. He's a good man."

"Does he know about Willa?"

"No. And he never will. No one will."

Lydia turned to her and Madeleine stepped back involuntarily, afraid Lydia would strike her. But Lydia remained where she was by the crib. "All right" she said. "But understand this: once you leave, you can't come back to this house. Don't contact us. And don't ever expect to see Willa again. I won't allow it."

Madeleine started to go past her out of the room, but Lydia stepped forward, blocking the doorway. "I just want you to understand this, you tramp. Your father's a weak man. What he did is a sin, and he will have to answer to God for it. But you—from the time you were a little girl, I've watched you manipulating him, wrapping him around your pretty finger to get anything you wanted from him. That he came finally to want that from you—and believed he had a right to it—is not beyond my understanding. He has the temperament of a child, not a man. I've known that since the first day I met him. He does only what he thinks he can get away with. What he did was unforgivable, but it would never have happened if you hadn't let him believe it could. You let that man dream, girl."

Madeleine stared at her, unable to respond.

Lydia stepped aside. "Now get out. Go to your lover—and be damned forever. I'm going to erase your memory from this house."

Madeleine went past her, then stopped in the hallway. She turned. Tears coming to her eyes, she asked "And you? You think you had no responsibility? You always protected him—never me. Where were you when he was crawling all over me? Do you know what I think? I think you knew and didn't mind, because then he'd have me to screw and you wouldn't have to do it with him anymore." She went down the hall to the stairs and ran down them sobbing.

Lydia stepped back, closed the door. Then she heard Emil hurrying down the attic stairs, and she realized he had been listening there. She reached for the doorknob, but her hand remained there. She listened to him going down the stairs and out of the house, then opened the door and went down the hallway to Madeleine's room.

She went to the window and stood behind the lace curtains. She saw the car on the road, the man inside it in shadows. Madeleine was struggling with the suitcase toward the car when Lydia saw Emil following her. He called to her, but she did not stop. She began running and then he was running too until he came close to her and half turned her around with his hand on her shoulder. He was shouting at her, pleading, when she turned and swung the suitcase and caught him in the shoulder, sending him off balance and forcing him to release her. She hurried on, but Emil was again behind her, and this time when he caught her and forced her to turn around facing him, he held her there by the sleeves of her coat. She tried to hit him again with the suitcase, but he held her arms fast so that she could not lift it. She struggled to release herself, then dropped the suitcase and pulled one of her arms free. She slapped him with full force, but the blow did not free her. Both of them stopped struggling as Madeleine watched Emil slowly— hands holding her coat as they slid down it—sink onto his knees. He had stopped talking, but he was still clutching the coat, his face lifted to Madeleine, waiting now. She slapped him repeatedly with both hands, but he did not attempt to avoid the blows as he knelt before her.

She stopped, yanked the coat free, and picking up the suitcase, strode off to the car as Emil watched from his knees. She spoke shortly to the man inside and he got out quickly; Lydia watched the portly black man take the suitcase and put it in the back of the car. When they got into the car and it started, Lydia heard Emil scream the girl's name. He kept calling it until the car's headlights disappeared through the trees, and seeing him kneeling in the silence that followed, she thought that even the night had forgotten him. She waited a while, then went down to retrieve him.

18

On Willa's first visit to the Little America Café she had seen a movie on the television about a beautiful woman who worked in something called a brothel in a city named Memphis and rode in a funny car that made a lot of noise and who wore long dresses and walked around with a colored umbrella when it was not raining. Willa knew she was a nice woman because she laughed a lot and did kind things for people, but the other women in the city did not like her and kept trying to harm her. Since at that time Willa did not know what a brothel was or what the woman did there that would make the people of the city want to hurt her, she had decided it was because she charged the men that came to the brothel a dollar to go to her room with her so they could look at each other with their clothes off. It had seemed to Willa a strange thing to do, but what she understood from the movie was that some people thought it was a sin and others thought it was fun. The ugly women of the city called the nice woman a harlot, and since that was a word Willa had heard her grandmother use sometimes when she quoted from the Bible, the next day she had asked the old woman what a harlot was. But the only explanation her grandmother would give her was that Willa's mother was one and that women who became harlots went to hell.

By then Willa did not believe in heaven or hell, and since the movie had shown that harlots made men happy, she had decided it could not be a bad thing to be.

■ ■ ■

Early Wednesday morning Willa and Mary were seated again in the large living room. Josephine had come for her before daylight, laid out the clothes she was to wear, and told her that after she bathed and dressed, breakfast would be served by the cook in the small dining room. She had told her that then Mary would see her.

Because of the erratic hours kept by those living in the house— hours determined by Mary's inability to sleep except for brief periods— Willa had slept little since she came there. But no matter how tired she was, whether roused from a short nap or awake waiting to be summoned by Josephine, she hurried each time to her meetings with Mary, happy that she was going to be with her again. The previous night, however, overcome not only by exhaustion but by the wine and the cigarettes and the extreme and confusing emotions Mary's powerful presence created in her, she had drifted off even as she sat happily at Mary's feet listening to her tell her stories.

Minutes later Mary had roused her. Straining with the effort, she had leaned her bulk forward in the chair, gently easing Willa onto her feet. Mary's fingers had communicated: they drew Willa toward her, then up, where Willa came to rest in Mary's lap. Mary had put her arms around her, and in the warmth of the big woman's body, Willa had drifted off somewhere into the region between sleep and fulfillment.

Mary had talked on, her voice lower now as she told Willa about that time and place she had known with Willa's mother.

Before they had all gone to bed at around three in the morning, Mary had given Willa a pipe and matches and what looked to her like a pellet of black clay wrapped in tinfoil. She had told Willa how to use it. She had said it would give Willa sleep like a devotion and a playground of dreams.

She had dreamed of white horses—wild, majestic large horses with long quivering manes and high tails like geysers, rippling flesh and legs as if carved out of ivory—cavorting in a moon-bright field of broad night, heads raised and rearing as if to gnaw on the stars. She floated onto one of the horses and it sprang into the air, off the earth past the night into a constellation of streaking stars where, like a vaulted ceiling, the bountiful firmament awaited her.

This morning, having appeared promptly, Willa hoped that the purpose of this early-morning meeting would be for Mary to tell her that she had located her mother—or at the very least that there was some progress to report. For although Mary talked willingly about Madeleine in the past, the only time Willa had asked Mary about the search for her mother, Mary had told her she must not make inquiries, that her methods in such matters involved others and must remain confidential. She had asked Willa if she trusted her.

"Absolutely," Willa answered.

"Sometimes" Mary informed her "trust must be proven by silence. Just know that I care for you and have your best interests at heart."

Now Mary was waiting for her in her chair. She signaled Willa to her chair and indicated a decanter of wine and glasses on the table. But Willa shook her head, for there was something in Mary's demeanor and in the formality of this meeting that suggested there was indeed news at last. She sat gripping the arms of the chair and waiting.

She was still waiting minutes later. Mary had not spoken since Willa entered the room, nor had she made any movement except for her slow breathing. She sat in the chair like a monument. Minutes more went by before Willa cleared her throat. She did it a second time, more loudly. She waited a moment longer, and when there was still no response, she leaned forward, peering at her, for she knew Mary sometimes fell asleep sitting up for short periods. Mary's small eyes were closed in deep pockets of flesh, but Willa saw that it was not sleep but thought Mary was engaged in. As Willa watched, the eyes slowly opened. They held Willa's, for Willa was always drawn to their serenity; they were like dark flowers on still water. Willa leaned back in the chair as Mary began to speak.

"We may have news of your mother" she said.

Willa held her breath. She held on fiercely to the words that followed.

"I want to caution you that it is not definite yet, but we have reason to believe she moved to a city in another state years ago, where we hope to locate her by the end of the day."

Willa felt like shouting, jumping, dancing around the room. But she knew better. She understood Mary's warning for caution at this point: not to celebrate her hopes prematurely. And she wanted to please Mary more than she wanted to express her belief that her mother had been found and would soon be reunited with her. She let the tears fill her eyes, but that was as far as she dared go. She just nodded, then, when she was able to, smiled.

She said "Mary, I don't know how to thank you. I mean, even if this doesn't work out, I couldn't do enough in a million years to pay you for what you've done for me already. I've been wanting to tell you, Mary, that I think you're a great woman, and that it's been a privilege to know you."

"Willa" Mary said, "you have made me very happy just with your presence. As I have come to know you, I have also come to love you. But you would make me happier still if you would come sit on my lap as you did last night."

Willa left her chair and climbed onto Mary's lap. Mary eased

Willa's head down against her large breasts, and Willa's hands crept up onto each of her shoulders. She might have been a climber clinging to the face of a cliff.

Mary reached over and opened the silver box on the table and took from it one of the cigarettes and the lighter. Willa heard the lighter click on and off, heard Mary draw her long breaths in and out. She lowered the cigarette to Willa's mouth, where Willa drew the smoke in and out in turn with Mary. In that way, they shared it.

An hour later she returned to her room, drew the drapes and lay down in the dark. She tried to sleep, but her mind churned with vague images and imprecise plans now that the perfection of dream had turned into a distant reality. Where was her mother? Was she married? Did she have other children? What was her life like? Until now her mother had been the faceless woman in white in the dream, or the girl of Willa's age in the photograph. But the beautiful woman in the dream had only been an ideal, and now the girl too had vanished into the obscure face of a woman. She listened with nerves tingling, breath strained, in happiness and foreboding, for footsteps in the hall, a knock at the door, Josephine entering to tell her whether the search had ended.

A knock at the door startled her. She sat up instantly. "Come in!" she shouted.

It was Heather. She stood in the doorway in a sheer white negligé. Although it was probably the smallest size made, it was still too large for her, the hem touching the floor, one strap falling from her shoulder, and collapsed in front of where another's breasts would have filled it. Her puny shoulders pointed forward like arrowheads. She was so small and thin she made Willa feel robust by comparison.

"What is it?" Willa asked. "Does Mary want to see me?"

Heather did not answer. She stepped into the room, closed the door behind her. Willa watched her dim figure go to the bedside table, take the ashtray and sit down on the floor with it beside the bed. She pulled a book of matches and one of the cigarettes from the neck of her negligé and laid them next to the ashtray. She had made a small encampment in the dark.

Willa turned on the light. She watched as Heather lit the cigarette, drew on it deeply again and again. Bursts of smoke wandered back like tendrils into her hair. When she looked up, Willa saw the new, vague, distant eyes—so unlike the eyes of the girl who had first greeted her at Madeleine House—eyes that were never intended to belong to a young girl's face.

"What do you want, Heather? Did Josephine send you for me?"

"Josephine doesn't tell me what to do. Only Mary does." She sounded drunk; her voice was intended to convey ill humor and toughness. It occurred to Willa that she was trying to show Willa that she was more important to Mary than Willa had thought she was. Heather had been such an inconspicuous presence in the house before then that Willa had not thought much about her.

Heather said "I killed a girl once."

Willa did not believe her.

"I'd kill you too if you took Mary away from me" Heather said.

"Why would I want to do that? I only want to find my mother."

"That's what you say now." She spoke in the strained distant voice of a smoker struggling to hold the smoke in while speaking through it. Willa watched as she smoked the cigarette down to a stub, then held it between her fingernails as she drew the last distillations from it. She extinguished the remnant in the ashtray and dropped it down the neck of her negligé. Willa noticed then that the negligé was dirty, rumpled and stained, as if she had been wearing it for a long time, or slept in it in unsavory places.

"Do you have another of those cigarettes?" Willa asked.

"*Cigarettes?* Why do you always call them cigarettes? They're pot, grass, bombers for chrissakes! Don't you know *anything?*"

"Do you have another one?" Willa asked again evenly. "Mine are all gone."

"Tough titty" Heather said.

Willa held her silence, reluctant to offend the strange girl who was so close to Mary and seemed to have some influence over her when Willa wasn't there.

"Why don't you go away?" Heather said. "Just leave us alone. Ever since you came here, Mary's been living in the past with those people, your mother, again. Only now she forgets sometimes it's not real. When she got sick, when the doctor told her she'd die if she didn't retire and she turned the running of the business over to Jo, she started doing that: reliving those days. I was the one who brought her back. She even began following the doctor's orders and stopped drinking and doing dope. Then when she heard about you, that you were that woman's daughter and were coming here to see if she could help you find her, it started all over again."

"What's wrong with her?" Willa asked.

"The last couple of years she started putting on all that weight. It was freaky. She didn't look like that two years ago. Then something went wrong with her heart. She's already had two operations. They said she had to have another one, but she wouldn't do it. She was all right, though, until you showed up. Look, what if I told you I might be able to put you in touch with someone else who could help you find your mother? Would you go away then?"

"Who?"

"That Chatto Hoffman."

"Do you know him?" Willa asked.

"No, but he used to work for Mary. And I heard Penny Markman at Madeleine House mention him a few times. If he had any connection with Madeleine House, Penny would have his address there in the files."

"If Mary knew where he was" Willa said "she'd have told me."

"Maybe she does and doesn't want you to know."

"Why would she do that?"

"Look" Heather said, "I'm only offering so I can get rid of you— get things back to the way they used to be. Now do you want me to find out about him or don't you?"

"I don't have to see him now" Willa said. "Mary just told me they found out where my mother's been living and she'll have all the information by the end of the day."

"And if Mary doesn't find her? If you never find her? What will you do then?"

Willa stared at her.

"People disappear all the time" Heather said. "They jump into the river and get eaten by sharks or get washed out into the ocean. They're murdered and their bodies are sealed up behind walls. Or they die on the street and if no one comes to claim them, they're buried in a grave with all the other bodies no one has a name for."

"Not my mother!" Willa said.

"You've got to face facts. That's what could have happened."

For the first time Willa considered what would happen to her if the search failed. The only sanctuary she could hope for was the one she was now in; the only one who cared whether she lived or died was Mary. She already knew what a cruel place the world was. Mary's story of the woman behind the wall would have convinced her of that if nothing else did. Now she thought of what it would be like to be without money or friends in its harsh streets.

"That won't happen!" she said.

Heather got up. She went to the door, opened it, turned back. She said "You put all your eggs in one basket. But just don't plan to live here if they don't come home to hatch." She left.

Willa stared at the door. Her mouth opened and closed, but there were no words to give her courage in this land of uncertainty.

* * *

She waited all morning and all afternoon. When she would hear footsteps approach, she would run to the door, stand next to it listening. The footsteps would always pass. Distant voices would drift toward her, then drift away. In between, there was only silence. By seven o'clock she was hungry and started for the kitchen to bring something back to the room to eat. To get there she had to pass the door behind which she had first seen Mary under the blue light. The door was closed. As she turned into the dining room, she saw Josephine coming down the floating staircase carrying a tray holding two syringes lying on a towel.

The servants had gone home, but Willa made a sandwich and drew a cup of coffee from the large metal urn that was kept heated day and night on the sideboard.

As she was hurrying back to her room, she saw that Mary's door had been opened and left ajar. She heard voices coming out of the room, and she stopped and looked in. She was hoping to hear something about her mother.

The first thing she saw was Heather, still in her negligé. She was lying on the floor, head propped against the wall at the side of the divan. She was staring into the distance. She was smiling. As Willa watched, Heather raised her hand, and Willa drew back, thinking she might have seen her and was about to wave to her. But the girl's hand went instead to in front of her face, where her fingers began moving as if weaving something out of air. She smiled at her fingers as if she had brought them there to entertain her.

Mary was seated on the side of the divan, the sleeve of her caftan pulled up, a rubber tube tied above her elbow. She had the muscles of a man.

Josephine performed like a surgeon, her movements quick and precise. But she stopped with the needle now above Mary's arm. She said to her "Never again, Dr. Myers said."

"That was before she came."

"Then she should go."

"No. There are moments—it all comes back. But this time, as it could have been. Do you still love me, Jo?"

"You know I always have."

"Then do it. There's so much pain there, too."

Heather began counting her fingers.

Willa watched as the needle sank into Mary's arm and a bubble of blood rose in the syringe. The bubble descended, rushed with the clear liquid to its point of rejoicing. Josephine waited. Heather was still counting her fingers. Then Josephine slid the needle down. Mary sighed. "Tonight" she murmured. "Tonight it will all be as it should have been. Dreams end, but other dreams take their place. There is nothing else in between."

Willa waited until she saw Mary lean backward. Josephine helped her onto the divan, placed her head on a pillow. Then she straightened up and turned the blue overhead light on, extinguishing the white light beside the divan. While she was gathering the works back onto the tray, Willa slipped past the door and down the deep carpeting back to her room.

When Josephine came for Willa that night, she brought with her a long box with the words *Chic 'n' Freak* on it and dressed her in its contents of a white wedding gown, white gloves and a veil. When Willa arrived in the living-room doorway, she saw Heather seated at Mary's feet in a white pantsuit, white shoes, white man's felt hat, white-on-white shirt and white tie.

"Come in, Willa" Mary said. "We're having a party." When Willa sat down beside Mary's other leg, she and Heather looked like marble statues at the foot of a cenotaph.

There was food and wine and the silver box filled with the cigarettes open on a table next to Mary's chair. Mary poured Willa a glass of wine and handed it to her, along with a cigarette. She lit it for her with the gold lighter. She was also in costume: a priest's cassock with a silver cross on a chain. She was drinking gin from a tall goblet.

Ten minutes later Josephine arrived, carrying a small box. She was dressed in a tuxedo complete with tails and a top hat. With her hair swept up under the hat, the tall woman looked to Willa even more impressive than before. She sat down in the chair across from them. It seemed to Willa like an assembly, which Mary then convened.

"Let me tell you this story, Willa" Mary said "before we begin. It is especially appropriate that I tell it tonight, because it is a story of mother love.

"Back then there was this young woman who had a child out of wedlock. Her lover deserted her before the child—a girl—was born, which was possibly the reason she loved her daughter so passionately, made such sacrifices for her. She was a delicate woman in ill health (I believe, for one thing, she was consumptive), but even so, although she had opportunities to have other lovers, even marriage if she chose it, she never did, choosing instead to give all of her love to her daughter. She was the sort of young woman common among us in those days: without much education, with no profession or skills beyond a slight talent for playing the guitar (which an earlier lover had taught her) and singing, and with no desire for anything more than singing her songs of love and brotherhood and sisterhood and peace to those who would listen to her on the streets and in parks and pay her with small contributions put into a cigar box at her feet.

"She had a family somewhere, but they had long since disowned her. Parents did that in those days: disowned their children for believing in peace and love. There were other reasons the parents gave for doing this, but it was also because they were embarrassed and made uncomfortable by their children's public declarations of those ideas. No one likes to be taught that he does not know how to love. These children, then, learned how to be independent—as was the young woman, even until that time when her declining health made it more and more difficult for her to earn a living for herself and her daughter on the streets with her music. No doubt, she went without, denying herself food and, toward the end, even the medicine she needed, in order to provide all she could for her child, who by that time had grown into a beautiful, dark-haired girl of three."

She stopped. She looked off. She had lit a cigarette, and now she was staring through the expanding smoke as if she could see the woman and her child on the other side of it. As when Mary had told the other story, Willa now had the feeling Mary was no longer telling it to her but to herself, bringing it back in a memory.

"It was a beautiful thing to see" Mary resumed minutes later, "the lovely child and her mother always together, the girl so caring, so loving in return. They were content to have only each other. Because they were so poor, they lived in the worst section of the city: drug addicts, pushers and thieves everywhere, children of twelve and thirteen making love on the landings. People defecated in hallways and rats as large as cats came out of the alleys and sewers attacking people on the streets. The police would seldom venture there, taxis never after dark. But I visited them in that apartment once, and although there was no way to control the cockroaches, which bred endlessly and were part of the very skin of those old buildings, that apartment was kept as immaculate and shining as any you could find anywhere. Nor did they seem to be affected by the violence that went on all around them day and night; they were never threatened or harmed by the other residents, who preyed upon one another as the poor and disenfranchised often do. It was not that they were accepted, brought into the world of the people of the street, but as if a special place which was by common agreement inviolate had been created for them."

She stopped and stared off again, and when she at last brought her quiet eyes back to Willa again, Willa thought she could see that mother and daughter's love reflected in them.

Mary smiled at Willa before she resumed. "How delicate love is! How perishable! Time withers memory, and so with it love. Perhaps it was this thought that was in the woman's mind during those last months, in which she became finally too ill to go onto the street even for a few hours to make enough money to sustain them. She would have known anyway by then that she was dying. She had gone earlier to the welfare people as a last resort to see if she could get temporary relief, but when the interviewer began asking questions about the daughter— how she was cared for, the surroundings and conditions in which she was being raised—she had left and never gone back, for fear they would attempt to take her child away from her. When finally she had been unable to pay the small rent on the apartment, the landlord turned off their gas and electricity and threatened to evict them. Who knows how they survived during those last weeks? All that is known for certain is that the child was fed and healthy and as immaculately groomed and prettily dressed as she had always been.

"But the woman, on the other hand, declined alarmingly, becoming very thin, more ravaged than her mere twenty-odd years could have made her. She had begun to look old. Only once during those last days was she seen on the streets playing her guitar and singing while the child stood, as always, quiet and obedient beside her. But by then it was winter, and people no longer gathered in the parks; and how many would stop to listen to someone singing songs of love and brotherhood on those cold streets? Someone later recalled seeing them there that day and thinking the woman was drunk, for she was unsteady on her feet, staggered, and nearly fell several times.

"Not drunk" Mary went on after another long pause, "but perhaps intoxicated by inspiration at the end—one of those epiphanies of such luminosity that they abolish reason or make reality irrelevant, and which surely had to do with a faith more pure than any intoxicant can induce. For it was shortly after that, on one of the coldest nights of the year (the temperature near zero), that she and the child went out at midmorning to a nearby park, which was already lean and hardened by that fierce winter. It was there, it is certain, that they had a picnic, for the remains of it, with their overcoats, were found nearby on the grass the next morning. They were discovered frozen upright on a bench, their arms around each other. They were smiling. The one who found them said that at a distance, with the sunlight falling on them, their skin shining, he had thought at first they were statues. The snow that had begun that morning had turned their hair white, making it look as if they had grown old together overnight."

* * *

Willa had been holding up her bridal veil, smoking the last of the cigarette and drinking the wine, when Mary had come to the end of the story. Now she lowered the veil. The others seemed to think the story beautiful, but what Willa felt now was its sadness. Its message was one of death as beautiful, ornate. Death as a beginning. But what the story had created in Willa was fear.

The others were happy. One by one they turned to her, their faces strangely smiling. Heather said to Willa "Mary's like that mother. I wouldn't want to live either if she died."

Willa looked at Mary, whose eyes were tranquil and dreaming. She looked down at Willa, smiling gently. She gave no sign that she was aware of Willa's fear.

For the first time, Willa felt she was being excluded in their company, that there were things being said and done that the others understood but of which she had no knowledge.

"Heather" Mary said, "dance with Willa."

When Heather turned to Willa, her face looked even smaller, more pinched and insignificant under the large fedora. She got up and went to Willa. "Do you want to dance, Willa?" she asked.

Willa shook her head.

"Come" Mary said to her, "this is a party. We rented these costumes, planned it all for you."

"I don't know how to dance with somebody" Willa said. "I never learned how."

"Heather will lead you" Mary said. "You danced so beautifully the other night. Now do it this way for me."

"There's no music" Willa said.

"We'll clap. We'll keep time."

Mary reached down and touched Willa's shoulder, urging her onto her feet. Willa stood. She closed her eyes, because there was something in the room now that she did not want to see. She felt Heather take her hand. Heather put her other hand on Willa's waist.

"Lift your gown off the floor" Mary's voice came to her. "It's what a bride does when she dances with her groom."

Willa raised the heavy dress above the floor with her free hand. Then she heard the clapping begin.

It was a steady, simple rhythm: controlled and repetitive but becoming more lively as it went on. Mary clapped more loudly than did Josephine, who was more inventive, interpreting Mary's clapping, at times anticipating it, subduing it in its moments of greatest enthusiasm.

At the first sound of the clapping, Willa was pulled forward by Heather, stumbling. Eyes still closed, Willa at first failed to follow

Heather's lead; their bodies jerked apart and collided like two irreconcilable components in a mechanism. But after a few minutes Willa began to anticipate Heather's movements, to hear the music behind the soft meeting of hands. She began gliding with Heather as she felt the girl's fingers sending instructions to her flesh. Heather held her tighter, moving faster with her, and Willa's nervousness faded as she blended into the dance.

She surrendered to it, let herself be carried away by it, as if fluid movement and the insistence of the clapping hands were voices whispering to her of the pleasures of peace. She forgot time and place, became one with the dance as Heather led her smoothly, now effortlessly, through its further intricacies.

After a while Mary's clapping grew faster, more insistent. It became louder, so that she had to call above it. "Whirl her! Whirl her!" she shouted to Heather.

Heather obeyed, and Willa felt herself being transported in ever faster and widening circles.

Willa's head snapped back at the end of each tight turn; her body arched, the gown whispering behind her, as Heather took her in circles of trailing sibilance away from, back to, then away again from the clapping hands.

"How lovely!" she heard Mary say. "How beautifully they dance together!"

The clapping stopped and Willa opened her eyes and became instantly dizzy. She staggered, nearly fell, but Heather caught her and held her upright by the arm. Her returning vision focused on Mary leaning forward in her chair, eyes alive and bright with a vision. "Come here, Willa" she said.

Heather released Willa and she went staggering to Mary. She stood in front of her.

"I want to kiss you" Mary said.

"Why, Mary?"

"Because I love you. Let me lift your veil." She reached forward and pulled the veil up over Willa's head. Her large hands enclosed nearly all of Willa's head as she pulled Willa's face toward her. All Willa could see were her eyes and the large fleshy lips as they came to her. Behind the eyes the blurred face was like a fish swimming to her underwater. But the lips when they touched hers were warm and trembling.

Mary released her and leaned back as Josephine rose from her chair and came to Willa with the box she had been holding. Josephine opened it and put the lid aside on the table. She unfolded the tissue paper inside it. Willa watched as the woman lifted a baby doll from the box, turned to Willa and placed it in her hands. It had blonde hair and small, perfect painted fingernails. Its arms were raised to her.

"A baby" Mary said to her. "The gift of love. Had your mother been here, this is the child we would have adopted and raised together. Now you are here. Rock your child, Willa. Show it that we love it."

She began rocking it.

Mary had given her another of the black, claylike pellets. But after Willa smoked it in the pipe, sitting up in bed, the horses that came to her in a dream this time were black and ravening. They had eyes like white windows.

She awoke later to the sound of her bedroom door opening as Mary's dim outline filled the doorway. Mary came forward in the darkness and looked down at Willa.

Willa sat up. "What is it, Mary? Have you heard something?"

Mary's head bent like a stone precipice over her. Her eyes revealed nothing.

"What is it, Mary? Tell me."

"We've heard. Madeleine—your mother—is dead."

Willa moaned. She began crying, full of loneliness, lost in the night.

19

t that moment Vernon was standing in the closed doorway of a store across from Mary's house. He had been watching since dusk. He saw the light behind the drapes in a second-story window go on and minutes later go off. Then the house was dark.

He had walked back and forth on that side of the street several times, not daring to stop for fear of causing suspicion among the few people still on the street. He was in a highly agitated state of mind, for except for the one time through the window, he had not seen the girl in three days. Now, the house dark and the street empty, he wanted to know that she was all right, for he remembered the scene through the window, the marijuana she was smoking, and that conclave of women grouped like hunters around her. He thought if he could catch a glimpse of her he could cease his watching for the night. If for some reason he could get her to come to the door or even out onto the street—

Next to Mary's house was a condemned building, and beside that was a corner lot in which Vernon could see a twisted metal bed frame and a broken bureau kneeling in remnants of bricks and rubble. Plastic garbage bags, some of which were ripped open and spilling rotten fruit and vegetables, formed a small mountain, while others were strewn about the lot.

Vernon's mind, like the minute hand of a clock, moved slowly but inexorably, seizing its moments. He looked at the vacant lot, the garbage bags, the relics of flown lives, the gutted building beside it, and the courtyard that separated Mary Vandel's house from it all. Then he stepped out of the shadows and walked back three blocks to where he had parked the car.

He did not get in. He opened the trunk and took out of it a can of gasoline he had put there the day he began following the girl. He started to lower the trunk lid, then stopped. He replaced the can and closed the trunk and locked it. He stepped back onto the pavement and looked down the street at a neon sign four blocks away: Night Owl Market. He started toward it.

The sign outside the Night Owl Market had an owl's face designed into the O; Vernon passed under it through the store's automatic door. The door made a hissing sound in front of him and hissed again as it sealed itself behind him.

He did not have to search for what he wanted, for he saw immediately that they were sold at the checkout counter, behind which a young woman was reading a paperback novel with a picture on its cover of a man and a woman kissing in a hurricane. He went up to the counter and stood there until the woman put the book down. She seemed disturbed to see him. The market was empty except for the two of them. She asked "Can I help you?"

One of her hands had slid under the counter; it remained there. He looked at it, then back up at her. He said "I want to buy a package of cigarettes."

The hand emerged. She waited, as if expecting him to say something more, but his attention had been drawn to the book and the picture of the lovers kissing passionately in the midst of the hurricane. He reached out and pushed it aside.

The woman's hand went back under the counter. "What brand of cigarettes did you want, sir?" she asked.

He was not expecting the question. After a moment he answered "I'm just starting."

Her free hand pulled a pack from the display rack beside her. She put it in front of him and snatched back her hand. "Take these" she said, her voice rising.

He waited.

"Did you want something else, sir?" she asked.

"The matches."

He heard her sigh of relief. "They're extra" she said, and her hand went to a jar on the counter marked Matches, 2¢. She slid a pack toward him.

He paid, put the cigarettes and matches in his pocket, and had turned and was on his way to the door when he stopped. He looked back at her. He said "Only a fool makes love in a hurricane." Then he turned again and went out the door.

She watched him slide into the shadows and disappear.

* * *

He threw the cigarettes into the street two blocks away. When he returned to the car, he took the gasoline can out of the trunk and fit it under his overcoat.

Cradling his swollen belly with his arms, he moved quickly now until he arrived at the edge of the lot, where he hesitated. Objects closed in darkness brought back old memories, fear of things he was alone with in the night. He who was consummate in darkness had once known its terrors, too.

He stepped up onto the lot. Tilting on bricks, he moved among the plump bags that dotted the lot like giant mutations of flowers grown especially for the night. He arrived at the foot of the small hill of bags.

The ground was smoother there and unimpeded. Unseen soft objects yielded under his feet. He sank with each step. Sliding the can from his coat, he uncapped it, tilted it, and the gasoline trickled out, sliding over the bags' slippery surfaces, burrowing into crevices. The fumes rose to him and he pushed the can farther away, letting its contents flow freer, scattering it. Then he stopped. He became still. He had heard something move.

He listened. No sound. But when he resumed pouring, he did so quickly until the can was empty. He flung it to the top of the mound and stepped back.

He waited until the fumes subsided, then took out the book of matches and struck one. He had creased the flap so that it was steady and firm in his one hand, and with the other hand he touched the flame to the unused matches. They sputtered and became a single bright flame, which he raised like a flag, then flung off. It fell between two bags. Seconds later a thin arm of fire reached out of the crevice and around, becoming longer. Its fingers reached over the bags as if feeling them. Leaving by the same path, he heard the fire begin whispering behind him.

He returned to the doorway and waited to hear the fire engines arriving, see the lights come on again in the house, the girl open part of the night at a window, perhaps come out to watch his gift to her.

The lot was illuminated now by the fire. It looked as he imagined hell would look. He watched bags opening like bellies, disgorging their fiery contents onto the lot. Then he saw something else.

Breaking the fabric of darkness, he leaned out of the doorway on tiptoe to see better. What he saw were dozens of rats emerging from the base of the pyramid of bags: wriggling free, then scurrying away into tunnels of refuse and debris, which began trembling above them. The rats started appearing above, some sliding down the slippery flanks of the bags, others dropping softly onto the ground, where they looked startled for a moment, then rushed off.

The area around the bags was soon congested with frantic rats as they jockeyed for position to escape through the debris from the flames which now licked at them, spurring them on. He could hear them shrieking as they began forming lines expanding outward. Seconds later the first of them came in sight in waves seesawing on broken bricks and tin cans and bottles toward the lot's edge. They paused there, then tumbled off the lot's rise and scattered.

He watched as dozens of them came streaking across the street, some slithering along the curb out of sight, others struggling up, lifting themselves onto the sidewalk. The larger ones leaped there.

He flung himself out of the doorway and down the street, gesturing like a madman chased by terrors only he could see.

20

Madeleine heard something calling in the night. She got out of bed, where she had been lying awake next to the sleeping Orlo, and in nightgown and bare feet went out of the bedroom and through the small living room into the kitchen all the way on linoleum. The faint sound was clearer from there.

She did not turn on the light. She crossed the narrow kitchen into the fall of moonlight from the window above the table, thinking she would have to buy bedroom slippers soon. Her feet stuck to the cool linoleum and made sucking sounds beneath her.

She climbed onto the table to see out the high window, drawing the long nightgown up in front of her. She opened the window outward by its handle and looking out saw only the faceless sides of buildings. The cries—a repetitive, plaintive calling—grew louder.

She leaned out the window to where, at the bottom of the airshaft, she saw a kitten. It must have fallen there. It raised its face to her as it tread softly in circles, one paw collapsing repeatedly beneath it. Its hindquarters were twisted to the side.

She knew there was no outside access to the airshaft, and all of the windows were dark. She decided there was nothing she could do to help it.

She pulled a chair onto the table and sat listening. Around dawn, it stopped calling.

The first thing Madeleine had done the previous morning, after she and Orlo had arrived in the city, was clean his apartment. She had scrubbed the floor and beaten dust out of the overstuffed chair and couch, which except for a coffee table and a small portable television set was the only furniture in the living room. She had scoured the toilet and sinks removing months' worth of grime, and the bathtub, ridding it of its ring. She had hung her clothes alongside Orlo's in the narrow closet of the small bedroom. She had pulled down the newspapers he had put over the windows, which were the only other windows in the apartment, and had gone out and bought curtains and hung them in their place. Elevated trains passed so close to the windows that she could see the passengers' faces clearly. The bed trembled as each train passed.

Now, after Orlo's alarm clock went off, she pretended she was still asleep until he left the apartment to go to his job at the garage. Then she got up and made coffee and carrying her cup into the living room, found a five-dollar bill on top of the television set, along with a note from Orlo telling her it was to pay for food and other household expenses.

She bought frozen dinners for them, then spent the rest of the money on hamburgers and a root beer at a sidewalk refreshment stand. She passed the rest of the afternoon sitting in a small, dirty park, an island in the middle of a wide street in which derelicts lay sleeping on benches as the city rushed around them. When one of them approached her begging for money, she hurried away amid a swirl of pigeons.

As she crossed under the elevated platform to return to the apartment, she looked up at the long belly of a train going by. The ground trembled beneath her, and the structure shook with its passing.

He left five dollars for her on top of the television every morning after that. She sat in parks and went to movies to pass the time. Each day she returned with something for dinner that was frozen or canned and needed only to be heated. He did not care; he ate anything she served him. In the evenings she watched television much later than he did, hoping he would be asleep when she went in to bed.

His lovemaking was perfunctory; quickly satisfied, he sank into a noisy, troubled sleep minutes later. She felt nothing during the lovemaking and stayed awake for hours afterward watching the light from the elevated trains creeping across the walls. He tried to win her with presents of flowers and cheap boxes of candy and told her he loved her. He was afraid of her and so conquered her momentarily in sex.

She got up one night when he had gone to sleep after sex, and taking her pillow and a blanket, she spent the rest of the night on the couch. She did that after sex for a week, until one night she told him she could not sleep sharing a bed, and after that slept on the couch. When he came into the living room in the morning, he always found the television still on next to the couch, where she had fallen asleep watching it. One night he asked her to remain in bed with him for a while after sex, but she refused. She knew he thought he had done all he could to make her happy and wanted to understand what it was he still needed to do, but she could not tell him. He was a decent man who suffered because of his unreturned love for her, but she could only respond with indifference or annoyance when that love made him most vulnerable. At the end of the second week she stopped having sex with him.

Two nights later he came to her from his bed and tried to lie down with her on the couch, but she pushed him away. "No" she said. He sat there for a few minutes, then got up and went back to bed.

"I love you, Madeleine" he told her the next night while they were watching television.

"I know, Orlo."

"And you don't think I'm as good as dirt."

She pretended not to, but she could see the tears in his eyes.

He did not come to her on the couch again, nor ask her to join him in bed. She was surprised when she realized that he was relieved to have accepted at last that sex was over between them.

One day she discovered his savings bankbook, which stated a balance of over six thousand dollars. That night she demanded that he give her more money for the apartment and food, that he stop pretending they were poor. He looked hurt when she told him she needed money for clothes and winced when she suggested the amount of two hundred dollars.

He gave it to her—two new hundred-dollar bills left on the television—and that day she bought a white dress and white shoes she had seen in a shop window. It was her first purchase in white.

She modeled the new outfit for him that night. It accentuated her dark good looks, gave her a swarthy, madonnalike quality she saw reflected in his worshipful gaze.

That night he came to her on the couch while she was sleeping. She had her back to him, but she awoke immediately, knowing he was there. When she turned to him, she saw only his head and shoulders, for he was kneeling on the floor. She said "Please, Orlo, go back to bed."

She could see he was trembling. His voice trembled too when he spoke. "Please, Madeleine, let me kiss your feet."

She hesitated, then thrust her feet out to him from under the blanket. He lifted them and rubbed his cheeks over them as she watched. Then he lowered them to the side of the couch and bending, kissed them. She watched him until he half rose and moving quietly in shadows, returned to the bedroom.

The next day she bought a white purse with a strap, a cream-colored sweater and a long pleated white skirt. That night she asked him to take her out where she could wear them. She understood now that there were demands she could make of him by granting him the small favor that was his adoration of her at night.

He took her to "the neighborhood," a place with a century-long history of residents who were in the arts. There they came upon a street of bright lights, noisy bars and coffeehouses and outdoor food stands where they saw crowds of people parading in costumes: a barefoot Jesus in a bed sheet, Indians and cowboys and young girls in long dresses offering flowers to strangers. Street musicians played for money on every corner—young people mostly, slightly mad with life, giddy with freedom. A girl with a face full of sparkles passed her, and another with a shaven head painted white brushed her aside in the dense traffic. She saw transvestites dancing with their lovers in the street and other white women arm in arm with black men.

They ended the night at the High Note, a nightclub with a long bar by the door and tables in back where people gathered to listen to live jazz being played on a small platform.

Orlo was taking them to two seats at the end of the bar when a woman called to him from a table where she was sitting with a large black man. Orlo was reluctant to join them at first, then guided Madeleine to the table.

"Have a drink with us, Orlo" the woman said.

He nodded to her and they sat down.

The large woman was wearing slacks and a man's shirt open at the neck; her short black hair was cut in bangs, her sole attempt at femininity. "Orlo," she said "you've been a stranger. And this lovely girl must be the reason. I don't blame you for hiding her."

Although speaking to Orlo, she kept looking at Madeleine. She raised an arm at a passing waitress, who took their order. Then Orlo introduced Madeleine to her.

The woman said to Madeleine "I'm Mary Vandel, and the philosopher sitting next to me is Big Brown." Madeleine nodded to Mary's large black companion, who nodded back. He had a shaved head and large, bushy eyebrows. Beneath an expensive chalk-striped suit with wide, pointed lapels, his broad shoulders and thick arms seemed straining to break loose. But like most powerful men when inactive, he appeared placid and lacking in energy.

Mary said to Madeleine "You're exquisite. Like—moonlight. May I call you Moonlight?"

"Call me Madeleine" she said.

The black musicians had been on a break, but now they returned to the brightly lighted platform. Those who sat waited at their instruments while the others picked theirs up or strapped them on and experimented with notes that ended in sudden clarity. They tuned up separate from one another, casually and unhurried; but when they began to play, it was without a signal and suddenly as one.

Madeleine had never heard music like it before. There was none of the showmanship of a Coley Wilson—none of his posturing and over-elaboration—in their playing. They allowed the music to go its own convoluted and intricate way. When it became too intense, they reexamined it. Its excitement was the intellectual charge of invention and discovery. They were looking for the unexpected. Now and then someone would call up to them, not loudly, never shouting, "Yeah, man, go," but the musicians did not pay any attention. They smiled sometimes, but briefly, at the end of their solos. Their only communication was between one another and their instruments.

When Madeleine heard raised voices, she turned away from the musicians to a short black woman nearly as wide as she was tall standing on the bar. She was a homely woman with wild hair, and even drunk she was remarkably agile as she began dancing in her bare feet. Her wide hips swung out and around, and her large behind shifted from side to side like loose cargo on a ship. She obviously thought herself beautiful as she danced up and down the bar.

"Who's that?" Madeleine asked Orlo.

He started to speak, but Mary answered her for him. "That's Mau-Mau Sue, the black Sally Rand. Watch."

The customers at the bar were clapping; even the two bartenders did not interfere until she lifted a sacklike dress over her head and flung it off. Then both bartenders lunged for her.

She dodged their hands and danced nimbly away in panties and brassiere. When she reached the end of the bar, she unhooked her brassiere and flung that away too. Her breasts dropped halfway to her stomach, then rose like arms waving as she spun out of reach of the bartenders. She stopped in the middle of the bar long enough to step out of her panties, and twirling them over her head, she sent them billowing into the tables. Then two men came rushing at her and caught her.

They lowered her off the bar. Someone had retrieved her dress and given it to one of the men who now lifted Mau-Mau Sue by her arms and legs and ferried her away. She smiled and waved amid loud applause.

Madeleine had been aware of a man standing at the bar ignoring the performance as he stared at her. There was no flirtatiousness in his expression, none of the arrogance of a man staring at a strange woman in a bar: it was a look of quiet confidence which seemed to tell her that no matter what she might think, he alone of those there had discovered her and knew who and what she was.

He was a well-built man of about thirty, with copper-colored skin that glowed in the light at the bar. He had sharply defined features like those seen on heroic statues, a suggestion of Indian blood somewhere in his ancestral line. He was the handsomest man at the bar, but he dressed and carried himself in a way that made her understand he was indifferent to his good looks. He had not smiled at Madeleine; he had made her understand that it was unnecessary to communicate anything between them with looks or signals. A pretty blonde girl was leaning over him and talking to him in an attempt to regain his attention, but she might as well not have been there, for all the notice he gave her. He could be cruel, Madeleine thought, and indifferent even to those who loved him. His gaze was relaxed but so steady she forced herself to look away.

She tried to concentrate on the music again, and had almost succeeded when she felt him standing behind her. Without asking permission, he sat down across from her. Big Brown stirred, as if trying to decide if he should do something about the intrusion, but the man ignored him. He ignored Mary, too, and Orlo, who opened his mouth to protest, then apparently thought better of it. The man spoke only to Madeleine, and then only one sentence:

"You're so fine I could eat you without honey."

Then he got up and returned to the bar.

There was silence at the table after he had gone, until Madeleine asked "Who was that?"

Mary answered her. "Chatto Hoffman. A poet."

Orlo got up. He put his hand under Madeleine's arm. "Come on" he said. "Let's go. I gotta get up early."

She returned to the neighborhood the next day, walking the streets and browsing in the windows of jewelry and clothing shops, which displayed unusual, handmade items. The bars and nightclubs were quiet. The people on the streets—some of the couples with children, the men with long hair and beards wearing jeans and sandals and a few of the women in Mexican serapes—were obviously residents. It was a place of peacefulness and some beauty in the daytime.

She entered a section of the neighborhood with narrow cobblestone streets and sidewalks, old brownstones, and houses hidden in cul-de-sacs and pocketlike courtyards. When she came to a restaurant with a sign in the window—Waitress Wanted—she stopped. She looked in through the window, then entered.

She was hired on the spot by a middle-aged Greek who, she learned later, had once been a successful fashion photographer but had quit to write poetry and pursue his own interest in photography; some of his pictures of landscapes and cities (in which she saw he was photographing the spaces in between objects rather than the objects themselves) were displayed on the walls. He told her to start the next day at eleven; she would work until seven at night. The fact that she had no experience as a waitress did not seem to concern him.

It was a clean, cheerful place with the paintings of local artists displayed on the walls. A large window gave her a view of the street and the people who lived on it: young men walking small, pampered dogs on leashes, bearded artists, prosperous-looking lesbians with young mistresses. She soon knew them all, liked them and was well liked in turn. She enjoyed the lively conversations and the relaxed atmosphere, even at noon and dinnertime when the restaurant was crowded and she did not stop for a moment. She liked the work and quickly became efficient at it and made good money in tips.

Chatto Hoffman came in three times her first week there. He avoided sitting at one of her tables but spoke to her twice—briefly, casually—each time making her laugh.

When she returned to the apartment at night, Orlo was always watching television, withdrawn and looking hurt and betrayed. He had not wanted her to work and was jealous of her job and the independence it gave her.

She made him take her to the High Note again, where she wore a new white skirt and sweater. When they arrived, the bar was again crowded, and Mary and Big Brown were at the same large table. When Mary signaled to them to join them, Orlo bent close to Madeleine and whispered that they should sit elsewhere. But Madeleine insisted and they went to the table, where Mary again bought them drinks.

They had been there a half-hour when Madeleine saw Chatto come in the door. He ordered a drink and leaned against the bar looking over the crowd, but he stopped when he saw Madeleine. She turned away when she saw him coming toward them.

He put his hand on her arm. "Come with me" he told her.

Orlo leaned forward. "Now one minute, Chatto—"

"Shut up" Chatto interrupted him without taking his eyes from Madeleine's.

"She's with me, man" Orlo said.

"Shut up, I said."

Big Brown started to get up from his seat, but Mary put her hand on his arm, restraining him. Chatto did not bother to look at Big Brown. "Let's go" he told Madeleine.

She got up and with Chatto's hand on her arm, went with him through a doorway at the rear. They passed the ladies' and men's rooms and continued along the corridor to a heavy iron door. Chatto opened it for her, and she preceded him out of the bar into a walled courtyard. She was standing against the wall of the bar when Chatto closed the door behind him and went to her. He pushed back the unruly curl on her forehead, but he did not speak and neither did she. His eyes held hers for a moment. Then he kissed her. She felt as if she had leaped forward. When he withdrew his mouth from hers, she gasped.

"Take off your panties" he told her.

She did, stepping out of her shoes first. He folded her panties and put them into her purse. Then he lifted her skirt above her hips and from the back spread her legs at the upper thighs. He unzippered himself and entered her standing, thrusting into her powerfully. She gasped again and put her arms around his neck. She clung to him, staring wide-eyed past his shoulder, then moaned and seconds later cried out as she felt herself coming apart piece by piece.

When they reentered the bar, they were walking side by side, she with her head on his shoulder and he with his arm around her.

They returned to the table and sat down. Madeleine held Chatto's hand as Orlo looked on. She seemed not to see Orlo or anyone else at the table, and only when the others broke their silence did she notice that Orlo had gone.

She never returned to the apartment, except once with Chatto during the day to get her clothes. She left Orlo's keys on the television set.

The first week they were together, they stayed in the loft apartment of a friend of Chatto's who was out of town. It was illuminated by klieg lights mounted on the whitewashed ceiling and walls. Madeleine enjoyed the feel of the polished wooden floor on her feet. She liked to wander barefoot through the large, high-ceilinged rooms whose sparsely furnished, highly acoustical spaces carried every sound she and Chatto made, so that she felt they were never far apart. Their shadows merged in doorways while passing, grew large as heroic murals on the walls. He never asked her about her past, but in time she learned something about his.

He was from Chicago, the only child of a prominent white Jewish lawyer who had married Chatto's black mother while they were both working for the NAACP. Chatto's mother, a well-known educator and

pioneer author of black children's books, had come far despite her origins; her mother was a poor Tennessee black woman and her father was
a Cherokee Indian poet and radical activist for Indian and black causes
who was shot to death by unidentified white assailants.

It was Chatto's Indian grandfather who had most deeply influenced
him as a boy, whose name he had taken at twenty in preference to his
given name of Charles, and whose wild blood he felt was the true pulse
in his own veins, progenitor of his own fierce poetry later.

At eighteen he had entered Fisk University, where for the first time
he saw southern blacks living under segregation, which his upper-
middle-class upbringing had not exposed him to before. The university
had tried to isolate the students from the poor blacks around it, but
Chatto had made friends among them and spent most of his free time
with them. At school he had excelled in athletics and majored in sociology and philosophy, graduating with top honors. On his own he read
W. E. B. Du Bois and studied the teachings of Marcus Garvey. Denmark
Vesey and Nat Turner, along with his Indian grandfather, became his
triumvirate of heroes. By then he had decided to become a writer.

For several years he had been estranged from his father, who had
renounced his youthful belief in revolutionary world socialism in favor
of moderation and peaceful change; Chatto saw him as a failed man who
had betrayed his dreams. After Chatto's graduation, the uneasy truce
between them was canceled when Chatto publicly denounced him.
Chatto had come to believe that all white people were morally inferior
to blacks and that their corruption had resulted in a racial weakness that
he could only despise. He loved his mother, but he was never able to
reconcile that love with the resentment he felt because of the taint of
whiteness she had inflicted on him.

He had published three books of poetry, which fused dark humor
with a barely controlled rage; a collection of essays entitled *Black Writing and Revolution,* which had been reviewed widely with both outrage
and extravagant praise and which hovered in the middle of the best-
seller list for six weeks; a highly technical history of the blues; and now
during the day he worked on a play, based on the murder of his grandfather, at his small portable typewriter in the alcove kitchen of the loft.

Among the few pieces of furniture in the loft was a large bed raised
two feet off the floor on a platform. Madeleine and Chatto spent most
of their time together in it. She cooked for him and washed his clothes.
She bought him shirts, a pair of boots, and a brightly colored silk ker-
chief, which he wore knotted loosely at his neck. She took pleasure and
pride in enhancing his good looks.

In the warm evenings they brought a blanket onto the fire escape and drank wine while a loudspeaker pumped jazz to them. They made love there and afterward lay watching the stars. It never occurred to her until much later that except for his hatred of the white race, he seldom revealed his feelings or thoughts to her.

He made her laugh with a wry humor he seldom displayed before others, made fun of her for what he called her secret vice of vanity. His lovemaking was fierce, even frightening to her at times. For the first time she experienced sexual pleasure and fulfillment; he always knew what would excite and please her. She sometimes thought he could read her mind.

On Saturday—a half-day off for Madeleine—he took her to a large park where tourists and people from the neighborhood came to promenade around a fountain flowing into a round basin. They sat on a bench in the sunlight where Chatto seemed to be waiting and watching for someone, while Madeleine listened to folk singers perched with guitars on the edge of the fountain and black men and women dressed in brightly colored African robes beating bongos in fast rhythms. People stood on boxes shouting to small crowds against the war and the evil deeds of the government.

A young couple entered the park wheeling a baby carriage. Chatto stood up. "Come on" he said to Madeleine.

The young couple made slow progress ahead of them, for every few minutes someone approached them; they would stop and the newcomer would lean with the woman into the carriage, then quickly leave, and the carriage would resume its journey around the park.

Chatto took Madeleine's arm and they walked up to it. "Hey, Chatto" the man at the head of the carriage said. "What's happening?"

Madeleine leaned forward to look at the baby. It lay under a blanket sucking on a bottle filled with a brown liquid. It stared up at Madeleine with wide, startled eyes.

Chatto pulled her back. "Let's see the baby" he said to the woman. He leaned into the carriage and the woman bent with him. Her hand went under the baby's blanket, withdrew, and taking some money from Chatto's hand inside the carriage, put a small plastic package into it.

They returned to the loft, where Chatto spread a blanket on the floor. He got a dish, a magazine and a razor blade and sat on the blanket with the package in front of him. Madeleine joined him. He emptied the contents of the package onto the plate.

"Is that marijuana?" Madeleine asked.

"Some people call it that, baby. I prefer to think of it as an antidote to all the bullshit."

She watched him separate the twigs and seeds from the leaves, chop the leaves into small pieces with the razor blade, then slide them onto the magazine and from there into the plastic bag. He used his fingers to salvage the residue.

He got up and went to his duffel bag, which contained all his possessions except for the typewriter, and returned with a book of matches and a small pipe with a short stem. He had put on some records, and as the music began he dropped some of the pot into the pipe and lit it. He drew in the smoke several times, then passing the pipe to Madeleine, instructed her on how to get it down smoothly. They smoked in silence, communicating without any need for words. She became aware of time as an entity and the shape of sunlight as it changed on the walls and floor.

A Billie Holiday record dropped onto the turntable. A sorrowful, sweet voice invaded Madeleine with its acceptance of sorrow:

> Good morning, heartache,
> You old gloomy sight.
> Good morning, heartache,
> I thought we said good-bye last night.
> I turned and tossed until it seemed you were gone.
> But here you are with the dawn.

After they had smoked two pipefuls, Chatto got up from the blanket. Madeleine watched as he dropped his clothes on the floor until he was naked. He turned and walked to the shower stall next to the kitchen. He was meticulous about his grooming and showered two or three times a day. He appeared to Madeleine to move like someone not bound to the earth.

His dark body was trim, hard and muscular. Just the sight of him naked always made her tremble and become breathless. Now her heart leaped, sad with the loneliness of its need. She undressed and went to him in the shower.

They went to a party that night in another loft. As they approached the building on the darkened empty street, they saw the large windows all alight five stories above them. The sound of music filled the cavernous street with echoes, and some of the partiers leaning over the fire-escape railing called to them.

They went up past the locked doors of factories on worn wooden steps, past signs with arrows pointing upward beneath the words *To the party* to a heavy metal door which as Chatto opened it, let out the full force of voices and the band's music.

Madeleine wore a white pantsuit she had bought for the party and a white ribbon falling the length of her long hair. Chatto had put on dark glasses and Madeleine wore a pair with white frames he had bought her. She had never used more than a little light lipstick, but several days before Chatto had told her he preferred women who wore more makeup, and to please him she had begun that night with bright red lipstick, powder and mascara.

Inside the door, in the middle of the long loft and away from the band, a woman in a man's suit sat in a chair with a dozen girls at her feet. She had a flattened nose and the face of a veteran prizefighter, but the girls were all looking at her adoringly. She held a guitar in her lap and she was barefoot. Her feet were big-boned, solid as objects carved from a rock; she paid no attention as one of the girls ran her hand caressingly over them. She lifted the guitar and began playing a few chords as Chatto whispered to Madeleine that she was a well-known lesbian poet who wrote and performed exclusively on her one subject: feet.

The woman brought her hand down hard, striking a loud, annunciatory note on the guitar. Other people had arrived to hear her, and one of them passed a joint to Chatto, who smoked it and passed it to Madeleine as the woman began singing in a deep voice coarsened by cheap whiskey and cigarettes. A lighted cigarette was fitted under the strings at the top of the guitar.

Look down, she began to intone. She struck a new, harsh chord on the guitar.

Look down! She repeated it. Then in a longer, quiet, lyrical run:

> Look at your feet.
> They are the universe.
> If you love them, the world will love you.

Then a loud, crashing note:

> Visions in time reside in them,
> And God reveals himself

One of the girls began clapping in time to the words:

> In feet, in feet, in feet, in feet,

The other girls joined in, clapping softly.

> In feet, in feet, in feet, in feet.

Shrugging and smiling at Madeleine, Chatto turned her away and into a bathroom, where some people stood around a bathtub filled with cans and bottles of beer on a bed of ice. He picked up two bottles and offered one to Madeleine, but when she shook her head he threw it back. He lifted a bottle opener on a string tied to the spigot and opened the bottle. He drank, and she took a sip from his bottle before they left.

They stood in the doorway looking out at the party. Chatto removed her arm from around his neck. "Circulate" he told her. "Don't stay around me all the time."

She watched him go off to where some people were waving at him and calling his name. Feeling conspicuous standing there, she went to a long table filled with snacks and gallon bottles of wine. She poured wine into a paper cup and stood trying to appear as if she were waiting for someone; but after ten minutes during which no one spoke to her, she finished the wine, poured a new cupful and moved off into the crowd.

"Hello, Moonlight."

She turned to face Mary Vandel. "Hello, Mary."

"I was hoping to see you at the High Note."

"We've been busy."

"You and Chatto. I heard. How long have you been together, a week? That's a record for Chatto. You're the envy of half the girls in the neighborhood."

Madeleine did not respond. The large woman seemed to loom over her. Madeleine looked at the floor. Her cup was empty.

"I was hoping we could talk, just the two of us, sometime" Mary said.

"About what?"

"Life. Death. Love. The eternal cosmos. Are there any other subjects worth talking about?"

"I wouldn't know."

Madeleine turned and went back to the table. She filled a new cup with wine. Mary appeared beside her. "Moonlight—" Mary began.

"Please don't call me that."

"All right. Madeleine. Madeleine, if you're as bored with this party as I am, we could go somewhere else. I know a place where we could go dancing."

"No thanks."

"You're worried about Chatto? He won't mind. He'll be too busy being loved whether you're here or not."

"Excuse me, Mary" Madeleine said. "I see someone I know." She hurried away.

She wandered from group to group for an hour, listening to talk of literature and art, music, politics and philosophy, but never speaking herself on things of which she had little or no knowledge; she refrained because she felt inferior to those people who spoke with ease on such subjects. She wanted to participate and learn, but she was ashamed of needing to learn. And no one she met looked sympathetic. She saw that there were other women there who stood quietly by their men letting the men do most of the talking: adjuncts to the men and apparently content to be only that. But she knew she did not want to be like them or seek them out as friends. She would learn, she determined. She would go to a library the next day and start reading again—for her own sake and to be worthy of Chatto, who, from what she had observed, was a star in his world.

Several people in the groups had passed joints to her, and she had been back to the table three times for more wine and was on her way there again when she saw Chatto sitting on the side of a bed. A pretty Spanish-looking girl sat beside him, her arm over his shoulders as he talked to the people standing in front of him. Madeleine filled her cup at the table, then went and sat down on the other side of him as the others laughed at something he had said. He did not acknowledge her, continued talking, but he put his arm around her waist as a tall blonde man wearing a corduroy jacket with leather patches on the elbows approached them. He held an unlit pipe in his hand.

Chatto looked up, but the man had already begun to kneel on one leg in front of him. He held the pipe by its bowl on his other leg. "Chatto" he said, "I'm Roy Stone. I've read your books and wanted to talk to you for some time."

"Talk" Chatto said.

"Well" the man began, "the thing is, I'm no authority on poetry— don't pretend to be. I'm a teacher—sociology—which could probably be described as the science of what is here now, while you work in the realm of art, which is the study of what always is." He paused to let Chatto absorb his wit. A few of the others laughed, but Chatto just looked at him as if expecting something more.

Roy Stone went on. "But I think you'll agree that black writing today is as much a subject for the social sciences as it is for literature."

Madeleine saw Chatto's eyebrows raise, but although the man paused to allow him to reply, he was silent.

The man hesitated, then went on. "I'll dispense with the dreary old argument of form versus content. I'd be the first to admit that the raw power and energy of black writing today—which no matter what it lacks in literary sophistication and subtlety it more than makes up for in conviction and unbridled imagination—makes that argument irrelevant. And—"

Chatto spoke then, interrupting. "Are you sure you're not a literary critic trying to pass?"

The others laughed and Roy blushed and laughed too. "No, I make no such exalted claim for myself. I'm only a teacher."

"You sure could'a fooled me" Chatto said. Madeleine noticed his intentional lapse into the black vernacular.

"Seriously, Chatto" Roy continued. "Seriously now." He tapped the stem of his pipe on Chatto's leg. Chatto did not look down. "As I said, my area of expertise is sociology, and so I abdicate any right to criticize on literary grounds your work or that of other black writers." He put his free hand over his heart and smiled. "I swear I had no intention of misrepresenting myself on that score. But I'm sure you and the other black poets and prose writers have preempted the critics by taking your work out of the realm of literature yourselves."

Chatto's eyebrows lifted again as Madeleine felt his arm withdraw from around her waist. The man did not seem to notice the tightening of Chatto's facial muscles, he was so caught up in his own words.

"Let me get to the point, Chatto. My brief is short and simple, but, I think, one worth considering. Simply put, you, Jimmy Baldwin, LeRoi Jones, Ted Joans and the others—you're all so intractably angry. Unreasonably so, I might add, and to your disadvantage, if you really want to achieve your goals. The progress made in civil rights in just the last few years, the demonstrated good faith of a large portion of white society—especially its intellectuals and artists—seem to go unnoted or dismissed out of hand by all of you. Look at me. I'm a reasonable person. I care. Tolerance, fairness, is a two-way street, is what I'm trying to say. And that correcting the present black condition, the solution to the problem, is a joint enterprise."

He stopped. His hands and the pipe he held were trembling; his speech had ended in a passion that seemed to surprise him. He blinked, as if he had been carried away and just returned. He had not noticed that during his speech Chatto had begun to lean forward until their faces were now nearly touching. When he saw Chatto's face so close to his, he seemed relieved that Chatto was smiling.

Chatto did not say anything for what seemed to Madeleine a long time. Then he spoke, still smiling, face still in front of Roy's. "Do you know what I think, Roy?"

"What, Chatto?"

"What I think, Roy" Chatto said slowly, drawing out the words "is that you suck cocks."

The man's mouth opened, but he did not speak. He looked like someone who had been struck hard in the face.

The reaction from the others was delayed, but now they started laughing. But Chatto did not laugh, and he was no longer smiling.

Chatto said "You cunt, what the fuck do you know about the *black condition*? Who put you in a black skin that you know anything about it? And where was your honky ass while it was happening? Where will it hide when the real shit goes down? And do you want to know about black *literature* today? It's *alive*. It's *here*. We ain't doin' the white man's number no more. We ain't doin' minstrel no more, Charlie. You dig?" His hand went around the man's neck as, standing, he brought him to his feet. He turned him so that he was staggering backward out of the crowd, which parted before them as Chatto said "Get away from me, honky faggot. Just get the fuck out of my sight."

The man backpedaled several steps, then turned and hurried away.

Chatto returned and sat down again between Madeleine and the Spanish-looking girl. He looked up at the others. "Can you believe that shit he was laying on me? Some day I'm going to get a gun and show morons like that how wrong they are."

Madeleine said "Chatto, he didn't mean any harm. He was just expressing a point of view."

He turned to her so quickly it startled her. "So now you're an expert on the subject too?"

"Of course not. But—"

He stood, bringing her up roughly with him by the arm. "Come with me. I want to talk to you."

He moved her through the people, who parted again to let them pass, and across the loft to the wall on the other side of the door. He jerked her around so that she was facing him. He said "Don't you *ever* say anything like that to me again in front of my friends. Understand?"

"Yes, Chatto."

He walked away.

She returned to the table for more wine. She had drunk three cupfuls before she allowed herself to feel anything again. "Screw you, Mr. Perfect" she murmured to the absent Chatto. "I'm going to have a good time no matter what you want." She smiled, looked around and was surprised to see someone smiling back. She filled her cup again and aware that she was unsteady on her feet, made her way carefully to the black man sitting alone on a couch, which was the only piece of furniture in that part of the loft. She sat next to him.

He was a handsome man of about forty in a blue suit and tie. His clothes looked expensive, and although his suit was conservative, he wore highly polished maroon boots with zippers and dark glasses. He was smoking a joint.

"Did someone dump you too?" she asked him.

"Not really."

"Well, someone dumped me. How do you like that?"

"It's probably not an irreversible tragedy."

"Do you think I'm pretty?"

"Very."

"Men have always told me I'm pretty, but he just dumped me like an old bag of garbage." She pointed to his half-finished joint. "Could I have some of that?"

He passed it to her, and she leaned her head back on the couch, smoking it. She studied the ceiling. As she handed the joint back to him, she said "My name's Madeleine."

"I'm Jason."

"Hello, Jason."

She leaned out and looked down the long loft to the other end, where the band was playing in front of its reflection in a wall of full-length windows. She was squinting behind her dark glasses. She licked her lips, which were suddenly dry, before she asked "Would you like to dance, Jason?"

"Dance?" He looked around. No one was dancing.

She gestured for the joint, reached for it where it was held tenuous and distant in his hand. Her fingers missed it and he placed it in her hand. She raised it carefully to her lips, where she smoked it down to a stub, then opening her fingers slowly, let it fall onto the wooden floor. She raised her foot and lowered it slowly, grinding the roach beneath it. "Sure" she said. "Dance."

She started up out of the couch, fell back onto it. She tried again and managed to stand up. She planted her feet firmly on the floor, smiling at Jason, arms out to him. She began moving in place. "Dance with me" she said.

He got up, and she moved into his arms. She put both of her arms around his neck, her face against his, and then both of them were dancing in place. She closed her eyes.

She was humming along with the band when she felt a hand drop heavily onto her shoulder. Her eyes opened in surprise as the hand spun her around to face an attractive black woman. Jason had taken his arms from around her; now he stepped back.

The woman moved forward, pushing her body against Madeleine's. She raised a fist in front of Madeleine's face. Long metal earrings shook as her hand shook. "Girl" she said, "you put your hands on my old man again and I'll pull your tits off."

Madeleine stepped back and raised her hand to her face for protection; but the woman turned away and pulled Jason to her and went off with him, her arm in his.

Madeleine tried to hold back her tears, but a few escaped. She had wiped her face clear of them before she realized the woman had scared her almost sober. She drew back her shoulders and with a self-conscious attempt at dignity went looking for Chatto.

She found him talking to a young couple between the door and the band. She spoke to his back. "Chatto, I want to go home."

He turned to her. "In a little while" he said.

"Please, Chatto. Take me home."

"I said we'd leave in a little while" he said. He turned back to the couple.

She stamped her foot. "Chatto, I want you to take me home this minute. Now, damn you!" She was shouting.

Chatto spoke to the couple. "Excuse me" he said. Then he turned again and with his hand firmly on Madeleine's elbow he moved her to the door. He opened the door and pulled her into the threshold. "You want to go?" he said. "Go." He pushed her, and she stumbled onto the landing. He closed the door in her face.

She stood for a moment looking at the closed metal door. Then she kicked it. She kicked it again, hurting her foot. "Goddamn you, Chatto, you bastard!" she screamed at the door. No one responded; the sounds of the party continued as before, and after another minute she went down the stairs to the landing. She sat down on the steps, waiting. She began nodding off. She wrapped her arms around herself, adjusted her body for what comfort the hard steps could provide. She leaned her head against the railing and in minutes was asleep.

She awoke several times to people passing, talking about her on their way from the party. Someone shook her, asked if she was all right; she opened her eyes, nodded and closed them again. The next time she awoke it was to the sound of laughter going down the stairs. After that it was quiet.

It was the silence that woke her finally—that and a rain of dirty light falling onto her through a skylight. She stood up, confused for a moment, wondering how she had gotten there.

She was stiff, and her foot ached as she went up the stairs to the loft door. She opened it, but she did not go in.

Chatto was sitting on the floor with a dozen other people in a circle. They were talking. She watched as a joint passed from hand to hand. The band had gone, and they were the only ones remaining in a hushed conclave that seemed to her secretive, excluding her. She closed the door slowly and left the building.

When she got back to their loft, she pulled the blanket off the bed and sat on the floor beside the bed with the blanket wrapped around her. She did not sleep, did not even close her eyes. Her need for him translated itself into fear. If she lost him, she knew, the loneliness would be too much to endure. She pulled the blanket tighter around her.

An hour later she heard him coming up the stairs. When he appeared in the doorway, she went to him on her knees.

■ ■ ■

The next day, with the help of Johnny Thanopolous, she found a furnished ground-floor studio apartment for them which was on a quiet side street with lean trees and red brick pavement. Johnny advanced her the extra money they needed for a month's rent, and Chatto got an advance for an article he had agreed to write for a magazine so they could buy what was lacking to make the small apartment comfortable and cheerful. Chatto did not much care where they lived or in what circumstances, but Madeleine was determined to make a home for them, and even he was pleased when she had finished.

The first time she saw him reading in the apartment, he wore glasses. He had been wearing them for a month, he told her, but only now for the first time in front of her. She was the only one who knew about them, and it made her feel closer to him when he asked her not to mention them to anyone.

A week after they moved in she bought a pipe she saw in the window of a head shop and carried it in her purse with a small stash when they went out; she smoked it while she cooked and did the housework, but only enough to stay mellow during the day. Chatto provided a phonograph and a box of used records; he did not tell her where they came from and she never asked, but after that, on the evenings when they did not go out, they sat smoking their pipes and listening to music in the light of a red bulb they turned on when they smoked.

Chatto finally unpacked his favorite books from his duffel bag and put them on the bookshelf. Dusting them the first day they were there, Madeleine saw a piece of paper fall out of one; on it was written the words *Hide; be smart; never love anyone*. She replaced it and never mentioned it to him.

He set up his typewriter on the large table where he worked on his play during the day and where they ate at other times. The table was in front of the apartment's only window, and although there were iron bars on the window, it looked onto a fenced-in yard with grass and a stunted tree which valiantly produced a few leaves.

Now on the nights when Madeleine could not sleep or slept for only a few hours, she left the sofa bed she and Chatto slept on and sat in his chair at the window smoking and looking at the tree and a portion of sky she could see over the top of the wooden fence. On those nights the tree reminded her of something out of her past, but she could not remember what it was.

She began to write poetry again with the pipe and the silence to help her. She wrote mostly about the loneliness and uncertainty of love, but it was a new kind of poetry for her, discovered in the books she was reading on her own and with Chatto's guidance. Gone were the rhymes now, the young girl's derivative rhythms and forms, the lofty themes; the new poetry roamed as easily as a cat over the surface of her life as she now lived it. The one poem that was not about love or the domestic details of her life was about the tree. She entitled it "The Memory Tree," and it had in it the only lines she had written that she liked well enough to read over now and then:

> Memory is gone.
> It lives in an old tree now.

She never showed her poems to Chatto, whose books she had read; hers seemed trivial and ephemeral compared to his. She hid them from him in the bottom of a drawer.

She began collecting things off the streets: discarded objects such as candy wrappers, empty matchbooks and coins. She kept them in a coffee can in the back of the closet and sometimes, when Chatto was not there, went over them as if they were treasure. She bought Chatto a pair of silk pajamas, which he wore only once, preferring to sleep naked; and on those nights when he went out alone and did not return until late, she slept with them under her pillow.

In mid-September Chatto finished his play. A week later Mary Vandel began sending Madeleine flowers with notes asking her to meet with her. The flowers always arrived when Chatto was absent. Madeleine tore up the notes and flushed them down the toilet and put the flowers still in their boxes into the garbage can in front of the building. After two weeks during which Madeleine did not respond, the flowers stopped coming. During that time Big Brown was arrested for beating up one of their girls so badly that she nearly died. But the matter was settled by Mary, and the girl dropped the charges against him. Big Brown had begun drinking heavily, and after beating up a bartender and the bouncer at the High Note, he was barred from there for life.

Madeleine began drawing pictures of trees.

* * *

They went to the High Note together on those nights when they had money left over from the household expenses; on other nights Chatto often went out alone. She had been accepted into the ritual of drugs passed among the club's habitués, but except for the joints handed to her beneath the table, she never participated; she was content with the pot and the red wine she drank exclusively.

One night a man called Dr. New commented to her that she seemed very nervous for one so young, and she confessed that she had trouble sleeping. The next night he passed her a packet of Valiums beneath the table, and she took one later in the ladies' room.

Dr. New had graduated recently to the status of intimate at the High Note by dispensing free drugs and writing prescriptions for the jazz musicians, whom he admired and tried to emulate, and those girls who slept with him in exchange. He was a slight man in his forties who had crew-cut hair and wore Indian headbands, buckskin jackets and pants with fringes. He sat in on drums with the musicians when they jammed after hours and would let him; he bought drinks for the musicians and those at the tables he joined, often only for the company of the younger people he enjoyed being with. He was generous, spent lavishly, and lived in the apartment he owned uptown with a series of young girls he had met at the High Note. In the few months he had been among them, he had become an increasingly frequent user of his own drugs, and in combinations that even the others avoided.

Dr. New liked Madeleine, and since he never attempted to have sex with her, she accepted the Valium prescriptions he gave her whenever she needed one. When later she told him of feeling enervated, he supplied her with prescriptions for Dexedrine as well. She discovered Dr. New to be discreet, for he kept his word not to tell Chatto about the prescriptions he gave her in private.

One night Mary Vandel followed Madeleine into the ladies' room. She stood at one of the sinks and waited until Madeleine came out of the stall. Madeleine went to the other sink, and Mary stepped up behind her and put her hands on her shoulders. When Madeleine turned to shrug her off, she found one of the large woman's hands on her breast. She pushed it off. Mary tried to kiss her, but she pushed her away.

Mary said "I love you, Madeleine. I'd do anything for you."

"Then find somebody else to love" Madeleine said, and went past her out the door.

The next night, after Chatto left the apartment, Mary appeared at the door. She was drunk. She said quickly "I can't think of anything but you, darling. Come with me. I'll treat you better than Chatto ever—"

Madeleine slammed the door in her face before she could finish.

Another night Madeleine was waiting for Chatto at the Bucket of Blood and Mary came in and asked her to dance, but she refused and left.

For a week Mary followed her at a distance to and from work. When she approached her one night, Madeleine ran away. Mary stopped following her.

Three days later Madeleine was leaving work, still in her waitress uniform under her overcoat, when someone in a cream-colored Eldorado sounded his horn at her from across the street. Big Brown leaned out the window and waved to her to come to him. She crossed the street and stood by the car door.

"Hello there, Madeleine."

"Hello, Big Brown."

"Me 'n' Chatto's up at my place all alone, drinkin' some good brew. He wants you should come join us."

"Why didn't he come for me himself?"

"I had to go out for a minute on business. I said I'd pick you up."

Madeleine did not answer, hesitating. Big Brown smiled. "Come on, girl, get in. It's too cold out here for this skinhead of mine."

She went to the other side and got in beside him. A large hat was on the seat between them, but even when he wasn't wearing it his head nearly touched the roof. "I either got to get a bigger car" he said "or start wearing smaller hats."

He drove the car smoothly onto the street and took an eight-track tape from a batch of them over the dashboard and inserted it into the tape player. Rock music began blaring in stereo front and back. He had to shout for her to hear him over it.

"I can't stand that namby-pamby jazz like they play at the High Note. I like rock, don't you? Listen here." He began pounding the steering wheel to the music with a hand that was twice the size of hers. He shouted in time to the music "I like white music, white Cadillacs, and—ooohee!—those fine white women!" He threw back his head and laughed.

He turned onto a residential street and drove past an alley next to an apartment building. He stopped in the street alongside two large garbage cans standing ten feet apart next to the curb. He said "The only thing wrong with this neighborhood's you can't get a parking space and the nearest garage is four blocks away. Them's our cans. The police try to look out for me, but I put them there just in case. Last sucker moved them cans rode away on four flat tires."

He laughed again, got out and moved the cans back onto the side-walk. Then he pulled into his space, turned off the music and opened the door for her. She got out.

They went into the apartment building and through a foyer full of mirrors on thick carpets and up three floors in an elevator next to a stairway. Big Brown was silent, smiling down at her in the elevator.

He used his key to get into the apartment. Madeleine was surprised to see that the large living room was tastefully decorated: the furniture was spare but expensive-looking; there were throw rugs on the polished oak floor. The effect was of spaciousness. There were shelves full of books, abstract paintings and prints on the walls, and at the far end was a large picture window looking onto the street, a small dining table in front of it, and two high-backed wooden chairs on each side of the window. There was no one else in the room.

"Where's Chat—" she began. Then she heard a lock click and a chain put in place behind her. She turned. Big Brown stood in front of the door, his suit coat unbuttoned.

"We can do this nice" he said "or you can get hurt. Mary gave me permission if you need some convincing." He pointed to a closed door on his left. "Go into the bedroom, girl. She's waiting for you there. If you give her any trouble, I'll come in and join you."

Madeleine backed away. "Let me out of here" she said.

"Oh, girl" he said in a sad voice, "how many times you think I heard that before?"

He came forward and reached out with his long arm, his hand grabbing her coat collar before she could move out of the way. She turned sharply and he yanked on the coat; one by one its buttons came off and clicked onto the floor. He pulled at the coat again, and it tore around her; but before he could get his other hand on it, she slipped out of it and ran out of reach.

He seemed surprised for a moment that he was holding an empty coat, then flung it away. As he came toward her again his hands went to his belt. He opened the large silver buckle and pulled on the belt; it came hissing out like a snake.

Madeleine turned to run, but the belt caught her, hissing until the metal bit into her bare leg. It whipped into the flesh of her leg again as she tried to dodge it. Big Brown was smiling. When she backed into the end of a couch, her fingers went to a heavy glass ashtray on an end table; she threw it, but he avoided it easily and kept coming. Then she picked up the end table itself and threw it at him.

It caught him unguarded and distracted him long enough for her to run past the couch and around the small dining table to the window.

She picked up the table in both hands and turned with it to the window.

He did not move, just stood in disbelief as the table left Madeleine's body and went crashing into the window. Large pieces of glass fell onto the floor and the windowsill as the rest of the window collapsed outward and out of sight. Cold air filled the room as she heard the window shattering below.

"Shit!" he murmured as the table tottered on the window's edge for a few seconds, half in and half out, before sliding slowly forward and down. They both heard it crash into the sidewalk.

"You crazy?" he shouted and began to move toward her again when he was stopped by the sight of the four chairs, one after the other, following the table out the window. She turned to him, her expression one of fury, not fear.

"Will you let me out of here, you moron?" she screamed. He raised his hand but did not answer, so she turned back and picking up a floor lamp with one hand, yanked it out of the wall socket by the cord with the other. She heaved it, and it flew through the window. The cord slid across the floor, then followed the lamp, whipping the windowsill like a tail.

"Will you open that door and let me out now?" she screamed again. She looked around, but there seemed to be nothing left to throw until she saw some paintings on the wall. She yanked one away and threw it through the window. It went sailing, then dropped. As she reached for a larger painting, she heard him scream behind her. "*All right,* you crazy bitch!"

She yanked the painting down anyway and was holding it when she turned and saw him at the door, unlocking it. She stayed where she was. Mary was at the bedroom doorway watching. She was either smiling or in pain.

Madeleine advanced several steps. "Open the door" she said.

He opened it wide, flinging it back in disgust.

"Now get back" Madeleine said. She pointed to Mary. "With her."

He moved into the bedroom doorway with Mary.

She moved to within ten feet of the open door, the painting under one arm. "Get into the bedroom, both of you, and close the door" she said.

They stepped back into the bedroom. The door closed quietly after them.

She ran through the doorway and down the hallway, where she dropped the painting before she got to the stairs. She went down them two and three steps at a time until she reached the foyer and ran past her reflections in the mirrors until she was back on the street.

She began trembling and felt the pain in her bleeding leg as she limped the six blocks back to the apartment.

Chatto was reading in his chair at the table when she came in. He took off his glasses, put down the book and stood up.

"What happened?" he asked.

She ran sobbing into his arms.

"What the hell happened?" he demanded.

She sat on the side of the bed and told him. She had expected sympathy from him. Instead he stood looking at her coldly when she was done. Panic came upon her, but she did not know why. When Chatto asked "Why did you go there with him? Didn't you know they're both pimps? That she's a dyke?" she began crying again.

"Answer me" he said. He was standing over her. "Are you so dumb you didn't know what they wanted? Or is it that you're as naive as those silly poems you write?"

She looked up. "You read my poems, Chatto? You had no right."

"What makes your kind think you can write poetry when you feel nothing, know nothing, *care about nothing* that matters to anyone but you? Must I strip you of that conceit too before you realize how little you matter?"

She put her hand up in front of her face as if to protect herself. "Chatto, please" she begged. "Don't."

He went on. "Or maybe the thought of Big Brown fucking you excited you? You wouldn't be the first white girl to come around here queer for black men."

She jumped up screaming. She tried to hit him, but he turned her around easily and pushed her back onto the bed. She had stopped crying. She was glaring at him now. They were both silent.

He took his coat off the back of the chair and put it on. He walked past her to the door. Then he turned back to her. "Head fuckers" he said. "I've seen your kind before."

"What's that mean?"

"That you're a lousy piece of ass, Madeleine."

"Is that all I am to you—a piece of ass?"

"Just barely that" he said, and opened the door and left.

She lay back on the bed, arm over her eyes. Then she took it away and stared at the ceiling. She sat up on the side of the bed and reached into her uniform pocket and took a folded tissue out of it. She picked the three remaining Valiums from it and let the tissue fall to the floor.

She went into the small kitchen and washed the pills down with water at the sink, then went back and lay down again on her side. She drew up her legs and buried her head in her arms. Twenty minutes later her breath began to come more regularly. She slept.

She was still sleeping at two-thirty in the morning when Big Brown's Eldorado drew up opposite his parking space outside his building. It stopped. Both of the large cans had been toppled, their contents of garbage and refuse spilled next to the curb. Cursing, he drove down the street and out of sight around the corner.

A half-hour later he came walking around the other corner. When he passed the alley, Chatto stepped out of its shadows behind him. "Hello, Leonard" he said. He was holding a baseball bat at his side.

Big Brown whirled around. "Who the—" he began, but when he saw the bat he did not finish. His hand reached for Chatto's throat.

But Chatto had raised the bat at the same moment, bringing it down with such force from above his head that when it met the arm as it rose, he heard the arm break at the elbow. Big Brown screamed as the lower half of his arm dropped away, swinging like a pendulum. He reached over with his other hand to hold it, but the bat had come around again and he screamed louder this time as his wrist splintered and his hand jerked outward at an angle. It twitched twice, then was still. It took two blows for Chatto to break Big Brown's leg below the knee, but he did not scream this time, just whimpered as he dropped onto his other knee. The huge man was kneeling before Chatto; he swayed, but he seemed determined to remain upright. He was silent except for his breath coming in gasps; what he must accept, they both knew, was less important now than how he accepted it. Then the bat came down again on his other kneecap, shattering it. He grunted as the leg folded under him. Then slowly, as a tree falls, he fell.

Chatto threw the bat into the alley and stooping, undid Big Brown's trousers.

A pair of garden shears appeared in Chatto's hand. Lifting his prize, he waited until Big Brown's eyes opened. Then he lowered the shears. This time Big Brown's scream could be heard blocks away. Then he was silent.

Chatto threw the darker object into the alley, then stepped over Big Brown and walked away.

Madeleine could not find a white overcoat to replace the one left in Big Brown and Mary's apartment, so she bought a serape of white and gold with another loan from Johnny Thanopolous. She began wearing Mexican jewelry with it.

After six months in the hospital, Big Brown left town on crutches. While he was still in the hospital, Mary bought him out of his share in their business. She had planned for a long time to get it off the streets, open a house where she could introduce special services to a select clientele. Dr. New had helped launch it by bringing her customers from uptown. She began making money and a reputation in a spectacular way.

A month after Big Brown was found in the alley after being attacked by rival pimps (it was his explanation, and although they all suspected and Mary knew who the real assailant was, no one challenged it), Madeleine and Chatto moved into a much cheaper apartment in the poorest section of the neighborhood. Madeleine regretted the loss of the apartment, but her debt to Johnny Thanopolous and the cost of nights at the High Note and a steady supply of pot and Madeleine's pills made a choice necessary between the apartment and those daily expenses, and neither she nor Chatto hesitated to choose the latter.

The door to the new third-floor apartment opened into the kitchen; a large bathtub on legs stood just inside it. The front room, overlooking the street, was large, the one bedroom small and window-less. There was no furniture; they had to buy a used bed and mattress at the Goodwill, and the pieces they already had were so few that the front room with its large unshaded windows looked barren. The linoleum in the kitchen was encrusted with grime, and the rotting wooden floors in the other rooms were uncarpeted. There was a tin lid that fitted over the bathtub where they placed two wooden chairs side by side to eat and where Chatto set up his typewriter when he worked on his poetry during the day; his play had been optioned by a man named Max Kemmelman who still had not produced it after four months, despite his initial enthusiasm. There was an old-fashioned pull-chain toilet in a wooden stall in the kitchen. Nothing Madeleine did rid the apartment of cock-roaches, and at night they could hear rats scrambling between the walls. But what she missed most from the old apartment was the tree.

One morning Madeleine watched from their window as workmen hoisted a concert grand piano on pulleys from the street through a window of the apartment below theirs. That night they heard their new neighbor, Billy Tyler, playing jazz and classical music beautifully on it. The sound rose to them clearly through the floor.

Madeleine had seen Billy Tyler perform with his trio at the High Note. A talented, classically trained jazz pianist, Billy seemed uncon-cerned—or bore with humor and forbearance—the fact that his recent popular success was due in part to his being a dwarf. Madeleine had noted that while he included a great deal of humor in his performance, none of it derived from his physical appearance. He had to hop down from the piano bench, and his misproportioned body waddled when he walked, in the manner of all dwarves, but other than that, everything about him overshadowed his deformity. A few minutes into his playing, even the tourists who came to the High Note to see a curiosity forgot that he was a dwarf.

Madeleine's insomnia had returned now, no matter how many Valiums she took, and on those nights when Chatto went out alone and she could not sleep, she turned off the lights and sat smoking pot as she listened to Billy Tyler playing. She had asked Chatto, who knew him, to introduce her, but he refused. She knew the reason was that Billy Tyler was a white man making money playing the black man's music in a business where most of the great black musicians had died in obscurity and poverty. One night when she and Billy were both alone, she took her pipe and stash and knocked at the little man's door.

They became friends that night. They had affinities: both had known loneliness and rejection. But Billy's defense against it was to satirize the normal world, which in so many ways excluded him; he made Madeleine laugh.

Billy had fashioned a sumptuous personal world for himself in his apartment. Thick purple drapes hid the windows and the street from sight. Instead of lamps, he had placed dozens of fitted-glass globes of all sizes and colors around the front room; when he turned off the overhead light, it was like sitting in the midst of a galaxy. There was a red velvet-covered couch and deep scarlet chairs with Oriental carpets in every room. A large metal gong and a wooden hammer stood at the foot of his canopied bed. A mink-covered toilet seat and a replica of the great dwarf Voltaire's death mask were on the walls.

In the privacy of his apartment, Billy assumed a different persona— which, like all parody, was part yearning. He wore ascots with velvet smoking jackets, spats and long monogrammed silk dressing gowns. He smoked cigarettes through a long carved ivory holder, and hashish in a hookah.

Madeleine often curled up on the couch while he played for her— not just jazz and classical pieces, but show tunes as well. He loved to sing the old standards—Cole Porter, Jerome Kern and Gershwin—and with his high-pitched voice he convulsed Madeleine with laughter each time he imitated Noël Coward singing the uncensored version of "Let's Fall in Love."

One night she met a girl there named Sylvia Rosenberg. She was quiet, made herself unobtrusive, but was obviously Billy's lover. She left a few minutes after Madeleine arrived.

They were talking one night—Madeleine on the couch and Billy in a chair across from her—when someone pounded on the door.

"Who is it?" Billy called from his chair.

She recognized Chatto's voice. "Madeleine, are you in there?"

Billy struggled to get out of his chair, but Madeleine rose first. "I'll get it" she said, and went smiling to the door.

The moment she kissed Chatto as he stood in the doorway, her smile died. She began trembling.

"Get out here" he said.

"Billy was just—"

"I don't give a fuck what Billy was doing. Get your damn ass out here."

Billy left his chair and came toward them as if intending to intercede for her, but Chatto turned him around with a look. Billy hopped back into his chair.

They returned to their apartment in silence, where Chatto got his duffel bag out of the bedroom closet and began shoving his clothes into it. Madeleine moved cautiously into the doorway. "What are you doing, Chatto?"

"I'm tired of all this bullshit: that fag downstairs, all those pills you think I don't know you're taking, your moodiness. We used to have a few laughs together. Well, it's time to check out now."

"Don't leave me, Chatto. I'll kill myself if you leave me."

"Go ahead. Do something right for a change. Get your stupid white ass out of my life forever."

"Please. I'll do anything. I know I was wrong to go down there. I won't see Billy again."

He turned to her. She looked down at the floor. She waited. When he spoke, it was softly, no longer angry. "Do you understand now who the master is in this house?"

"Yes, Chatto."

"You'll obey me from now on?"

"Yes, Chatto."

"Kneel in front of me, then."

She went to him and dropped to her knees.

Later he replaced his things out of the duffel bag while she sat on a chair watching him. When he left without speaking to her again, she took five Valiums and the pipe and the plastic bag from her purse. She swallowed the Valiums without water and lit the pipe with a match. She waited for Billy to begin playing, but he was silent too.

She learned the next day that Chatto's play had been rejected by the producer as too controversial. He had never offered to let her see it and by then it was too late to tell him she had read his carbon copy and that its power and poetry had impressed her as nothing else ever had.

She used the Dexedrines during the day and the Valiums at night. She still drank wine only moderately at the High Note but now kept a bottle of wine hidden among her clothes for when Chatto was not there and she was too nervous for the pills alone to help. It was to keep a balance, to keep the tightrope from swaying. She could sink into her skin and look outward from a world that was colorless and enclosed her. When the outer world began screaming, she could silence it.

Being alone became no different than being among people. She was roused only by Chatto's increasingly infrequent lovemaking. On those occasions when he did make love to her, there was a viciousness in it now that precluded any thought of her pleasure, and even defied her to feel any. She could not tell him that his indifference to her feelings excited her. She sometimes pleasured herself when he was not there so that she could feel even less worthy of him.

Because she thought it would please him, she wore rouge and eye shadow when they went to the High Note. Mary Vandel still showed up for a few hours every night, but now her table was filled with some of her wealthy customers and celebrities she brought there. Madeleine knew that Chatto had begun working for Mary in some capacity that seemed to be known only to a few of Mary's inner circle; he had already turned down her offer that he recruit new girls for her house, so it was not that. But even so, Madeleine was surprised when one night they joined Mary's table at the High Note.

Madeleine sat looking into her lap; she spoke only when Chatto spoke to her. He had sat across from her, beside Mary, and most of the time he ignored her. She was looking down as the others were all laughing and talking when she became aware that Chatto had become silent and was watching her. Then the others at the table became silent too. When she looked up, she saw that they were watching Chatto, who was holding his hand out to her. When he told her to kiss it, she did it without hesitation.

Dr. New was arrested in the spring for illegal trafficking in drugs; Madeleine heard about it at the High Note. At first she was unconcerned that his absence ended her source for the pills: it was a problem, but one she managed to put away in that place where she kept all problems that were not immediate. But when there were only a dozen pills left in each bottle, she forced herself to face the fact that she had to find a new supplier.

She knew that no doctor would prescribe them for her in her condition and in the amounts she required; the pushers on their street only dealt in marijuana and heroin; Billy Tyler was too frightened of Chatto to help her; and the only others who could do so were those people she knew at the High Note. So that night she went alone for the first time, when she knew Chatto would not be there.

They assured her they would not tell Chatto she had asked, but denied they knew anyone who could get them for her. She understood what they were really saying: Chatto had put out the word not to help her. She had taken a chance even to ask, and now she was too frightened to pursue it further.

She left, bought a bottle of wine, and drank it that night with six of the remaining Valiums. It was enough so that she was asleep before Chatto came in, and the next day half of the Dexedrines got her through work and into the evening. The rest of the pills were in her purse, and before she and Chatto left that night for the High Note, she went into the toilet and took two Valiums. Her hands shook so badly that she dropped the bottle cap into the toilet. She was perspiring and for a moment was afraid she would throw up and Chatto would hear her.

She did throw up later, in a stall in the ladies' room at the High Note; then she dry-heaved a dozen times before she felt well enough to come out and put water on her temples at a sink. Mary came in while she was drying her face with a paper towel. Still clutching the paper towel in her hand, Madeleine backed away from Mary against the wall. "Stay away from me" she warned.

Mary kept at a distance. "You look like hell" she said. "I heard about your problem."

"You? Oh, God, does Chatto know too? Did someone tell him I was here?"

"No. No one wants to bring bad news to Chatto. But I make it my business to know what's going on."

Madeleine threw the crumpled paper towel at the wastebasket. It hit the rim and bounced back to her feet.

"Can I help you?" Mary asked.

Madeleine straightened. "I don't need anything from you" she said and went to the door.

"If you change your mind" Mary said as she was leaving "let me know. Just give me twelve hours' notice."

Outside the door, Madeleine bumped into Sylvia Rosenberg going in. She almost knocked her down.

"Are you all right, Madeleine?" Sylvia asked.

"Yes. Fine."

A small girl carrying a book and wearing tie-dyed jeans and love beads, Sylvia did not drink, did not take drugs—did not do anything, as far as Madeleine knew, except come every night to the High Note and sit alone at a table close to the musicians, waiting to see which one of them would take her to bed at the end of the evening. Madeleine had heard that sometimes the musicians cut cards for her. On those nights when no one wanted her, she went away looking forlorn. She was said to have recently had an affair with Billy Tyler, but now she was back at the High Note. She put her hand on Madeleine's shoulder and said "You look sick. Can I help you?"

"No, Sylvia. I'm all right. Thank you. Excuse me."

She hurried back to the table.

The last six Dexedrines helped her through work the next day; she actually felt good walking back to the apartment. Then she stopped in the middle of the sidewalk. She was looking up at a tree a half block away in which she saw clearly dozens of children hanging by their hands from its branches. She closed her eyes, then looked again. They were still there, some of them swinging back and forth. They were smiling at her. One of them waved. She ran.

She rushed into the apartment, leaving the door open behind her, and into the stall where she fell onto her knees beside the toilet and heaved into it again and again. Nothing solid came up, but even after she felt better and wanted to stop, she could not. When she did finally stop, she lay with her cheek on the side of the bowl, breathing heavily. Tears came to her eyes, but she was not crying.

She took the last three Valiums at the sink and had time to smoke two pipefuls of pot before she heard Chatto coming up the stairs. She managed to make dinner, and although her hands shook and he kept looking at her, he did not say anything. He left an hour later, telling her he had a job to do for Mary and would not be back until late.

She went to the High Note at ten o'clock, the hour Mary usually arrived. She ordered a glass of wine and sat at the bar watching the door, fearing Chatto might walk through it at any moment.

He did not, but Mary arrived an hour later. Madeleine caught her eye, then went to the ladies' room and waited.

Mary entered minutes later. They waited until two women finished and left. Madeleine asked "Why do you want to help me? You won't get anything for it."

"I'm used to that from you. Maybe it's because I feel sorry for you. What difference does it make?"

"All right" Madeleine said. "I'll trust you this time."

"What is it you need?" Mary asked.

"Dexedrine and Valium—and sleeping pills. I can't sleep most nights."

"Come to my apartment after you leave work tomorrow."

"Your place?" Madeleine looked alarmed.

"If you want me to deliver them too, then to hell with you" Mary said. She started to leave.

"Wait!"

Mary turned back at the door. She did not speak.

"All right" Madeleine said. "I'll come."

Mary opened the door.

"Mary?"

"What?"

"Can you get me something in the meantime? To hold me over?"

"I thought you would never ask" Mary said. She took a plastic packet from her slacks pocket and handed it to her. There were four pills in it.

"What are they?" Madeleine asked.

"Quaaludes. Be careful. They're strong."

Mary was half through the door when she turned back. "Didn't you ever learn to say thank you?"

"Thank you" Madeleine said softly.

"You know" Mary said, "there was a time when I believed in things like goodness, decency and human dignity. Then I lost it. Never mind how. You were my last hope to get them back." She left, leaving Madeleine staring at the door.

Madeleine was there on time the next night. She knocked and heard Mary call "Come in, it's unlocked." She went in but left the door ajar behind her. She looked around.

"You needn't worry. We're alone" Mary said from where she sat on the couch in a dressing gown with dark slacks underneath.

Madeleine went to her but stood on her side of the coffee table that separated them.

"Do you want to sit down?" Mary asked.

Madeleine shook her head.

"Do you like the new furniture?" Mary asked, smiling. "Some of it's new, anyway."

Madeleine did not answer.

"Moonlight, Moonlight" Mary said. "Where have you gone? It seems like such a short time ago that you were my moon goddess. I loved you. I could still love you if you let me. What do you say to that?"

Madeleine remained silent.

"All right" Mary said. "Here." She took three bottles from the pocket of her robe and held them out to Madeleine, who took them across the coffee table and put them in her purse.

"How much do I owe you for them?" Madeleine asked.

"Nothing."

"I want to pay for them."

Mary sighed. "If you insist. Twenty dollars will cover it."

Madeleine put the money on the coffee table, then started for the door.

"Is that all I get for my trouble?" she heard Mary say.

"It's all you asked for."

She found her safe world again. Deep, without reflections, where her fears could be silenced. Mary kept her supplied with pills, which now, she was surprised to discover, were always nearly gone.

It took a week during which Chatto did not make love to her before the anxiety began that with that last bond between them gone she would lose him. She could not talk to him about it—just the thought was enough to raise the anxiety to panic. So that night when he came home in the late morning and thought she was asleep, she turned over in bed and drew close to him. She reached under the sheet and fondled him and his eyes opened looking at her, but nothing happened. She was naked and she lifted his hand and put it on her breast, but it just lay there. She kissed him and his eyes remained open, but his lips were closed and unresponsive. He turned away from her. "Please" she whispered. She waited. Then she accepted it. She raised herself up, then got onto her knees. She drew down the sheet, which was all that covered them in the July night. Then she went on her knees to the foot of the bed and bending, kissed his feet again and again.

A week later he did not come home at all. The next day she was so nervous she repeatedly made mistakes at work and asked Johnny Thanopolous if she could leave two hours early.

She rushed home, but Chatto was not there. When she took the bottle out of her purse, she could not believe there were only two Valiums left. She smoked a pipeful of pot, then lay down on the bed fully clothed. She pulled the sheet over her head. I'll wait, she thought. I've learned how to wait.

She had not. She was at the High Note at seven o'clock, but although the club was open and the bartender and waiters were setting up for the night's business, there were no customers. She asked the bartender if he had seen Chatto, but he just shook his head as he went on drying a glass with a towel.

She hurried out and went to the Bucket of Blood a few blocks away. It was where the older Italian and Irish residents of the neighborhood mixed uneasily with the newer, younger ones. A place of rough people and drunks where Chatto had taken her and sometimes went without her. There was sawdust on the floor and an old jukebox where Bing Crosby and Perry Como coexisted uneasily with Thelonious Monk, Miles Davis and Charlie Parker. Mau-Mau Sue was drinking gloomily at the bar.

Madeleine sat at the bar next to the fat black woman and ordered a glass of wine. When the bartender was not busy, she asked him if he had seen Chatto or knew when he would be in, but he just shook his head, as if there were a rule against bartenders speaking when asked such questions.

She looked in all of the other bars where he might be, had a glass of wine in each. She had taken the last two Valiums in the ladies' room of the first bar, and an hour later her hands were shaking. At nine o'clock she hurried back to the High Note.

Chatto was not there, but by then she was thinking not just of him, and by ten-thirty, when Mary came through the door, she was thinking of him even less, preoccupied as she was with her own nervousness and anxiety, which had reached a new level.

At the sight of Mary she jumped up from her stool at the bar. She stumbled and her wine glass toppled, bleeding on the bar. She signaled Mary, then went to the ladies' room. She turned, watching the door. Minutes went by. She paced, passing, then repassing a woman's feet on the floor of a stall. The woman came out five minutes later and washed her hands. She combed her hair and put on new lipstick. Madeleine wanted to scream at her to leave. She did leave, but slowly, lingering with her reflection at the mirror, turning reluctantly away from it at the last second as Mary passed her coming in.

"What is it?" Mary asked. She stood with her back to the door.

"Do you know where Chatto is?"

"No." She turned to leave.

"Mary, wait! I need pills. Tonight. I'm sorry. They just—went. You can get them for me tonight, can't you?"

"No." She started to leave again.

"Please, Mary!"

"As a matter of fact, Madeleine" Mary said with the door open, "I'm not sure I can have them for you tomorrow either. My connection left town." She left.

When Madeleine got back to the apartment, she drank a glass of wine standing at the kitchen sink. It made her feel better, her hands shook less. She carried another glass of wine and the bottle into the living room and, sitting at a chair by the window, took her pipe and private stash from her purse. She shook the plastic bag, held it up to look at it in the light. There was only enough left for one pipeful, but Chatto had bought an ounce two days before. It began to rain, and she watched as the first raindrops fell, slowly expanding on the window. She finished the pipe and got up to get the new stash.

She looked in the drawer under Chatto's clothes where he kept it. It was gone. She pulled everything out of the drawer, letting it all fall to the floor, but the pot was not there. She did the same with the other drawers. Then she searched the apartment.

It was then she noticed that Chatto's typewriter was gone too. She sat down where she was, on the floor by the window. The Dexis are working at least, she thought. The raindrops sounded like bombs now. Cars passed on the street, their lights flashing on the window like signals.

She finished the wine, then took two Nembutals; but for a while the sleeping pills and amphetamines only caused her to lie there, eyes wide, as the ceiling slid back and forth over her head. Then it stopped. She curled up on the floor and slept.

She awoke to a horror of waking: fear of everything. It was daylight. Voices and the sounds of traffic came to her from the street, and they frightened her.

She spent most of the day in bed, only hurrying out at ten o'clock to call Johnny Thanopolous and say she was sick and could not come to work. She threw up in the hallway on her way out. She got nauseated again in the phone booth and minutes later stepped into an alley, where she bent retching, then stood with her sweating forehead against the brick wall. She bought two bottles of wine, but when she returned to the apartment, the first taste of it sent her running to the toilet and onto her knees, vomiting into the bowl. She tried later to eat but could not hold down food either. In bed she alternated between fever and chills.

By early evening she managed to eat a piece of toast and afterward drank half a bottle of wine. She got dressed and, perspiring, hands shaking, went down onto the street, where she saw a young Puerto Rican standing in the doorway of an apartment building. She had seen him before and knew he dealt drugs on that block. He watched her as she approached. He was wearing yellow shoes and a crucifix on a long chain.

"Would you sell me some pot?" she asked.

"Sure, baby. Come in here."

She looked past him into a dark hallway. "There?"

"Yeah."

"Bring it out."

"The heat's down. Nobody's dealing on the street now, chicky. It's in my apartment."

She backed away from him.

"What's the matter, baby? You think I'm gonna rape you? You could trust me. You want a hit too? It wouldn't cost you. We could work something out."

She hurried back to the apartment.

She held out until midnight, then went to the High Note. Chatto was not there. Others she knew at the bar turned away as she passed them.

Mary was at her table with some of her customers. Madeleine went to the table, where they kept talking, and stood at Mary's side, waiting to be noticed. Mary ignored her until she spoke. "Mary?"

Mary looked up. The others became silent. "What is it, Madeleine?"

"Could I talk to you?"

"About what?"

"It's private, Mary."

Mary got up and, without looking at Madeleine, went ahead of her to the ladies' room. Madeleine followed in silence.

They waited until a woman left. Then Mary asked "What is it now?"

Madeleine was shaking again. "Please, Mary, you have to get some for me. I'm sick. I feel like I'm dying."

Mary was silent.

Madeleine began crying. All of her body was shaking. "*Please help me*" she said between sobs.

Mary watched her in silence for a minute, then said "You're really strung out now, aren't you? Do you need it that badly?"

"Yes, Mary."

Mary made a sound like sighing. "All right. Be at my apartment in an hour."

She was there pacing the hall when Mary got off the elevator. She followed her into the apartment, eyes lowered.

Mary went to the couch and sat down. Madeleine waited on the other side of the coffee table. This time Mary did not invite her to sit down. She lit a cigarette, then sat smoking and looking at her. Finally she spoke. "Come closer, Moonlight."

Madeleine moved to the side of the coffee table closer to Mary.

"You're a wreck, aren't you?" Mary asked.

"Yes."

Mary said quietly "Take your clothes off."

She undressed, putting her clothes on the coffee table. Then she stood with her arms at her sides, head bowed, waiting.

Mary continued smoking, watching her. She said "If I asked you to go to bed with me now, would you?"

"Yes."

Mary leaned forward and put out her cigarette in an ashtray. She said "Where did your arrogance go, Moonlight? Where is your pride now?"

Madeleine was silent.

"You can put your clothes on" Mary said.

Madeleine looked up to see Mary taking the familiar three bottles from a drawer in the coffee table. She held them up for her to see. Then she threw them at Madeleine's feet. "This was a lesson. Pretty soon those pills won't be enough. You'll want something stronger. I'll keep you supplied. But the next time I ask you, be prepared to come here as my lover. Chatto won't mind. He's finished with you. No one else will help you. I'll see to that. And when I'm through with you, maybe I'll put you to work for me. You see, Madeleine, the difference between what you were and a tramp has always been a very fine line. Now get dressed and get out of here."

As Madeleine was leaving, she saw another large woman Mary's age watching her from the bedroom doorway.

She took five Valiums sitting on the stairway below Mary's apartment. She stared at the sky through a window. A hummingbird came to the window, hung in the air, then flew off. It could have come there to look at her. Minutes later she wondered if there had been a hummingbird at all.

She returned to the High Note. When she opened the door, the sounds of a new band came out to her, a tenor saxophone screaming in notes building higher. She saw Chatto immediately and began pushing through the crowd along the bar.

He was sitting at the bar with an attractive blonde girl. He had his back to Madeleine, his arm over the girl's shoulder. She was caressing his face. She leaned forward and kissed him.

Madeleine shook his shoulder. "Chatto—"

He turned to her, but in his own time. "What do you want?"

"I need to talk to you, Chatto."

"Leave me alone." He turned back to the girl.

Madeleine put her hand on his shoulder again and tried to pull him around to her. He shook it off. "Leave me alone" he said. "I'm through with you."

"No, Chatto! Please." She was shouting. The girl turned away in embarrassment. "Please, Chatto, give me another chance. Just come home. I'll change. I'll be anything you want me to be."

He turned back to her. "You don't understand, do you? I've already gone."

"Chatto, please! Don't do this to me." She began crying. People turned to watch them. "I'm sorry" she went on. "I'll be better. Chatto, I love you. *Please don't leave me.*"

He got off his stool. He brought the girl with him, holding her arm. He moved her ahead of him past Madeleine, then started past her himself, pushing her back. Her hand had gone out reaching for him, but he avoided it. It hung there. The girl had gone into the crowd, but before Chatto started after her, he said "All you ever loved, white bitch, was my black cock."

She watched his head advancing in the crowd, people pushed aside around him. It reached the door and stopped, facing the blonde head. Then the door opened and they went out together.

Madeleine stood watching the closed door until passing customers moved her back against the bar. She turned away and slid onto the blonde girl's empty stool.

She did not move. The bartender kept watching her, but he did not come near her. She stirred only after a voice next to her asked for the second time "Are you all right?"

She turned to it; it belonged to a black man about thirty in a gray business suit. He might have been a bank clerk or a salesman. "Are you all right?" he asked again.

She nodded. Then she said "Yes." She smiled at him. "Would you buy me a drink?"

"Of course. What would you like?"

"Whatever you're drinking."

He held up two fingers and called "Scotch and water" to the bartender, who served them in silence.

The man held up his glass in a toast. "To good times still to come."

"What?" Madeleine asked. Then seeing his raised glass, she smiled at him again and touched her glass to his. They both drank. He had put his arm across the back of her stool, and when he moved his hand onto her shoulder she did not object. She was looking into her glass when she asked "Would you like to go somewhere else?"

"Where?"

"To my place."

He finished his drink, got up. "I'll buy a bottle" he said.

She went ahead of him to the door, where he held it open for her.

As she passed onto the street, the saxophone began screaming again behind her.

She waited outside the liquor store until he came out with a pint of scotch in a paper bag. When he attempted to put his arm around her as they walked, she let him.

When they arrived at the apartment, she told him to go in ahead of her. She passed close to him in the darkness and went to the doorway and turned on the wall light switch on the other side of it. "Go in" she said. "I'll pour us some drinks." She was standing back in shadows when he passed her going into the living room. He handed her the bottle on the way.

She turned on the kitchen wall switch and in that light took down two glasses from the cabinet over the sink. She lifted the bottle from the bag and put it next to the glasses on the sideboard. She was calm, her hands steady. She was smiling when she turned back, but her mouth was dry. She felt the fear and excitement starting in her stomach. She went through the doorway into the living room.

The man's back was to her as he stood looking out the window. He did not turn around when he heard her. "Excuse me" she said and moved into the bedroom.

She went to the bureau and opened a drawer and took her cosmetics bag out of it; it held the lipstick, eyebrow pencil, powder, rouge and eye shadow she wore when she went out with Chatto at night.

She passed through the living room, where the man was still standing looking out the window, went into the kitchen and entered the stall, where there was a small mirror on the wall. When she came out of it ten minutes later, her face was made up in garish imitation of a whore's face. She was smiling.

She crossed to the sink and poured scotch into the two glasses. She picked up the glasses in both hands, then stood holding them. She stared at the wall. She shook her head and lowered the glasses back onto the sideboard.

She went to the wall switch and turned the light off in the kitchen. Then she reached through the doorway and, feeling for it on the other side of the wall, flicked the switch off in the living room too. She stepped into the doorway.

The only illumination was from the windows. Shadows hung on the walls, and as the man stood facing her now in the middle of the room, his face was in shadows too.

She went to him and sank to her knees in front of him. Her hands went to his belt. She began opening it. "Just stand there. Don't say anything" she whispered as her fingers touched his zipper. She drew it down slowly.

She fondled him, then raised it and lowered her head to feast on her sorrow.

He was gone. He had disappeared like a shadow, leaving her there on her knees. She did not feel anything now. The self-loathing she had felt minutes before had cleansed her. The fear had not begun yet.

When she arose from her knees, it was as if a shadow had come to life in the room. She went to the chair by the window and lowered herself slowly into it.

She did not look out the window; she stared at the wall opposite her. Nothing impressed itself on her eyes; thought had shriveled inside her. When an hour later she became aware of the noises from the street, she was surprised they were there. Her hands began trembling again. The feel and the taste of it returned to her with clarity. She saw herself again on her knees. She gasped and threw up her hands in front of her face to push the image away, but it persisted.

She went into the kitchen, turning on both lights along the way. Her purse was on the sideboard where she had left it. Looking for the Valiums, she saw three bottles. She did not have to think about it; she took the new bottle of Nembutals and put the purse aside. She picked up one of the glasses of scotch and went into the bedroom, turning on the light. She sat down on the side of the bed.

She opened and tilted the bottle of Nembutals. The capsules slid into her hand. She did not count them. She knew there would be thirty of them there.

The moment she held them she felt calm. Peace intensified into perfection. Everything frightening vanished before the promise in her hand.

She washed them down with the scotch and lay back on the bed, her head on the pillow, her arm over the side of the bed, still holding the empty glass. Her fingers relaxed, opened. The glass fell to the floor without breaking. She closed her eyes.

She heard the kitchen door open, voices in the apartment, and was roused enough to open her eyes again. When she saw Chatto and the blonde girl standing in the doorway, she stretched out her arms to him. She raised her emblazoned face from the pillow. She heard him say "The bitch is here. Look at her face. She's crazy" and he and the girl turned in the doorway, began fading, then soared off.

Her head lowered back onto the pillow, her eyes closed. She felt warm as she floated away.

I should have saved the kitten, she thought.

21

When Willa was four she ran away three times. She had little knowledge of the world outside the house and did not know where to go, except that she could not travel where grown people were or she would be taken by the kidnappers and lose her freedom forever.

The first time she left she went through the woods close to the highway hoping she could cross it and find a haven on the other side. She stood behind a tree looking cautiously out. The sounds frightened her then so did the sight of cars and trucks roaming the highway like sentinels patrolling it.

The second time was when the idea came to her that other children must have run away and, unable to go to the cities, could be living together farther into the woods than she had ever dared go. That time she prepared for flight by taking with her a bag of food from her grandmother's kitchen. She went for hours through the woods without encountering runaway children or a sign that any had preceded her. She got to the Whitewater River, which, with its mills and factories on the other side, seemed to her like the beginning of civilization. There she retreated back into the woods, going in another direction. She had not gone far when she came upon an amazing sight.

Years before torrential rains and hurricane winds had beaten the countryside for days. The river overflowed and swept shacks and small houses and boats away. Winds pried open the roofs of houses and sent them whirling, and farm animals floated by as drenched carcasses or were swept away bellowing and squealing. The rain collapsed the roof on an old woman's shack, killing her, then carried her out the door on her wooden bed to the top of a hill. Rescuers took the old woman away, but the bed remained like a strange landmark for months. Most of the loss, though, was only to property, but it was sufficient to discourage the return of the squatters who had been living along the river for years.

Now Willa stepped into a small clearing where she saw remnants of that storm. Much of it was unrecognizable, baked by the sun in matrices of mud or pressed into shapes no longer identifiable. She picked up what she recognized as a pillow and it crumbled in her hands; she approached a couch lying on its side whose stench was like something long dead. Ribbons festooned the upper branches of a tree, and a broken mirror lay on the ground reflecting imperfect parts of the sky. A doll hung in the branches of a tree, and above that was a child's shredded dress, as if its owner had been blown out of it by the storm and risen unwillingly and in great tumult to heaven. Only a wooden hobbyhorse remained upright and undamaged in the midst of the devastation. Willa went to the hobbyhorse and sat on it to better contemplate what she saw.

What interested her most was a small house trailer upended aslant against a tree. She knew that no one could have lived in the clearing for years, but the house trailer suggested to her that it had once been inhabited. It could have been a settlement of runaway children who had been surprised by kidnappers in the night.

She got up to inspect the trailer. Its windows were broken, its door hanging down on a twisted hinge. Wildflowers were blooming on its rear tires. When she pulled the hobbyhorse up to it and, standing tiptoe on it, looked in, she saw a tangle of furniture and other objects at its lower end. The smell of mildew rose to her. There was no evidence that anyone had lived in it for a long time.

The devastation saddened her—the violent manner in which the settlement had been destroyed by those who, she decided, wanted it to remain as a warning to other runaway children who thought they could hide.

On the chance that other children who had heard of the settlement might show up, she slept on the ground next to the hobbyhorse that night and the next day sat rocking on it and waiting in a silence interrupted occasionally by birds and small animals scurrying around her. She finished the last of her food and, several hours before nightfall, started back to the house.

This time when she returned her grandmother had her grandfather put locks on the refrigerator and kitchen cabinets to keep her from taking food with her if she thought of leaving again. He nailed shut her bedroom window and locked her door from outside at night. But that was not what prevented her for a time from leaving again, for she could easily have run away during the day; rather, it was the depression that came over her whenever she considered the chances of runaway children living in a world that so ruthlessly hunted them down.

The third time she left it was in angry reaction to her grandmother's strict guard over her—proof that she was still a worthy participant in that contest of wills that existed between them at the time.

But that time she traveled so far—emerging from the woods only when they ended in private properties and trails, and returning to them as quickly as possible—that by nightfall she had to sleep in a cemetery before starting back.

Since she could not read at that time and would not have known what a cemetery was anyway, she thought it was a place where people came and sat on the grass couches to look at the beautiful stones and statuary. While the wind whistled through the orifices in the statues she slept peacefully on one of the grass couches, under the gaze of a stone angel.

Until she was old enough and knew better, she continued to believe in a community of runaway children out there yet to be found.

■ ■ ■

Mary sat on the bed next to Willa, and Willa clung to her after hearing the news of her mother's death. Mary tried to comfort her: she told her she could stay on and they would be together for as long as they both lived. She told her she would call her lawyer that day and leave the house and her money to her in her will; and that after she was gone Willa could live there until the end of her own days, never wanting for anything. She would open the house again, she said, and they would have friends and parties and a wonderful life from then on.

She held Willa while Willa wept, and when she was calmer she put one of the clay pellets in Willa's pipe, lit it, and held it for her while Willa sucked on it. In a little while Willa slept.

Mary got up and laid Willa back on the bed, pulling the covers over her. "Moonlight" she whispered, "I have you now in your daughter." She leaned over Willa and kissed her. She was smiling. She felt she could remake the past now with Willa beside her, be as she had been before she went to the Apollo Hotel, where she lost her soul.

When Willa awoke it was still dark, the house silent. She heard fire engines on the street, sirens low and droning as they moved off slowly in the night. When she turned on the light, she saw that Mary had left her pipe and another pellet on the night table for her.

She remembered Mary holding her, soothing her with her voice, and now she needed to be with Mary and hear those words of assurance and love again. She got out of bed and went to find her.

But when she arrived in the living room, no one was there. She had never known the house to be so quiet. She decided to wait for Mary there, rather than disturb her in her room, where she would be sleeping.

She went to the television set and sat on the floor in front of it and turned it on. It came alive quickly, like a face appearing suddenly in front of her. On the screen were three strange men who did things to each other—slapping and hitting one another on the head and spilling buckets of paint over one another—that she knew were supposed to be comical but that to her were not funny at all. She turned the dial and a preacher confronted her, yelling and screaming. She switched him off quickly. She twisted the dial again to where men were killing one another shooting guns on a street, and she turned that off quickly too. She settled back on the carpet when the next picture revealed a pretty child playing with her dog in a field full of grass and flowers. She watched the girl put her arm around the big dog's neck and kiss it, and Willa was filled with sadness and longing but happiness too for the girl's happiness. But after fifteen minutes there came a scene showing the dog going along a road, and she knew from the way the movie kept going back and forth from the dog to a speeding car on the same road what might happen. She sat up. She looked terrified, her face twisted, as the car speeded closer to the dog. Then the picture was of the girl running toward the road calling the dog's name and trying to get there in time to save it, and Willa experienced a moment of hope. But the girl was too late, and with a cruelty that the camera not only recorded but abetted, the car struck the dog with a terrible thud and a squealing of tires. The dog yelped, then lay still. Willa's fingers went out to the screen, and when the next image revealed the girl sitting in the road holding the dog and crying as it lay dead in her arms, Willa wept too. Then she turned the television off.

She got up. She wandered the room, touching objects absently as she went. She got into Mary's chair and sat staring off.

Sighing, she got back out of the chair. She started for the doorway. She was going to get the photograph of her mother, which was in her purse in her room.

In all the time she had been in the house, Willa had not looked at the photograph once, as if the house and Mary and her stories had swallowed the mother she had known in the photograph and replaced it with another who was not of Willa's dream. Now Willa felt the need to restore the mother of the dream so she could say good-bye to her.

She passed Mary's room on her way to her own and stopped and listened for a moment at the door, but there was no sound from within. She found the photograph and returned to the living room with it.

Sighing again, she climbed back into Mary's chair and propped the photograph against the cigarette box on the table next to the chair. She put her arms around the chair's cushioned armrest, laid her cheek against that. She sat looking at the photograph. Then she got down from the chair. She stood in front of it. She began to dance.

It was a slow, sad dance. She took small steps, her body bending and unbending like a willow branch in the wind. Her arms lifted, then slowly descended as she lowered her body at the waist toward the floor. She swayed there, fingertips brushing the carpet, long hair falling, head low in an act of obeisance to a deity yet to be heard from. It was a dance of pain, and finally of surrender.

She stopped dancing, went to the window and, for the first time since coming to the house, looked outside. It was morning. In the flush of sunlight and with the fountain now turned off, she saw the face of the naked stone woman clearly for the first time.

It came to her gradually, but when it did, her eyes went wide. She pressed her face to the window to look closer, then went to the table and brought the photograph back to the window. She compared the face in the photograph to the one on the statue and there was no mistaking it: they were the same, both Madeleine, her mother.

A new fear came over her that nothing was constant or real in the house, that everything changed according to Mary's fancy. It was ruled by ghosts and things that might never have been. She dropped the photograph onto the floor, turned away from the window and returned to her room.

She sat down on the side of the bed, empty of emotions now. They had been spent so extravagantly and in so short a time that she was exhausted.

She got under the covers and smoked the pellet sitting up in bed. She replaced the pipe on the night table, then lay back. With her eyes closed she saw a rain of the white horses hurtling past in space. Then she slipped into a dark tunnel, where she slept.

She awoke into the full flowering of depression. She stared up at the ceiling, near to tears again. Then she turned onto her side and stared at the heavy drapes covering the window.

Someone knocked at the door.

"Go away" Willa called.

The knock came again. "Go away" she called again.

The door opened and closed and she heard someone in the room coming toward her. She did not bother to turn around.

She heard Heather's voice. "Willa?"

"Go away, Heather" she said.

She felt the girl's hand on her shoulder, shaking her. "Willa, turn around and look at me. I have something important to tell you."

"I already know" Willa said. "Mary told me. My mother's dead."

"Willa, listen to me. Mary lied to you. She doesn't know whether your mother's alive, dead or what. She couldn't."

Willa turned, but slowly, afraid that when she looked, Heather would not be there, would not have spoken, and Willa would find that she was in a dream the pipe had made for her. But Heather was there, leaning earnestly toward her at the side of the bed. Willa sat up quickly. She stared at Heather.

"It's true" Heather said. "Mary couldn't know that about your mother because she never looked for her. No one has." She held out a slip of paper to Willa. "Here's that address I said I'd get for you. Now you can go."

Willa looked at the writing on the paper. She saw the name Chatto Hoffman and an address. She looked back up at Heather, too stunned for the moment to ask the questions that raced through her mind. Heather helped her.

"Last night" Heather said, "when we were dancing together, I was pretending. I was going along with Mary, stalling, until I could get that address and get you out of here. I knew everything all along, and so did Jo, but last night I knew it had all gotten out of hand, that somehow Mary had gotten you and your mother so mixed up—"

"I don't understand" Willa said. "The time I talked to Mary on the phone—why didn't she give me this address then? She hadn't seen me, couldn't have thought I looked like my mother then."

"Because" Heather said "she's afraid of Chatto Hoffman. She's been afraid of him for a long time. It has something to do with what he did when he worked for her. I never knew Mary to be afraid of anyone before, but she's afraid of that man. She told me—and listen close, Willa, so you'll be careful with him—that this Chatto, he did terrible things to people when he worked for her. And she said once that there were people after your mother disappeared—Orlo Haines was one of them—who thought he murdered her. They were all afraid of him, so no one did anything about it."

"Does Mary think he killed her?"

"She doesn't want to. She always needed your mother to be alive as

280 / LESLIE GARRETT

much as you do. But Mary's out of it now; Mary's mad, Willa. Didn't you see that last night at that crazy party? She's gone."

Heather stopped, forcing back her emotions at her last words. But she recovered. The girl Willa had thought of as weak now seemed strong. "Mary's mad, Willa" she repeated "and that's another reason you have to leave now, while she's asleep." She hesitated, then said "Willa, I love her. But I'm afraid now of what she might do. I can't control her. I can't help her anymore."

"What will happen to her?" Willa asked.

Heather hesitated again before saying "I'll take care of her. Like I took care of her before. I know what she would have wanted, and what I have to do for her." She looked at Willa. "Are you all right now?"

"Yes, Heather. Thank you. I don't know what I would have done if you hadn't told me."

Heather went to the door.

"Where are you going now?" Willa asked.

"To Mary."

Heather had her hand on the doorknob, was turning it, when Willa asked "Won't Josephine try to stop me from leaving?"

"Jo's over at Madeleine House investigating a burglary. Someone broke into Penny's office last night." She smiled. "But you better hurry. I don't know how long she'll be gone." She opened the door, then turned to Willa. "Just go now, Willa. You don't belong here. You never did."

She left, closing the door behind her.

Willa got out of bed and went to the closet. She opened it to reveal the white clothes and white shoes she had worn since coming to the house, was wearing now. At the far end of the closet were her own clothes, which she could now reclaim. She was about to change into them when she remembered the photograph she had left on the floor of the living room.

She left the room and hurried down, relieved to find the photograph where she had dropped it. When she turned with it, she was facing Mary's empty chair.

There were no longer any ghosts congregated around it. It was just a chair now, in a room lit with morning sunlight. As she turned away from the chair for the last time, she knew that no matter what Mary had done, she could not hate her. What Mary had done, she understood, was try to make her mother love her in a dream.

She was at the door, about to return to her room with the photograph, when she stepped back out of sight. She watched as Heather—as Willa had seen Josephine do—came down the spiral staircase carrying two syringes on a tray. There was an air both private and processional about the girl as she descended, as she went past the doorway and down the hall to Mary's room. She entered without knocking, then closed the door quietly behind her.

Willa returned to her room and changed into her own clothes. She hung the white dress she had been wearing beside the others. When she closed the door, the clothes whispered behind it.

She was going down the stairs when she heard the front door open. She stopped. She listened to footsteps coming along the hallway toward Mary's room, a knock at her door. "Mary" Josephine's voice called through it.

Willa stayed close to the wall near the bottom of the stairs. She heard a second knock, much louder this time, then Josephine calling "Mary, I'm coming in. I have to see you."

Willa heard the door opened, then flung back, banging against the wall. There was a moment of silence before Willa was startled by Josephine's scream. Then her cry: "Mary! Oh, God, no!"

She heard Josephine rush out of the room, go running down the hall, then the rattling of the suspended spiral staircase as she ran up it and down the upper hallway toward her office, where the only telephone was. Willa waited, then went down the rest of the stairs.

When she got to Mary's room, the door was open. She looked in.

Mary and Heather were lying on the divan, both still, Mary smiling in a peace past longing now in Heather's arms.

Willa turned away and ran out the front door.

She went out the gate and started walking in the direction of the bus stop. She was in sunlight again, and although she had the paper with her mother's former lover's address on it, she was too exhausted to continue. She would go back to her room and rest, and see Chatto Hoffman later.

She looked back a last time at the house.

22

Sitting in the rocking chair across from the mannequin the next afternoon, Vernon had tried to explain to the mannequin why he no longer wanted to remain the nonentity that followed the girl. He had already begun to speculate on that time when her search was over and he could tell her about the intimacies they had shared.

But now he thought that having fled the rats when he had wanted to stay and help her, he had proved he was unworthy of her. For the first time since he began his underground life—submerged his identity by taking on the lives of others—he was dissatisfied with it. He had hidden his own feelings for so long that now, when he wanted to express them, he no longer knew how. The unhappiness he felt because of his cowardice he could not even explain to the mannequin in words.

He got up and took down the small oval mirror from the wall. He had moved it there from its original place behind the bureau when he first came to the room so that he would not see himself in it. There was no other mirror, and he tried never to look at his reflection anywhere. Now he returned to the rocking chair with the mirror and stared at himself in it.

The face that looked back at him revealed nothing: none of what he was feeling so intensely. The large eyes blinked slowly, but none of the fear, the loneliness, the suffering was in them. He wanted the girl to see those feelings and understand that the first emotions of his own he had felt in so long were because of her. But just as the words were not there to make the mannequin understand, his emotions were not present in his face for her to see.

He needed to show her himself as he was, naked, no longer hidden behind the borrowed lives of others.

* * *

He came out of his building just after dark with the overcoat buttoned to his chin and his collar up, even though it was a mild night.

He went down the street and turned off it along the alley to behind the girl's building, where he had gone periodically during her absence to see if she had returned. Where he had once stood by the tree watching her in the window.

She was back. The light was on and he could see her standing in front of a mirror, combing her hair. He moved his hands over his own hair in imitation of her. Then he stepped out of sight behind the tree.

A moment later his overcoat fell to the ground. His shoes, socks and trousers followed it. When he moved away from the tree, he was naked.

He moved into the light as close as he could to her window. Had she gone to the window and looked down, she would have seen him in full view, his arms raised to her.

But she did not come to the window. After a few more minutes in front of the mirror, she went to the door, turned off the light, and left.

He cried out to her.

23

Chatto had returned for his possessions. When he saw the empty Nembutal bottle and realized Madeleine's condition, he went to a bar and called an ambulance. He sent the blonde girl away, then waited outside for the ambulance to arrive. After Madeleine was taken off unconscious on a stretcher, he packed his things and left in another direction.

Madeleine awoke two days later in the drug and alcohol ward of a hospital. She heard later that her first words were "Oh, God, I'm still here."

With her resistance lowered, her condition was complicated by double pneumonia, and she was transferred back to the intensive-care unit, where during the crisis she saw herself leave her body and hover over it, watching. Then she was flying above a field of flowers and trees, peaceful, released, when at the end of it she came to a cemetery with row upon row of tombstones passing slowly under her. She tried to read the names on the tombstones but there were no inscriptions, all wordless and immemorial, until she saw one that bore her name in clear letters. She cried out and awoke, drenched in perspiration. The crisis had passed.

She went back and forth between delirium and brief periods of semiconsciousness; later her one clear memory was of waking in what must have been early morning, the room dim and silent except for hospital sounds around it. She saw a girl in the uniform of a hospital orderly standing over her, looking at her. She was a stout girl, homely, with a kind face. She took Madeleine's hand and held it, and it was that sensitive gesture, the girl's concern for her, which caused Madeleine to say "Everyone I ever loved left me." The girl began weeping, very quietly, and Madeleine said, consoling her, "Don't cry. I'm going to be all right."

She slept holding the girl's hand, but when later she tried to find out the girl's name to thank her for her kindness, no one knew who she was, and Madeleine never saw her again.

She gained full consciousness a day later. Only then did she realize there were tubes inserted in her mouth and nose; when she tried to talk, she could only make garbled sounds, and later she communicated erratically in a voice that was not hers. When she tried to move, she found she was tied to the bed at the wrists and ankles. A nurse passed near and she called out, trying to say "Please untie me" but the nurse ignored her and left. She was bound too tight and the circulation had gone from her wrists, and her arms and legs hurt. She was thirsty and she called out for water, but no one answered her. Only when she began thrashing around on the bed trying to free herself did a nurse hurry to her. The nurse held her down as she said "Don't do that. That's so you don't pull out the IVs in your sleep. Now be a good girl and don't give us any more trouble."

Madeleine signaled frantically with her eyes. The nurse bent near her and Madeleine managed to say "They hurt. Too tight." The nurse loosened the cloth straps. "Water" Madeleine said. "Thirsty."

The nurse straightened. "You can't have anything to drink yet. You're being dehydrated. They had to pump out your stomach."

She made angry sounds behind the tubes, began fighting against the straps again, and the nurse held her down roughly and said "If you're going to be a troublemaker, we'll have to put you in full restraint. Now stop giving me a hard time."

She stopped resisting, but she glared at the nurse before she turned and went off. The light went out and she was left alone in the dim room.

She saw three other beds with shapes of people huddled in them. An old woman coughed, then gasped for breath. She continued gasping, a high sound that was a desperate searching for air. A nurse came and gave the old woman an injection, and soon she slept.

Madeleine slept too, but awoke later to voices whispering across from her and saw a doctor, a nurse and two male orderlies gathered around the old woman who had been gasping for breath, and Madeleine knew she was dead. They lifted her, wrapped in her sheet, onto a gurney and wheeled it away. An orderly came in, and fresh sheets went billowing above the bed, leaving it like a tombstone. Madeleine closed her eyes, and when she awoke in the morning, someone else was in the dead woman's place.

She began remembering: about Chatto leaving her, her unhappiness during the past year. She lay with tears flowing but soundless in the light of morning.

Chatto did not visit her. No one did except someone she hardly knew, who arrived with flowers that afternoon. Sylvia Rosenberg had brought a vase too, which she filled with water, and arranged the flowers in it on the bedside table. She drew up a chair and sat down.

Madeleine noted again what a quiet, soft-spoken and gentle person she was. She wore granny glasses now as she sat across from Madeleine. Madeleine realized she was older than she had appeared to be at Billy Tyler's and the High Note: in her midtwenties. There was about her the manner of one who had matured early.

"How are you feeling, Madeleine?" she asked. "They tell me you're going to be all right."

Madeleine signaled with her fingers for Sylvia to come close, and Sylvia rose and bent over her.

"Write" Madeleine managed to say, and made a gesture of writing with her hand.

Sylvia reached into a large bag she had with her and took out a pen and a pad. She put the pen in Madeleine's fingers and held the pad as Madeleine scratched on it in large, erratic letters: WATER   THIRSTY.

There was no glass or pitcher beside the bed, but Sylvia signaled to her that it would be all right; she was leaving but would be back.

Five minutes later she returned with an ice cube in a paper napkin. She wet Madeleine's lips with it, then held it for her as she sucked greedily on it.

Sylvia visited her every evening after that. She brought her a pen and a writing pad of her own. Madeleine did not ask about Chatto, and Sylvia never spoke to her of the neighborhood and the people they both knew. Sylvia read to her—mostly poetry—and Madeleine communicated to her that she had poetry of her own with her things at the apartment, which she was afraid would be gone by the time she was released from the hospital. Sylvia told her the apartment had been rented but she had gotten the key from Chatto, packed Madeleine's personal possessions and taken them to her own apartment. She told Madeleine she could stay with her when she left the hospital until she found a place of her own. When Madeleine inquired why Sylvia was being so kind to her, she did not answer. She seemed embarrassed by the question.

As Madeleine recovered, her nervousness returned. When she asked a nurse for a tranquilizer, the nurse seemed outraged and refused. The insomnia returned. One night Madeleine heard voices in the corridor. A group of doctors and nurses were talking too far away for her to hear them, but she heard them anyway. Their conversation revealed that they were members of a secret organization that selected people guilty of unmentioned transgressions and performed an operation on them that reduced them to mindless entities. Then she heard her name spoken as a candidate for the operation. She could not escape and she knew she must not let them know she had overheard them, and so she lay terrified all night, waiting to see if they would come for her. When early the next morning a nurse arrived to remove the wrist and ankle restraints and the tubes from her nose and mouth, she began kicking and screaming. When the tubes were out, she shouted "I'll be good! I won't be bad anymore."

They returned her that day to the drug and alcohol ward.

She was put in a room with one other woman. She was given a new hospital gown and cardboard slippers, and as long as she obeyed the rules and did not cause any trouble, she was left alone. She begged the attendant to give her something for her nerves, but she refused curtly.

Both Madeleine and the other woman had chairs next to their beds, and during the day when the other woman was gone, Madeleine sat alone in the chair for as long as she could remain still, then got up and paced the hallway until she was tired enough to return to the chair. She kept asking for a pill or an injection to put her to sleep, but her requests were always met with outrage. On the third day she attacked the head matron, and others came and held her down on the bed and strapped her into it. When she continued screaming, they fastened a gag around her mouth. She stopped struggling and lay whimpering. Then someone put a tube in her arm.

That night she saw a dog she knew could not possibly be there wander into the room and climb onto her bed, where it stood on her stomach baring its teeth at her. It disappeared but was followed by a bird, which flew all over the room, diving at her repeatedly; she screamed behind the gag, but no one came.

She could barely move behind the tight leather restraints, but her efforts to free herself so exhausted her that by midmorning she slept. When she awoke, the other woman had already gone off and the daylight through the window looked softer and warmed her, and her nerves, although still bad, had ceased screaming. The hallucinations stopped.

She was thirsty again, but she had learned how to get along there, and she made no requests and was obedient when the attendant came the next morning and talked to her; she thanked the big woman when she removed the gag and tube, and when the straps were taken off she thanked her again, with tears of gratitude streaming down her face.

She paced the hall that day and most of the next, only returning to the room to sit in the chair, which was fastened to the floor with its back to the wall. That afternoon while she was sitting in the chair staring at the opposite wall, her roommate—an old woman who, Madeleine realized then, had not said a word to her in all the time she had been there—wandered into the room. Seeing Madeleine sitting there, she sat in her own chair with its back to the wall and, with only a bed separating them, stared at the wall too. When Madeleine got up and began pacing the hall again, the woman followed a few steps behind her; she returned to her chair when Madeleine returned to hers and followed her again in the hall when Madeleine went out again.

Madeleine could see the old woman was harmless, but her attachment to her only made Madeleine's nerves worse. Rather than scream at the woman and bring the attendants again to put her in restraints, she went into the lounge area for the first time, where the woman separated from her and sat down on one of the couches where other patients— men and women—were watching television.

That night she slept for a few hours, and the next morning her nerves were calmer, her mind clearer. She ate most of a full breakfast— the first solid meal she had eaten since her arrival at the hospital—at a long table next to the recreation lounge. But when a young man sat down next to her and attempted to talk to her, she hurried away with her tray to the other end of the table.

No visitors were allowed in the ward, so Sylvia could not come see her, but she sent a message through the head matron that she would come for Madeleine when she was discharged. When Madeleine asked the matron when that would be, she told her in five days if she continued her good behavior and the psychiatrist–interviewer agreed to it. Later Madeleine tried to calculate how long she would have been in the alcohol and drug ward by then, and although she was uncertain, she estimated ten days. She would have been in the hospital nearly three weeks.

That day, for the first time, she noticed others newly arrived who, as she had done, became violent and were restrained by attendants; others shook like puppets and were unable to remain in one place for more than a few minutes. Some wandered dazed and silent, future ruin in their eyes. She had been one of them—was one of them.

That night she was unable to sleep again. Fear kept her eyes open, staring at the ceiling. What she feared was the world waiting for her outside.

On the day she was discharged, Sylvia arrived with a change of clothes for her and her makeup. As they were leaving, the head nurse stepped out of her office and wished Madeleine good luck, and Madeleine thanked her in a voice that was little more than a whisper. She stood with her head bowed until the woman left.

Sylvia had a small apartment in a pleasant neighborhood; she made up a bed for Madeleine on the couch. When she saw that Madeleine only responded to her when necessary and did not initiate conversation, she did not press her to talk. When Madeleine sat at the window for hours looking out and only joined her for meals, Sylvia did not comment on it. She had a job during the day and left Madeleine alone in the apartment with her own key.

Madeleine did not go out; she sat by the window or in a chair, staring off. There was a phonograph and records, books and magazines and a television, but she had no interest in any of them. She did not ask Sylvia what plans she might have for her—where she would live, how she would support herself—and showed no interest in anything beyond the moment. Sylvia had told her that the psychiatrist who had interviewed Madeleine had recommended she undergo psychiatric evaluation and treatment and had given Sylvia a card with the address of a clinic where she could be seen without charge. But Madeleine appeared frightened at the mention of it, and Sylvia put the card in Madeleine's purse so she would have it if she changed her mind later.

On Madeleine's first day there, Sylvia had given her an address and told her to write a letter asking for a copy of her birth certificate. It arrived the day after Madeleine's eighteenth birthday, and the following morning Sylvia took her to the public assistance office, where for the first time Madeleine learned that Sylvia was employed there as a caseworker. When they walked through the door, Madeleine pulled back at the sight of all the people jammed into one room waiting to apply for assistance; she tried to leave, but Sylvia told her it was necessary that she have public assistance until she was able to work again. She took Madeleine to the receptionist's desk, spoke to the woman there about her; the woman nodded and Sylvia took Madeleine to a chair where she waited with the others. Then Sylvia went to her office.

That day Sylvia guided Madeleine through the intricacies of applying for welfare, came out and held her hand and encouraged her when she panicked and tried to leave. It took all morning, but in the end Madeleine left with a check for emergency aid, and the following week she received the first of her regular checks.

A week later Sylvia found her a furnished apartment so inexpensive that Madeleine could afford to live there on the checks from public assistance. She bought Madeleine a small used television set and gave her linens and towels and dishes and pots and pans from her own apartment. Then she moved Madeleine and her possessions there in a taxi, gave Madeleine her phone number to use if she should need anything else or want someone to talk to.

As Sylvia was leaving, Madeleine for the first time realized how much Sylvia had done for her. They had never been friends, and Madeleine had not even known her well before she appeared at the hospital. Sylvia had asked nothing in return, not even Madeleine's friendship if she chose not to give it. Why, then, Madeleine asked her, had she done all she had for her?

They were standing together in the doorway when Madeleine asked the question. But although Sylvia did not answer it this time either, when she looked at Madeleine her eyes misted behind the granny glasses. And because she would not—or could not—answer her, she turned instead and hurried away.

■ ■ ■

She was alone. It was what she had wanted all along. Even in the face of Sylvia's generosity and kindness, she had wanted to be free of her too, to be where no one, nothing, could touch her again and hurt her.

The apartment was in a slum neighborhood of Puerto Ricans, blacks and whites. A Puerto Rican bar across from her apartment blared Latin music from a loudspeaker all night and into the early morning. It was a neighborhood of deteriorating former mansions built in the last century and now divided into apartments. The old houses retained remnants of grandeur: wide staircases, high ceilings and ruined stone embellishments on their facades. A wide stairway with large concrete railings rose from the street to the high, wide doors of her own building.

It was a large apartment with a long hallway from the door to the front room, which was both living room and bedroom; it had a kitchen and a bathroom with an old-fashioned iron bathtub raised inches from the floor on iron lion's claws. The only furniture was a table and two chairs in the kitchen, a bed, a table, and a wicker rocking chair and floor lamp next to high, wide windows in the front room. The first thing she did after Sylvia left was pull down the shades on the windows; after that she lived day and night in artificial light. Then she sat down in the rocking chair and turned on the television set Sylvia had given her.

There was a crack in the plaster of the wall opposite where she sat, and when she was not in bed, she sat looking alternately at the crack and the television. She could not remember from one minute to the next what she had been watching on the television. She changed channels frequently, and her mind kept drifting off. Only the crack interested her, for it had endless variety and suggested things profound. She went to the window now and then and looked out from behind the shade to see whether it was day or night.

Sylvia had supplied her with groceries, but when a week later there was nothing left to eat, she was forced to go out for the first time to a *bodega,* where she bought the cheapest food she could find with the food stamps the public assistance office had provided her in addition to the checks. On the way back she saw a liquor store and she went in and bought a gallon of the cheapest red wine she could find. On her way out she had seen a Puerto Rican man who lived in her building dealing pot on the stairs; returning, she saw him again, and although she had hesitated at first, the fact that he lived there and did not seem threatening gave her the courage to approach him. He sold her a dime bag and welcomed her to the neighborhood.

When she got back to the apartment, she found the pipe Sylvia had packed away in her suitcase along with her other possessions from the old apartment. She took the pipe and the plastic bag with the pot in it to the table in the front room, got a plate and an old newspaper and one of her razor blades and, as she had watched Chatto do many times before, cleaned the pot.

After that she sat day and night sipping wine and staying high enough on pot to short-circuit the world outside the apartment. She still stared at the crack in the plaster and watched those images on television that were all the same to her and which she forgot seconds after they appeared. But now she began rocking, and once in a while she smiled.

One morning a month later she hurried out of the building on her way to the liquor store. She never spoke to anyone she did not have to speak to on the street, and she bent her body and head as she walked, as if fighting a strong wind. She feared the street and what was on it. When she reached the curb, she stopped.

She had crossed the street many times, but now she just stood there. Other people crossed around her, but she was immobilized by fear. She thought, Nothing is there. She put a foot onto the street, then drew it back. She looked across and saw people on the other side going about their business as usual. She thought, It's me. They're not afraid. Look at them. The street ordinarily had little traffic on it; children played in it; and when she looked, there were only a few cars approaching, blocks away. But when she tried to hurry across it, she got only a few feet before rushing back. She had been certain that one of the cars, which was too far away to overtake her, would speed up and run her down.

She would have returned to the apartment had she needed anything but wine, but she had to get to the liquor store, a block away. She tried to cross several more times, but each time she had only one foot on the street before pulling back. Even when there were no cars in sight, she stayed there, fearing one would appear suddenly out of a side street. Finally, when there were no cars in sight for several minutes, she ran—and was surprised to find herself safely on the other side. She hurried to the liquor store.

She went down the familiar aisle to where her brand of wine was kept, but when she got there another problem confronted her: she had always bought the red Don Quixote brand because it was the cheapest, but now she saw two new brands that were even cheaper. She reached for one, but there was something about the label that made her uncertain whether it was the right choice. She reached for the other new brand, but that too seemed suspicious to her. She decided she should not take a chance on unknown wines and started to take down a bottle of Don Quixote. The higher price stopped her, and she went back to debating between the two others she had already rejected.

She stood there for twenty minutes trying to make a decision: deciding, then finding another reason to buy one of the others instead. She left the store unable to choose but remained outside looking through the window to where the wine bottles were.

She wanted to cry, but she wanted the wine more. She went back into the store and up to the owner, who had seen her many times leave with the same item. But this time she asked him for a gallon of the cheapest red wine—as if she had never been in the store before. He hesitated, looked at her, then went and brought her one of the cheaper new brands.

She hurried back to the apartment with it and poured wine into the glass she kept on a chair next to the rocker. She filled her pipe and turned on the television. She smoked and sipped wine, leaning into the light from the television screen as if she had discovered something there she had never seen before.

She went to bed around midnight but awoke at four in the morning certain the house was on fire. She ran down and huddled on the cold street. No one else was there, and she could see no fire.

Near dawn she went back into her building. She checked every floor for fire and smoke, venturing into obscure areas she had avoided before but which now held lesser terrors for her.

She returned to the apartment, but she did not go back to bed. She kept the door open and moved the rocking chair into the doorway of the front room, where she could watch down the long hallway for signs of fire or smoke. She closed the door when she heard other doors opening, people rising in an ordinary morning.

She told herself later that there had been a fire, but it had gone out by itself, and she was the only one who knew about it. She moved the rocking chair back in front of the window.

As she sat rocking for the rest of the day, every loud noise from the street frightened her, made her jump up from the chair in panic.

That night there was a loud knocking at her door. She went to the head of the hallway and shouted "Who's there?"

A man's muffled voice answered her in Spanish.

"Who is it?" she shouted. "What do you want?"

He answered her again in Spanish, more impatiently.

"If you don't tell me what you want I won't open the door" she called.

He answered with a question that contained someone's name.

"I don't know anyone here" she yelled.

He knocked on the door again, much more loudly, angrily.

"Go away! I don't know anyone!"

He shouted through the door.

"Go away!" she cried. "I don't know you!"

He began cursing and calling her names through the door as he continued knocking on it insistently and angrily.

"*Please go away*" she screamed. "I'll call for the police if you don't leave me alone."

He kicked the door and, cursing her again, went off.

She returned to the rocker trembling, afraid he would come back. "He knew what I am" she murmured to herself later. "He knew all about me. That's why he wanted to come in." She went to a corner of the room and crouched there for several hours. She started whimpering, she was so afraid.

That night she took off all her clothes, raised the window shade all the way, directed the light from the floor lamp onto herself, and stood naked at the window in full view from the street.

The next night she pulled the mattress off the bed and after that slept naked on the springs. When she got up in the morning, her body was bruised and had small cuts on it. She bound her wrists and her ankles so tightly with wires that they bled.

A week later she had to go to the neighborhood laundromat. She had put it off for as long as she could, for the Puerto Rican men frightened her and she knew their wives looked on her, a woman without a man, with suspicion and contempt. Even their children frightened her. But this time she went at the dinner hour, when it was usually deserted. She was the only one there.

She put her laundry into a front loader and sat on the bench waiting for it to complete the cycle. The sound of the machine soothed her. Her mind drifted. She was tired. She closed her eyes.

When she opened them, a tall, handsome Puerto Rican man was leaning on the washing machine next to her own. He had evidently come in off the street, but he did not have a laundry bag or hamper with him, and the only machine in use was hers. He was looking at her with arrogance, even confidence. She felt a sensation that was part fear, part excitement at the thought that his expression was based on the fact that without ever having met her, he knew her, knew even those secrets she had tried to keep hidden from herself since the night she attempted to kill herself. When he smiled at her, she found it difficult to turn away.

Then her machine stopped, and when she turned back he was pointing to it, smiling. She stayed where she was.

"Your stuff's done" he called. "You better come get it."

She got up and moved cautiously along the row of machines toward her own.

"What's your name?" he asked.

She stopped. He had moved to the machine next to hers and leaned on it. She watched him smiling at her with large, perfect teeth.

"Hey, what's your name, baby? You too shy to say your name? I see you around here before. Pretty girl like you, I couldn't miss you. How come I never see you with a man? You live alone?"

"Please, go away" she said.

He straightened. "Hey, baby, you don't want me to go away. I know that."

"I do."

"Look" he said. He was holding a joint up for her to see. "Pure Panamanian. Great stuff."

"No" she said.

"Hey, look" he said, "I don't offer this to just anybody. I want you to have some because you're special."

"No" she said.

"I know what's the matter. We're not introduced. My name's Jesus."

He held out his hand to her, but she did not take it. "Hay-sooz?" she asked.

"Yeah. J-E-S-U-S. Like the one you pray to. You ever pray to Jesus? Lotsa girls, they prayed to Jesus."

She moved back several steps, but she could not take her eyes off him now. He kept smiling.

He crossed to a door in the wall, took a key from his pocket and opened it. He reached in and pulled a string, and a ceiling light went on. She could see a broom and a mop and pail inside. He put one foot inside, held up the joint again, and motioned for her to join him.

"Baby" he said, "come on. We go inside here, see, close the door so we can be alone. We smoke this great shit. Then I want to see you pray to Jesus. You know you want to." It was a cruel smile now, suggesting greater cruelty to come. He wiggled a finger at her.

She wet her lips. She could hear her own breathing. She began to feel the excitement again, the anticipation of the pleasures to be known in sorrow and shame. The feeling became so intense it was finally like madness. She moved forward until she was standing in front of him in the utility-room doorway.

"That's right" he said. He put his hand on her shoulder and turned her to face the doorway. He nudged her forward.

At the last moment, she stepped back. "No" she said.

"Hey" he said. "What the fuck you—"

"No!" she shouted, then turned and ran.

She did not sleep that night, did not even lie down. She had to fight her need to go out and find him. Kneel. Pray to him.

She drank wine and smoked pipe after pipe, and by late evening she was so drunk and high that she had trouble standing, but the fear did not go away. Nor did the excitement, the need. Had he been there, she knew, in the room with her, what she feared would have come to pass.

At midnight she got up and got the razor blade she cleaned the pot with and returned to the chair with it. She held it over her wrist and then drew it across a vein. Blood rose. She watched it. She did it to another vein, but deeper, and the blood poured over her wrist. She thought, That's my life. It's my life flowing out of me.

She ran into the bathroom and wrapped the wounds in a towel. The towel turned red and she got another one and wrapped that around her wrist. She went back to the living room and sat holding the towel to her wrist. She wept. Then she screamed. "Please" she shouted, "somebody save me! I don't know what happened to me."

She kept drinking and smoking and crying until she crept exhausted onto the mattress on the floor and passed out.

At nine o'clock that morning she found the card Sylvia had given her and called the mental health clinic and made an appointment for that afternoon. She began crying again when she hung up the receiver in the phone booth.

She sat in a deep chair across the desk from Dr. Crane at the Brown Street Mental Health Center. He was a good-looking man in his early thirties with a large mustache. He wore boots and brightly colored flannel shirts open at the neck and looked more like a lumberjack or a seaman than like a psychiatrist. He had a quiet voice and gentle eyes that seemed always to be searching.

"I'm nothing" she told him.

"Everyone is something, Madeleine. What's my name?"

"Dr. Crane."

"And what am I?"

"A psychiatrist."

"What's your name?"

"Madeleine."

"And what are you?"

"A tramp."

"You see?"

She looked at him.

She went three times a week to the clinic for sessions with Dr. Crane. Each session was painful to her, and after a particularly difficult one she began to withdraw again. Some days they sat without speaking through the entire hour. The first time he probed too deeply, she backed away instantly. She got angry another time and threatened to leave and not return when he asked what had happened previous to the first suicide attempt. She drank and smoked just enough before leaving for their sessions so that she could get there and get through them. At the end of two weeks, she told him he could not help her. But by then she had told him some of her story.

"How do you feel about your father now?"

"I don't remember him."

"Are you sure?"

She arrived at one session drunk and he sent her home. She called him later and screamed over the phone that he too had betrayed her.

She stopped bathing. On the outside she was as neat and well dressed as ever, but underneath, as the days passed into weeks, she could feel the accumulations of dirt between her toes and in her armpits and loins. On the bus going to the clinic, she smiled secretly at what those around her would say if they knew. When she was alone in the apartment, she put her fingers in those parts of her body where the secretions were thickest, then raised her fingers to her nose and smelled them. She smiled. After the third week, the smell of her filth on her fingers made her giddy with pleasure.

"Can't you smell me, Dr. Crane?"

He did not answer.

"I've been sitting here smelling like this for weeks and you haven't said anything about it. I'm filth. I stink."

He looked at her sadly.

She started bathing again, but that did not change anything.

"Your daughter: do you miss her?"

She became silent. She slumped farther down in her chair.

"What are your feelings about your daughter, Madeleine?"

"She grew on a tree."

"What tree?"

"A baby tree."

"I want you to stop drinking, stop smoking grass and anything else you're using."

"I can't."

"You'll have to."

"I can't face it all without it. I simply can't, Dr. Crane. I would if I could."

"You have no choice, Madeleine. We haven't made any progress, and I see now we never will until you're sober. If you want, I'll arrange for you to go to the hospital to dry out again."

"No!"

"Then stop, or there's nothing I can do to help you. I'm going to prescribe Thorazine and Adapin for you. And Librium to help you stop drinking."

"No. I won't take them."

"It's either the hospital, you stop on your own or you'll die if you go on like this. Do you want to die?"

"No."

He started writing the prescriptions.

"Do you mean it? You're through with me if I don't stop?" she asked.

"I can't help you any other way."

He held out the prescriptions to her. She hesitated, then took them.

She filled the prescriptions with the card the clinic had given her and returned to the apartment. She got out the bottle of wine and the plastic bag with the pot in it. She put them onto the chair and sat in the rocker. She listened to the street sounds, voices in the building. She opened the windows and let air into the musty and uncleaned apartment. When she went to the toilet to pour the wine and pot into it, she felt a moment of panic. She closed her eyes as she flushed them away.

The first two weeks were the hardest. The Thorazine helped, but not enough to keep her from pacing when the scream started inside her that she knew could be silenced for a while with wine and pot. She experienced physical withdrawal, chills and fever and vomiting again, but not as badly as she had the other time. She paced and rocked and often cried for no reason now.

Dr. Crane gave her his home phone number. He told her she could call him at any time, day or night.

The Librium began working; she had less desire for wine. She went to the public library and brought back books and began reading far into the night to keep her mind off her withdrawal.

She began eating again. She ate ravenously for a while and gained twenty pounds. When she looked in the mirror, she saw a face that was more mature, had character in it and was no longer just the face of a pretty girl. She liked the solidity and depth the extra weight gave to her figure.

Dr. Crane had told her earlier "I'd like you to start keeping a daily journal, Madeleine. You said you used to write poetry. Perhaps putting your thoughts and feelings down on paper will make you more comfortable expressing them. You can bring it in and we can talk about what you've written."

Her first entry in the journal had been about death.
"What do you think about when you think about death, Madeleine?"
"It's like love is supposed to be. I'm not lonely when I think about it."
"Death is like a lover—a boyfriend or husband?"
"Better."

"You always refer to your daughter as 'it.' She has a name. What's her name?"
Silence.
"Do you remember her name, Madeleine?"
"I'm sick. I want to go home."

* * *

"You've always been stronger than you think, Madeleine."

She started going to free concerts and movies. Once a week she treated herself to a meal in an inexpensive restaurant. She read in the newspaper that tests were being scheduled in what was called a general educational development program for those who wanted to acquire the equivalent of a high school diploma. She took the tests and scored in the top ten percent.

She still had trouble crossing streets and several times had periods of indecision over simple choices, but they were less intense, and it no longer frightened her.

She had two serious setbacks: one two days before Christmas and the other just after the first of the year. The first time was when she was shopping in a supermarket and she felt the shelves moving toward her. She left her basket and ran out of the store. The second time was in the laundromat again when at first she was certain the Puerto Ricans were talking about her, then that they were about to attack her. She ran from there too.

There were nights when she had to fight the impulse to kill herself. They came at her the strongest after the setbacks. At times the desire to stop fighting, to give up, find peace in an end to it all, was so compelling that she had to force herself not to get the razor and slit her throat. Sometimes the struggle went on for an entire day, during which she sat in the rocker grasping the armrests to keep herself there, and twice she had to call Dr. Crane for emergency sessions that ended in tearful breakdowns.

She dreamed that Willa was dead, and when she awoke she called Dr. Crane from a phone booth at three o'clock in the morning before she could go back to sleep. At an emergency session later that morning, when she started to tell him about the dream, she wept so uncontrollably that she could not continue.

"Her name is Willa."

Dr. Crane did not say anything. He watched her start shaking.

Then it all rushed out of her in tears and anguish. At the end of the session she felt empty. She went back to the apartment and slept until the next morning, and when she awoke she was still frightened, but not as much as before.

* * *

She had taken the high school equivalency test so she could enroll in an evening secretarial course. She graduated in the spring and began looking for a job.

She found a job as secretary to the president of a small manufacturer of furniture. It was a dismal place to work and the salary was less than she hoped to make later when she had more experience, but she worked alone in the office and her employer was usually too busy in the factory to pay much attention to her. Most of the people there were middle aged or elderly immigrants, and since they kept to themselves, there was no pressure on her to make friends among them. She did her work efficiently and left alone every day.

She sent a money order to Johnny Thanopolous paying her debt to him but did not put a return address on the envelope.

She continued to see Dr. Crane. He stayed late so she could come after work. When she told him she thought she was well enough to discontinue the sessions, he recommended that she continue them for a while more. She told him her plan to go to college at night, get a degree, and become a social worker.

In late May she moved into a new apartment. It was smaller than the other one but it had one room she could use as an extra small bedroom. It was in a quiet neighborhood with trees and a view of the river from her window. Although it was furnished, everything was old or in need of repair, so she went to a store and put a down payment on her own furniture.

Dr. Crane smoked foul-smelling Italian cheroots, but during their sessions he could seldom find a match to light them. At the end of their last session in August she gave him a cigarette lighter with an inscription. They hugged at the door.

She continued to write in her journal occasionally.

24

Willa was four when her grandmother took her to Pineville in the taxi. She did not tell her where they were going or why, but said she must not talk to anyone, not answer questions from strangers, never reveal her name. She told her that if she did, she would leave her where they were going and then she would be on her own. At that time, being alone in that outside world her grandmother had taught her to fear was the worst thing Willa could imagine.

They stood at the side of the highway for an hour before a free taxi came by. Neither spoke. Willa kept looking around. She held her grandmother's hand tightly, afraid to leave her side. When the taxi stopped and the driver opened the rear door from inside, Willa pulled back, afraid to get in. She did not say anything, did not make a sound, but she clung to the door panel until her grandmother disengaged her and forced her inside. As the taxi pulled off, Willa pressed her face to the window, looking back in alarm as they left the only place she had ever known.

But curiosity soon overcame fear: on the highway she looked out trying to see the people in cars that were passing; she saw billboards and a radio tower and a hitchhiker for the first time. When the taxi turned onto the main street in Pineville, she saw tall buildings and restaurants where behind windows people sat eating at different tables. Houses she glimpsed on the side streets looked very small to her. The taxi stopped, then proceeded several times in obedience to changing lights of different colors hanging from wires over the street. Most of the people on the street seemed to be strangers to one another. Then she saw a black person, then others.

She remembered the black handyman, Lester, who had once

worked for her grandmother, but now she was amazed to see so many black people in one place. She had always thought that Lester was a rarity, someone whose skin color had come out wrong at birth. Living around animals, she knew about sex and reproduction among them before she knew very much about other people.

They stopped in front of a tall building, and her grandmother gave the driver money while still in the taxi, then walked her quickly into the building.

They hurried past people waiting in front of two closed metal doors beside each of which was a panel on which lighted numbers went moving up and down. They walked up a back stairway three flights into a hallway and to a door with writing on it. She could not read yet. They went in.

The only person there was a woman sitting behind a desk. Her grandmother spoke to her and the woman pushed a button, picked up a black object from the desk and spoke into it. She put it down. "He's been expecting you" she said to her grandmother, and they went through a door.

In the room were two men: one about her grandmother's age sitting behind a desk, the other a much younger man standing by a window. The older man got up, came around the desk and shook hands with her grandmother. "Nice to see you again, Lydia" he said.

"I hope you understood from my letter exactly what I want" her grandmother said to him. "Everything you asked for is in this envelope." She took a thick envelope from her purse and handed it to him.

He put the envelope on his desk. "As always" he said to her grandmother, "you've made your wishes very clear. There are details to be worked out, as I told you in my letter." He had been looking at Willa as he spoke. The young man at the window had been watching her since they came into the room.

Her grandmother said to the older man, indicating Willa, "This is the child, Willa." She spoke to Willa. "This is Mr. William Cass and his son, John. They're my attorneys."

The man shook Willa's hand. "Hello, Willa" he said.

She did not answer. She was following her grandmother's instructions.

Both men kept looking at her. The older man continued smiling. He had teeth that were too large for his face and did not look real. There was no hair on his head. Willa decided she did not like either of them. The room was full of stale odors. She backed away from the older man.

He said to her grandmother "It's best if she waits outside. This won't take long. The papers are ready."

Her grandmother took Willa into the other room. There, sitting in one of the chairs, was a beautiful, thin woman wearing jewelry, a yellow dress and a large hat.

"Sit out here" Willa's grandmother told her. "Don't move, and do exactly as I told you." She went back inside.

Willa sat down next to the thin woman. She looked up at her. She had never seen anyone dressed like her before. The hat she wore was so large it nearly hid her face. She touched the woman's dress. It was so smooth her fingers slid over it. When she reached up to feel the hat, the woman pulled her head back. "Please don't do that" she said. She turned her face away.

Willa continued to look up at her—she could not help it, the woman was so beautiful and dressed so exotically. She had long red fingernails. Willa had never seen painted fingernails before either. Shiny pieces of metal were hanging from her ears.

When Willa reached up carefully to feel one of the pieces of metal, barely touching it, the woman jerked her face quickly back toward her; she felt to make sure the piece of metal was still there. "Little girl" she said, "please don't touch me." She turned away again. A moment later she got up and sat in a chair on the other side of the room.

Willa had always felt that when she touched something she understood it better; she had not meant any harm to the woman. She was trying hard to obey her grandmother and not talk, but it was becoming difficult. She got up and went to the desk and stood in front of it.

She picked up several objects on the desk that were unfamiliar to her, examined them, then replaced them carefully. She moved to the side of the desk to look at a machine that had made a clicking sound every time the woman behind the desk had touched it minutes earlier; she was reaching out to touch it too when she saw the woman's hand motion her away. The woman was talking into the black object again, but her eyes were on Willa. Willa returned to the front of the desk.

Willa watched as the woman talked into the black object: she would listen, then talk, listen and talk again. Finally she laid the object back on its black box, then raised it again. She pushed a button on the box, spoke, listened, spoke again. When she replaced it a final time, she looked at Willa.

Willa had to know: "Can you talk to people through that?"

"Of course."

But Willa did not have time to ask her other questions, for at that moment the door opened and the older man called Willa back inside.

While her grandmother watched from a chair, the older man sat Willa in another chair. He backed up and lifted a black box and pointed it at her with his face behind it the way Willa's grandmother had when she took the picture of her in the rocking chair. But this time when he pushed the button a bright light exploded in her eyes blinding her for seconds. Then he took her to the desk and put ink on her hands. She looked around at her grandmother, but the woman did not say or do anything to help her and she knew she was not going to explain to her what was happening or why. Willa did not say anything when the man pressed her ink-smeared hands onto a sheet of paper on the desk, but she pulled away from him when he was done. She looked at her stained hands, then glared at him.

"Wash your hands" her grandmother told her, indicating a sink in a corner of the room. As Willa went to it, her grandmother got up and bent over the desk, writing on a paper.

They returned directly home in another taxi. Willa went into the woods where she sat under a tree for the rest of the day. It was then that she decided to find her mother and live with her someday.

■ ■ ■

Willa stood across the street from Chatto Hoffman's basement apartment. The lights had been off in the apartment when she arrived four hours earlier: she could see the hands on a church clock behind the building moving onto midnight. She knew she had come to the right place when she went to Chatto's door to knock on it, for beside it was a mailbox with his name on it so stuffed with letters and magazines and newspapers that no more could fit in; others had fallen to the ground beneath it. When she went to a window and looked in, she saw an apartment cluttered with odds and ends but only a few pieces of old furniture.

The church clock struck twelve sonorous notes, after which the street was silent again. A half-hour later she heard the sound of a cane tapping and a blind man came up the street on the other side.

Each night at the same hour Chatto left his apartment, and four and a half hours later he returned. The routine had remained unvaried for three years. He always took the same route coming and going, along the darkest streets, past alleys and doorways into which he could see only dimly, if at all. His steps were measured and slow, and he tapped the white cane more loudly and often than he had any need to, as if announcing his arrival and his nearly sightless condition to anyone who was waiting. He was waiting too.

The journey always took him to the same place: the Bucket of Blood. It was the only bar still operating among those he had frequented in the old days in the neighborhood, the only one that remained unchanged among those that had struggled for years to survive, heavy drinkers and ethnics being loyal to their haunts and resisting change. Even the High Note was gone, a health spa standing where it used to be. The jazzmen and their music had scattered and gone underground once more.

He always sat in the same back booth, where his drinks were brought to him. He put his cane on the table. Only there did he put on the dark glasses he usually wore now only in daylight. He sat facing the door, and now and then when it opened and someone entered coming in his direction, he looked up. What he saw was a blur, a contiguousness of shapes melting somewhere at the center of his vision.

Only the older locals knew him there now, and he seldom spoke to any of them. The others had all gone, died or drifted off. He and Mau-Mau Sue had been all that remained of them until a year ago, when she had fallen asleep drunk smoking a cigarette in bed in a cheap hotel. All that was left by which to identify her was a ring.

Once in a while a woman joined him, and sometimes he took one back to his apartment with him. But they were older women, often drunks. None went with him a second time, and later they told stories of how he had humiliated and frightened them.

At midnight he retraced his route home. Back on the streets of the neighborhood he passed memories, ghosts risen and sometimes speaking to him but no longer to be seen. Now and then he stopped at the entrance to an alley or opposite a darkened doorway; a sound or something displaced or foreign in the atmosphere catching his attention, he raised the cane and waited.

He was waiting for his assassin. Not Big Brown, who, he knew, had been shot to death in a bar in Pittsburgh, but some other from among the many he had maimed and scarred and humiliated when he worked for Mary Vandel. He sometimes remembered the one he buried up to his neck in a deserted barn on an isolated field and left for two days. When he returned for him, the man had gone mad. And another who had owed Mary money and refused to pay whose fingers he had cut off. They thought he was insane, so they all feared him. He smiled when he recalled them. He had declared a private war on the white world—especially on those who had power and money—but it had been over for years. Now he sometimes thought of himself as a dinosaur roaming among other unmentionables on the dark side of history. He did not know who would come for him or when. All he was certain of was that he would not hide.

Recently a thought had occurred to him that was the only thing that had ever frightened him: that no one would come, or wanted to anymore, to challenge him on his nightly journeys.

Willa had not expected the blind man to turn and go down the steps to Chatto Hoffman's apartment; he already had his key out and the door open when she started down the steps toward him. Then he stopped.

He turned, his cane raised. He did not speak, did not ask who it was, just stood facing her with the cane ready to strike, she knew, if she came within range of it. She stayed where she was when she asked "Mr. Hoffman? Are you Chatto Hoffman?"

He did not answer, but she could see by his expression that he was surprised.

"Mr. Hoffman, my name's Willa Rhineman. I've been looking for you."

"Why?"

"I'm Madeleine Rhineman's daughter."

"Who?"

"Madeleine. She was your girlfriend a long time ago. She disappeared back then and I came here to find her."

"How old are you, girl?"

"Sixteen. I was only a baby when you met her."

"Who sent you?"

"No one sent me, but a friend of Mary Vandel's got your address for me."

"Your friend could get hurt for doing that."

"Mary's dead, Mr. Hoffman."

He lowered the cane then, pushing his door wide open with it. He reached inside on the wall, and a bright light came on in the apartment. Then he stepped back to make room for her. "Go in" he said. "Stand where I can see you."

Willa came down the steps and went past him into the apartment. She turned and faced him.

He leaned forward looking at her. Then he laughed. "So she had a kid" he said. "That explains a lot."

He stepped into the apartment, closing the door behind him as a shadow at the top of the steps detached itself from the other shadows there.

"Sit down" Chatto said.

Willa sat on a couch the other end of which sank nearly to the floor. There were hundreds of books and magazines on shelves all around her. Empty wine bottles and beer cans were everywhere, as well as plates with the remains of meals on them. Photographs of angry-looking black men hung in frames on the walls.

He pushed some clothes and a beer can off a chair and sat down in it across from Willa. He leaned forward on his cane to look at her, but he could have been looking through her.

"I'm sorry you lost your sight, Mr. Hoffman" she said. "How did it happen?"

She found it difficult to believe that the man she saw was the same one she had heard about: the man Orlo Haines and even Mary had feared. She could see he had once been a handsome man, but now his face was very thin and his features were pinched. Where his body was not thin, the muscles were turning to fat. The black hair that came to below his shoulders had wide streaks of gray in it.

He said "It's called an astigmatism."

"Can't it be fixed? An operation or something?"

"I let it go too long for that to be likely. Anyway, I don't have the money and I won't take their charity." Then suddenly he said "But what do you care?" He leaned closer to look at her again. "I can't make you out even in this light. Do you look like Madeleine?"

"It's funny. Mary Vandel thought I did, but Orlo Haines didn't think I look like her at all."

He leaned back in his chair. "So old Mary is dead. A lot of important people are going to breathe easier now. I heard she got herself a smack habit."

"I wouldn't know about her habits" Willa said. "I liked Mary. She was unhappy because she loved my mother so much is all that was wrong with her."

"Your mother was a woman who couldn't stand to be loved."

"Oh, I wouldn't say that."

"What the hell would you know about her if you never saw her?"

"I didn't know anything about her until now. But these last days I've learned a lot. Such as that she loved you. Did you love her, Mr. Hoffman?"

She saw his body stiffen. His hands gripped the cane tightly. "She meant nothing to me" he said.

"Maybe you're the one who couldn't stand to be loved."

He got up. He shook the cane at her. "What do you want?"

"I want to find my mother. I thought you would help me."

"Why is it you white people only come to us when you have a problem? If it wasn't for the fact that you need us now and then, we could rot for all you care."

"I don't know about other white people, Mr. Hoffman. I just want to find my mother."

He sat down again. "I haven't seen Madeleine since the night they took her to the hospital" he said.

"When she was sick, you mean?"

"Sick? Is that what Mary told you? Your mother tried to kill herself that night."

This time it was Willa who stiffened. "She must have been very unhappy" she said quietly.

"What do you white people know about unhappiness?" he asked. "Try being unhappy in a black skin sometime."

"Maybe my mother learned about being unhappy too good. You couldn't exactly have been a pleasure to live with."

He laughed. Then he stopped. He turned his face to the window and motioned to her to be quiet.

"What is it?" she whispered.

He did not answer for a moment. Then he turned back to her. "I thought I heard somebody out there."

She looked at the window: "There's nobody there, Mr. Hoffman. Who are you afraid of?"

"I'm not afraid of anyone. You'd better go now. I can't help you find Madeleine."

She did not move to leave. "There's one other person who might. Did you know a woman named Sylvia Rosenberg?"

"I knew about her. I met her once. Why?"

"After my mother got out of the hospital, she stayed with her for a while. Do you know where she lived?"

"No."

"Do you know anybody who did?"

"Half of the musicians at the High Note knew her. But none of them are around now, except one. Now that I think of it, if anyone knows where to find her, it would be him."

"Why?"

"She had a kid by him. It died a year later. She must have been pregnant when Madeleine was living with her. Would you believe a girl who would ask a man to give her a baby without wanting anything more from him?"

"Why did he do it?"

"He wanted to prove he was a man."

"Why did she?"

"You'll have to ask her that."

"How do you know about it?"

"The creep went around bragging about it. Look, Willa, I can call him, make him see you. But that's all I can do. Then I want you to get out of here."

She nodded.

He got up and went into a bedroom. A minute later she heard him talking on the telephone.

She got up to look at the photographs on the walls. She was standing near the door when she turned and saw a man's shadow on the wall outside the window. It moved, leaning closer to the window.

She looked toward the bedroom for Chatto, but he was still talking on the telephone. She could have gone to him, but she was much closer to the door. She opened the door partway and called out of it. "Who's out there? What do you want?" The shadow on the wall withdrew, and she stepped outside to see who it was.

There seemed to be no one there at first. She was about to go back inside when she saw him standing in partial darkness near the top of the steps. All she could see of him were his shoes and the top third of his face. She was at the bottom of the steps looking up.

"Who's there?" she called again.

He did not move, was so still she would not have noticed him except for the light from the open doorway and the street, which revealed him at the top and bottom. His eyes looked down at her, frightened, asking her not to come nearer.

It was so dark at the foot of the stairs that she had to look down to find the first step, then use the handrail to ascend to it; when she looked up again, he was gone. She went back in and sat waiting for Chatto.

He came in a minute later with a piece of paper in his hand. He held it out to her, and she got up and took it. A name and address were typed on it. She folded it and put it into her purse.

He sat down again in his chair. She remained standing.

"That address is ten blocks from here" he told her. "Go north for eight blocks, then east for two. He's waiting for you. Now get out of here, and don't come back."

"Thank you" she said. She went to the door. Chatto remained seated looking straight ahead.

"I should tell you, Mr. Hoffman, you were right. There was someone out there by the window."

His face lifted to her.

"He's gone now" she said.

He did not show any emotion at her news.

"Did you hear me, Mr. Hoffman?"

"I heard."

"Good-bye."

He did not reply.

When she got to the top of the steps, she watched him through the window as he got out of his chair, went to the wall and switched off the light. Then he returned to the chair and sat down in darkness.

■ ■ ■

After confirming the street number on the piece of paper Chatto had given her, Willa entered the old building and went up two flights on concrete steps and knocked on a metal door with the name on it. It opened slowly in the small hands of the dwarf who stood inside looking up at her.

"Are you Mr. Tyler?" she asked. "I'm Willa Rhineman."

"Yes, yes" he said. "Come in, child. Excuse the appearance of the place. We had a party, and I've had such a frightful hangover all day I haven't had a chance to clean it up."

It looked clean to Willa except for glasses and trays of food here and there. A large piano stood at one end of it in front of purple velvet drapes that covered the windows. She had never seen so many statues and paintings and stuffed animals in one place. Against a far wall was a life-size doll of a fat black woman with large breasts wearing an apron and with a bandanna around her head.

Billy Tyler hurried up behind her. "Sit down, sit down" he said.

She sat on a purple velvet couch. All of the furniture in the room was either purple or crimson.

Billy twisted up into a chair opposite her. He had to reach up to place his arms on the armrests. "Would you like something to drink? I don't have any milk or fruit juice. Perhaps a glass of wine with some water in it in the French manner? I always thought it quite sensible of the French to give their children wine. The water would probably kill them." A glass of wine and a wine bottle were on a table next to him.

"No, thank you" she said.

His bare legs pointed at her straight out from the chair. He pulled the hem of the Japanese kimono he was wearing over them before saying "Well, so you're Madeleine's girl."

"Yes, sir."

"Your mother and I were close friends. She used to come see me, sometimes sit on that very same couch you're sitting on now. We'd drink wine and laugh and just dish the night away. She's a lovely person. So genuine and open. But, in light of what happened, perhaps too sensitive for her own good. Of course, I was *shocked* when I heard she tried to take her own life. You don't look a bit like her, by the way, if you don't mind my saying so."

"I don't mind."

"Your mother—she had an ethereal quality. You appear to be more earthy."

"I'm pretty earthy" Willa agreed.

"It was that sensitivity that made your mother so vulnerable. That's how we became close friends. We're both artists and much too sensitive for this harsh world we live in. Have you read her poetry, by the way? She wrote *such* beautiful poetry, but *oh,* so sad. But she could laugh too. Oh, my, how she could laugh! I suppose we were pretty silly sometimes. You know: mugging and clowning and corny jokes and all of that. We just let our hair down and *were.*"

Willa was wondering why the little man looked as if at any moment he would burst into tears. He grabbed his glass and drank down a full glass of wine. He refilled it, drank some more, then smiled weakly at her. She did not know what to say to him.

"Do I bring you down?" he asked. "I'm sorry. It's just that lately—" He took a handkerchief from the pocket of his kimono and blew loudly into it. Then he smiled weakly at her again. "Child" he said, "don't ever fall in love. It's just not worth it." He smiled bravely. "When you see Madeleine," he said "send her Billy's love. And tell her he's happy. Will you do that for me?"

"Yes."

"Good friends are all that matter. Don't forget that."

"Mr. Tyler" Willa said, "Chatto Hoffman told me—"

He put a finger to his lips to silence her. His small hand motioned to her to lean nearer; he moved to the edge of his chair and leaned forward too so that their heads nearly met halfway.

He whispered "My friend Giorgio is in the next room. He mustn't hear this. And you must never tell him about Sylvia and our baby. He simply wouldn't understand, and he'd never let me hear the end of it. In fact, although I'm glad I did so now that I've met you, if it had been anyone else but Chatto Hoffman that asked me to do this I would have refused. But that man has always terrified me. He is a cruel, cruel person, and I was fearful of what he might do if I didn't see you. Your mother, Lord knows, suffered enough at his hands. So I'm going to call Sylvia and ask her to meet with you, but you must promise never to bring up the subject again."

Willa nodded.

"Good" he said. "You're really a very understanding person for one of such tender years. Now I'll just go and freshen up and then make that call. You make yourself at home. Look around if you like."

He climbed out of the chair and, body twisting as he walked, went through a door in which she caught a glimpse of a naked young man asleep in a bed. He closed the door behind him.

Willa waited. Minutes later she heard Billy and someone else arguing. Then she heard Billy yelling, then crying, and finally running off. A door slammed. Then it was quiet.

She looked around. On one wall was a framed photograph of a younger Billy in a tuxedo sitting at a piano. Next to it were album covers with his name on them. Several posters announced concerts of his. And finally there was another photograph of him at a piano with two other musicians in what looked like a nightclub. The glass was broken and someone had slashed his face in the photograph with a sharp object.

She waited in the silence. After a while she became aware of the large doll; when she turned to it, it seemed to be looking at her in the dim light of the room. It held a slender, ruby-red glass in one hand and a small silver dish in the other. A broad smile was painted on the fat black woman's face, but its eyes were solemn and did not fit the laughing face. It looked so lifelike she almost expected it to move suddenly and walk across the room to her. She got up and went to it.

She touched it: it was made of metal and wood. Up close, she saw that the red glass was a phial with a hole in its top. From behind the doll curled out a cord which fit into an electrical socket on the wall; on the doll's side was a metal box with two buttons. She pushed the button marked "On." The doll moved.

She stepped away at the first sound of the doll's loud voice: "HA-HA-HA, HA-HA-HA, HA-HA-HA."

It was bending at the waist toward her; at the same time, the hand with the phial in it and the one holding the silver dish began moving together. "HA-HA-HA, HA-HA-HA, HA-HA-HA" it kept saying in a hollow voice.

She moved back to it, reaching for the box to shut it off as its face descended close to hers shouting into her ear "HA-HA-HA, HA-HA-HA, HA-HA-HA." She found the button as the hand with the phial in it tilted over the dish: a white powder fell from it onto the dish a second before she could push the button marked "Off." "HA" it went and was silent, still bending.

She waited. She expected Billy or the young man in the bedroom to come out, but neither did. She decided to leave the doll as it was and went back to wait in Billy's chair.

She could sense the doll looking at her again. Doors opened, then closed. She imagined the two men going into and coming out of rooms endlessly. She wanted Billy to return so she could leave.

The door opened and the young man, who she saw now was about eighteen, stood in the doorway. He was slender and tall, with a face of such startling serene beauty as she had seen only in pictures of angels. He had blonde hair to his waist and the whitest, most perfect skin she had ever seen. He was completely naked. He came toward her.

He moved with the sinuous self-confidence of a beautiful woman. He showed no hint of self-consciousness about his nakedness; that state, he seemed to announce, was not only natural to him, it was his right. When he looked at Willa, there was in his expression the recognition not of her but of himself in her eyes. He sat down across from her as gracefully as he walked, arms out full length across the back of the couch, legs apart. His expression close up, Willa saw now, was not serene but absent.

"Hello" he said. "My name's Giorgio. Are you a friend of Billy's?"

It took Willa a few seconds to gain her voice. "Not exactly" she managed to say.

"I am. We've been living together for a year. He worships me. He thinks I'm the most beautiful creature on earth. Do you think I'm beautiful?"

Willa stared at him. She did not know how to answer such a question from a man. He stared back at her, either unaffected by her silence or indifferent to anyone's opinion in the face of such an obvious truth.

"I found a blemish this morning" he said. "Would you like to see it?"

She nodded and he leaned forward, his arm bent and held up for her inspection. She could not see anything.

"There" he said. "Just above the elbow."

She looked closer and saw it: a brown spot the size of a pinhead.

He leaned back, arms outspread again. His limp penis hung over the edge of the couch. She tried not to look at it.

"As blemishes go" he said, "it's not much, but it's the beginning. When my time comes, I want to look like an ugly old hag. It will be nice not to be wanted anymore. All my life men and women have used me. You can't imagine what it's like to be desired by everyone only because you're beautiful."

Willa did not know how to reply to such a statement. Also, his expression and manner did not match his words. She wondered if he had read what he said in a book or heard it somewhere.

But the fact that she had not commented did not seem to matter to him. Although she had only said one sentence to him, he appeared bored with her already. He had apparently dismissed her from his mind when, without moving his body, he looked over at the doorway seconds before Billy appeared in it. Willa had not heard him.

Billy came to the couch and climbed onto it next to Giorgio. "Willa" he said, "I want to apologize. Giorgio has no shame. He is always doing this. He likes to shock my friends." He looked up at the boy, who was pointedly ignoring him. "Go put some clothes on" Billy said.

Giorgio rose, but not until seconds later, while Willa and Billy waited. He moved off slowly and as if he were the only person in the room. He paused in the doorway, pointed his melon-shaped behind at Billy, and wiggled it. Then he went into the other room, slamming the door behind him.

"Child" Billy said, "I'm so embarrassed. You have no idea how that boy loves to torment me. If I didn't love him so, I'd throw him right out on the street. But what can I do? Someone else would destroy him. Such beauty begs to be defiled."

Willa said "Mr. Tyler, I'm sorry to hurry you, but it's late and—"

"Of course. Of course, Willa. Forgive me. My trials are no concern of yours." He took a piece of paper from the pocket of his kimono and gave it to her. "I spoke to Sylvia. She'll see you there tomorrow morning at ten."

"Thank you." She got up.

Billy followed her to the door. He opened it for her. "Remember to give Madeleine Billy's love" he said. "And tell her he misses her."

As she was going down the stairs, she heard the doll laugh again. "HA-HA, HA-HA-HA, HA-HA-HA."

She went faster.

25

Vernon had to hurry to the bus stop where the girl was waiting; he did not have time to return to his room and dress. When he drove back to the bus stop, he was still half-naked under his overcoat.

His state of undress was what caused him to make the mistake he would never have made otherwise. He who was a follower knew about the treachery of shadows; he had learned always to be conscious of his. When possible, he gathered it around him like a second overcoat—when not, he avoided places where it would betray him. When he followed, his shadow was another Vernon, always under his control. But that night it exposed him.

When they arrived at the girl's destination, he waited in the car a block down from the street where she stood on the sidewalk waiting too. He had learned by then that she had the same patience and single-mindedness he did. She too knew how to wait alone and in silence.

He was tempted to leave the car and enter a doorway close to her, to breathe as she was breathing, move as she moved, perhaps let his shadow touch hers in a brief embrace. But he knew he could not risk it on such a lightly trafficked street.

He saw a blind man come up the street and start down the steps toward the house she had been watching. When she crossed after him, Vernon got out of the car.

It was then he realized that his near nakedness would interfere with his following: he was too aware of it—and of the possibility that a passerby would detect it—to do as he always did, merging his presence with his surroundings. He considered going back to his room and waiting for her to return; but if he did that, he would not know what happened during the rest of that night in her search for her mother. She could even disappear again, perhaps permanently this time. He realized then that he would miss her. He had never felt that before about anyone he followed.

He watched them through the window as they sat talking; he saw the blind man get angry and stand up, shaking his cane at her, and for a moment he was frightened for her. He leaned closer, his ear near the windowpane, trying to hear them. He understood a sentence here and there, but most of what they said was unintelligible to him. He moved closer, and it was at that moment that one of the buttons on his overcoat clicked against the window.

He drew back an instant before the blind man turned to the window. Vernon knew the man could not have seen him even if he had had perfect vision, but the sound had alerted him. They had stopped talking. No one Vernon followed had ever heard him before.

He waited several minutes after they had resumed talking before he moved back to the window, but before he got there he withdrew. He had lost his fluency, was no longer one with his subject. He stayed where he was against the wall of the house. He listened, but he did not dare go nearer.

Then they were silent again. There was no sound from inside for minutes. Moving slowly, holding his breath, he looked in at the edge of the window. They were both gone. He leaned farther out to see if they were in another part of the room, and it was then that he became aware of his shadow on the wall opposite him. He pulled back, but not before he heard the door open and the girl call "Who's out there? What do you want?"

He had no alternative: for the moment, she could not see him, but if she stepped into the entranceway, came around it—He tried to get away up the steps.

He was almost to the top of the steps when he knew she was coming out. He stopped. He moved back as far as he could into the shadows.

When she came to the foot of the steps and looked up, he knew she could see him. She did not know who it was, but she knew someone was there. She was looking into his eyes. He had wanted her to recognize him, but not like that—not as the follower. He begged her with his eyes to go away. Instead, she started to come up the steps.

It was that moment in which she had to look down to find the first step that saved him: he was gone onto the street before she could look up again.

26

The day after Madeleine left for the city with Orlo Haines, Lydia decreed that she never again be mentioned in the house by name, and that any questions Willa had about her parentage be referred to her.

She packed all of Madeleine's possessions in boxes and stored them in the old stable. She had Emil disassemble Madeleine's bed and take it and the other furniture in her room to the stable too. She put the family photo album in one of the boxes, along with every other picture of Madeleine she could find in the house. Madeleine's room remained bare until Lydia moved Willa into it.

When she had divested the house of every trace of her daughter, she began on those objects she decided had contributed to the household's corruption. Magazines and books, except for the two Bibles, were burned. Every picture that was not of a religious nature was taken from the walls and disposed of. A deck of cards, a chess set and other board games Emil and Madeleine had once played were destroyed. She allowed the radio to remain, but now the plug was pulled and it was turned on only at her direction and in her presence, the dial fixed at the one station that broadcast religious programs. She emptied the bathroom cabinet of all aids to grooming and beauty: she deemed vanity, more than any other, the vice that had corrupted her family. She had Emil take the television to the stable, where it came to rest in the farthest corner, broad-shouldered in shadow where dust eventually shrouded it, its pale eye stilled. The stable now held a community in disgrace and exile, Lydia's passion expressed in a metaphor of objects. Nothing was sold or given to charity, as if to do so would have let their evil loose on the world. The car and pickup would join them within a month, and following that the telephone was taken out. On that day when the family was cut off from the community, Lydia had Emil take the tires off the two vehicles and burn them and put a new lock on the stable. She kept the only key.

It was at that time that Lydia told Emil what he needed finally to be told, what she had withheld from him for seventeen years, partly in the name of discipline and partly because there was no need for him to know it and he had never asked: she told him how they had lived in relative comfort and raised a daughter too all those years on Emil's salary and minuscule government pension and the small income from crops and livestock; how that large house had been maintained, the taxes paid on it.

He sat listening in silence as she told him that in two weeks he would be retired three years early from the mill, that she knew this because she had arranged it, as she had arranged that he go to work there in the first place: because she was a minor silent partner in the mill.

He had suspected it. He had perhaps even known it but had never wanted to face it. He remembered the night she had rescued him from the bar owner in Milltown after he had beaten up the whore; how that night she had faced down the man who had obviously heard of her and knew she could accomplish that threat with which she had forced him to cover up the incident and save Emil from jail.

She told him now what he had only wondered about once or twice in the early years: that contrary to what Lydia had told him the first day they met—that her first husband had died leaving her only the house and a small amount of money—she had been the sole benefactress of a cash bequest which, after death taxes, was in excess of thirty thousand dollars. That when a group of local businessmen had decided the time was right to reopen the mill, those friends of her late husband's had approached her with the offer that she use the bulk of her inheritance to go into it with them. She had accepted, after consulting with her husband's lawyer, William Cass—with the provision that she be a silent partner, although one who would be kept informed of all major decisions and whose advice during those early years proved to be shrewd and farsighted. It was her strategies that had contributed significantly in keeping the union out of the mill for a decade.

The mill had prospered under its new ownership, and although it had meant that for a while most of her capital had been tied up in it and yielded her only a moderate income, she had invested the profits shrewdly, through Cass, in stocks that had appreciated steadily over the years, so that, as she now informed the silent Emil, they had a net worth of over two hundred thousand dollars.

He did not say anything when she had finished, did not ask any questions. Instead, he went out of the house and onto the porch. She watched him through the window.

He stood very still. He looked slightly bent. He remained there until the sun had gone down, when darkness further diminished him.

The day Emil retired from the mill, he drove to Milltown. He had not seen it since that night seventeen years before.

He hardly recognized it. Some of the bars still bore their original names, but now instead of ramshackle wooden structures they were buildings constructed of stone and steel and glass; and instead of the frail light in their open doorways from kerosene lamps and bare bulbs inside, he saw now fluorescence lighting them within and neon without. The bumpy dirt road was covered over with the sameness of asphalt, and there were concrete sidewalks where before there had been stubbled soil. Where the nested cabins had once been there was now a parking lot and motels. The whores were still there, but they no longer looked and acted like whores, and the raucous music that had served to introduce them to their customers, the live bands of drunken musicians, were replaced by rainbow-lit jukeboxes whose songs told of the same urgencies, but no longer wildly. The wooden shacks and cribs of black women where darker passions once fed were now gone; and although a black church was there bearing the same hieratic name, the precarious wooden structure had been replaced by another of stone, whose vertical lines ending in twin spires seemed metamorphosed from the stone cliff on which it stood. No joyful music or black women dancing ecstasies were framed in its windows, which now were of stained glass—containing joy, instead of sharing it with the night.

He revisited those bars he now recognized only by name. He sat alone at the tables. He did not drink any alcohol, did not laugh at any of the jokes he heard told or tell any of his own, did not flirt with the whores and pretty young women who still came there.

He returned home around midnight. Lydia never asked where he had been. When he awoke the next morning, their isolation had begun.

Until Willa was three—in the beginning out of necessity—Lydia dressed her in clothes that had been hers when she was that age. Willa during her early years was a replication of Lydia. When one day Lydia saw Willa in a pinafore and sunbonnet she had worn in her own childhood, she realized it was her ego that made her dress Willa that way. She prayed that night, and the next morning she put all the clothes back into the trunk. But not before she retrieved the camera from the stable and photographed Willa sitting in her rocking chair wearing the pinafore and sunbonnet.

After that she made Willa's clothes herself: overalls and dresses of cheap cloth she had dyed black and dark gray. She combed and pinned the child's hair back similar to the way she wore hers: not in emulation of her this time but as a guard against future vanity. She made a trip by bus to a distant town where she bought Willa sturdy, sensible shoes. During the summer she let Willa go barefoot.

As Willa grew older, she became more aware of the man she knew as her grandfather but who lived apart from them in the attic. He almost never spoke to her, but then, although he ate his meals with them, he seldom spoke to her grandmother either. Those occasions when he did spend more time among them were when she saw him doing the one thing he obviously enjoyed: working with his hands. He had made the bed she slept in and all of the furniture in her room; and she had even seen him smiling while repairing things around the house with the tools in the long box he kept in the upper hall closet. She was intrigued by the fact that although there was no one there to steal the tools, he kept a key in his wallet with which he locked the box when he was finished using it.

One summer morning she sat barefoot on the back steps watching him replace the hinges on the cellar door. He worked slowly and meticulously, and when he was done, he ran his fingers lovingly over the shiny new hinges. Then he locked the box and got up from his kneeling position. When he turned, he saw Willa. He stared at her entwined toes, which looked like more than the five toes they actually were. He surprised her by sitting next to her on the step. Then he surprised her again by speaking to her in an intimate way.

"Do you know how you got your foot?" he asked her.

"I was born with it."

He put his finger to his lips to caution her to be quiet. "I'll show you a secret" he whispered. He leaned over and took off one of his shoes and sock. She had noticed that he limped, but she had not known why before: what he showed her was that he had only half a foot.

"Go ahead" he said. "Touch it if you want to."

She reached down and touched it.

As he was putting his sock back on, he said "It never slowed me down any. I was as quick as most men with two whole feet. Quicker at some things." He reached for his shoe to put it back on. "I lost my toes" he said "when I was a young man. Now it looks like they turned up on you." He smiled at her as he leaned over to tie his shoelaces. Then he stopped. He looked quickly up and around, aware before Willa was of her grandmother standing at the screen door. His smile was gone. He looked frightened. He bent hurrying to tie his shoe when her grandmother spoke through the screen door.

"Emil, come in here!"

He did not speak to Willa again nor look at her as he picked up the box and, bent over slightly, went into the kitchen. A minute later she heard her grandmother scolding him, but in a voice too low for Willa to understand what she was saying.

After that he avoided Willa. It was the only time she had shared a close moment with him, but that day she understood they had something in common: he hid things from Lydia too.

One day when her grandmother was out of the house and Willa was coming up the stairs, she turned into the hallway in time to see him go into the closet and close the door behind him. She went to the door and looked in through the keyhole.

He had turned on the overhead light. She could see him clearly. He was sitting on his long box reading a Bible. She was about to conclude that going into a closet to read the Bible was just another of his eccentricities when she saw him take something from it. She recognized it as a photograph, although she could not see of whom or what. She continued to watch as he sat looking at it for a long time. He touched the surface of the photograph once with his fingers. Then he put it back into the Bible. He put the Bible into one of the drawers in the side of the box and locked it. He was turning out the light when Willa slipped away and back down the stairs.

There were other times when her grandmother was not there that Willa saw him go into the closet and sit looking at the photograph. He seemed lonely there, and although she wanted to know what was in the photograph, she could not see it from where she sat to peek at him, and he never left the box unlocked for her to find out.

When Willa was twelve, she saw her grandfather, who was lifting a heavy piece of machinery in the back yard, suddenly stop. He staggered forward a few steps, then dropped it. He fell to his knees, where his body jerked several times as if in pain. He pitched forward onto his face.

Her grandmother came running out the kitchen doorway. She knelt by him and turned him over. His face was white.

She told Willa to go to her room and stay there, then hurried off in the direction of the roadside store.

Willa went to her room. She was frightened. She had never seen anyone near death before, but she knew that was what was happening.

Twenty minutes later she watched from her window as a long car with revolving lights on top drove into the yard. Her grandmother got out of it along with two men dressed in white coats, who minutes later carried her grandfather away on what looked like a thin cot.

When her grandmother returned that night, she told Willa he would live but that he had had an aneurysm.

He was gone for three weeks. When he returned, he was weak and much thinner. His hands shook and his eyes showed the fear of one who knows that death is near.

That was when Emil's eccentric behavior began. He came down to breakfast one morning and, abruptly but in a quiet voice, asked Lydia "Where's Madeleine?"

It was the first time he had broken the rule; it took Lydia a moment to control herself. "She's gone. Don't you remember, Emil?"

"Oh, yes. Do you think she'll be coming back soon?"

Lydia had been raising her coffee cup to her lips. She put it down. She looked at him intently, thinking for a moment he was trying to deceive her; but the eyes looking back at her were without duplicity. She wondered not for the first time at the fact that except for being thinner, even with his illness he did not look much older at fifty-seven than he had when she first met him. Now his mind too was becoming younger than his years. She considered the irony that she, who considered herself sinless, looked like an old woman, while despite his many sins, he was in some ways more youthful than before. That morning he looked innocent; he had about him the reticence of a child.

The next morning he did something he had seldom done before: he went out to the mailbox before Lydia could. When he returned, she asked him what he had been expecting.

"I thought there might be a letter from Madeleine" he said.

She made him sit down. She sat across from him. "She's gone, Emil" she told him.

"I know."

"I mean, she won't be back or writing us, ever."

Willa came into the room at that moment. She had been standing in the doorway. She might have been listening. When Lydia got up and led her away, Willa looked back at her grandfather, who sat staring off.

That winter they heard Lester Kane on the radio. For years Lydia had been bringing news back to the house—from newspapers and magazines where she had first seen his name at the roadside store, and from buying trips to neighboring towns—of the handyman who had left them ten years ago to take over the stewardship of the Mount Calvary Baptist Church of Jesus Joyful in Milltown. During that time he had become famous and powerful, the friend of presidents and world leaders everywhere, first as a civil rights activist in the sixties, then, after Martin Luther King's assassination, as one of his successors who had continued to champion the cause to the present day. The church on the cliff had become famous too, brought through his leadership from its impover-ished beginnings to world prominence as the base to which Lester Kane returned from his forays to stir America's social conscience. Those sto-ries that pleased Lydia most were criticisms of him as one who had abandoned religion to further his radical (some claimed communistic) political goals. There had been such an escalation of those charges against him in recent years that he had announced his return to full-time participation in his church for five years to "reassess my relationship with God and seek counsel from my conscience." Now for the first time his weekly sermons were being broadcast nationwide from Milltown.

They gathered in the parlor, where Lydia always made Willa join them to listen to the religious programs on the radio. Usually Willa day-dreamed, bored by the frantic men who seemed to her to say the same things over and over. She had years ago rejected God—not necessarily as unlikely but at best as one who had only a remote interest in human affairs—and she was certain her grandfather did not believe in God at all. It was one of his secrets. But this time she was attentive, because she had heard her grandmother denouncing Lester Kane to her grandfather. She had called him "a disgrace to God-fearing colored people" and "the antichrist." Now Willa sensed that something unusual was happening in the room.

Lester Kane's sermon was not much different in content from the hundreds of other sermons Willa had been forced to attend there: he had stated its theme as sin and something he called "redemption." What was unusual was that from the moment the voice of their former handy-man came into the room announcing with his first words "I have been witness to sins the likes of which might have turned even the heart of Jesus to stone" she had seen a look of fear come over her grandfather. Her grandmother, sitting rigid and resistant in her chair, did not notice, but Willa was certain that her grandfather's fear came from the fact that he believed Lester Kane was talking to him. He put his hands up once as if to push away the voice, but her grandmother did not notice that either. Willa watched his jaw trembling. Tears came to his eyes. He looked around as if for someone to help him. There was only Willa.

When the program ended, Lydia, her curiosity satisfied, announced that she had heard enough. Lester Kane in his sermon had included among those sins that of repression of black people in America. Now she declared that "even a dog has more gratitude than to bite the hand that feeds him." Never again, she announced, would they listen to Lester Kane.

A month later Lydia discovered that a box of envelopes and another of stationery were missing from her desk drawer. It was the second set of each that she kept there, and she would not have noticed they were gone if the first had not run out. Each box contained a hundred envelopes and a hundred pieces of stationery. There were no stamps missing.

She had suspected Willa first but, after questioning her, was convinced she had not done it. She found them later in a shoe box under Emil's cot in the attic. There were ninety envelopes, all with names written on them in Emil's hand, all sealed: thirty to each of three parties.

She put on her glasses and sat on the side of the cot, where she separated them into three piles. When she was done, she had opened and read all of them in less than five minutes.

The first envelope she opened was addressed to Lester Kane. The letter was signed by Emil and it contained only two words: *I'm guilty.* The other twenty-nine addressed to him were identical, except that each bore a different date, covering a period of thirty days.

The next batch was addressed to "The Authorities" but had no address. These consisted of the dates and three sentences: *Lester Kane knew back then. He has judged me. Punish me.*

The third pile had Madeleine's name on each of the envelopes, and inside the dates again, but the pages were blank. They were unsigned, but on each sheet was a drop of blood. His pocket knife was in the box too.

She put the letters back into the shoe box and carried it down to behind the house, where she burned them in the oil drum in which they burned trash.

She confronted Emil later in the attic. She stood over him where he sat, head bowed and hands folded in his lap, on the side of the cot. "What did you think it would accomplish?"

He did not answer.

"Did you think it would wipe it all out?" she persisted.

He still did not answer.

"After all I've done for us, now this." She said "You are dangerous, Emil. Do you want me to lock you up here? Is that what I have to do to protect us?"

He looked up. He shook his head.

"Then swear that you won't do anything like that again."

"I swear it" he said.

She turned to go. Then she turned back. "What's done is done. We live with it."

She left.

She checked periodically to make certain there were no more letters; there were not. She told him that from then on she would take Willa with her to the roadside store.

He was all right for the rest of that year and into the following summer. Then he stopped making repairs to the house. Lydia did not insist and began doing those repairs she could herself. He would not let her use his toolbox, but he gave her the tools. He seldom left the attic. Then he stopped coming down for his meals.

She brought a tray to him in the attic, but when she returned for it the food had hardly been touched. After that he ate only enough to sustain life. Although she continued to bring a full tray to him, she did not try to force him to eat.

One morning she brought up his breakfast tray and found him sitting in his rocking chair with one of her steel knitting needles pushed through the flesh of his upper arm.

She searched the attic and confiscated every object he could use to mutilate himself. She told him if he tried to harm himself again she would tie him to the cot for his own safety. She knew he would be terrified of that.

Later she found him standing at the high, small window, looking out. He was there every day after that. He almost never spoke to her anymore.

He began leaving bread crumbs on the window ledge, watching the birds when they came for them. When she came in one morning and found bread crumbs in front of the rocker where he was sitting and birds there feeding on them, she nailed the window shut.

He returned to watching at the window.

When late that year his strength began to fail, she took him to the neighboring town of Lebanon and the doctor who had attended him at the hospital. She had been praying for him, but by then his deteriorating condition overcame her lifelong distrust of doctors.

She locked Willa in her room with food and water and went to the roadside store, where she called a taxi and rode back to the house in it to pick up Emil, who was waiting in the parlor.

The doctor examined him in his office. His name was Summers. He said that Emil might have a damaged aorta as a consequence of the aneurysm, and there was evidence that he was suffering from Alzheimer's disease. He told Lydia that Emil should return to the hospital for tests, but when Emil heard that, he begged Lydia not to send him. Being alone there the last time without Lydia to look after him had made him terrified at the thought of going back. The doctor recommended it again strongly, but all Emil would agree to was treatment at home and periodic visits to the doctor in his office. Not even Lydia could persuade him to go into the hospital.

The doctor put him on a special diet and a regimen of light exercise. He gave Lydia prescriptions for medication, which she had filled before they left Lebanon.

She brought his cot down that afternoon from the attic to her room. He waited in a chair, and when she came in with it he asked that she put it next to her bed, which she did.

That night after Lydia turned out the light, he asked her if he could lie with her for a while. It took her seconds to answer. "Yes. For a while."

He climbed under the covers with her, wearing his pajamas. He was so thin they no longer fit him. He turned to her. "Thank you, Lydia" he whispered. She did not answer. But when he asked her to hold him, she did.

He was trembling. "I'm afraid, Lydia" he said. "I don't want to die."

In the spring he began sitting in her rocking chair on the front porch. He never rocked, and his fingers moved in his lap as if he held prayer beads there. On those days when it was cool, he asked to wear Lydia's shawl.

The doctor had recommended walks, but he could not get farther than the edge of the woods before tiring. Several times he sat down to rest in the grass, which had grown so tall that it hid him. When he returned to the porch, there were grass and leaves in his graying hair, which Lydia picked out.

He kept bread crumbs in his hands. Birds flew into his lap and fed out of his hands, but when too many of them came, Lydia put an end to it. When some of the birds returned the next day, he opened his hands to show them they were empty.

He slept a great deal there, and Lydia noticed that he smiled in his sleep. On the last of the cool days he wore a blanket over his lap as well as the shawl.

* * *

As the sun grew warmer in the approach of summer, he began to regain some of his strength. He took longer walks, and once he went to the copse. He picked wildflowers on the way. He did not go in; he stood just outside it. He lifted his hands high and, in a gesture that could have been a benediction or a summoning, showered the air with flowers.

The next day he told Lydia he was going to start a garden and named the seeds he would need. She got them for him at the roadside store.

There were other, less arid places where he could have planted the seeds, but the spot he chose was only ten feet from the porch. He got the pick and shovel from the barn, and marking the boundaries with sticks and string, he began turning up the rocky and sandy soil where, Lydia knew, it was unlikely anything could grow.

It took him a week, for he could only work an hour a day without tiring. Then he planted the seeds, which in other soil would have bloomed into peonies, chrysanthemums and roses. Lydia watched, uneasy. Every day he watered them, got onto his knees to tend them. Who could say what resurrection he hoped for?

June came, then July, and each day he tended the garden, then went onto the porch and waited for the flowers to appear. Nothing grew there. Nothing.

She heard him cry out one night from the cot: "Who am I?" Another time he woke her with a shout: "Where's the road?"

It was in late August that Lydia returned from her bath to find Emil awake in the cot, the covers pulled up to his chin. She went to the bureau to lay out her underclothes for the next day. She was in her bathrobe and her hair was down and wet from washing. It was pure white, but it was still full and beautiful. Emil watched her as she took a fresh pair of stockings and a slip from the drawer. He was smiling. She lifted a brassiere and a pair of panties, then hesitated. She put them on top of the bureau and looked into the drawer. When she appeared to be counting something, Emil stopped smiling and pulled the covers more tightly around him.

She went to him and yanked the covers off him. He was naked except for a pair of her panties and a brassiere.

Early the next morning he went to the attic and opened Lydia's old trunk. Among the other clothes, she had kept a long garden dress and a sunbonnet once worn by her mother. He put the dress on over his own clothes and tied the large sunbonnet on his head. Then he went down to work in his garden.

When Lydia came out later, she watched him watering the garden. From that distance he could have been mistaken for a tall woman. When he turned and saw her, he smiled and waved at her. She hesitated, then waved back.

She watched each day from a window or the porch as in the long dress and sunbonnet he continued to work in the garden. He was happy. Perhaps for him the flowers were blooming.

Only once did he wander off in her mother's clothes; he had started down the dirt road before she reached him and led him back by the hand.

On a morning in September she came down to see the familiar figure sitting bent over in the garden. She was passing the screen door on the way to the kitchen when she stopped. With his bent back to her and the sunbonnet covering his head, she could not see his face, but his arms hung loosely at his sides, and as she continued to watch, he remained motionless.

She hurried out of the house and down the porch steps, but as she drew near to him she slowed down.

She had not expected the loneliness she felt when she saw he had died peacefully there, tending his flowerless garden.

27

A wkward, ungainly, unaccustomed to the pubescent body sprouting upon her, Willa sat on the couch in the parlor wearing the black dress her grandmother had made her for the occasion.

The old woman stood in front of her, also in a black dress. She held her Bible, out of which she had just read from 2 Corinthians: "For He hath made Him to be sin for us, who knew no sin; that we might be made the righteousness of God in Him."

And from Romans: "For the wages of sin is death; but the gift of God is eternal life through Jesus Christ our Lord."

Now she said in her own words "He was a dreamer without a dream. And so I provided one for him and made it come true. He didn't understand it—he couldn't—but the happiness he had at the end, I gave him. He would have died early and in sin except for me. Remember that: my duty is the protection and well-being of my family, of which you are the last member. Let him be at peace. The Lord has him now. Pray for him with me, Willa."

The old woman bowed her head and stood for a moment in silence. Then she looked up, ending the private service. Telling Willa she would trust her to stay in her room while she was gone, she left for the place where they were putting Willa's grandfather in his hole in the ground.

Willa did not go to her room. She went around the parlor peering behind objects and opening drawers. She searched her grandmother's desk. Then she went upstairs. She was looking for something. On the way she shed the dress, leaving it behind where it fell on the floor in the hallway.

She found what she was looking for on the bureau in her grandmother's bedroom: her grandfather's wallet. There was no money in it, but that was not what she had been searching for. Some cards lay on the bureau beside it, the wallet stripped of its contents as if he had never belonged to it. But as Willa had hoped, her grandmother had not found the small key he kept in the separate compartment.

She went to the hall closet and, as her grandfather had done, turned on the overhead light, unlocked the toolbox and opened the side drawer, where she found the Bible. She sat down on the toolbox with it.

She opened the hollowed-out Bible and saw the little packages like the one the man in the clearing had used with the girl the time she watched them from the tree when she was eight. Her interest now was not in them but in the photograph. She picked it up, and for the first time saw her mother's face.

■ ■ ■

When Willa left the next morning to meet Sylvia Rosenberg, the sun was shining in a cool clear sky. Good sign, she thought. She swung her purse as she walked.

Now she was at the gate of a school yard in which a woman was attending a group of children. The woman was about the right age, Willa thought, with stooped shoulders and short black hair salted with gray. She was wearing jeans, a necklace of colored beads and small round glasses such as Willa's grandmother had worn. She looked too old for her style of dress.

The woman began to run after one of the children, who was wandering off. She caught it and picked it up and it hung limp and submissive in her arms.

Willa looked at the other children, who were all bundled up in sweaters, scarves, coats and woolen caps. They lumbered on hidden feet like balloons blown into the school yard. Only when they looked at Willa as she came through the gate did she see their faces. Their heads were held lopsided, as if uncontrolled by their bodies, and the eyes trying to watch her usually wound up looking elsewhere. Some of them were drooling.

She was about to proceed when the woman saw her. She came to Willa, one of the children following her. It wrapped itself around her leg and was clinging to it as she spoke. "Are you Willa, Madeleine's daughter?"

"Yes, ma'am. Miss Rosenberg?"

"Yes. I'm sorry. I'm due to be relieved in a few minutes. Why don't you wait for me over there on the bench?"

Willa went to a wooden bench next to a sandbox and swings. She sat on the bench. Only days before, she thought, she would have sat on a swing.

Another woman came out of the building and went up to Sylvia, and a minute later Sylvia was sitting next to Willa on the bench. She adjusted her glasses, which had slipped. The small round lenses reflected the sun.

"I don't know what I can do to help you" she said. "I didn't really know your mother very well."

"I heard she lived with you—that you helped her" Willa said. "Why did you do that if you weren't her friend?"

"Yes. That's true. How much do you know about me?"

"Billy Tyler, Chatto Hoffman and Mary Vandel told me some."

"Yes. Billy said you have a quality that creates trust and inspires confidences. And if I know Billy, he probably told you a great deal more than you needed to know. Are you aware how much I detest Billy, by the way?"

Willa thought it best not to answer. She let Sylvia go on, because she seemed willing to talk. Perhaps she had never spoken to anyone about it before. Willa knew about the loneliness that comes from keeping things hidden.

"To answer your question" Sylvia resumed, "the night your mother attempted to commit suicide—"

Willa stiffened. That information was still too new to her. It still disturbed her. But she did not want to interrupt Sylvia.

"—I had decided to do it myself. If they told you about me, then maybe you know what I mean when I say I had finally done something that disgusted even me. You've seen Billy. I had his baby inside me. There's a time when self-loathing has to end or become madness." She looked off. She was squinting behind the glasses. "I knew about Chatto Hoffman" she said finally, "and I knew your mother slightly at the time. But like the others who either didn't care or were afraid of him, I didn't do anything to help her." She looked off again. "Your mother" she continued a moment later "was the only one of them that treated me with respect. That night on my way out of the High Note, I heard she had done what I was intending to do that night. Thinking about it later probably saved my life. The next day I decided that if she survived, I would try to help her. I just gave her some kindness back at a time when she needed it, and in the process helped myself."

"Maybe Billy told you" Willa said "that my mother disappeared back then. You're the last person I know who saw her after she went into the hospital. If she lived with you, maybe she said something that would give me a clue to where she went."

Sylvia shook her head. The glasses slipped again and she fixed them. She squinted through them. "Nothing. She stayed with me for a few weeks, but it's amazing how little I learned about her all that time. She was very withdrawn, and I didn't press her to talk. I helped her move into an apartment, but I understand that building's now a home for wayward girls."

"And that was the last place she lived?" Willa asked.

"As a matter of fact, no. She did call me about a year later to tell me she was well and had moved into a new apartment."

Willa leaned forward. "Where? Do you know the address?"

She shook her head again. "She told me the address, and after my son died, I wrote her about it, but the letter came back marked 'Moved. No forwarding address.' I thought she must have gotten married or left the city."

"Do you have that letter now? Or remember the address?" Willa asked.

"Heavens no. I threw it away. As for the address, all I remember is that it was somewhere on lower Sheridan Street, near the river. I remember that because I knew it to be a nice neighborhood, and I assumed she had a job and was well situated at last. I remember it too because she seemed especially pleased to be living near the river. She said she could see the river from her front window." She sighed, looked off again. "That was such a long time ago, and I've tried to put it all behind me. There was something in the air then. Hysteria. The whole country seemed to have gone mad. People pursued freedom as if it were salvation. There is only one true salvation. If I hadn't been born again, taken Jesus as my savior, who knows if I would have had the strength to survive? After my boy died, I wanted to die too. Then I found Him. Jesus is our redeemer, Willa." She turned back to Willa. She was squinting again.

Willa got up. She held out her hand, but Sylvia did not appear to notice it. A child had gone off from the other woman, tilting this way and that until it got to Sylvia. It began eating its scarf, but Sylvia did not notice.

Willa dropped her hand. "Well, ma'am" she said "if you can't remember anything else—"

Sylvia looked up. "Those others you saw—what happened to them?"

"Mary's dead, Chatto's going blind, and I guess you know, Billy loves a boy named Giorgio."

"They're all doomed to hell eternal unless they've accepted Jesus."

"Yes, ma'am."

"Tell them I'll pray for them."

"Yes, ma'am."

"I once hated them all, but now I love them."

As Willa turned to leave, Sylvia was pulling a length of scarf out of the child's mouth, but she did not seem aware she was doing that either.

She found lower Sheridan Street, but it was lined with buildings for as far as she could see. None of them had Apartment for Rent signs on them.

She began knocking on doors, but few people answered and those who did had either never rented out apartments or did not know her mother by name or recognize her from Willa's photograph. And she had not even seen the river yet.

She had been coming out of a building on the second block when that thought came to her. She stopped. She slapped her head with the palm of her hand. "Dumb, Willa" she said to herself. "You're getting real dumb in your old age." She hurried north up the street.

It was twelve blocks away. It was a wide river, twisting under bridges for a half-dozen blocks until it straightened and pointed like an arrow at the horizon. She stood where Sheridan Street ended, looking south and sloping on grass down to the water. She studied the buildings. She saw only four blocks of them, and half of those were not high enough to see over the taller ones to the river. She started back down the street, ringing bells and knocking at doors again to ask her questions, but passing by those buildings she now knew did not have a view of the river.

It was past noon when she came to a house that looked older and less well-cared for than the others. The shades were drawn on the bottom-floor apartment, but after ringing three times, she saw one of the shades move and a woman look out at her. She waved her hand for Willa to go away. Willa turned and pressed the bell two more times. She waited.

The shade moved and the woman looked out at her again, but this time Willa pretended not to see her. She stared ahead at the door until the shade closed a second time.

A minute later the door opened. Willa smiled at a tall, thin woman in her sixties. She had copper-colored hair that was white at the roots. She was wearing worn bedroom slippers and holding a beltless frayed bathrobe around her. She did not return Willa's smile.

"Good morning, ma'am" Willa said. "I'm sorry to disturb you, but do you rent apartments here?"

She shook her head. "I don't rent to single women anymore. Anyway, I don't have any vacancies and don't expect to have any."

She started to close the door, but Willa leaned into it. She smiled again as she began opening the purse. "I'm not looking for one" she said. "What I'd like to know is if you ever rented an apartment to someone named Madeleine Rhineman."

The woman shook her head.

"It was a long time ago" Willa said.

"How long?"

"Fifteen years."

"Oh, for Christ's sake!" The woman tried to shut the door again, but Willa moved farther into it.

"It's very important, ma'am, otherwise I wouldn't bother you." She held up the photograph to the woman's face. "This is her." The woman glanced at it, then shook her head.

"Look again, please, ma'am" Willa said. "Madeleine Rhineman. A pretty girl older than me. Lived alone. Very quiet."

The woman looked at the photograph closely. She looked back at Willa.

"It's not a good picture" Willa said. She waited.

The woman pulled the neck of her bathrobe tighter. She seemed angry. "What's she to you?"

"She's my mother. I'm looking for her."

"Well, good luck! She skipped out on me too. She still owes me a month's rent."

The photograph began shaking in Willa's hand. She lowered it. "You remember her?"

"Now that I recall. You look a little like her. She signed a lease for six months, but she didn't stay but two or three. Ran off with some man, I thought at the time."

"She didn't leave an address? Or give you some idea where she was going?"

"I told you: she just left. She left behind some old pieces of furniture I had to give to the Salvation Army because I didn't have room to store them. Are you willing to pay me that month's rent she owes me?"

"Ma'am, I don't care about the furniture. But if you help me find her, I'll see you get paid for the rent."

The woman opened the door wider. She seemed to be thinking, then said "I don't know how I can do that, unless there's something in that old suitcase that's still in my cellar. And there's nothing but clothes and odds and ends in that."

Willa controlled her excitement. "Ma'am, do you remember if there were any letters in it? Or maybe an address book?"

"No. Nothing like that. There were some poems and a notebook

that had writing in it that didn't make much sense to me. I only glanced
at it."

"Things *she* wrote, you mean?"

"I guess so."

Willa's hands were trembling visibly now. She put them in her dress
pockets. She said slowly, so as not to betray her excitement, "Ma'am, I
would be happy to take that suitcase off your hands for you."

The woman's eyes narrowed. "She still owes me that month's rent.
And I'd have to charge you for storing that suitcase."

"How much would that be, ma'am?"

"Well, I'm not a greedy person. I think five dollars a year for the
storage would be more than fair. And I won't charge you interest on the
sixty dollars rent, or for the inconvenience and trouble I went to on her
account."

"I appreciate that" Willa said. She waited while the woman calcu-
lated aloud.

"Let's see. Five dollars a year for fifteen years is seventy-five dollars.
And the sixty for the rent makes it one thirty-five."

Willa's spirits plunged. She knew how much money she had left in
her purse: thirty-two dollars and change. She said "I don't have all that
much on me, but I could come back later and pay you if—"

The door began closing—firmly this time. "Fine" Willa heard the
woman saying behind the door. "You come back when you have it."

Willa thrust her arm into the opening in time to prevent the door
from closing. She could not see the woman's face now. "Ma'am!" she
shouted. "Ma'am! Just one minute."

The door opened, but cautiously, and only a few more inches. Willa
spoke through the opening. "Ma'am, could I just go down in your cellar and look at that book you mentioned? Read it there?"

The door began closing again.

"Ma'am!"

It stopped.

Willa could feel herself perspiring, despite the cool weather. She
took a deep breath to regain her control, then said slowly "Ma'am, I've
got thirty-two dollars on me. I'll give you that if you'll just let me read
that book."

The woman answered unseen behind the door. "What do you take
me for? I'm an honest woman. All I want is what's legitimate owed me.
You come back when you have the whole one hundred thirty-five."

Willa withdrew her arm before the door closed on it.

She stood for a minute looking at the door. It took an act of will
for her to turn away, but finally she did.

She walked slowly to the edge of the sidewalk and looked up at the two top-floor windows: those behind which her mother had once looked out at the river. She had never felt so near and at the same time so far away from her. Tears came to her eyes: the hundred thirty-five dollars, she knew, might as well have been a million. She walked away from the building.

Vernon stepped out of a doorway of the building next to her mother's after she had passed by, but she would not have seen him anyway through her tears.

Two hours later she was lying in the bathtub on her floor of her rooming house, only her head and shoulders visible above water. Her wet hair hung limp in the water. Steam rose all around her, and beads of perspiration dripped off her. It shrouded the window and the mirror over the sink.

She had been there for an hour, constantly replenishing the water, as hot as she could stand it. She did it with her toes. She had been taking hot soaks since she was ten, whenever her nerves got bad or depression descended upon her.

She licked steam from her lips. It leaked from her eyebrows over her eyes. Then she slid under the water, holding her breath.

More than a minute passed, after which the sound of the water began pounding in her ears and lights started flashing in her head; but she did not emerge, because it was also peaceful there. She looked up at the room, which was now a faint blur. It swayed. Her skin was tingling and lips of water were kissing her. It was like lying in a coffin, she thought. It must be what dying was like. Death would come peacefully, kissing her.

She held on until the sound in her head was like hammer blows. Her eyes grew large, her cheeks blew up like balloons. Her heart raced like an engine and her head felt like it was going to explode.

She emerged gasping and spitting. Water poured over her head like a wig. She wiped it away, still struggling for breath.

She sat up and looked down at her knees. Her dark pubes floated on the surface of the water, and her small breasts had emerged like tiny volcanoes. She was a woman of sorts.

She lifted herself farther out of the water—but slowly, something else emerging with her: an idea. She had done it once for money; she could again to get the notebook. There was no other way, since she could not imagine what kind of job she could get. She pulled the plug chain with her toes and the water started gurgling.

She stood up in the tub, a thin instrument but sufficient for what she needed to do. She stepped out of it, dripping water onto the floor. As she reached for the towel, she thought, But not for any dollar this time. She was more worldly now, knew something about such things, although she was still hazy on details, such as how much women really charged.

The other times, she thought, she had not felt anything then or afterward. She could have picked flowers while she waited for the boys to finish. But when she had dried off and was reaching for her dress hanging on the doorhook, she felt a new surge of depression at the thought of doing it again. She understood then that the price paid for the loss of innocence is uncertainty.

She finished dressing and took the suitcase out of the closet. She put it on the bed and opened it, took the remaining four condoms from the Bible and put them in her purse. She slipped into her loafers. She was ready.

She went to the door, but she remained there for a few minutes with her hand on the doorknob. Then she went through it and onto the street with her long hair lank and glistening in the sunlight.

She remembered seeing them in the center of the city when she circled the block the night she arrived: women standing outside a large bus terminal talking to men who passed looking at them, then taking money from them. They went into the hotels on the street with the men, and after Willa had walked past there a few more times, the same women were back waiting.

Now she approached the bus terminal, where women were again rallying. She took a place at the end of the line.

The first thing she realized was that she was not dressed right. Her pleated party dress was in contrast to the tight clothes the other women were wearing. They wore stockings, while she had on white socks. Hers were the only loafers in the line, and her small purse was a glaring exception to the large bags the others carried. She was unadorned by makeup, which was splashed over the whores' faces. And to further announce what was already an obvious anomaly, she was much younger than the others.

Men approached the line, selected women, and went off with them. None asked her. She waited, but she might as well have been invisible. She did not know how to stand, either, so she tried imitating the others: she put one hand on her hip and tilted the other hip. She leaned her head back against the wall and lowered her eyelids in a fixed look that was her approximation of seductiveness; she even raised her eyebrows at the men who passed assessing the line of whores from the corners of their eyes. But none of what she did created the reaction in the men that it did for the others, and she finally gave up, standing with her arms at her sides and looking straight ahead. She continued looking ahead as other women went off with men.

She blinked, disbelieving, as the largest, fiercest-looking black woman she had ever seen detached herself from the line and walked up to her. Her shadow completely covered her. She began trembling the moment she heard the black giantess's angry voice.

"You belong to the union, girl?"

Willa had been trying to pretend she did not see her. Now she had to look far up to answer her. Her own voice was weak. "What?"

"Who's your agent?"

"I—"

"Well, if you don't belong to the union and don't have an agent, what're you doin' here, girl?"

"Waiting for someone."

"He ain't comin'."

She moved to the end of the block. She felt even more vulnerable there. Some of the whores continued to lean out of the line, glaring at her. She held the purse to her chest for fear someone would take all the money she had left.

Ten minutes later a fat man wearing a suit with a long chain looping across his vest came down to her. He looked at her. She forced herself to look back and he went to her hitching up his trousers. He leaned near her and whispered "Do you do French?"

"I don't know any foreign languages" she answered.

He went back to the other women.

She realized then that she had more to learn than how much to charge.

A tall bald man came down to her from the line. He was wearing a suit and vest too and was carrying a briefcase. He licked his lips several times, then moved closer to her to ask "Do you dress up?"

She just stared at him.

"Well, do you? I only have an hour."

She opened her mouth to speak and, because she had no idea how to answer him, was relieved to see a tall Spanish-looking man in his twenties arrive in time to answer for her. He spoke to the man as if he knew him. "Not today, Marquis. This peasant girl ain't been broke in yet. Try Natalie this time."

The man hurried away hugging his briefcase, and the tall man— who, Willa saw, would not be so tall without the high-heeled boots he was wearing—turned to her. He had a pleasant smile. She relaxed somewhat. He leaned down to her, supporting himself by his hand on the wall.

"*Muchacha*" he said, "the girls tell me you don't have any representation. Now, you're a cute-looking piece, and once you get set up proper—get rid of that freaking dress and purse and so on—Raul will be glad to act as your agent. Ask any of the girls. Raul takes care of his pieces. You don't, baby, you don't work around here. *Capisch?*"

She nodded.

"OK. Now the rules. One: you charge twenty bucks straight, thirty for French. Anything else you check with me or one of the other girls. Two: you pay your union dues every night to me, which is half of everything you make. For that you get protection and Raul's undying affection. If you think that's not fair, consider that furthermore, I buy all your clothes and business necessaries and bail you out if you get busted. Three: you hold back any gold on me or get out of line any other way, I bust your head. So if you want to work, Raul can start you tonight. If not, I see you peddling it and I break your arms."

Willa sighed. She lowered the purse from her chest. She looked up at the line again sadly. "I don't think so" she said, moving off. "I only wanted to make some money quick to get something."

"Don't we all?" she heard him call to her as she hurried to cross the street.

28

Vernon followed her back to her rooming house, where after an hour he decided she would not be leaving again soon. He had never seen her as discouraged as she looked now.

Her search had reached a dead end: she could not do any more until she got her mother's suitcase from the landlady. And where could she hope to obtain that much money quickly?

It was an opportunity he had not even dreamed of: not only to help her in the search, but to gain her gratitude when she discovered later that he had been her benefactor. He already knew what he would do when that day arrived.

He went to his bank first, where he withdrew three hundred dollars, all that was left in his savings account except for five dollars. He used a bank envelope and pen, and standing at the desk wrote on the envelope "For the girl in the red dress." He took a sheet of bank notepaper but hesitated at how to identify himself to her. First he wrote *a friend,* then crossed it out. He thought for several minutes before substituting *a distant admirer,* but crossed that out too. He tried *The boy who is waiting for you,* but ran the pen through that quickly and enough times to completely ink out the words. *The one who will be coming for you* was as quickly obliterated. He settled finally for the ambiguous *A good Samaritan* and folded the paper over the hundred thirty-five dollars.

He was about to put the envelope in his pocket and leave when an idea came to him. He turned the envelope over and in the lower right-hand corner where it would not be easily seen, he wrote so small that it was unrecognizable except when looked at closely, the words *I want you.*

* * *

He went next to Miller's Discount Department Store, where he bought a gray suit, a white shirt and a blue tie. He had never owned a suit: not in the orphanage, nor after he left there and came to the city. He could not have imagined an occasion where a suit would be necessary. But now there was one. On the way out he saw a display of plastic flowers and bought a dozen of those.

He returned to his street, where he put the letter in the girl's rooming-house mailbox, then went to his room. Taking his suitcase out of the closet, he put it on the bed and opened it. He lifted the suit from its box and, folding it carefully, laid it out on the bottom of the suitcase. He opened the bag that contained the shirt and tie and put them on top of the suit. The plastic flowers went in next. Real flowers would not have lasted long enough.

He returned to the closet and took down his extra blanket and put it in the suitcase. There was no telling now where the girl's search would take her, how long he would have to wait in the car. All he knew for certain was that whatever its outcome, his day was near. He closed the suitcase and put it back into the closet.

Then he sat down to wait.

29

Lydia came down at first light. She had loosened her hair and put on her best black dress, and although she carried herself with the resoluteness that had sustained her through all her life, the pain that had been eating at her for over a year had bloomed during the last month to make her movements slower and her posture bent for the first time. Her hands shook when she reached for the arms of the rocking chair, and her body yielded to a momentary frailty as she lowered herself slowly into it to face the rising sun.

It had not come as a surprise to her: that insidiousness that had tormented her mother in her last year she had thought would be calling her too one day. She was grateful it had waited this long.

No one knew, except Dr. Summers; not even her granddaughter. She carried the pain like an invisible crown, as she had borne all her life's tribulations—as if they were personal tributes to her. When she saw her hands shaking in her lap, she locked her fingers to still them. The sun inched upward, her only witness.

Then the pain came again and she rose in the chair, her hands gripping its arms as her entire body tensed beneath her. When she eased back into the chair, her face was drenched in perspiration. She withdrew a handkerchief from her sleeve and wiped her face dry, then held it balled in her hand. She smiled.

She had for the last month elected to stop taking the pills Dr. Summers had prescribed; the morphine syringes had been put away in a drawer before that. Their beneficence had lured but not seduced her.

Just as Emil had chosen two years before out of fear to forswear the same doctor's advice and accept his fate, she had chosen to wrestle pain, outwit it, and in so doing, hasten its end. She had welcomed the challenge, even knowing it was the last of all those challenges she had surmounted. A hopeless battle, she believed, fought in solitude and silence, was among the noblest of endeavors.

She could hold on longer, but there was no need. Emil was gone, their secrets safe, and Willa grown, the child's future determined by her years before.

Her last uncertainty had come in the unexpected reemergence of Lester Kane, who had continued to work for them for two years after Willa's birth. He could only have caught glimpses of Willa during that time, and she had told him the child was the daughter of a widower brother they had taken in. Her one mistake, she realized later, was that she had allowed herself to be fooled by his Negro cunning all those years; she had not understood that he was a sentient factor, taking things in, perhaps spying, while hiding a sophisticated mind she could not have imagined him possessing then. Even the morning she fired him she had not known it, although, she realized much later, he had given her a hint. He had lowered the mask for a moment when he replied distinctly "I was leaving soon anyway, Mrs. Rhineman." It had surprised her, but it had not alarmed her. That came later, when she started reading about him.

But whatever he might have seen either was not enough to arouse his suspicions or he had chosen to keep silent about it. Respect—or fear, call it what you will—once implanted, lasts forever.

So it was done, her duty accomplished. All that was left to do was the dying. She took out of the pocket of her dress a letter and a note wrapped around it with a rubber band. The letter was stamped and marked Special Delivery, and the note was to Willa, instructing her to give it to the mailman when he came later that morning. It would reach lawyer Cass that afternoon at the latest. Should it not happen today, she would come down again tomorrow.

William Cass had the will and her written instructions; the other papers had been in his care for twelve years. He would see to it that Willa was put in a responsible professional home and taken care of for the rest of her life with the money Lydia had provided. The house and land would be sold, the past and its secrets put to rest forever.

Her tombstone had been purchased and inscribed "She served God and her family." It was to sit next to Emil's more modest memorial in the twin plots at Quiet Oaks in Lebanon, that town that had provided her needs after her abnegation of Pineville.

She held the letter in her lap now. She knew she would not let go of it. She began to rock.

Emil's pick and shovel were where he had left them beside his failed garden. His last illusion, last dream. She still thought of him every day.

She smiled again, because she was sitting now where she had been sitting that day when he first came up the path with his jaunty walk and that guileless smile, which, she had no doubt, even then had already broken too many hearts. She had not then conceived her dream yet—that united family that had been denied her mother in her lifetime—but by the time she had, she knew that no more malleable material could have presented itself to her to fulfill that part of it. That he had shown some backbone, put up resistance, had only made it more satisfying in the long run. If it had not been for the girl (she still would not even think of Madeleine by name) and the one sin of which she had never thought he was capable, it would all have been accomplished years ago.

Birds had begun nesting on the roof during the warm months; some were there even now: she could hear them at night. They reminded her of Emil's strange affinity with birds during the last months of his life. They had come to him, trusted him, clustered around him, and toward the end they were all over him. She would come out and they would be in his lap, on his shoulders, perched in his hair. They flew onto the palms of his hands. He had sat so still: like a statue, smiling.

She stopped rocking and leaned forward, looking at the unusual small mounds of earth in which he had planted his sterile seeds. She had not noticed it before, but she saw now the resemblance they bore—each of them, in rows—to unmarked graves. She got up to look at them more closely.

She had reached the steps when she was struck by the worst surge of pain yet. It lifted her off one foot and left her shaking and grasping the porch railing. Then another, even worse, and she cried out for the first time. "Oh, God!" When it had passed, she murmured "Please, Lord, make it soon." She barely had strength to get back to the chair and collapse into it.

She withdrew the handkerchief from her sleeve, where she had replaced it, and wiped the perspiration that covered her face. Her hand trembled so that she had trouble getting the handkerchief back into her sleeve. When she looked up, her vision had become blurred. She glanced down to see the letter crushed in her fist.

She took her glasses from her pocket and put them on. She leaned back, too weak to get up again. She straightened out the letter and began rocking. She felt at peace once more. She closed her eyes.

Only she, she thought, of the three of them who had begun it—she, Emil and the girl—had remained uncorrupted. But she had succeeded in exempting Willa from corruption. She smiled at the thought of her granddaughter, who had come finally to obey and respect her.

She had not given her a moment's trouble since those rebellious years when she was a child.

I'm ready, she thought. She opened her eyes and looked up, still rocking. "My duty is done, Lord" she whispered. "But I'm tired now. I'm old and in pain. I want to rest at your bosom, a good servant."

She continued rocking. Now, she thought.

Now.

Now.

■ ■ ■

Willa found her two hours later still upright in the chair, eyes open but directed sightless at the sun. She stood still in the doorway for a few minutes looking at the lifeless figure of her grandmother. Then she came onto the porch, the screen door screeching behind her. She had never seen a dead person before, not even her grandfather. She went to her.

She reached out and touched the dead woman's hand. The skin was hard and wrinkled, and there was no warmth in it. She did the same to her face, running a finger down the woman's cheek, and nothing human imparted itself to her. The staring eyes bothered her, and she tried not to look at them. The old woman's glasses were crooked, slipped down on one side, and she lifted them off, folded them, and put them in the pocket of Lydia's dress, as she had seen her do many times.

She sighed. She was alone now. But she was ready. The day had come, and already the old woman was irrelevant to her as she felt the excitement building inside her. She looked up to judge the time by the position of the sun. She thought she had better get started right away, because she had a lot to do.

Then she noticed the letter in her grandmother's hand and she reached for it. But the old woman held it so tightly that she had to pry her fingers from around it before it came loose.

She read the note that was addressed to her first, then the name on the envelope. She was puzzled until she remembered it was the name of the lawyer her grandmother had taken her to meet in Pineville. She recalled the stale smell of the office, the two men watching her, studying her. She recalled it all, even the papers her grandmother had signed at the end of it. She had known even then it had something to do with her future, and although she did not know what it was the old woman had planned for her, it did not matter. She had her own plan now. She tore the letter into small pieces and tossed them off the porch. Then she turned back to the dead woman.

She put her hands on her hips, studying her grandmother. "I guess I can't just leave you there" she said to her.

She went to her and pulled her forward by the shoulders. She put her arms under the dead woman's arms and started to lift her. She had her half over her shoulder before she stopped. "You sure are heavy" she said to her. "Well, it has to be done." The chair rocked one more time as Lydia came out of it.

She disposed of her grandmother's remains the only way she knew how, then hurried back to the house to get ready to leave for the city and find the mother who, until now, she knew little about except her name and what she looked like in the old photograph.

Birds gathered on Lydia's unmarked grave.

30

When she awoke the next morning, Willa saw the envelope sticking out under her door. Her landlady must have put it there, but who would write her?

She got out of bed naked and picked it up. It was heavy. There was something in it that did not feel like a letter. She sat on the side of the bed and opened it by tearing it apart as she had the only other letter she had ever received: the one from Orlo Haines. Money fell out of it onto the floor.

She stared at it a moment, disbelieving. Then she picked the bills up and counted them. She nearly shouted for joy when she saw it was the exact amount the landlady had demanded for the suitcase. She was grinning.

She picked up the sheet of paper that had fallen out of the envelope with the money. She knew who the good Samaritan was from the Bible, but who was this one? Whoever it was, he had sent her exactly the amount of money she needed so desperately—which was the one thing that bothered her. How did he (or she) know not only about her need, but the amount as well? She became uneasy about her unknown bene-factor. She had had the feeling of being followed when she had first come to the city, and when she remembered the man in shadows on the steps outside Chatto Hoffman's the other night, she decided she might have been wrong: he had not been spying on Chatto, but on her. Her grandmother had warned her about dangerous people in the city. She would have to be careful from now on. But now she did not care. She stacked the bills evenly, then kissed them. Then she folded them and put them into her purse.

Ten minutes later she came out the front door onto the street. She looked around to see if someone might be waiting to follow her, but the street was empty. She began walking. Then she ran.

This time when she rang the bell, the shade lifted and the woman looked out, but seeing who it was did not wave her away. A minute later the door opened.

"I have the money" Willa said. She patted her purse. "I'd like to have my mother's suitcase now."

"Come in."

Willa followed her down a hallway to a door across from a stairway. She looked up at the stairway before going into a small living room full of sturdy furniture that looked like it came from another era. An old upright piano was against one wall next to a fireplace, above which a gallery of old people in framed photographs looked down at her from the mantelpiece. A floor lamp with a tasseled shade provided the only light in the room. She sat down on a large couch whose cushion sank slowly beneath her, making her feel smaller. She had to reach up to put her arm on an armrest with a lace doily pinned to it.

"Did my mother come into this room?" she asked the woman, who was going through a desk drawer looking for something. She found it: a key.

"She came in here to pay the rent" the woman answered.

Willa's head rotated, taking in all of the room. She ran her hand over the seat of the couch.

The woman watched her, then said "I'll get the suitcase" and left.

Willa got up and circled the room. She sat for a moment in each of the three chairs. She ran her hands over the armrests. Then she went into the hall and to the foot of the stairs. She looked up them. She slid her hand up the railing, then stepped onto the bottom step. She whispered "Hello, momma." She stood there for a minute looking up before going back to the room. She returned to the couch, where she became aware for the first time of a clock ticking on the mantelpiece. Her heart began pounding. She had never experienced happiness and fear simultaneously.

The woman returned, carrying an old metal suitcase. It was dented and looked like it once must have done a lot of traveling. The woman said "I dusted it off, but it's still pretty dirty from being down there all those years."

Willa jumped off the couch. "I don't care about that!" She had not meant to shout.

"Lord knows" the woman said "why I didn't throw it away years ago. There's nothing of value in it except all those white clothes she always wore. Now why would someone always dress in white?"

Willa did not answer. She took the money from her purse and handed it to the woman. The woman counted it, then put it into the pocket of her dress. "I seem to have misplaced my receipt book" she said. "Otherwise, I—" She looked up to where Willa had been standing, but she was no longer there. She was in the doorway, the suitcase in her hand.

"I don't care about a receipt either" Willa said. "This is all I wanted." She turned and left, leaving the woman standing there looking puzzled, perhaps anxious that she had overlooked something of value in the suitcase.

Willa opened the suitcase on the front steps. The notebook was on top; she read the title on the cover: *Journal of Madeleine Rhineman*. She opened it and saw page after page in her mother's handwriting. Tears clouded her eyes, but this time they were tears of happiness. She closed it and put it back into the suitcase. She closed the suitcase and picked it up.

She started back to her room, grinning. She said aloud "It looks like me and my mother have something in common: all both of us own we can put in one suitcase."

Sitting on the side of the bed, she opened the notebook to the first page. Her hands began shaking again. She looked away for a minute, then back, as she wiggled to get more comfortable. She read the first entry, dated October 23, 1966:

Dr. Crane told me to keep this journal. What should I write? There's only this: The presence of death is near.

Willa went on to the next entry:

October 25, 1966. I don't feel anything. Life is appalling. It is a palling. Words too. Look at them lying there like little corpses. Dead babies. Babies better not born. I used to have such wonderment. I can hardly remember back to then.

Willa looked away. She drew a deep breath before she went on:

October 29, 1966. One thing I know for certain. I won't go back to that damn hospital ward again with the drunks and junkies and crazy people, where you have to ask permission even to go to the toilet and where they keep coming around snooping, reading our thoughts, raping our minds. I told that dyke head matron I'd kill her if she touched me like that again. Little Jack Horner sat in a corner eating his own—shit!!!!!!!!!!

October 30, 1966. I pissed in the bed there purposely. When I did it again, they locked leather panties on me and I pissed in them. I growled like an animal because they treated me like an animal.

Willa put down the notebook. It was minutes later before she could continue, and she skipped pages until she came to:

November 6, 1966. Dr. Crane wants to fuck me. I'll tell him tomorrow what I'll do for him instead. I can't wait to see his face!

November 7, 1966. I couldn't say it. I was wrong. All he wants to do is help me. He's like a big brother. A big bear! I've been used so often no wonder I feel dirty with all the handling. Chatto's a pig, but I know I'd crawl back to him on my knees if he'd have me.

November 8, 1966. No. I mustn't even think about going back to Chatto. I have to talk to Dr. Crane about that. No going back! I have to be calm. My nerves are screaming. Calm. Calm.

November 9, 1966. Damn him! Damn him! Damn Emil. Father/lover. You made a baby in me, you prick! I'd cut it off! I'd bury it! Do you know what you did to me, Daddy?

Willa looked up from the notebook. She sighed. So now she knew who her father was. All the time he was there—the quiet, sad, gentle man she knew as her grandfather. Who had sat beside her on the porch steps and showed her the missing part of his foot he said she got from him. He had wanted to tell her then, she now realized. How many times had he wanted to tell her and been afraid? She could not hate him—not even for what he did to her mother. The house's secret was now clear to her. It explained all the rest. She read the next entries.

November 10, 1966. I got drunk last night.

November 16, 1966. I had to concentrate this morning to remember my name. Madeleine. Magdalene.

She turned more pages until she came to:

January 29, 1967. I actually noticed the sun today. The grass looks green again!

She skipped over pages again until she arrived at an entry in large letters:

March 12, 1967. Dr. Crane said I'm making progress at last! No more pot. No more wine for—how long? It's like coming out of a fog—or a horror movie in my head. Maybe there's a life after death after all.

There were more pages she would read later, but the last entry was the one she turned to and read next. Her heart leaped at the sight of her own name for the first time in her mother's hand. Then her lips began trembling as she read:

September 12, 1967. I made up my mind. I'm leaving by bus tonight. I'm going back and get Willa and bring her here to live with me. She's my daughter and I love her.

She closed the notebook. So she came back for me, she thought. She loved me. And after that nobody saw her again.

She opened the notebook and looked at the date of the last entry again: September 12, 1967. She was three then. And the only people who might have seen Madeleine that day were both dead. It was the end of the search. She closed the notebook and sat staring ahead.

Then her eyes slowly widened. She jumped down off the bed and grabbed her purse. She checked the money in it; it should be enough.

I was wrong, she thought. There was somebody else who might have been there that day. Somebody who could have seen her, even talked to her. Somebody back there who all along might have been able to solve the mystery. And she knew who he was and where to find him.

She ran out of the room and out of the house. This time, in her haste, she did not stop to check if anyone was following her.

The whores were there again by the wall, but if any of them recognized her, they gave no sign of it. She went past them and into the busy large bus terminal, where she stood at the end of one of the long lines at the ticket windows. She smiled at the thought that a week ago when she left she had not even known there were buses she could have taken to the city.

She tapped her foot as she waited for the line to move forward. She hugged the purse to her and kept looking out and around the line to see how many people were still ahead of her. "Keep moving. Keep moving" she whispered to the back of the man in front of her when he did not advance quickly enough with the line. When it was finally her turn, she had to stand on tiptoe to reach the counter.

She said to the man behind it "I want a ticket on a bus that will take me to that big store in New Jersey on the highway this side of Pineville."

"What's it called?"

"I never knew it had a name. It was just 'the store' to us. But the driver can't miss it. It's the only one around there." She kept moving up and down and rattling her purse on the lip of the counter.

"You say it's near Pineville?" the man asked.

"Not near. Pineville's about three miles from where I want to go."

The man opened a book and turned slowly through it. He stopped and drew a finger down a line of print just as slowly. The purse began beating more rapidly on the counter until he looked up. "There's no scheduled stops between Brewton and Pineville. You'll have to pay the full fare to Pineville."

"All right."

"But the driver will let you off where you want to go."

"That's good. Tell him to do that for me, will you?"

The man looked at her steadily for a moment. Then he said "You just tell the driver when you board the bus where you want to get off. He'll do the rest."

"Yes, sir. Thank you, sir. Could you sell me one ticket, please?"

"Round trip or one way?"

"One way is all I need right now."

"That'll be five eighty-five."

She opened the purse and counted out six of the one-dollar bills. She pushed them toward him.

He took the money, gave her change, then touched a button. There was a whirring sound, and a ticket jumped up out of a slot under her chin. She took it and put it in her purse. She asked "What time does it leave?"

"Seven o'clock at gate twelve."

"Thank you, sir."

She left the window and looked up at a large clock on the wall; it was only noon. It won't take me but a few minutes to pack, she thought. What'll I do all that time? She decided she would walk around the city for a while. She had been so busy since she arrived that she had not had a chance to do any sightseeing. Then later she could go to one of those movie houses she had seen around the corner.

She was hurrying toward the exit when a young man wearing lizard-skin boots fell in step alongside her. He smiled as he bent down to her. "Hello, girlie" he said. "You just leave home?"

"No. I'm going back!"

31

Mrs. Friendly had been Vernon's landlady for three years and had never had any reason to think of him as anything but the most exemplary of roomers. She often said she wished she had a dozen more like him.

That is why she had not checked his room for years—as she did those of her other exclusively male roomers—for signs of cooking, drinking or bringing women in at night. She did that with the others, and unexpectedly, and so that there would be no complaints, she informed them when they applied that she would do so. She had told Vernon of his exemption from the inspections in a rare rush of warmth for the only tenant who had never given her a moment of worry or trouble. She even permitted him to change his own linens and clean the room instead of having the maid do it, as she did for the others. She never doubted for a moment that he would keep the room spotless, for she had never known anyone so meticulous and clean.

But lately she had heard talking and unusual noises coming from Vernon's room, often at night. She had hesitated to break her word to him, but the reputation of her house, she felt, justified her doing so. When she heard him drive off in the car a while ago, she had decided to make the inspection.

The room was as she had imagined it: faultlessly clean and neatly kept. She did not smoke and had a keen sense of smell and the only objectionable thing she could find was a stale odor that was vaguely familiar to her but which she could not identify.

She looked through his drawers first: his clothes were carefully folded and separated. When she opened the bottom drawer, she saw that his used shirts were still stiff. She wondered why he put so much starch in them. The odor was strongest there, but she still could not place it.

She looked behind the bureau and went to the window, where she pulled the curtains out to see if food had been stored on the windowsill. She ran her finger across it and there was not a speck of dust on it.

She went next to the bed and got down on her knees and looked under it. She knew that was where they sometimes hid hot plates and food. She had once found an empty wine bottle under a bed. But there was nothing under Vernon's bed, and she rose slowly and carefully, because of her rheumatism, and looked around once more. Then she looked at the bed.

Mrs. Friendly disliked thinking it about Vernon, who was the last person she would have expected to have a female visitor overnight, but if such were the case, the evidence might be there. She drew down the covers and looked closely at the sheets and pillowcases. There was no sign that a woman had lain on them. She remade the bed and, when she was finished, saw she had not done it nearly as well as Vernon had.

She opened the drawer in the night table, but there was only a pad and a pen in it, and no writing on the pad. Nor were there any of those shocking magazines she had once discovered in a young man's night table. She was beginning to think she was hearing things in her old age, or that Vernon had started talking in his sleep. Vernon, she decided, was as nearly perfect a tenant as any landlady could hope for.

There was only one place left to look: the closet. She went to it and opened it.

She gasped when she saw the hatted figure looking out at her. Then she screamed.

III

THE BABY TREE

32

Vernon followed the girl's bus until it pulled alongside the closed store, where it stood like a large animal in a dark cave, panting.

The girl and the driver got off and the driver opened the belly of the bus and took her two suitcases out of it. He reboarded the bus and it pulled away, its broad shoulders hunched against the prospect of night. She stood holding the suitcases, watching it, then turned and struggling with the weight, entered a path in the woods and disappeared from sight.

Vernon turned on the car's headlights, pulled off the side of the highway, and drove onto the lot in front of the store. He watched where he saw her head bobbing under the limbs of trees on the uneven path. He got out, locked the car, and followed her at a distance.

He waited in the woods as she crossed a dirt road and went up another path toward a white house. She climbed the porch steps to where he could no longer see her, but where he heard a screen door open, then close. A minute later a light went on in the front room. He had never traveled in the country before—certainly never followed anyone there—but already he felt as if he were familiar with it. He waited, and when she did not come out again, returned to the car.

He drove back along the highway until he found a road turning off it through the woods, and minutes later he was on the inner road, from where he saw the lights in the house beyond more trees. He pulled onto the side of the road to watch from there. When ten minutes later the lights downstairs went off, then went on in an upper window, and after that were extinguished there too, he turned away.

He opened a paper bag in which there were two thermos bottles—one filled with hot soup, the other with milk—and some sandwiches. He opened the thermos of milk, unwrapped a sandwich and sat chewing slowly and drinking while he watched the dark house.

The quiet of the country was new to him: he heard every sound. The woods seemed to breathe in the wind, and the moonlight changing between the slowly moving limbs of the trees resembled a carnival being held in the trees.

When he had finished eating, he replaced the thermos in the bag, unfolded the blanket on the seat beside him and wrapped himself in it in preparation for sleep. But first he looked up through the windshield at the room where the girl had settled down for the night too.

A night bird called shrilly, startling him.

33

Willa was so tired from the search and the trip back, and having slept in her own bed for the first time in eight days, she arose late. Standing in the kitchen, she ate dry cereal and an apple that had not turned completely rotten. Then going out the back door because it was nearer, she made her way down the path toward the highway.

There was little traffic on Sunday morning, but she did not try to get a ride from the few cars that passed; instead, she walked the mile and a half to the sign she had seen on her first attempt in the pickup to get to the city: Milltown, 1 mile. An arrow on the sign pointed down a paved road, and she turned onto it. Fifteen minutes later, she entered Milltown.

There was activity there: people and neon signs flashing in daylight and music coming out of the bars. The sun was bright in a crystal sky, and passing a drugstore whose window displayed inexpensive dark glasses such as she had seen people in the city wearing, she went in. She emerged minutes later wearing a pair of the dark glasses.

She continued down the long street past buildings made of glass and chrome, a motel with its blinking neon sign advertising day rates for short stays. She did not have to be told now what the motel's principal trade was. She kept going, because she was looking for black people, and there were none there.

She found someone at the last house on the street. The house was a curious holdout, a one-story wooden cabin with tape patching a cracked window and loose boards where there had once been a porch. Four cinderblocks led up to a doorless entrance, and a fence lay half-broken in an attempt to separate the property from the street. She stopped outside it, where in a yard full of broken objects and refuse, an old black woman sat on a wooden chair smoking a pipe as she watched the parade of people on the street. She lowered the pipe when she saw Willa. Her eyebrows raised. "You lookin' for me, chile?"

"No, ma'am" Willa said, "but I was hoping you could help me."

"Come in. Come in. We see what hep ole granny has in her pockets today."

Willa walked through the broken fence and approached the old woman, who did not look so much small as shrunken. The sun through Willa's dark glasses hung like a white plate over the woman's shoulder.

"Come close, chile" the woman said "so's I can see you clear. My glasses is broke and the welfare won't fix 'em."

Willa moved closer.

"Ah" the woman said. "That's better." She took a pair of spectacles from the pocket of her dress and looked up at Willa through a broken lens. The other lens was missing. "You looks like someone I seen" she said. "Is you a movie star?"

"No, ma'am."

"Then maybe it's just the resemblance. I been here since before Milltown started. Wouldn't sell then and won't now. And I guess I seen most people traveled through here sooner or later. I had three daughters worked in the houses once. Two died of the consumption, and one run off with a musician passin' through and I ain't heard from her since. But I'm still here. They'll have to carry me off dead. Now what kind of hep can ole granny do for you, chile?"

"I'm looking for a man named Lester Kane. He's a black man who preaches in a church around here."

"I know Dr. Kane well. Knew his momma and daddy before him. I don't have no truck with all that Jesus stuff, but he's a fine man. He's gettin' things done for the poor black peoples. Too late for me, but he's doin' it!"

"Do you know where I can find him?" Willa asked.

"Fine him? You standing in the shadow of his church, chile."

Willa looked up the cliff, where she noticed for the first time the church standing in sunlight.

"You just go on up there" the woman said. "That church ain't segregated. He be up there. You can't hardly miss him, even iffen you wants to."

"Thank you, ma'am" Willa said.

The old woman nodded. She lifted the pipe, relit it with a kitchen match struck on her thumbnail and resumed smoking. She watched Willa as she went off, then as she stepped back through the gap in the fence shouted "They's a path on the left there goes right on up to it."

Willa stopped, nodded, and went on. She heard the woman shout behind her "Iffen you takes off them dark glasses, you'll see a whole lot better."

She was not the only white person in the church, but most of the people there were black and some turned to look at the latecomer sitting in the back row wearing dark glasses.

She recognized Lester Kane immediately: heavier now than he had been, somehow taller, much grayer. He was in a blue business suit and wore tortoiseshell glasses as he leaned across the lectern or paced back and forth delivering the sermon.

"So what is that which is sinned against you but a test of your strength? What is injustice but a test of your endurance? I tell you, brothers and sisters, we have the strength, we have the character, we have the endurance to stand firm against that injustice. Three hundred years of forging that steel! Three hundred years of bending before we learned to stand upright! Three hundred years of waiting before we learned to raise our fists and shout 'No more! No more! No more!'"

"Amen to that!"

"Amen!"

"Are we going to bring down the walls of our spirits' prison?" he called.

"Yeah!"

"Are we going to cast off the chains of compromise and lies and delay?"

"Yeah, man!"

"And are we going to stand up and shout 'This is my land too, my heritage; my sweat built it too, and my rights are as important as yours'?"

"Oh, yes!"

He held up his hand for silence. "Some will tell you" he continued "that the trial will be held up there in God's throne room. That if we just wait, God will see we get justice there. Well, God never said that, never intended it, brothers and sisters. That's what the man says he said, but we know different, don't we?"

"Sure do, Reverend!"

"We know it!"

"The trial" he concluded "won't be held up there, because it's going to happen here. It's started! It's happening! Praise God, it's ours, and it's now!"

He turned like a prizefighter who has received a hard blow and staggered back, so that Willa could not see his face as the congregation rose applauding, some with fists raised, all shouting.

An organ sounded as amid the shouting he returned to the lectern. Perspiration poured over his face, and his glasses were clouded as he raised his fist to join theirs. Then he lowered his arm, and gradually the noise died down and the congregation began to return to their seats.

He announced "Now I know you'll all be happy to hear from our sisters of the Joyful Choir as they sing for us," then sat down in a chair. He took a handkerchief from his pocket and wiped his glasses and his face as a group of black women and girls arose to the left of him and began singing a hymn, all in the same dresses, all clapping and swaying on their feet like fans from side to side.

Willa watched Lester Kane. It was difficult for her to put the two together: the assured, forceful man who had so aroused the congregation and the quiet hired man she recalled living like a shadow in the corners of their lives. As the singing ended and she got up with the others to go down and meet him, she was no longer confident she could get him to talk to her and answer the remaining question of what happened that day at the house.

She stood to the side waiting. The others ignored her, but after ten minutes Lester Kane glanced over at her several times. He was talking and listening to those who came to shake his hand, but he was watching her. As the line got shorter and the people were wandering out, she stepped into it behind the last of them.

He offered his hand to her more tentatively than he had to the others. She took it, and he folded his other hand over hers. "It's a pleasure to see you here today, young lady" he said.

"I enjoyed your speech and the singing" Willa said "but I came here for a different reason. I'm Willa Rhineman, Madeleine Rhineman's daughter, and I'm looking for my mother, who disappeared years ago, and I'm hoping you can answer a question that might help me find her."

He drove her through Pineville in a shiny black car and into a suburb of houses with stately trees, sculpted gardens and long lawns rolling down onto immaculate sidewalks, then into the driveway of a large gray house. She followed him into a vestibule where an elderly black woman was waiting to take his coat.

"Thelma" he said, "this is Miss Rhineman. We'd like some tea in the study. And please, no calls for a while."

It was a large room, two walls of which were lined with books from floor to ceiling. There were plaques, framed documents and signed photographs of Lester Kane with important-looking people covering all of a third wall. At the far end of the room was a desk, behind which were two long windows with venetian blinds drawn over them. Lester Kane sat behind the desk in a tall chair and signaled Willa to sit in a deep leather chair in front of him. He folded his hands on the desk and sat for a minute looking at the girl he knew now for the first time had not been a distant relative of the Rhinemans', but the daughter of the only member of the family he had liked. "Now, how can I help you?" he asked.

"Sir" Willa said, "I'm hoping you were there on a certain day—" she opened her purse and took a small notebook from it and read— "September 12, 1967, when I think my mother came back to our house to take me away with her."

"That was a long time ago, Willa."

"Please try to remember."

He leaned back in the swivel chair. He folded his hands under his chin. Willa noticed how long and graceful his fingers were and how beautifully the nails were kept. He looked at her over them. "You say that was September 12?"

"Yes."

"She was there" he said quietly.

Willa leaned forward. She wanted to get up in her excitement, go to the desk to be nearer to him, but she restrained herself.

"But I didn't see her, Willa."

"Then how do you know she was there?"

"Because I heard her—heard her and your grandmother, precisely. She must have arrived late, because I was asleep when I first became aware of them."

"You heard them all the way out back in the shed?"

"They woke me. They were quarreling."

Thelma came in with a tea service on a tray. She put it on the desk and served Lester Kane his. She asked Willa "Do you take cream or lemon, miss?"

"Just black, please" Willa said, without taking her eyes off Lester Kane.

Thelma handed Willa her tea and left, and Willa leaned forward without tasting it and put it on the desk.

Lester Kane looked at the dark glasses, behind which the girl was watching and waiting for him to continue. The past reappears in unusual guises, he thought. He thought he had left that house and the strange Rhineman family behind forever. Left Emil Rhineman standing naked at his bedroom window watching him. Left the fearsome and obsessive Lydia Rhineman, who in her intolerance of all that did not shape itself to her conceptions and strong will, had been the model from which so much of his later portraits of white arrogance had been drawn. Left too what he had suspected then was going on between father and daughter. Now this intense child was sitting here who was conceivably their—his mind turned away in revulsion from what Willa conceivably might be.

"Sir! Sir?"

He returned to find the girl talking to him. He composed himself. He folded his hands again under his chin, which was one way he had learned to draw attention away from his face when he wanted to hide what might be revealed there. "Yes?"

"You said you heard my mother and grandmother quarreling. What about?"

"As I said, Willa, I had been awakened from sleep and was not fully aware, and from that distance I could only hear snatches of what was being said; but as nearly as I could determine, it was about you. It seemed, as you said, your mother had come to take you away with her, and your grandmother opposed this. They were shouting at one point and perhaps even physically battling, because I heard something fall in the fracas."

"What happened then?"

"Nothing. After that it grew quiet. I went back to sleep."

"And that was all?" Willa asked. "That was all you heard?"

"No. I was awakened again by someone going into the old stable where the tools were kept—which I thought was unusual at that time of night. Then later—once more awakened—I heard them passing the shed in the direction of the woods."

He got out of his chair, went to the window and opened the blinds to look out. His back was to Willa. I am fighting something here, he thought. Evading again. That accursed weakness that has before afflicted me at those times when courage was most needed. Caution, he thought. The world thinks otherwise, but I am a man of caution. I lack that indispensable quality Dr. King had: to go beyond what is my normal capacity for courage. It is sometimes called lack of faith, and it has brought me back here to this retreat from the wider public arena, which I call a period of assessment. The decision has to be made, the step taken finally to return, even though I know it means they will destroy me, as they destroyed Dr. King.

"Sir?" he heard again. He turned back to the girl, who was now standing behind his chair. He looked again behind the dark glasses to those eyes that saw his, he thought, more clearly than he wished.

"Sir" she said, "wasn't that pretty unusual too? Late at night, I mean, going into the woods?"

"It was. That's why I got up and put on my robe and stepped outside."

He turned back to the window with a motion uncharacteristically uncoordinated. I knew what was happening between Madeleine and her father, he thought. I knew. And I should have known who this child was then, and why Mr. Rhineman retired so young, and why the secrecy, the withdrawal of them all. That woman's explanation of the child: it was designed to deceive an idiot, and I was not an idiot. I knew—or suspected, at least—that much, but chose not to recognize it. Their lives seemed so sordid to me, and compared to my people's suffering, insignificant. Even Madeleine, who was worth helping, and who, I knew even then, was becoming their victim. She even sought out my friendship, and I held her off. Because I believed then—as I know now—that there are no white friends in this country for us yet. Only those who pretend to be, and those who think they are until the time of real testing comes: those whose good intentions I have used. So why should I have jeopardized our future for any of them—even for that nice white girl, whose intentions were more genuine than most white people's? I was a man of God—and as such, of the faith that all are God's children, all equal in his sight, black and white—and yet my convictions could not bend to satisfy my faith; *I* could not bend to it. So I retreated. Then that night: What did I retreat from again into silence? Now this child is here, come to me, asking my help. And although I know little that is certain about that night, I am again considering silence and denying I saw anything at all.

"Sir. Sir."

He turned back to face her.

"Are you all right?" she asked. "Are you sick?"

He put his hands on the back of the chair: "No. No. I am well."

"Are you sure? I could get Thelma for you. You look sick to me."

"I am quite well. I was thinking."

"Then could you tell me if you saw anything when you got outside? Did you see my mother?"

He looked off. Willa waited on the edge of the chair. She waited so long she became afraid there was something wrong with him after all. Then he turned back to her and spoke.

"I saw her. At least, I think it was her. You see, by the time I had put on my robe and gotten outside to see what was happening, I could only catch a glimpse of them from behind as they entered the woods. It was, I'm certain, your grandmother and grandfather, but the woman walking between them—I only glimpsed part of her for a second."

"Did you hear them say anything?"

"They were silent."

"What was she wearing?"

"What?"

"What color dress was the woman wearing?"

"It wasn't a dress. It was one of those suits women wear. And, yes, it was white."

Willa leaned back. He heard her sigh as he turned again to look out the window. Then she asked "Did they stop in the woods? Did you see that much?"

He answered with his back to her. "I could see that white suit—like something floating between the trees—until it was gone."

"Gone into the woods?"

"No. For a long distance as it got smaller and smaller, through the woods and beyond them. I went back to sleep after that. I never heard them return. But the next day, your mother was gone, and you were still there."

He still spoke through the blinds, but now as if to himself. "The next day your grandmother fired me. Some lame excuse. But I was leaving, as I always did at the end of that month, anyway. Only this time permanently, to assume the ministry of my church. I never went back." He closed the blinds.

When he turned back, the chair was empty and the door was open. She was gone.

34

Willa waded up to her hips through the tall grass, pushing waves of it before her. The dark glasses glinted reflections of cold suns. When she got to the edge of the copse, she stopped.

It had been there inside her all along. All through the search, and in the years before that, it was she who held the answer: what the child of three had known and then refused to acknowledge again until now. All those years she had been carrying her mother inside her. Now, in a sense, she knew it was time to give birth to her.

Inside was the baby tree, dripping with its rich flowers: that tree that held birth and death in its long fingers.

She could not go in yet. She lowered herself into the tall grass. It swelled, then swallowed her.

■ ■ ■

That night she had awakened in her crib to voices arguing below.

"No one knows I came here. If anyone asks, I'll say I boarded Willa out."

"And later? What will you say later when she needs to know where she was born and who her father is? No. She's mine now. We had an agreement, and you will abide by it."

"Damn the agreement! You won't get away with this. I won't let you. Get out of my way. I'm going up."

"I'll see you dead first."

There was a noise that was like someone stumbling, then falling. Then she heard someone coming quickly up the stairs. A woman's voice called her name: "Willa." The door opened.

She was frightened, so she closed her eyes. She heard the bars of the crib being lowered, then someone shaking her.

"Willa" the woman said. "Willa. Wake up. You're coming with me."

When she opened her eyes, a beautiful woman dressed in white was bending over her, her arms out to her. She was smiling at her. She reached up to her, but before they could join, she saw her grandmother rush into the room, go behind the woman and throw her arms around her. The woman struggled, but her grandmother was the stronger as she wrestled the woman back through the doorway. The door closed behind them.

She turned onto her side looking at the door, waiting for the woman to come back. When she heard them struggling again at the top of the stairs, she climbed out of the crib barefoot, in her cotton nightgown, and went to the door to listen.

"Get out of my way" the woman said.

"I warn you, girl, take one more step and I'll—"

"Get out of my way, damn you!"

"Whore!" her grandmother shouted, and there was the sound of a blow and the woman cried out. Then no sound at all for moments, then a second blow and a cry and something heavy tumbling down the stairs.

She waited in the silence that followed. When she heard footsteps hurrying down the stairs, she opened the door and went to the side of the stairs, where she stood out of sight listening. She heard her grandfather's voice for the first time.

"Oh, Jesus! Oh, dear God, Lydia, you killed her!"

A long silence. Then her grandmother's voice. "There's a faint pulse."

"Thank God."

"Be quiet, Emil. I have to think."

"Think? What's there to think about? I'll go for an ambulance, someone—"

"Will you be quiet?"

"Lydia—"

"*Shut up, Emil.*"

His voice came from farther away then, near the door. "I'm going for help."

"Get back here."

"I'm going." She heard the screen door opening.

"Emil!"

It stopped.

Then her grandmother's voice. "There's nothing that can be done for her. She's barely breathing. It's too late."

"You don't know that."

"I know this: if she leaves here now, goes into a hospital and dies there, it's all over for you, for us. It will all come out, everything. And think of Willa. What will become of her then?"

"I—"

"Prison for you, Emil. And perhaps for me too now. Is that what you want?"

"I don't—"

"Don't think, Emil. I'll do that. Just stay here with her. I have to go to the stable."

She heard the screen door open, then close. Then it was silent again for a long time until she heard her grandfather's voice. "Madeleine" he said. "Daughter, I'm sorry."

That was when she knew who the woman was.

Her grandmother came back. She heard the screen door open and close. She put something heavy down. "Come help me" she said.

"What are you going to do?"

"You don't need to know. Just help me get her there."

They began lifting something, then carrying it across the room. The screen door opened, closed behind them as they left the house.

She ran back to her bedroom and looked out the window, where she watched them carrying her mother upright between them across the yard. Her grandfather was holding a pick in one hand and her grandmother a shovel and rope.

They were entering the woods when Lester Kane came out of the shed and stood watching. When he went back into the shed, she went down and out of the house to follow them.

She saw them crossing through the tall grass at the other end of the woods. She hurried behind them as they reached the edge of the copse. They disappeared inside it.

She went to the edge of the copse and looked in. They were stooping. Then her grandfather arose and turned and hurried back toward where she was watching. She stepped to the side and back out of sight. He passed so close she could have touched him. The grass erupted around him as he began running. A minute later he was gone.

When she looked back into the copse, her grandmother was standing. She threw one end of the rope over a high limb of the tree, then stooped again and placed the looped end over her mother's head. She stood and began pulling on the rope. The white form began rising like a secret resurrection. Then it just hung there, swinging.

She backed slowly away as her grandmother tied the rope to another limb of the tree. Then she began digging. The white form kept swinging. The last thing she saw was the grass rushing beneath her bare feet.

When she awoke the next morning, she remembered nothing of the night before. Her year of silence began.

The tall grass swelled again as Willa arose out of it. Then it receded. Standing in it, she took off the dark glasses and put them into her pocket. She entered the copse.

She advanced slowly at first, then began running. When she reached a patch of earth beside the tree, she threw herself onto it. She pressed her cheek to the ground, arms out and palms touching it.

"Momma?" she said. "Momma, I found you."

She sat under the tree until dark. One hand remained on the ground beside her, touching it. She thought she could feel the earth breathing. The condoms hung like a strange roof over her head.

The voices began that she had heard a year ago in the lonely reaches of that winter. They faded, as if saying good-bye, then stopped.

As the copse filled with the dimness of coming night, she drew her legs up to her chin. She put her arms around them and lowered her head onto them. She pulled her body tightly together. As the copse got darker, she seemed to become smaller and smaller.

When she left, she did not look back. It was cold, and she was shivering when she returned to the house.

35

After she turned on the light in the parlor, she put on the dark glasses again. She did not move for several minutes. When she did, she went slowly.

The heat had been off in the house when she arrived, but she had not noticed it until now. She was cold. She went to her grandmother's room and found her robe and put it on. She tied the sash and pulled the robe tightly around her. It was so large on her that she had to roll up the sleeves halfway and hold up the hem to get back down the stairs.

She went into the kitchen where, standing in the dark, she ate more dry cereal and another apple. She chewed slowly, looking out the window. As she tried to replace the cereal box on the shelf, it slipped from her hand to the floor, spilling its contents around her. She did not pick it up. She walked through it.

She returned to the front room and sat in her grandmother's chair. She did not move there either for a long time.

When she began to feel something again, it was fear. The search and the dream were over and she was alone. Her mother was dead. She had lived with her mother's presence inside her for so long that now that it was no longer there, nothing else occupied her. She had seen what the world outside was like, and she knew it was not a place she wanted to return to without the dream to sustain her. That world frightened her now as it never had when she was there.

She sighed, then got out of the chair.

She returned to the kitchen and got a chair and brought it into the parlor. She placed it under the ceiling light, then stepped back and looked up at the light fixture. She went to the wall switch and turned off the light. She climbed onto the chair and in the light from the window slipped the sash from the robe.

She was no longer afraid.

36

As Willa had watched her grandmother years ago in the copse, so Vernon had watched the girl there and followed her back to the house. He understood that the search was over. He waited, watching the window from the road, then went back to the car.

He opened the suitcase on the back seat, put the plastic flowers aside on the seat and changed into the shirt, tie and suit. When he came out the door, he was holding the plastic flowers in one hand and getting into the other sleeve of the suit jacket with the other. He buffed his shoes on the back of his trouser legs, closed all three buttons on the jacket. He tried to push down his wild hair with his hand (he did not own a comb and had not thought to buy one), but it sprang up again. Not trying to hide now, staying in the middle of the road, he walked down it to the path leading up to the house.

The lights were out. For a moment this confused him, for he had not thought the girl would go to bed so early. He considered returning to the car until morning, but it was cold and the night promised to get colder, and he did not want to sleep in the car again. He decided that if he could get into the house, he would wait in the front room until she came down in the morning. He had waited this long. He could wait another night.

It was full night now. There was only a burnt-orange moon going in and out of clouds, so he went more slowly up the path to the front yard. He was nearly at the porch steps when his foot hit something soft on the ground. He stopped. He looked down. It was a dead chicken. He pushed it aside with his foot and went onto the porch steps.

The wooden steps creaked beneath him, but as quietly as he could, he went up them to the screen door. He knew it screeched, so he opened it only a few inches and put his hand through to see if the other door was unlocked. It was not. He went back down the steps to the side of the house, where he ascended on creaking steps again to the door. There was a screen door there too, but the inner door was wide open.

He tried the screen door and found it unlocked. It screeched; but by opening it a fraction of an inch at a time to the minimum space that allowed him to slip through, he was inside in minutes. He was standing in a kitchen.

He could see well enough by the light from the open doorway and window to cross the kitchen without stumbling into anything. Then something crunched under his foot. He stopped, then stepped over it, moving toward the doorway.

He was in the girl's home at last, closer to her and far more intimate with her than he had dreamed of being when it all began. She was sleeping upstairs, unaware he had come for her.

But she was not asleep, or even upstairs, and he knew what it was hanging there in the front room even as he stood in the doorway. The flowers fell to the floor, and that arm lifted as if searching for something in the air. It came down slowly, fingers extended.

He moved into the room and, running his hand over the wall, found the light switch and turned it on. He turned but kept his back to the wall as he looked at her.

With the hem of the girl's robe touching the floor, it looked as if in his absence she had grown very tall and was standing there waiting for him.

He moved close. His arms went up to her, then fell back to his sides. He turned away and started to moan; then he wept. All those emotions he had buried deep inside him years ago and thought were dead came to life. When he was done weeping, he turned back and looked at her.

He returned to the kitchen, found a knife and cut her down. He carried her to Lydia's chair and sat her in it. Bending over her, he removed the sash from around her neck and threw it into the fireplace.

He straightened her in the chair and drew the robe around her. He placed her arms on the armrests, took off her dark glasses and put them on the table next to the chair. He knelt, arranging her legs, but seeing that she was wearing only one loafer, went back to where he had cut her down and found it on the floor. He returned to her and, kneeling again, replaced it on her foot. Then he went to the doorway and picked up the plastic flowers. He rearranged her arms so that when he placed the flowers there, she seemed to be holding them. Then he turned out the light and went to Emil's chair.

They sat like that all night, across from each other. Birds flew onto the roof and perched there, as if keeping guard over them. As morning arrived, it slowly revealed her out of the shadows that had hidden her. Only then did he move. With sunlight on her, holding the bouquet of flowers and dressed in the long gown, she looked to him like a bride.

He smiled at her. "Good morning" he said. "Do you remember me? My name is Vernon."

Then he told her the story of his life.

CODA

Vernon buried her that afternoon alongside her mother. He put the plastic flowers on her grave and, standing beside it, recited a prayer they had taught him in the orphanage. He wanted to stay longer and talk to her some more, but for the first time he felt he was intruding. She was with her mother. Instead, he left and returned to the city.

On one of his deliveries a month later, he met an older woman who owned a small printing business; seeing that he had the qualities of thoroughness and attention to detail, she offered him a job as an apprentice. She had been a widow for twelve years, and after she took him as her lover a year later, they married and he moved into her house in the suburbs. When after six years of marriage her health began to fail, she turned the running of the business over to him, and several years later when she died, he inherited it. The business had grown under his care, and eventually he married a schoolteacher who was nearer his age.

He never went back to the street, but now and then he followed someone.